DARK WATER

Also by Elizabeth Lowry

The Bellini Madonna

DARK WATER

BEING A HISTORY BY
DR. HIRAM CARVER
OF BOSTON, MASSACHUSETTS

And written by

Elizabeth Lowry

LONDON

Printed for riverrun:

An imprint of Quercus Books, *Carmelite House, 50 Victoria Embankment*

MM.XVIII

riverrun

First published in Great Britain in 2018 by

riverrun
An imprint of

Quercus Editions Limited
Carmelite House
50 Victoria Embankment
London EC4Y 0DZ

An Hachette UK company

A CIP catalogue record for this book is available
from the British Library.

Hardback 978 1 78648 562 5
Trade Paperback 978 1 78648 563 2
Ebook 978 1 78648 565 6

10 9 8 7 6 5 4 3 2 1

Typeset in Monotype Fournier by CC Book Production
Printed and bound in Great Britain by Clays Ltd, Elcograf S.p.A.

For my children,
and for Romaine, friend indeed

And darkness was upon the face of the deep

Genesis 1:2

PART ONE:

Rising Tide

ONE

Superintendent's Office, Asylum for the Insane, Charlestown, Massachusetts, January 1855

I DATE MY PROFESSIONAL INTEREST in what I call the dark water, or submerged aspect of the human mind, to an incident that befell me as assistant surgeon of USS *Orbis* in 1833, shortly before I came to work at the asylum.

This was when I first got to know William Borden.

I was just twenty-one, and until then I'd never been to sea. We'd embarked at Boston in the fall of the previous year. After successfully navigating the long haul around Cape Horn to the Pacific, the *Orbis* had meandered from port to port up the Chilean coast. Now we were following the line from Chorrillos in Peru on a cruise that was to take the ship past the Marquesas, round the Sandwich Islands, and then back home on nauseatingly rough waters. We began this leg of our journey in early May. Our intolerable passage (I suffered badly from *mal de mer*) was to last a little under nine months.

Five days after setting sail from Peru the ship reached Hood Island in the Galapagos and anchored in Gardner's Bay. It was dead noon by ship's time when Captain Barnard sent a party on shore to capture a hundred or so of the island's giant tortoises as meat for

3

our voyage. These beasts lived in a cactus-filled valley some two or three miles inland. The beach was bleak, a sickle of leprous white. When the hunting party straggled out into the saltbush and thorny mesquite fringing the bay I decided to remain behind, since I still felt sick to my stomach, and explore this dismal place on my own.

It was like stepping out onto a distant star. All around lay ridges of a black porous rock that was so blasted and dustless that it appeared to have been baked in a furnace. Picking up two stones, I struck them together. They rang like dull bell metal. The hot, still air retained the sound mournfully.

The noise disturbed something in the scrub: there was a rustling and a thrashing, followed by a low hiss, as if the rock underfoot had sprung a geyser.

I lifted the heavy limb of an acacia bush with my stick and found myself looking at the hard socket of an eye, a scrolled and cracked lip, a horned forehead encrusted with a scab of salt.

In front of me crouched a hideous lizard, a devil of darkness snorting seawater from a cavity in the middle of its face. As I stood gazing at it the thing raised itself on its forelegs and began to slither towards me across the lava with a slow waggle of its squamous hips. Revolted, I lashed at its head, bringing my stick down as hard as I could on those empty eyes. It retreated, neck lowered, jaws gaping in a soundless cry.

My heart was beating fast as I scaled the crest of the ridge and arrived at the sweep of sand on the other side.

That was when I saw Third Lieutenant Borden. He was sitting motionless about a hundred yards away on an outcrop of rock. His profile was turned to me. Behind him stretched the apparently infinite sea, sequined with sunlight.

4

Borden's arms were raised horizontally, like a spar. To my astonishment they were covered from shoulder to wrist with clusters of the long-beaked mockingbird native to that spot. There must have been twenty or more of these birds, twitching and bobbing on their perch like old tars sunning themselves on a wharf. The rock at Borden's feet was thronged with feathered bodies, shingled gray and brown, nestling against his legs in the sunshine. While I watched, one of them approached him, climbed his thigh by hooking itself up and over it with its curved beak, and scrabbled onto his shoulder.

This was strange enough. But the expression on Borden's face was even stranger. It was one of anguished delight, as if the nip of each claw were an exquisitely tender caress.

Was he *weeping*? Something about his eyes, a pinchedness, suggested tears. At that distance it was hard to tell. I was coming closer when, without moving his head, Borden raised the palm of his left hand, as if to say: Stop. No further.

I'd had no suspicion that he'd even seen me. Embarrassed, I retraced my steps to the site of our anchorage. There I vomited copiously onto the sand. I also managed to kill a snake and found at least fifty more of those demonic lizards. I tried to stun a few with my stick, but they proved too agile for me.

When we were on board ship again I stuttered an apology to Borden for having intruded on him, but the look in his eyes was so raw, and so odd, that I dried up in mid-sentence.

Yes, I decided. They had quite definitely been tears.

*

WHEN I NEXT SAW Borden alone it was midnight. I'd gone up on deck a night or two later, unable to sleep. Earlier that day I'd exchanged angry words with the ship's surgeon, a superannuated old peacock whose medicine was as old-fashioned as his manners, and I keenly regretted the weakness that tempted me, however briefly, to let slip the tight grip I usually kept on myself.

To tell the truth, I was already experiencing the first of those doubts about my stubborn choice of career that were to haunt me throughout that wretched journey.

Was it this that made me so susceptible to what was to follow?

We were dawdling somewhere east of Charles Island, having met the whaleship *Grace* of New Bedford and given her our letters (I'd written just one, to my sister Caroline in Boston) to carry home. The next morning we'd start beating west.

That night the windless sky was bright with crude constellations. An orange moon lolled on the mizzenmast. In the starlight the vast bulk of the ship was magnified, a floating metropolis whose avenues sprouted masts rather than trees, with the spar deck spread like a park in the middle. In the midnight stillness, broken only by the slap of water, I could hear the distant scratching of the tortoises amidships.

When I reached the quarterdeck Borden was standing there, foot propped on a shroud. He was officer of the deck for that watch, and he was looking out at the tinseled ocean. I felt suddenly uneasy at coming across him unseen in that way, as if I'd again interrupted him in a private moment, instead of the common round of his duties. I thought of the docile birds, the black rock, those distantly glimpsed tears. Had I, after all, imagined them?

I knew a little about this third lieutenant of ours, naturally, since we messed together in the wardroom, but on a busy and tightly organized frigate of that size — with its ranks and social strata and orders of precedence, its regulations and rituals, it resembled nothing so much as a small continental principality — I'd seldom had the opportunity to speak to him privately, and then never beyond a few hurried words.

He was a Nantucketer of about thirty-odd, around six foot four and well-knit, with a quietly self-possessed air. Narrow hips. A deep chest. His back and shoulders were sprung tight with muscle; his gaze absolutely direct. Under a crown of coppery-bronze hair he had widely set eyes and a high nose, with a broad bridge, like the muzzle of a lion.

It wasn't arrogance, this self-possession of Borden's, for the way he held himself was perfectly open, but something else: a hushed concentration, an inward focus that was almost meditative. Though he wasn't a Quaker he occasionally had the Quaker's habit, often found among Nantucketers, of addressing others by their given names, and he had the Quaker's taste for silence.

I recall that there was a melancholy in Borden that gave his self-possession a conspicuous weight. That leonine face was grooved from mouth to chin with the marks of an entrenched sadness. He seldom smiled, and his smile, when it came, was utterly startling, like the unlooked-for dazzle of sun on tar. I've never before or since encountered such an effect of calm and tragic authority in any other human being. Even the captain spoke to Borden in a tone of respect, which was all the more noticeable since Borden was only a junior lieutenant.

That Borden had made the rank of lieutenant at all was unusual. He'd come up through the hawsehole, as the saying went – just over a decade earlier, from 1818 to 1821, he'd still been an ordinary seaman on USS *Providence*.

But I didn't yet know the story of what had taken place on that ill-fated ship. I knew nothing.

In every life, I now believe, there is one event that is the wellspring of the fundamental agony and decision in us. It lies beneath the sunlit layers of the present moment, throwing its shade across the foundations of our being, forming the self to come. If grasped and brought to the surface, it can save us or destroy us.

I only realized this later, once I was in possession of the shape of Borden's story – much, much later, after I'd wrestled it from the depths, and fumbled it into my shaking hands.

Later. Too late!

On that particular night I still had no inkling of it. A sluggish breeze, mazy with salt, crawled along the bulwarks. The great moon slid from her spar, dashing her metallic light over the wooden thoroughfares of the sleeping city. As it did so a peculiar thing happened. Borden was transfigured. He wasn't a man but a pillar of silver, and I felt an unaccountable and completely irrational impulse to go down on my knees before him on the scrubbed boards of the deck. He seemed unapproachable, and at the same time I yearned, with a powerful spurt of shame, to touch him.

Needless to say I did no such thing, but simply stood in the shadows, hoping to creep away unobserved. I discovered to my horror that my penis had stiffened and that its swollen head was butting wetly against the flap of my trousers.

I was about to go below when Borden turned and addressed me.

'Why d'you torture yourself with this unhappiness, Hiram? Whose will keeps you here?'

It took me a moment to collect myself. Astounded, I replied that I was in the navy entirely by my own will; but how, *how* was it that he had guessed – ?

'It's just that you're such an unlikely sailor. You hate the sea. And you hate this ship.' He spoke, I remember, in a wide, rather common accent. His voice was rich and steady, however, and in the darkness its spacious vowels had a curious power. He was smiling his fleeting, unexpected smile now: I could see his teeth by the light of the moon.

'Yes, I do – I do hate it.' It was such a relief to speak these words aloud that I started to laugh. 'I hate it more than I can say.'

This struck me as so funny that I laughed louder. It seemed somehow wholly natural that Borden should laugh with me. In a few moments we were leaning together against the taffrail, and my cheeks were wet with hysterical tears. Borden looked at me with unprobing compassion. The melancholy droop had returned to his face. I felt it again: that shocking impulse to touch him.

He nodded – a light nod, as if he'd read my thoughts. I put my hand awkwardly on his, and he let it rest there without embarrassment. Really, it seemed the most natural thing in the world that we should be standing like that in the moonlight, fourteen feet above the still, dark water, hand in hand. After another minute I felt quite calm.

'Thank you,' I said. 'I'll take your advice.'

Of course, he hadn't given me any. We stayed like that a while longer, talking of inconsequential things, and then I said goodnight to him and went back below deck to my cot to sleep a dreamless sleep.

I SPOKE WITH HIM alone again about two weeks after that.

He was ill. He had dysentery. Nearly all the men and officers had contracted the disease; Borden was one of the last. I'd warned Surgeon Spalding that in the Pacific heat thorough daily washing of the coppers in which the freshly butchered tortoise flesh was prepared was a matter of necessity, but although the weather-deck was holystoned and swabbed and squilgeed without fail every morning before breakfast, our cooking vessels were given only the most perfunctory rinse.

'In thirty years I have never served on a ship, Dr Carver, where this has been thought necessary or even recommended, whatever the custom in these matters may be in Boston,' pouted the old curmudgeon.

'Not just in Boston these days, sir. Forschmann's principles of food hygiene state quite clearly that –'

'What is "Forschmann"?' he interrupted me.

'A book, sir.'

'Ah. *A book.*'

Our medical consultation ended there.

The symptoms displayed by Borden were characteristic of this debilitating ailment: bloody stool, abdominal cramps, fever. I was impressed with the remarkable strength of his constitution, which had resisted the illness until well after our fellow officers, including Spalding himself, had succumbed. In the officers' mess the tortoises had been dissolved down into a tepid stew.

The captain, who dined alone in his quarters on fancier fare, was unaffected – as was I.

I found myself uncommonly moved by the sight of Borden's helpless body stretched out in the grimy light of my sick bay, and undressed him as gently as I could. This precious moment was marred only by the splutter of onions from the galley and the jabber of the gun-deck cooks.

All around us the sea rose and fell, with an unceasing, see-sawing pressure that invariably made me heave. But now I was hardly aware of it. I felt an effervescent emptiness in my stomach, a hurtling tremor in the reach of my fingers –

As Borden lay there, naked to the waist, I saw again how well-made he was. His heavily muscled arms had a grace that seemed superhuman. His trunk, compact as a great cat's, shivered faintly as he drew breath. One wide hand lay curled on the dark pubic furrow that extended like a scepter from his navel to his belt. That regal face, burnt to honeyed brick through exposure to sun and wind, was sealed. He was fast asleep.

I noted a curious detail that day about Borden's body. His torso was covered with irregular, shallow scars: the remains of old sores of some sort, the size of dollar coins, with heaped-up rims. A particularly long scar, a serrated purple lozenge, traversed his left side from chest to abdomen. Beneath it was a single tattoo. It might have been a fish, or the figure eight lying on its side, or a serpent biting its own tail – it was so roughly done that it was impossible to say.

How, and where, had he got this? Stooping over him, I traced its outline with the edge of my thumb.

Borden flinched. I drew back in surprise, and met his wide-open eyes. In the unclean light their irises were an untainted straw-gold.

'Did I hurt you?' I asked.

'No,' he whispered. 'But your hands are cold. They're fair near frozen.'

He was sick and I was well, but I sensed that *he* pitied *me*.

'I'm sorry. I didn't think you were awake.' I rubbed my knuckles against the seam of my jacket. 'I'll warm my fingers.'

'You can't help your coldness.' His lips twitched with mild irony. 'Well, friend, will I live?'

'I'm afraid you've been poisoned by the bouillabaisse, Mr Borden.'

'Ah. But *you* ain't, Doctor. You never touched it.'

It was true: I lived by choice entirely on ship's biscuit, vegetables, pickles, and the occasional slice of salt beef.

Borden regarded me with those sad, other-worldly eyes. 'You're able to go without,' he said. 'Few are. But you've mastered your appetite. I salute you.' He began to retch.

I blotted the spittle from his mouth with my own handkerchief. Perhaps I pressed a little harder than was necessary.

'Don't speak,' I insisted. 'You should sleep now.' But I knew that my impulse to silence him was prompted not by concern, but by a sudden petulant sense that his words, though apparently benign, weren't really meant in admiration at all.

Although I couldn't say why, I felt rebuked.

TWO

WE HAD BEEN AT sea nearly a month and were nearing the Marquesas, driven on by steady trade winds. Except for the bout of dysentery that had swept through the ship, our voyage up to that point had been uneventful – or so I was constantly assured by those who were more experienced than I was, which seemed to be more or less everyone else on board.

At full sail the *Orbis* at times appeared to steer herself, bumping across the swell as if tugged on invisible wires. Below decks the air was clotted with the smoke of candles and tobacco, with mold, mildew, and the furtive reek of tar and waste swilling in the bilges.

Our sick bay was a stewing cubby-hole in the forward part of the berth deck, positioned directly under the chains and ship's bell and down from the galley. Its two ports were kept shut tight while the ship was in motion. All day mustard-green water leached slowly along the breasthooks and through the hawsepipes.

The odor of salt and rust and suffering human bodies and the fug of frying was suffocating; the clanging of metal was percussive torture. The rolling and lurching of the ship reduced me to a state of drunkenness. The only place I could sit for any length of time without vomiting was on deck, but I couldn't sit on deck without being tossed about in what felt like a gale. It was a choice between being choked and seasick, or seasick and strafed by thirteen knots of wind.

And all the while I stank. I stank as much as the ship. We all stank, but in my own personal stench I could discern the smell of fear, and desperation, and self-loathing.

'Not long now, Carver, old boy. In a few days we should be out of the way of the prevailing wind, and then you can unclench your stomach muscles.'

Blocking the gangway running from the forecastle was Cornelius Buskirk, our first lieutenant – a puffed-up son of patrician New York who had got his commission thanks to family cash, and fancied himself an old salt. I knew him before joining the *Orbis*; our grandfathers had served together at Fort Stanwix, and our mothers, in the way of our world, were remote cousins.

'Thank you, Buskirk. In the meanwhile, perhaps you would be kind enough to step aside and let me proceed to the quarterdeck.'

'What? Oh yes, certainly. You'll get your sea legs yet, old man!'

Buskirk often spoke of being launched upon the Great Ocean of Life. He would then belch up an allusion to the Glory of his Calling, as if he'd swallowed an encyclopedia of inanities. He tottered a little now with the listing of the ship, hands on hips, legs planted ostentatiously wide apart.

'Are you getting ready to dance a hornpipe, Buskirk?'

'Very funny, Carver. If you adopted a more nautical demeanor you might do better. Think about it, old man. Just think about it.' He tapped the side of his head.

'Thanks, old fellow. Though your advice is undoubtedly excellent, I have to mosey off. It's nearly time for my saltwater shower.'

'Look here, Carver. This daily washing in the old briny. Why don't you just have yourself a nice tub drawn every few weeks like the rest of us, with soap? There's plenty of rainwater left in the barrels. We don't have to economize. In fact,' he huffed expansively, 'I'm due to have a bath next Friday. You can take my turn.'

'That's generous of you, old man, very generous. But I side with my friend Hippocrates in this instance. No need for soap where there's salt.'

'Not sure I know him. Are his people from Boston too?'

'Kos, actually.'

'Where's that? Down south?'

'Yes, right down south. Near Athens.'

Buskirk looked briefly flustered. 'We're not acquainted with many southern families. Are they old money, or new?'

'Oh, old. Very old. Boys all went in for medicine.'

'Humph. Medicine.' I could see him weighing up whether they were worth cultivating, and dismissing the notion. 'Well, if you're going to adopt these southern practices, old man, maybe you could leave the pyrophylactic equipment alone? I noticed when making my inventory of the, ah, appurtenances this morning that one was missing. It's vital that I keep track. Captain's orders.'

I stared at him, dumbfounded. Then I realized what he meant. During my last saltwater shower I'd lost my canvas container while fetching water. I'd promoted one of the pails hanging in the hold to water receptacle; it was still among my things. I burst out laughing.

The captain had found a task for our first lieutenant commensurate with the Glory of his Calling. He had him counting the fire buckets.

*

I SUSPECTED THAT BORDEN was as irritated by Buskirk as I was, but his natural reserve – that seemingly ingrained self-possession – inhibited any outward expression of this.

I watched them closely.

Buskirk chattered about 'the Fatherland', by which he meant Holland – the bricks from his ancestral seat in Albany, as he was fond of reminding us, had been brought from Amsterdam before the last century's war. He made sure we were aware that he was the heir to 'an island property' (a clump of mud and rushes in the Hudson that his family had snatched from the Mohawk). He bemoaned the delicacy of his skin and went into stupefying detail concerning the softness of his undergarments, which were handwoven for him from lamb's-wool by lackeys in Hoboken. For an awful moment I thought that he was going to lower his trousers so that we could take a look.

Borden gave no sign that he found any of this impolite, absurd or even mildly amusing.

Our second lieutenant, Gilbert, was a child of sixteen who was devoted to Buskirk. He was a boy with the stamp of our class all over him, the peevishness and the pimples, the elongated shanks and fatigued air.

I considered that it must have been galling for a man like Borden to be subordinate to this pair. But when I hinted as much, he gave me one of his long, assessing looks.

'Mr Buskirk and Mr Gilbert are gentlemen by birth. They are as they are.'

'Yes, but aren't you tired of it? Aren't you tired of this – this – *this asinine sense of entitlement*? God knows I count myself a gentleman too, but why do we have to listen to the Lord of the Isle bragging about his drawers?'

Borden shrugged. 'You're a gentleman of a different sort.'

'What sort?'

'The sort who is always worrying away at the meaning of what he has. And you don't like Mr Buskirk having what you ain't got.'

'What's that, then?'

'Straightforwardness. I can see Mr Buskirk coming. With you, I ain't so sure. Be easy, Hiram, can't you? You can't persuade me otherwise, you know,' he concluded with his rare smile, answering a challenge I wasn't aware of having made.

'Ah yes,' I snorted. 'We must respect our superior officers.'

'That's it. We must.'

Nevertheless, his words sounded automatic. I was convinced that they didn't express William Borden's true feelings, and that, whatever they were, he didn't mean to let me discover them.

AS IT TURNED OUT, Buskirk was right about the wind. No sooner had we passed the distant crags of the Marquesas, and steered away to the north-west, than the breeze suddenly dropped.

At first Buskirk took a vexatious delight in the accuracy of his prediction, but as the days passed, and we still failed to make any progress, we heard less on the subject. He and Gilbert slouched around the quarterdeck, surveying the flaccid sails. Occasionally they would shoot rancid glances at me, as if I were personally responsible for this turn of events.

For fourteen days the ship did not move, but merely drifted in the way that the Ark must once have drifted on the Flood. The air jerked with heat. The leaden blue Pacific, flat and monotonous, lay all about us like a stain left by the leaden blue sky.

When one has been becalmed for an extended period, the mind begins to play strange tricks. Events that don't at first seem to have any clear meaning rapidly become all-important. And so an apparently minor change in shipboard routine became the cause of an unfortunate misunderstanding between Captain Barnard and me.

The incidents that led up to it, emerging as they did from the mood of stasis and torpor on board at the time, seemed hideously linked to the crisis that came later.

In our wooden kingdom, even under full sail, time was a prison. I had known tedium before, and the staleness that comes from repetitive action, but I'd never endured anything as barren, as shriveled, as this. From hour to hour, from day to day and from week to week, the same stroke of the ship's bell was chased by the same whistle, the same call, the same round of duties. The twenty-four hours were divided into six watches. At the end of the first half-hour of each watch, the bell struck one, at the end of the second, two – until at eight bells the whole maddening loop began again.

The whistles that followed the bells were just as maddening. There was one peep and parp for calling all hands, another for hoisting away, a third for hauling taut and belaying, a fourth for loosing sails, and a fifth for furling them, and so on and on and on, in a nerve-flaying tattoo that repeated itself as incessantly as the bells.

And then there were the calls of the men: a deranged litany that followed hard on the whistles. At a change of wind the officer of the deck would give the order, 'Lay aft to the braces!' The sailing-master then shouted, 'Lay aft to the braces!' 'Lay aft to the braces!' squeaked every boy midshipman on board. 'Lay aft to the braces!' trumpeted the boatswain's mate. 'Lay aft to the braces!' blared the captain of the tops. 'Lay aft to the braces!' bayed the hands. 'Lay aft to the braces!' gurgled the sick, tossing in their hammocks beneath the water-line. 'Lay aft to the braces!' mouthed the fish in that dense, unfathomable, encompassing dark, into which I would gladly have launched myself, except that it promised neither safety nor relief.

For all around us, held back by the thinnest of bulwarks, by a hull that was always leaking or cracking and needed constant caulking and repair, lay death, in the form of the sea. It trickled through the ports and pooled in the bilges. It dragged at the pump chains. It flung its dumb weight repeatedly against the bow, with a disintegrating boom that killed all coherent thought. We ignored it. We never mentioned it. We pretended that there was no danger in what we were doing, no risk involved in floating above that grave in the thinnest of shells, certainly nothing remotely unnatural; that our safety was a matter of course, rather than an illusion. We did not refer to the fact that we were on this vessel, trapped in this demented cage, *because we could not get off*: because – as long as we wanted to stay alive – there was simply nowhere else to go.

Oh, it was perfectly clear to me. The *Orbis*, with her proudly curved sides, her three tall masts of planed pine, her delicately tapering spars, her miles of cordage that criss-crossed each other in apparent confusion but were in fact cunningly arranged in the most rigid of patterns, was a madhouse. To work her forty-four guns she kept a captive population of some four hundred and fifty lunatics, but she was sailed by only three-tenths of those.

Another tenth ruled her.

In that ship of fools no one, including those in charge, escaped imprisonment. The officers and petty officers spent their every waking moment, like ladies at a ghastly, perpetual dinner dance, fussing over gossamer degrees of seniority. The captain could not speak directly to the boatswain. The boatswain could not summon the young midshipmen from the steerage. The midshipmen reported only to the officers of their divisions. The officers of their divisions could communicate only with the first lieutenant.

As assistant surgeon I was in an unfortunate position. I could speak to anyone, and anyone, it soon became clear, could and would waylay me with intimate accounts of his pain, pus, and blocked bowels.

The majority – the waisters who kept the potato-lockers and saw to the sewerage; the holders who attended to the stores and cables; the landsmen of the after-guard, the armorer's mates and carpenter's mates, the painters, tinkers, and the marines – were deck-bound; enslaved, in order that they should have no leisure to ponder the absurdity of this arrangement, with gun drills, standing sentry, raising and lowering the sails for practice, and 'keeping the ship in order'. The keeping of 'order' meant an unbending drill of sweeping and scrubbing her oatmeal-brown decking, varnishing her wood until she glistened like foul treacle – every ladder, every hatch and every handspike, was daily coated in lacquer – and doing 'the bright work'.

The bright work! Nothing could have been duller. Each day the belaying-pins and rings on the spar deck were scoured with vinegar and buffed with flannel; the brass on the capstan and the companionways rubbed raw with rags, the monkey-tails, iron axes, and cutlasses scraped clean. The very hoops of the gun spit-boxes were given this crazy spit and polish. And afterwards these poor dupes, some of whom were permanently crescent-shaped from stooping, grinned and knocked their foreheads and thanked the uniformed clod in charge for not flogging them.

I went about my days in a coil of dread and anger. My anger was partly caused by a rising fear that I would lose my mind under the pressure of this collective madness.

The men who really did sail the frigate were a wily flock of topmen and sheet-anchormen, old hands who performed the actual work of keeping her afloat. Enthroned on the forecastle, or roosting in the fore, main and mizzenmasts, they had a crow's-eye view of the lunacy of the spar deck. When passing underneath the yards I sometimes overheard them mocking the officers.

As Buskirk inflated himself at a midshipman for not coming to attention quickly enough, I heard one croak, 'Why, ain't he the biggest toad in the puddle?'

And once I caught them mimicking my own bleating voice: 'Cap'n Bah-nahd. Cap'n Bah-nahd.'

The captain, knowing their value, left them mostly alone.

They were never disrespectful to Borden. He was the only officer who remained untouched by the insanity of the ship. He seldom said much, but he talked with everyone, and he did it with the same naturalness and grace with which he did everything else. I felt a tingle of envy on observing the unaffected ease with which he spoke to these old birds; the way in which, when he addressed even the most base, his whole silvery being seemed to flow outwards and expend itself, exactly as it had with me that treasured midnight weeks ago.

The captain of the maintop was a Rhode Islander called Fryar, whom Borden treated with an undeviating, irksome courtliness. Fryar made my flesh creep. He was erect and lean, with bloodshot eyes, seed-like stubs of teeth, and listless black hair combed into an artful curtain. There was an alarming incongruity between that elaborate coiffure and Fryar's spare body, as if the head of an archduchess had been stuck on a spike. He wasn't just persnickety about his own appearance – he imposed a Euclidean dress code on his subjects, who all wore their hat brims angled to the right and their neckerchiefs with the ends pointing downwards. They feared Fryar's displeasure, but above all they feared his despair. He was prey to bleak moods in which his voice grew lorn and fretful, his bearing as pointed as a quill. If a rope wasn't hitched to his satisfaction he would have it retied four or five times, clacking his tongue and caressing the knot imploringly with his womanish fingers.

Soon after we were becalmed Fryar reported to me with a bruised wrist. I strapped it up and advised him to move his hand as little as possible.

Two or three afternoons later I was on deck. I'd come up from the fetid darkness of the sick bay with a headache, famished for any sight other than oak, for light and movement. But above there was only more oak, and the dirty smudge of the sky, indistinguishable from the featureless ocean. The water was as flat and impassive as a swamp. It stretched out, permanently and willfully insensible to all human ambition or effort, drawing me deeper and deeper into paralysis with every minute that I gazed at it.

As I stood at the mainmast, stunned and blinking, I was distracted by an unusual amount of noise coming from the top. Remembering Fryar, I looked up. But I didn't spot him at his post. The usual gang of maintop-men was being worked by Isaac Duffy from the fore-castle. Under Duffy's direction they were making repairs to the main topsail. They moved aimlessly, bunching and fondling the unlaced cloth with lewd catcalls and laughter. While I watched, one of them hitched up his frock and scratched the hairy pelt of his belly with a languid thumb.

At that moment I happened to glance towards the forecastle. Fryar was on lookout, eyes turned not on the horizon but up at the mast as mine had been, his bound wrist held close to his breast, like a priest watching the desecration of a shrine.

I felt a dart of disquieting pain. Seeing Fryar brought low was an odd sensation, like coming across my reflection where I'd least expected to find it.

Did I, that afternoon, faced by the tarnished, indifferent ocean, recognize in him the image of my own weakness and despair? I have often wondered about this. I would like to think that my actions were complex, and not simply vindictive, but the truth is that I can't remember.

I remember only that I wanted to raise my fist and smash that loathsome mirror.

A FEW DAYS AFTER this the men of the forecastle were eating their midday meal on a square of tarpaulin spread out between two mess-chests. I was on my way to the wardroom and hurried by, not wanting to attract their notice. (That 'Cap'n Bah-nahd, Cap'n Bah-nahd' still rattled in my ears.) But as I crossed over to the gangway, Fryar got up and saluted me. I remarked that his wrist was no longer bandaged.

'Assistant Surgeon, a word with you, if you will, sir.'

'Yes, Mr Fryar?' I replied curtly.

'Surgeon, my arm is mended again.' He held out the blotched limb as proof. 'Why am I kept on fo'c'sle watch? I am fit for my usual place,' he added in a strangled tone, 'completely fit.'

'Mr Fryar, I have no idea. Yes, thank you,' I said dubiously – as he still waved his forearm in my face – 'I can see that the joint has almost healed. Pronation? Supination?'

'I never did, sir!'

'No – I mean – can you jiggle it? Tsk, tsk. Just about. Who removed your binding?'

'I didn't need it, sir. I am fit. Oh, sir, was it you told the captain to move me?'

'No, indeed. Why would I do that?'

'On account of my injury, sir. Maybe you did not know that I was fit. Because, sir,' he grizzled, 'I am as fit as I ever have been. Please, sir –' he rocked from foot to foot, his face contorting – 'I ain't no great shakes at speaking. But you talk like a book, Doctor. Please tell the captain I am fit.'

I was pierced by repugnance at Fryar's intentness. That plaintive exterior concealed a prim ferocity that both galled and excited me.

'Well, Fryar. I will do my best. But the captain must have his reasons. Have you perhaps been remiss in some point of duty? Or even – let me see now – *respect*?'

Fryar's chin retreated. He said nothing; only swung his head from side to side. His frantic eyes were gratifyingly shiny. Behind us the thugs of the forecastle had begun to moo and snicker. Fryar ran the heels of his hands over his cheeks between furious sighs. I believe that he would have struck me if he could have got away with it. Then he threw himself on my mercy.

'Sir, I must get my position back from Duffy. I must. Because you see, sir –' jabbing his elegant digits at the maintop in an agony of frustration – 'he's even letting them wear *calico trousers*.'

On gaining the distant safety of the quarterdeck I was dismayed to run into Captain Barnard himself, concealed behind the mizzenmast. William Borden was with him. The captain held a declination table in one fist, and in the other, a spy glass, which he tucked under his arm. My pulse started to tom-tom in alarm. I suspected that the spy glass had, until a moment ago, been trained on me.

'Is there some difficulty, Dr Carver?' asked the captain. 'Is one of the men unwell?'

'No, sir. I was conferring with them – more generally.'

'Ah. Generally, eh? I would have sworn from the expression on Matthew Fryar's face that he'd swallowed some very bitter medicine. Quite certain you have nothing of that sort hidden about you?'

I made as if to pat my pockets. 'Ha, ha. No, sir.'

'Very good. I'll let you get on with your duties, then.'

'Well, sir, if I may speak frankly –'

The captain gave me a level look.

'I did wonder, sir, after my brief conversation with Fryar – well, sir, I wondered why the latter had been taken off maintop watch and put on forecastle watch instead. I wondered, in short, sir, if you'd had a specific reason for making this change to the usual routine.'

'It was an impulse, Dr Carver, an impulse,' he replied blithely. 'Most ordinary men are subject to 'em. Since we have been becalmed for so long I thought that varying the watches might alleviate the monotony for the men. He is not the only hand who has been moved. Does that satisfy you?'

'With respect, sir, it seems to have been too effective – they have become rowdy and unsettled as a result. I have observed them, sir, and I believe that a reliable degree of monotony, far from being deleterious, is in fact conducive to peace in the simpler sort of mind.'

'Do you, now? Well, Dr Carver, it is useful to have such an observant young man as you on board. I shall think over what you have said, indeed I shall. I understand from our surgeon that you have been most observant, too, in one or two other matters of general shipboard health. We note what you say, sir – we note it.'

This surprised me; I hadn't thought that Spalding was the sort of man to learn from his mistakes.

'I would, however, be much obliged to you, sir,' the captain continued, 'if you would henceforth allow the men to go about their tasks undisturbed. No, sir –' he checked me with a calloused forefinger – 'let us permit them an *entirely undisturbed* enjoyment of that monotony of thought and society which you have so helpfully established as essential to their wellbeing. If I catch you agitating them again, sir –' here he scrolled up the chart as tightly as if he were wringing the neck of a chicken – 'I'll have you confined to the dispensary for the rest of our voyage, counting pills. And I don't care who your father is. Do I make myself clear?'

When he had gone off, Borden, who had listened intently to all of this with his head bowed, grasped me by the elbow.

'Hiram, you must let Fryar alone.' He spoke with uncharacteristic shortness. 'He's too full of feeling. You ain't helping him by encouraging his fancies.'

'Feeling!' The tamped-down resentment of weeks caught light, flaring out along my ribs. 'What about me? Who encourages *me*? Why must I be treated like a gasket or – or a pulley?' The image seemed very original to me, which merely increased my indignation. 'Doesn't it matter that I am *miserable*?'

'You make yourself miserable,' grimaced Borden, 'because you want what can't be.'

'Am I to have no freedom here? No agency at all?'

'Freedom? You came on board this ship to find *freedom*?' Borden laughed incredulously; an unkind laugh, I decided. 'No. You cannot. That's what wanting *is*. The looking for what you cannot have.'

'Can't I?' I griped. 'Why can't I have it? All I want is to make my mark.'

His throat bulged with strain. 'You want to command. But you can't command before you have learned obedience.'

What did I want? What I wanted, right then, was to pummel the disdain out of his ridiculous kingly face, to harry his tightly buttoned chest – he was already turning away, as if I were nothing! As if we'd never shared a single moment out of the ordinary! – so that he'd open his heart and let me in.

BY THE TIME I reached the wardroom I was in a smoldering mood, made even worse by finding Buskirk and Gilbert at the only table, flipping quarters into two teacups balanced on a copy of Bowditch's *New American Practical Navigator*.

'Join us, do, old son,' said Buskirk. 'We are just conducting an exercise in navigational mathematics.'

'So I see.' I leaned in the doorway, trying to affect a disinterested pose, but then gave it up and sloped into a chair. 'The truth is, Buskirk, I don't feel all that chirk. I'd rather not converse, if you don't mind.' I let my forehead flop onto the cool wood of the tabletop.

'What's up, old boy?' asked Buskirk, sinking a coin with a plink and a splash. 'Weather getting to you?'

'That's nine to you, sir,' chirped Gilbert. I could hear him delivering a vigorous nick to the edge of Bowditch with his pocket knife.

'Well, actually, if you must know,' I drooled into the soothing grain, 'I've been given a blasting by Jehovah.'

'Bad luck, Carver. Never mind. You've become very thick with the Hero. I'd stick close to him if I was you. The captain won't hear a word said against him.'

'I have no idea what you're talking about, Buskirk.'

'Our Hero, my friend. Will Borden. The Angel of the *Providence*.'

I raised my head. 'Do you mean the third lieutenant?'

'Yes him. Handsome bugger, ain't he? Like a fucking winged seraph.'

Gilbert tittered nervously. I couldn't help smiling too, out of sheer pique.

'Have you never studied the Annals, old pal?' asked Buskirk.

'The what?'

'The Annals of our Service.' His next shot went wide and spun off the table. 'My turn again, Gilly.'

I groaned. 'As little as I can help.'

'Well, Borden's the patron saint of this squadron, don't you know.' Buskirk pretended to sign a blessing over me. 'He's been plowing the Pacific his whole career, ever since he started on the *Providence*, back in 'eighteen or 'nineteen.' He stretched across and adjusted a cup, leaving Gilbert to hunt for the coin.

'Yes, and what of it?'

'Well, course he was no one then. But the crew on the *Providence* rose up against their officers and a handful of men got out in a boat. Borden was one of them. He sailed them all the way back to South America. Took more than two months. Kept most of 'em alive, too.'

'No one? What do you mean, he was "no one"?'

'He was a tar. One of the hands. Ordinary seaman, would you believe. Testified at the inquiry afterwards on the captain's behalf, though our Billy was the only one who came out of the thing well. Got promoted pretty sharpish after that.'

'Forgive me, Buskirk, but it all sounds very unlikely. Are you sure you aren't getting this from a boys' periodical?'

'Certainly not.' He took elaborate sightings of the teacups along his thumb before preparing to fire again. 'Ask anyone. Ask Jehovah. 'Sakes, ask Borden. Ask the Angel Gabriel himself! Don't know why he never speaks about it. I would.'

'Pah, I'm sure you would.' I was sitting up now. 'But if he is as much of a hero as you say – and even if he isn't – it'd be quite out of character for him to allude to an episode so – so extraordinary. So harrowing!'

'Oh don't sound so high-falutin', Carver.' Buskirk launched his quarter with a flick. It wobbled through the air and fell into the nearest cup, knocking it over. Tea slopped onto the table. 'Ten!' gloated Buskirk. 'And *that*, Gilbert, is how you plot a trajectory. Lordy, what a mess! Clear it up for us, there's a good fellow.'

The boatswain's pipe drilled through the bulkhead, signaling the change of watch. Buskirk winked fraternally at me and smoothed his front hair. 'Borden is as set on getting a leg up as you or I,' he smirked. 'If he don't talk about it, it's for another reason, depend on it.'

I HAD NO INTENTION of asking William Borden any such impertinent questions. But I noticed, while the humid heat curdled the air like souring cream and the ship seemed to dip lower and lower in the water, as if under the aggregate weight of our despair, that the captain consulted Borden rather more, and Buskirk rather less.

I also noticed that Buskirk, while remaining civil to Borden in spite of this slight, followed him with an expression that shuttled between greed and fear. At times I was convinced that Borden knew that he was being stalked; that his somber indifference to Buskirk's circling was camouflage. He'd had to develop his lion-like imperturbability, I imagined, in part because his habitat was rife with jackals.

'G'day, to you, Mr Borden.' Here Buskirk was again, padding along the spar deck.

'Good day, Mr Buskirk, sir.'

'Damned inconvenient, being adrift like this.'

'Aye, sir.'

'Got any tips for raising a wind?'

Borden didn't say a word.

'No? I rather thought you were party to maritime secrets unknown to the rest of us mere mortals.' A hyena-like laugh. 'Voicepipe straight to Neptune's ear, that type of thing. Ways of saving this poor old flesh.'

It was the jibber-jabber of a pack animal – but Borden blenched. If Buskirk was afraid of Borden, then Borden, I realized with a shiver of surprise, was wary of Buskirk in turn.

Was Buskirk's story true? Had Borden really survived mutiny and near death on this stretch of water, and not just survived them, but withstood them – heroically, gloriously? I couldn't get a proper grip on him somehow, couldn't steer my way through the questions that came rushing at me. Whenever I tried to right myself, my thoughts were capsized by a wave of confusion. And I churned now in the wake of a new speculation: that Borden's reserve, his apparently inviolable self-sufficiency, was the result, not of self-discipline or of an inherently melancholy disposition as I'd at first assumed, but of an experience that was, to me, essentially and profoundly unimaginable.

I didn't want to care for his good opinion, but I did. Oh, I did. More than that, I craved his confidence.

THREE

For two weeks the ocean lay in that bewitched state that is often the harbinger of a dramatic change. The horizon was swagged with clouds that piled up overhead in a roiling mass, its black bole split by a purple artery trailing ghoulish light like blood from a wound. And still there was no breeze; not a whiff, not a flurry. It was as if the world had stopped turning.

On the second Sunday of this supernatural calm we were all gathered on deck in the waist before midday, at our prayers. The captain had led us in divine service that morning, but since this was a partial day of rest and the ship was already tacky with vinegar and lacquer, to fill the time between breakfast and dinner the entire company had been piped up for an extraordinary round of piety.

The men scuffed their feet drowsily. In the baking hush I could hear them draw slow breaths through their mouths.

'What are we praying for?' I whispered to Borden. 'I hope it's wind.'

He glanced down at me but did not reply. Ever since our exchange of words on the quarterdeck I'd been superstitiously anxious whenever I came near him, as though he might indeed have a way of reading my mind.

I was unprepared for the flatness of his eye. The violet light had walled it about with shadows. His skin had a coarse, mineral sheen; a muscle jumped in his cheek.

But I couldn't study him then. The captain lingered over each prayer, hands folded like a prize-fighter's. When he got to the Our Father he intoned it with challenging emphases, pointing his Bible at the haunch of cloud above us, as if at an unseen adversary.

At last the pipe struck up calling the hands to dinner. 'Well, let's hope all that praying has appeased the gods,' I blurted. 'Though I guess that nothing less than a human sacrifice is going to do the trick now.'

Borden twisted around so suddenly that I thought he'd lost his footing. I reached out my arm to steady him and for a second or two we waltzed together in an appalled embrace. His face, inert before, was wide open – alive with terror.

'Mr Borden!' I half shouted into his ear. 'Are you completely well?'

In another second he'd recovered himself and fended me off. 'Yes.' He sucked in a loud lungful of claggy air. 'Let me go, Hiram. It's the heat. Too much standing about. I'll go below for a moment.'

He slipped into the surge of bodies on deck and allowed the press of it to carry him aft towards the companionways, where I briefly made out the flash of his bronze head in the gloom. I tried to follow him, but couldn't take five paces.

Then I found my way deliberately obstructed.

'Doctor. Sir.' It was Fryar, gracious fingers shaping a spire, hair arranged about his ears in a lugubrious fan. He fossicked with his neck-erchief. His smooth jowls were quivering. 'I ask a word. Just a word, sir.'

'Look here, Fryar! I don't have time for this now.'

Keeping his eyelids coquettishly at half-mast, his neck sclerotic with fury, he simpered, 'When *will* you have time, sir?'

I was overwhelmed by an urge to do violence to that neck. 'Listen to me. I don't know what you have done to offend *Cap'n Bah-nahd.*' I stretched out the words as if I were dragging on a saw. 'But offend him you surely have. I can't do any more for you,' I hissed, ducking into the throng. 'I'm sorry.'

It was no good. Though I rowed hard with my elbows, I'd lost Borden. I was being forced forwards as if a great contraction of muscle were squeezing me from every side. I headed for the companionways, planning to make my way to the wardroom and find him there. But I hadn't got very far when I heard a shrill cry, succeeded by an outward ripple in the swell.

Near the hatches there was a jostling and hooting, and a general carnival atmosphere.

Isaac Duffy rolled about on the boards, mewling and holding his temples. Fryar stood over him, swiping at the air with one of the capstan bars. Behind them a knot of topmen and forecastle men had begun to gouge and prod each other. A few onlookers broke into a slow syncopated clapping while shouting out their approval.

In the middle of the tangle hopped Buskirk, his arms going around like windmills. 'Desist! Desist, I tell you!' There was widespread laughter at this, and faster clapping. 'Two dozen lashes, Fryar!' he yodeled. 'Put down that blasted bar! D'you hear me?'

'Ooh,' said someone. 'That *blarsted* bar!'

'Goddamn you!' Buskirk yipped. 'I'll have the whole company on rations for a week! All of you! Every last man! Mr Borden! Mr Borden, where are you? Assist me, sir!'

He was there, head blazing above the rest, as if he'd never left the deck. He walked up to Fryar and took the capstan bar from his hands. Fryar sank to his knees with a snivel. The men stopped their scuffling. In the abrupt silence all that could be heard was the low creaking and moaning of the stays.

'Thank you, Mr Borden.' Captain Barnard was already nudging his way to the front. He was bareheaded, and I saw that the top button of his shirt was undone. How old and worn he was! And what a little man, compared to Borden! The thought came to me unbidden.

'Two dozen lashes, is it, Mr Buskirk?' he asked in a parched voice.

'It is a first offence, sir,' said Borden.

'Very well,' agreed the captain. 'A dozen.'

'Flog him, Captain,' said Borden quietly. 'But don't impose rations on the others.'

'I have not heard you, Mr Borden.'

Buskirk was almost on tiptoe with agitation. 'Sir, if I may just say something also. This attack was unprovoked. I witnessed it all. And on the Sabbath too. A proper example should be set. Though twelve lashes may well be the standard –'

'By God, Mr Buskirk, I have had enough of your noise today!' Sweat dropped from the captain's stubbled scalp as he fumbled with his collar button. 'There is one master on this ship, sir, d'you mark me? One!' He ran his tongue over his lower lip as if trying to rid himself of a bad taste. '*Proper!* I am the law here, Lieutenant. Only I. Do you understand me? You will summon all hands at four bells. We will delay our dinner.' Before quitting the deck he turned his jagged gaze on me. 'And you, Dr Carver, will attend Mr Fryar at the mast.'

'Well, Borden,' ventured Buskirk, swatting at his lapels. 'There's no reasoning with him, eh?'

'I reckon you left him no choice but to starve the men,' said Borden, 'to save you from seeming an even bigger fool.'

With these words a membrane seemed to have been peeled away from the familiar world. How strange Borden looked – emptied out, exposed.

Buskirk scanned the rigging with careful insouciance, as if appraising the condition of the ship: her scorched timbers and webbed ratlines, her withered pennants.

'You think you're untouchable, don't you?' he said. 'But I tell you, Borden. You're not.' The last syllable came out as a falsetto. 'We'll see how much of an appetite they have after we're through with Fryar. Go and attire yourself as befits your rank, Third Lieutenant. That's what I propose to do.'

I felt suddenly short of breath. 'Is he decking himself out for a ball? Mr Borden. William. I think – that is, I don't rightly know. I may be to blame in this. I fear I am.'

Borden was trembling down the length of his body. His filmed eye stared directly at mine. 'Whatever you've done or not done, Hiram, it's too late.'

Panic sizzled through me. 'Oh God. What now?'

'Get straightened up. Go above when you hear the call. The steward will bring you your seawater.'

'Seawater? Christ, I don't want a shower at this time!'

'The water ain't for you, Doctor. It's for Fryar.'

It wasn't long before I understood what he meant.

*

AT FOUR BELLS OF the afternoon watch the captain strode out to the mainmast in full dress. Buskirk and Gilbert hovered about him like two bluebottles, their swords clanking together when they moved.

One of the hatchway gratings had been taken away and laid on the deck boards, close to the bulwarks. I stood beside it, in a soggy boil, as if on a stage. My hairline itched under the cockaded chimney of my hat, which sucked up heat and threatened to skate off, so that I had to keep poking at it.

The boatswain's mate dawdled on my other side, playing absent-mindedly with the knotted tails of the cat. He'd shed his jacket and draped it over the rail. He was wearing a pressed frock and brilliantly waxed shoes that squeaked. In the puce light pouring from the heaped cloud overhead I could count the warts on his neck: one, two, three; one, two, three. During the endless quarter-hour in which we waited for the ship's company to assemble I counted them compulsively.

There was a pail of brine at my feet, placed there by Ole Henry, who normally saw to my shaving water.

'Henry,' I'd pleaded, because asking anyone else, especially the boatswain's mate, was too humiliating. 'What am I to do with this?'

'Why, sir,' said Ole Henry with gentle exasperation. 'You gone wash Mr Fryar down with it, sir. Between stripes.'

'*Wash?*'

'Yessir. Wash.' He made a casting motion with his arms. 'Don't they teach you young peoples nothing these days?'

From time to time, to shatter the image of my face in its gritty depths, I nudged the pail with the side of my foot.

Prior to taking his place with the other officers Borden came and stopped near me. I recognized with a plunge of unease that he still had that remote, heavy-lidded look.

'Hiram.' His words were muted, and I had to strain to catch them. 'Fryar ain't been flogged before.'

I would have asked him something more, but the master-at-arms had appeared at the edge of my vision with Fryar and I was preoccupied with a billowing of my senses, coupled with the bizarre sensation that I was treading the air an inch or two outside my own skull.

Everything that took place next unfolded very swiftly while being performed with such deliberation that it seemed to exist outside time.

Fryar was led up to the grating and climbed onto it. He kept his head up until told to remove his shirt, which he did with a terrible, frail modesty. His skin was silken and hairless, his nipples large and crimped like two surprised Os.

The master-at-arms spread Fryar's ankles and strapped them to the crossbars, then tied his outstretched wrists to the hammock netting above.

I believe that my memory of that afternoon became lodged in my being in some way, for it has often returned to me in dreams and in disruptions of my waking life – the purple sheen on the sails, the sky drawing in around us, the buzz of a mosquito at my ear; the sullen faces of the crew crowded under the mainyard, the captain reading the Articles, Buskirk's order to the boatswain's mate to begin, the eternity before the first blow fell, and the incongruous red fan that flirted across Fryar's back in the same moment.

Fryar's mouth opened noiselessly, as if all his breath had been sucked inwards. He sagged in his constraints.

'One,' announced the master-at-arms.

The mosquito still hunted. Otherwise there was silence.

'Dr Carver,' prompted Spalding from the thicket of blue uniforms.

I lifted the bucket, took a step forwards, and threw salt water at Fryar. I must have hit him, because he shrieked then. His whole body bucked and yawed again. I stepped back.

The boatswain's mate tripped along on his loudly squeaking shoes, arm upraised. The second lash crossed the welts of the first in a crazy filigree. Fryar let out a choked whinny and turned his head until his cheek was rucked up against his shoulder. His bewildered eye looked straight at me.

'Two,' chanted the master-at-arms.

It came to me with a throb of astonishment that we were going to perform these actions over and over.

'Assistant Surgeon,' clucked Spalding. 'Look lively, sir!'

This time I had to advance on that watching eye. Once I was finished, Fryar's white ducks were stained pink at the waist.

It can't go on much longer, I thought. It will be done with soon.

I was wrong. It seemed to go on for the entire afternoon. From time to time a spasm of wind tossed the pennants on the maintop. The last of the unearthly light died from the sky, leaving a dull lintel of cloud that stretched from bow to stern. The gray air was pitted with rain.

Fryar lost consciousness after the fifth lash. We continued to perform our punctilious choreography on his unresponsive body for what might have been another hour, although rational reflection tells me that the whole thing could not have taken more than twenty minutes.

Then the captain called a halt.

'Dr Carver, please assess the prisoner.'

'Assess, sir?' I was mesmerized by my own reply. How considered my voice sounded! My mouth felt clogged, as if it were full of sand or rock. A delicious numbness, like the numbness brought on by alcohol, had come over me. Nothing I heard or said was remotely helpful to understanding. 'In what way assess?'

I saw Spalding approach the captain. 'Sir,' he said. 'If I may advise.'

The captain waved him away. 'No, thank you, Surgeon. This is Dr Carver's responsibility.' I caught the glimmer of his epaulets and decided, in my befuddlement, to fix on those. 'Assess the prisoner, Dr Carver. Is he fit?'

I remembered Fryar's words to me on the forecastle. *I am fit. Please tell the captain I am fit.* They seemed to have been spoken many years ago.

'Fit for what, sir?'

'Fit to withstand the rest of his sentence, you idiot,' cawed Spalding.

I regarded the pulp of Fryar's back, in which black ruts had begun to crisp. Only the tender declivities above the buttocks were unflayed. That part of him might have belonged to a different species of creature.

'Are you unsure?' snapped Spalding. 'Then say so.'

I tried my voice again. 'I think any more may kill him. Sir.'

'Thank you, Assistant Surgeon.' The captain nodded, not ungenially, at Buskirk, who gawped at us like an overstrained child waiting to be sent off to bed. 'Take him down.'

The master-at-arms threw Fryar's shirt over him and loosened his cords, at which Fryar spilled sideways onto the grating in a graceful curve.

A mad piping began on the quarterdeck. I felt quite empty except for the prickling of the sickness in my guts. To my mortification, they let forth a slow, seething sing-song. I plucked at my belt and saw that the buckle was sprigged with blood.

Borden came up to me as the company dispersed. 'The wind's rising, Hiram, see,' he said. 'It's nearly time for dinner. I hope you are hungry.'

FOUR

WE DINED AT THE pocked table in the wardroom. Above us the lamp searched out the corners of the darkening cabin with its swaying tongue. In the last hour the *Orbis* had begun to list and the air to taste of iron. As the wind rose her canvas grew plump; her woodwork chattered and sang. When the order came to make sail my stomach drew tight with dread.

Ole Henry brought in the soup, unleashing a savory fog that condensed to droplets on my crawling skin. 'You gone eat now, ain't you, sir?' he scolded. 'You nothing but grief and gristle.'

'I don't think I can, thank you, Henry,' I said. 'Maybe just some biscuit.'

Before coming to dinner I'd examined Fryar's back in the sick bay. There wasn't much I could do with the boggy meat of it and I was under instructions not to give him rum. When I offered him brandy from my own flask, he turned his face to the wall.

Henry made a clicking sound, as if chivvying a horse, and produced a basket of rolls. 'See now, sir. Cook been baking. You try a tiny piece of this for me.'

We ate joylessly. The splintered crust of the bread scratched my throat. Buskirk plainly had no appetite, but put on a great show of mouthing the soup – it was thin and brown, like tea – while gulping two glasses of claret. Gilbert dangled his spoon in his right hand and worried at a fat pustule on his chin with the fingernails of his left. Once in a while our four little midshipmen, as sensitive to the poisonous atmosphere as canaries, hazarded a watchful peck at a crumb. Only Spalding ate with relish, lifting his bowl by the handles and scurrying after the backwash. Borden didn't eat or drink at all.

We were still stalled over the first course when the vessel tipped sharply to her larboard side, sending the soup tureen tobogganing down the table. Henry staggered in a few minutes later bearing sliced beef on a platter, which he wedged against the salt cellar. He came back a second time carrying a dish of pudding and another of peas and cabbage, and had begun to ladle these out when there was a knock on the wardroom door. He opened it reluctantly, with much grousing.

Behind the door stood a huddle of men. One of them held out a pair of boiled potatoes in a skillet.

'Lieutenant Buskirk,' he said, 'I want to speak with you if you please.'

'Yes?' Buskirk, who had been tormenting a fold of cabbage, put aside his knife.

'Lieutenant, do you think these is potatoes enough for eight men?'

'Well, my man, if you are not satisfied with what there is, you can pass in your pan and go without any.' He added under his breath, 'Or you can piss in it.'

'Then I'll speak to Lieutenant Borden, sir, if you will,' the hand persisted.

Borden rubbed a finger steadily around the neck of the salt cellar, but didn't raise his eyes.

'I am the superior officer here,' said Buskirk. 'If you've anything further to say you can take it up with Captain Barnard in his quarters. Now be off or you'll find yourself up at the mast for insolence.'

'The captain warn't never one to cheat a man of food, sir,' came the rejoinder through the door's narrowing chink. 'And neither was Mr Borden. Not till you came.'

'Tarnation,' grunted Buskirk. 'We don't want to punish them, but sometimes they give us no damned leeway.' He stuffed a chunk of pudding into his mouth.

'What sort of soup was it we had tonight, Henry?' asked Borden offhandedly.

'It was turtle soup, sir. A big bull sea turtle. I caught him myself with a line just this morning.' Ole Henry gave a baleful sniff and sloped off with the tureen.

'There is no harm in a fast,' declared Spalding, siphoning up claret through his pursed beak. 'I have often fasted.'

Borden caressed the salt cellar with such force that it tipped over. We followed it with our eyes as it rolled along the tablecloth and thudded to the floor.

'The men are to do seven days' work on empty stomachs,' he said quietly.

'Hunger is a test of character, Lieutenant. It proves the true mettle of a man.'

'It proves nothing, Surgeon.'

'Consider my assistant here,' Spalding chuckled. 'He's an example to us all. No food ever passes *his* lips.'

Everyone except Borden turned to look at me. A slash of rain fell across the skylight. As the room tilted to starboard, the glass was lit up by a double burst of lightning.

All at once I knew that I would vomit if I didn't keep my body absolutely still, and my mind as empty as possible. The nightmare quality of the day seemed to have entered me as a monstrous hollowness, a blankness; a doomed recognition that all of it – not just what we had done that afternoon, but the whole cruise, our very presence in that room, on that ship, on that ocean – was a mistake, a sickening error, for which we could and would never be forgiven.

'It is a matter of justice, Mr Borden,' sneered Buskirk. 'Of a clear and, ah, adamantine principle. All *educated* naval officers have been schooled in when to apply it. Ain't that so, Carver?'

'I wouldn't know,' I mumbled, teetering from my chair. 'My naval schooling has mostly been in applying salve to the clap.'

Spalding leaned towards me. 'Young man,' he asked with a quizzical squint, 'are you entirely in your right mind today?'

'No, sir,' I burped. 'Excuse me. I think I'm going to heave up.'

'There's a storm breaking,' said Borden, getting to his feet. 'I'll come on deck with you and look at the staysails. With your permission, Mr Buskirk.'

Buskirk got up too. 'You'll stay and finish your dinner like a civilized man, Mr Borden. Sit down, sir. Sit or I'll order you to sit.'

They stood utterly still, facing each other over the cold cabbage while the lamp played zig-zags of shadow across the table. In the savage light Borden's broad frame juddered and leaped. His expression had the void fixity of a hunted thing. The skylight flashed its rectangle of angry fire, turning the room and everything in it – the table, our three abandoned chairs; every glass, dish and plate, knife, fork and spoon – to ash, before going instantly dark again.

I reached the thwacking wardroom door just as the lightning picked out Borden's extinguished face.

ABOVE DECKS THE SOLID world seemed to have dissolved. Mast-high walls of spray rose and tore like tissue as the men clambered about the rigging, securing sails that were so bloated with wind that their braces screeched at the belaying points. The spar deck was sheeted with water. I scudded to leeward, hugging the rail, and vomited liquidly over the side. Below me the ocean exploded in terrifying detonations, pure sound in the substanceless wet.

I don't know how long I hung there. I was clamped to the rail when one of the midshipmen came skidding up, his jacket ballooning around him. 'I've been searching for you everywhere, sir,' he yawped above the noise. 'Mr Buskirk needs you in the wardroom!'

I shooed him away. 'Tell Mr Buskirk that I'm still unwell, there's a good lad.'

'It ain't the lieutenant says so, sir, it's the captain.' His eyes, oddly black and bead-like, skipped in their sockets. 'Lieutenant Buskirk's been hurt. He can't talk at all.'

'Well, that's a mercy, at least.' I let go of the rail to take a better look at the boy. 'Whatever's the matter?' The ship pitched at the bow, tumbling us together and bringing my face level with his enormous pupils. It occurred to me, with a frisson of surprise, that he was in shock.

'I can't tell you, sir, I can't! The captain says to be quick. Mr Buskirk's bleeding like a stuck pig.'

46

I wasn't prepared for the freakish scene that met me when I got to the wardroom. The captain was indeed there, holding a white damask napkin to his lap. The table was pulled at an angle and several of the chairs had been overturned. A spoor of broken china and glass crunched underfoot.

Buskirk lay in the middle of the floor. His bouffant hair was haloed by a widening circle of blood which I identified first by its ferrous smell. It was so thick and so glossy that it might have been paint. The table legs were syrupy with blood. The folds of the tablecloth nearest to Buskirk were hooped with arabesques of blood. My immediate thought was that he was dead. But then I saw that blood was still pumping, with a rhythmical viscous rush, from a ragged hole in his neck.

Spalding knelt beside him, gauntleted in blood, sopping up the ooze with what appeared to be a shirt. 'Ah, Dr Carver. We have had a busy time of it while you were taking the air. Come and help me close up this laceration, sir.'

While the ship rolled and careened I dabbed away at Buskirk's wound with the saturated cloth. Spalding set about yoking the yawning flesh back together using a needle and a skein of gut. At the first stitch, Buskirk regained consciousness and began to utter drawn-out squeals, although he was too weak to move.

Then I realized that a shirtless Gilbert stood at the end of the table, quaking and crying.

'Mr Gilbert,' said the captain firmly. 'Mr Gilbert, you may turn in. Go, sir. Thank you for the use of your shirt. You are relieved of any further duties tonight.'

'I have staunched the bleeding, sir,' said Spalding after a while, sitting back. 'Mr Buskirk's throat is badly torn here and here – ah,

47

yes, and *here* –' he stabbed at the pulsing cavity with a bloody finger – 'but the artery is unharmed.'

'Good. Can you silence him?'

'I can give him something to relieve the pain, certainly.'

'The pain be damned. Shut him up, Surgeon. And then, Dr Spalding, I would like you to do the same for Mr Borden below. Keep him quiet. Take Dr Carver with you. Come to my cabin, both of you, once he's still.'

'Mr Borden?' I asked. 'What does Mr Borden have to do with this?' I looked around, still clutching the hardening rag, and saw that Borden was not there. 'Is Mr Borden hurt too?'

Spalding gave a sardonic cackle. 'Not unless he's dislocated his jaw.'

This made no sense at all to me. The strain of madness running through the evening now bloomed unchecked, infecting everything. 'Was there an accident?'

'No, no. No accident,' said the captain heavily. He had the loose-wattled pallor of extreme exhaustion. 'Mr Borden is unhurt. But he is a danger to himself. I have set a watch over him in the stores for the time being.'

The struggle of weeks left my body. I felt light-headed, uncaring, as if I'd been clinging on very tightly to the edge of a raft and was about to let go. 'I'm afraid I don't understand.'

'Assistant Surgeon.' Captain Barnard spoke like a man humoring a creature of limited intelligence, a lapdog or an infant. 'Mr Borden did this to Mr Buskirk.'

He seemed to notice the napkin in his hand for the first time, and wiped his mouth on it with weary revulsion.

*

WE FILLED BUSKIRK UP with tincture of belladonna and put him to bed. As an afterthought Spalding slapped a poultice of wet bread on his wound. He'd made an imprecise job of stitching up the outer tissues, not troubling to trim the edges, which were frilled like the rim of a pie. The entire area from Buskirk's left clavicle to his under ear would be scarred.

By this time I felt as if the sea had entered my brain and obliterated all meaning with its violent ticking. When we made our way down to the stores on the orlop deck, jouncing against the overhead beams at every step, I thought I would sink. 'But what *happened*, sir?' I cried.

'You can see what happened,' replied Spalding impatiently. 'Mr Borden has almost killed Mr Buskirk.'

'Then he must have been provoked! Buskirk must have done or said something to him first.'

'Mr Buskirk did nothing, other than to make pleasant conversation such as any gentleman might make. And for that he has nearly got his head ripped off.'

'I don't believe it!'

'Well, for your own self-preservation I suggest that you try, before we go calling on Mr Borden.'

'Ripped? *Ripped?*' I was bellowing now. Every roll of the ship was wrenching me further from myself, into irresistible chaos. 'But with what?' I couldn't remember seeing a weapon anywhere in the bloodied wardroom. '*What did Mr Borden use?*'

Spalding tapped a graying incisor and touched the skin of his crenellated neck lightly with his fingertips, as if to check that it was still intact. 'His teeth.'

Two marines loitered by the door of the smaller of the stores,

49

from behind which frenzied thumps and roars could be heard. Their hair was shaved along the sides, Indian-style, exposing bluish scalps. They were stocky and work-hardened and looked unconcerned either by the listing of the ship, the racket, or what they were about to be called on to do. They saluted Spalding, palms down, and stood to.

'So, boys,' said Spalding. He listened at the door, taking care not to put his ear too close to it. 'Prisoner still restless, I gather?'

''Bout the same as before, sir,' answered the burlier of the two men, who was called Mullins. He had a broken nose from which his face deepened in seams. His mouth corners were stained with tobacco juice. 'I reckon he's been breaking up them barrels for kindling.' The other man, a brawler named Flint whose forearms were covered in lavender veins, gave a rumbling laugh. A pair of irons swung from his hand.

Spalding tugged at his bloodstained cuffs. 'Let's not dilly-dally, then. Dr Carver is here to lend us his valuable assistance. After we open the door you are to go in front and hold Mr Borden down. I see you have irons – use them. Use a strap too if you have to.'

'Aye, sir,' said the men, cracking their knuckles.

'Dr Carver, if you would be kind enough to commandeer Mr Borden's shoulders and get his mouth open, I will administer the sedative.' Spalding flourished his phial of belladonna. 'Any questions?'

'How am I to manage that, sir?' I asked. The roaring and pounding were, if anything, louder.

'Good heavens, man, I'm sure you'll think of something,' he scowled. 'Jack it open with your thumbs if there's no other way. I trust that's all clear. Right, lads. Unlock the door when I say "now". Now!'

At first I could make nothing out in the darkness. It was hot, and rank with an overpowering smell of creosote and rotting cheese. Unnervingly, the pounding had stopped, and had been replaced by a high-pitched whine. The lantern on the stairs creaked. As I wavered on the threshold there came a flapping and thwupping noise, as if a wet sheet had snapped out towards us and struck a wall, except that there was no wall where we stood. Someone yowled in pain.

The door was kicked wide and in the influx of light I saw the two men grappling with what appeared to be a headless torso that reared and buckled and arched its back in fantastic shapes. Mullins, clasping it by the middle in a lopsided hug, was trying to drag it to the ground. His face was wet with blood. Flint parried the flailing legs. He wound his arms about the thighs, put his head down, and butted the crotch with his full strength.

The torso folded abruptly into a sitting position, revealing the distended jaws and blackened head of William Borden.

While Flint hobbled Borden's feet with the irons, Mullins twisted his wrists behind his back and wove a strap around them. Jogging his shins onto Borden's shoulders, he lowered himself with a steady, almost coaxing deliberation. After a minute or two Borden's skull jolted against the deck.

'Please remember, gentlemen, that you are handling an officer of the United States Navy,' sighed Spalding. 'Now, Dr Carver, if you would please step forward.'

'What in God's name is that black stuff on his head?' I asked. Though horizontal, Borden was still rollicking from one side to the other and emitting an inhuman whine.

'I believe it is congealed blood,' observed Spalding. 'Mr Buskirk's, if I'm not mistaken. So, sir,' he said, addressing Borden. 'You must be quiet. You are disturbing the captain at his dinner with your ravings.'

'Devil,' said Borden with shocking lucidity, tossing and turning until Mullins was nearly unseated.

'Dr Carver, step up, please,' commanded Spalding. 'You may relieve Mr Mullins here at the bow.'

Borden lifted his feet and brought the irons down on the boards with a crash, narrowly missing Flint's hands.

'Stop your dancing, sir,' said Spalding, 'and co-operate. And keep a civil tongue in your head, if you will.'

'He'll be dancing on nothing soon,' muttered Flint.

'Thank you, Mr Flint.' Spalding cast a glance at Borden's shuddering body. 'That's enough. Dr Carver, what are you waiting for?'

I made my way over to Mullins. As soon as I did, Borden stopped twisting. There was an awkward scramble as I knelt and shuffled my shins into place on either side of Borden's head instead of Mullins's, first the left shin, then the right. Borden lay perfectly still and watched me, his eyes gleaming in their black frame.

'Well done, gentlemen,' said Spalding. 'Mr Borden, I am going to give you some medicine. Medicine, d'you hear? It will make you feel better. I would like you to open your mouth and drink it, without any more of this foolishness. Dr Carver is going to place his hand on your chin, and when he does so I want you to open your lips. If you would, Dr Carver. Your hand. Firmly now.'

I extended my right hand and cupped it around the lower half of Borden's face. His skin was sticky and alive with heat, as if the blood there were his own, welling from some unseen source. His pulse skittered wildly under my palm.

'I said firmly, damn you,' whispered Spalding. 'Shove him down if he resists.'

I tightened my grip. Borden growled. His lip lifted a little.

'Good man. Here we are, now. Drink up.' Spalding uncorked the phial and attempted to dribble its contents down Borden's throat.

At once Borden raised his head in a sinuous movement and sank his teeth into the side of Spalding's hand. I think I tried to stop him, but it was like trying to stop a snake from striking. The chief impression I had was of slipperiness and an utterly unexpected grace. For a startled second I felt exhilaration, complicity, a harsh soaring in my chest. The phial shattered with a tinkle. The reek of the tincture, sweet as stewed pears, spread through the air as Borden shook Spalding's captive hand slowly to and fro. Apart from the shattering of the glass it was all soundless.

Spalding remained bolt upright, regarding his hand with an unconvinced expression, as if examining a badly sewn glove. After a few more shakes Borden opened his jaws and spat the hand out. It hung at Spalding's side, imprinted with a garland of furled teethmarks that began to bloom and drip.

Borden sat up. He spoke, deliberately and gravely. 'You, Surgeon, really are a cocksucking devil, ain't you? Cocksucking son of Satan. I absolve you. I absolve you of everything.'

Spalding stuck his damaged hand into his armpit and leaned, panting, against the wall of the store. He looked at Flint. 'Deck him,' he breathed.

Stepping across on the balls of his feet, fists held up, Flint hit Borden on the temple above his left eye. Then, when Borden's throat was exposed, he struck him again, very neatly, on the larynx. Borden coughed once and slid down onto the floor.

When I emerged from the stores, Spalding was on the staircase, binding his hand with his cravat.

'Are you all right, sir?' I asked.

'Yes, thank you, perfectly all right. Dr Carver, please note that a senior officer was insulted today.'

'It was not meant, Dr Spalding. I would swear, sir, that it was not meant. Mr Borden is not himself.'

'And bitten. And *bitten*, sir.' His injury was already seeping through its makeshift bandage. Exhaling deeply, he brushed down his coat, freckling it with blood. 'This is what happens when we allow the lower orders to rise up the ranks.'

'I fancy they could bite us just as easily without being promoted first,' I speculated.

Spalding made no effort to dissemble his disgust. 'Your impudence will be your downfall, my boy. Curb it.' He touched his bloodied hand to his chest, bandage flapping. 'I offer you this advice freely, out of the particular affection I feel for your mother.'

'Thank you, sir. Shall I send her your love when I next write to her?'

His nostrils flared. 'Do.' He was about to walk on, but pulled himself up and turned back to me, still dripping. 'Our little world here on board hasn't been much to your taste, has it, Carver? Bit of a disappointment for a clever young hobberdehoy like you. Not enough stimulus, perhaps?'

Fool that I was, I couldn't see where this was leading. 'Well, sir,' I said, 'I wouldn't dream of complaining.'

'Ha! Wouldn't dream. Wouldn't dream! Just as I supposed. So. Let us see what we can do to make things more interesting for you, hmm?' He revolved on his stacked heel, keeping his narrow rump in front of me as we made our way to the captain's quarters.

For an old humbug, and a wounded one, he could move surprisingly fast.

CAPTAIN BARNARD'S AFTER-CABIN WAS a square, airless room, barely larger than William Borden's cell. It was crammed with a sofa, a full set of curly-maple chairs, a craggy sea chest doing duty as a low table, and a writing desk. Through a door in the facing wall one could peer past this cramped splendor directly into a dwarfish bedroom equipped with a box bed, which was covered at the foot by a homely cotton nightshirt.

The nightshirt was well washed, and yellow around the armpits. I didn't want to see it, but I couldn't tear my eyes away. I was adrift after our struggle with Borden, and to this was now added a new and more obscure stab of discomfort at having gazed – or so it felt – on the captain's nakedness.

The captain was braced against his desk when we came in. 'This is a terrible business, Surgeon,' he said, indicating the sofa.

Spalding eased himself onto it with crackling knees. 'That fellow is depraved,' he began. 'He is vicious. I've seen dogs with better breeding.'

I made an involuntary sound of protest.

The captain gave me his forbidding look – a silent expiration of breath, chin doubled, eyebrows vaulting. 'Do you have an opinion, Dr Carver?'

'Why, sir, from what I have seen, I think he is very ill.'

'And how does Mr Buskirk fare?'

I squirmed morosely on my chair, remembering the botch we'd made of Buskirk's neck. 'Mr Buskirk will live –' though I wasn't at all sure of this. 'I'm afraid he may not be as pretty as before,' I rounded off stupidly.

'Gentlemen, I am at a loss,' said the captain. 'I have sailed with Will Borden three times. In all that time I have never seen him out of temper. Never. Not once. And this – this goes beyond anything I could ever have conceived.'

'I can't comment on his *breeding*, sir,' I interjected. From the corner of my eye I saw Spalding making a close-lipped note of everything I said. 'But I've heard that he has a good record.'

'Good?' exclaimed Captain Barnard. 'His record is exemplary. I'd say it's a damn sight better than my own. He was on the *Providence* with Fitzgibbon when he wasn't yet twenty. Something I wouldn't have wished on my most seasoned enemy. He saved the old devil from immediate death.'

Here it was, at last! 'Actually, sir,' I urged, 'I don't know the story.'

'Mr Borden isn't in the habit of saying much about it. But he thinks well of you. I noticed that he was taking some trouble to instruct you.' He paused expectantly. 'I did wonder if –'

'No, sir.' There was a burgeoning grief inside my chest. 'Not a word.'

'Ah. Well, Fitzgibbon was a scoundrel. He's gone now. What happened finished him off.' The captain picked up a pen from a lacquered tray in front of him and wiped it assiduously on the blotter, as if this familiar ritual might shield him against what he had to tell.

'In those days, though – this was a good fifteen years ago – he was quite the man. He was sent over here to our friends in Chile during her wars with Spain to protect our interests. But he was a chancer and a cheat. He didn't give a goddamn for the United States or her good name. All he cared about was money.'

'Filthy stuff,' droned Spalding from his sofa. The blood had traveled down his sodden bandage, leaving a gaudy smear on the upholstery. He looked as if he were ready to keel over, but as I would discover, this was sadly far from the case. 'The root of all evil.'

Captain Barnard considered this commonplace as if the truth of it had struck him for the first time. 'Indeed, Dr Spalding. Of evil. And, where Fitzgibbon was concerned, what amounted to the same thing – of conduct grossly unworthy of his position. At that time,' he went on, 'there were merchantmen trading in all sorts from Hamburg linens to jerked beef up and down the coast from Callao to Valparaiso. They were chock-full of gold and silver and without any place to keep it safe. The Chileans were hammering away at the Spaniards and claiming any ship they could get their hands on as the spoils of war. That's where Fitzgibbon saw his chance. He offered up his ship as a vault. He was prepared to lock up anybody's specie in the hold of the *Providence* – for a fee, of course. Which he pocketed. He ran that ship for his own personal gain. He ran it like – like –'

The captain dropped his pen and lifted his hands briefly before flinging them apart in mute contempt.

'Like a bank, sir?' I offered.

Spalding gave a thin sniffle.

'A bank, yes. Exactly.' Captain Barnard wagged his chin at me approvingly. 'He kept his midshipmen counting money, day in and day out. They were not serving their country. Only the monetary good of Captain Fitzgibbon. And then he got beyond himself. He fell in with the master of a British brig who was shipping in his cargoes on the sly.'

I was lost now, spinning out to sea. 'On the sly?'

'A smuggler, Dr Carver. Someone completely outside the law. He set off to meet this pirate in open water, miles away from even the most godforsaken coral outcrop, where the *Providence* had no legitimate business. This was at the start of 'twenty-one. By that time his men were thirsting to string him up. They knew that he was making himself rich and that they wouldn't see a brass fingernail of this money. Is it any wonder – led astray in the heart of this great ocean, by a skipper who had become, to all intents, a buccaneer – that they turned on him?'

I grasped at the one buoyant fact I was sure of. 'But Mr Borden didn't!'

'Borden bargained for Fitzgibbon's life. He persuaded them to put the captain out in a boat with six others. They had water and a little hard bread. Some pork. No proper instruments. No charts. It was a death sentence. And then he volunteered to go with 'em. Two months later they fetched up off the Chilean coast. Five men were still living. Fitzgibbon was one. But he was never the captain of that skiff. Never! Borden was. Every surviving soul in that boat worshipped him.'

'But how in hell did he *do* it, sir?'

As soon as I said this I was afraid of having spoken too crassly. Captain Barnard, however, seemed to welcome my incredulity, and breasted it without flinching.

'It was *hell*, oh yes, precisely. Those two months were a hell you and I will, I trust, never experience. But unlike the rest of 'em, Will Borden was a fisherman's son. He knew how to live off the sea. And while the others were blustering and standing on their authority he was thinking, thinking and planning ahead. He'd taken an ordinary dry card compass and a quadrant before he got in the boat. He could find his way using the stars.' The captain's voice was exultant, and its warmth bore me up on a thermal of hope. 'He was – he is – a sailor to his marrow, bred to the sea without pomp or affectation. He is what we all – well, what I, for one, wanted to be. Can you see it now, Dr Carver?'

That humble nightshirt!

'I can, sir. I can see it clearly.' In that moment, I truly thought I could. What can we ever see? I saw Captain Barnard's version of William Borden, which threatened to engulf my own. But I was about to go under, and I was grateful. I threw myself on the wave and let it carry me off.

'He was the brightest and the best,' the captain concluded. 'And tonight – this. What am I to do with him?'

'Does he have any relations?'

'A fiancée back on Nantucket. A Miss Macy. I understand that the young lady's family is well-connected.'

My heart stumbled. 'In that case the matter is plain. He's ill, sir.'

Spalding, who had been rubbing his bony thigh in silence with his good hand while the captain spoke, gave a derisive laugh. 'Ill! He's not suffering from any sort of illness known to man. He's either murderously wicked or stark, staring mad. He should be locked away.'

Captain Barnard faced him with fierce wet eyes. 'What, am

I to keep a jail here? I'll keep no jail, Surgeon. My ship is not a jail!'

Mad? I wanted to shout. Aren't *you* mad? And you? Aren't I? We're all mad. Here we are, piloting a wood-shaving over an abyss. Is there a better definition of madness?

'I believe, sir,' I flung out instead, 'that madness *is* an illness. And I also believe that, as an ill man, Mr Borden should be treated with the consideration we would give to any patient, until such time as he can be returned to his relatives or placed in a suitable medical institution. I am ready to care for him myself.'

'You vainglorious ninny,' gasped Spalding. 'Do you want to be killed? Shall we let your mother know that we've had to bury you at sea?'

I addressed my reply to the captain. 'Mr Borden won't harm me, sir. I'm certain of it. I will be quite safe. It is the correct, the *moral* course of action, sir. My father will endorse it,' I said recklessly.

'Moral?' Captain Barnard pinched the bridge of his nose between his forefinger and thumb. 'Your father, eh?'

'Yes, sir.'

'Your father.' He glanced at Spalding. 'So, Surgeon? Are you satisfied?'

Spalding barely inclined his wrinkled head. 'Very well, sir. You have asked Dr Carver for his medical opinion. He has given it to us.' He looked meaningfully at the captain. Then he struck home. 'I suggest that Dr Carver be relieved of any future duties in my sick bay. I recommend that he be assigned as personal physician to Lieutenant Borden below decks for the remainder of our voyage.'

*

THE WEEKS THAT FOLLOWED were some of the strangest, and in some ways the dearest, of my life. I no longer felt as if I was a part of that cursed ship.

I went to Borden's cell every morning after roll-call and remained with him until the last watch had ended. I remember the monotonous, pile-driving blows of the sea against the bows. I remember the deep chortle of the water as it sluiced through the bilges, and the inter-rogative cough of the pump, *eh, eh, eh,* and the echo of the life of the upper decks, which reached us as a series of distorted blows and magnified cries. I remember the remorseless rocking of the vessel, and my relief at discovering that it was possible to bear it by giving up the ludicrous pretense that I could remain standing under this repeated assault, and finally going down on all fours.

It hardly mattered if I crawled. There was no one but William Borden to see me.

Strangest of all, I remember — could it have been so, in the Pacific, in July? — I remember the sound and sensation of rain, as I hunkered down in our wooden hole, the stipple and gathering swish of it starting high up above us, its steady vibrations traveling along the ship's timbers and through her hull, and the sight of the discolored deck, much later, as I came up. Tropical rain, then. Trop-ical storms. How far removed from the world it made me feel, to sit there in that putrid store room with him and listen to the ghost of that rain!

Borden didn't notice it. He lay without stirring, collapsed on an old blanket. Far from posing any danger to me, he seemed hardly aware of himself. He exhibited none of the manic energy I'd observed immediately after his attack on Buskirk. It was as if all the life had gone out of him. His arms and legs were so slack that they appeared boneless. He never spoke, only smiled.

On arriving every morning, and before leaving him in the evening, I took his pulse. It stammered in his wrist.

'Oh, Will,' I whispered. 'Where have you gone?'

It was a curiously intimate time. He refused to feed himself, and so this task fell to me. He wouldn't open his mouth for meat, or the eggs I cadged from my own allowance. I persuaded our cook to boil up a kettle of porridge for him daily, however, and he took a few ounces of this. I had to insinuate the spoon into the trap of Borden's lips, while he smiled at me as if I were an imbecile.

When he had to relieve himself, or defecate – he shat pebbled pellets, like a goat's – I helped him, both of us crawling, to the pail which I carried up afterwards and emptied over the rail.

Once I'd made sure that he was comfortable, and still placid, I didn't know what else to do, so I talked. I talked about Boston. I told him about my home. I told him about my father and my mother and my sister. I started off by talking about things that anyone would talk about, seemingly harmless things, and ended up shouting so loudly that Mullins rapped on the door. Somehow, I told Borden about my boyhood dread of the cows on the Common, and the elm outside my nursery window, and my escape to sea. I remember that I talked and talked, and while I talked he gazed at me with that ineffably merciful, sad smile.

Around and above us the machinery of the ship ground on.

Sometimes I sang: fragments of old nursery rhymes, a patchwork of half-formed gibberish that arrived from I did not know where.

He slept a great deal. Sometimes we both slept.

The heat grew even more oppressive, but I felt frozen. I could not stop shivering.

Hadn't Borden said that I was cold, and couldn't help my coldness?

The hours passed. My head had grown too big, and was inexplicably light, as if it might detach itself from my neck and roll away. I ached all over. As the ship's bell tolled the watches, my life continued to shunt its pointless tides through my body. I lay and shivered on the floor of the stores, smelling my own sweat, caged by dry walls.

One noonday, during what felt like profoundest night, I seized Borden's corpse-like hand. How dark it was in that box! How close! 'Help me, William,' I yammered, like a madman. 'Help me.'

Tired at last of the sound of my own voice, I shut my eyes and leaned back against the lurching wall of the cell – and found myself standing a great distance away from the *Orbis*, on the gray water, with my feet planted in the waves. The chill in my limbs spread outwards until I couldn't tell where my cold blood, my cold self, ended and the world began.

With this came a scrabbling fear of being left behind, and I tried to walk back towards the ship. The task was torture. At each footstep of mine the water turned to ice. I slipped and slid, flailing the whitening air with stiff arms. From a long way off, someone was calling me.

Hiram, the voice said. Hiram, come back.

I am coming, I answered, although I seemed unable to make the proper sounds. I am coming! Wait for me.

But the ice seized me with dead fingers, in a grip that held me rooted to the spot. I was soldered to it, unable to move. I lunged and twisted this way and that. As I struggled I felt my bones crack.

Or was it the ice cracking? It split wide open, with a ferocious roar like the roar of torn silk, with a roar of red, with a roar like my life breaking.

I seem to remember vomiting a stream of blood, a hot arched jet of it, across the boards of our cell. Was Borden laughing? I think I remember – unless this was still part of my delirium – trying to stand, and failing, and rolling on my back, and fetching up beside him, and rubbing my bloody face against his, and his patient, puzzled, hooded stare as he let me. I remember that I howled like a cub, a foundling. I remember crying tears which seemed to pour out of me like a bottomless Pacific. I remember a pounding at the door, which may only have been the pounding of my heart. I remember being carried up, up, away from the sullied air of that hutch, and being set down on a bunk, still howling, in the sick bay where I had once hoped to rule.

And that is all I remember or want to remember.

FIVE

I HAVE BEGUN BY RECORDING, as faithfully as possible, what I recall of my first meetings with William Borden. Yet even in the act of putting pen to paper I am aware that such a record is laughably imperfect. At times my work on human memory – my life's work, no less – strikes me as the most unreliable I could ever have undertaken.

We think of our memories as having fixed properties and clear outlines; vulnerable to distortion or loss of focus, to be sure, but still in some sense objectively there, if only we had the tools to recover them. We feel that though we can't remember, given time we could – oh, we could!

The truth is that memory is not like a shoe or an umbrella or any other thing that we have mislaid, and which is lying in a corner, waiting for us to stumble across it. It is not a *thing* at all. It is a process, forever in flux. It is not solid but liquid. It is inherently unstable.

If memory resembles anything physical, then it resembles water.

Even under ordinary conditions a constant shifting and displacement is at work, a blurring of detail, a rearrangement of the depths. The surface looks continuous, but underneath, all is dissolution and change. What we want to remember will quite literally *no longer be there* in the same form a month or a year later, let alone the two decades that have passed since the events which I will now try to retrieve.

This gives me reason to pause.

I write: *I remember this, I remember that. He said, I said. I thought, I believed. I felt.* With this haphazard trawling I hope, somehow, to dredge up an account of what happened that has the semblance of wholeness, of unity. Of truth. And as I write I fear that the shape I am giving to Will Borden is not his true shape, that it has been digested, disfigured, in the acid element of myself.

Yet however corrupted my story may be, however corroded my recollection of Borden as he was then, however uncertain I sometimes am of its final meaning – whatever the twists and the turns of it, it always leads me to this moment. To myself. Here. Seated, as I am, in this straight-backed, over-upholstered chair, the chair of a rational man, a superintendent of the insane, a protector of the vulnerable, a respected and needed individual, dipping his pen into his inkwell as the lights go out around him in the Bartlett mansion and darkness gathers in the long carriage avenue.

I am the one solid, it seems, in a perspective of shadows, a rock in the dark current.

Borden was ill, and I am triumphantly, almost indecently well.

I cling to that fact.

I HAD NO REAL memory, then or later, of my last months on board the *Orbis*. Or rather, they were like the memory of a dream, weightless and uncertain. When I thought of the weeks I'd spent with Borden in the stores, and then confined to my bunk with fever, I appeared to be lying in my own coffin as the whispers of the living mingled above me like mist.

For the remaining stretch of my tour I ran a high temperature that came and went without warning. While it was at its height I was tormented by barbaric sweats that were about to split my bones, and a mouth that was full of blood. The more I spat, the more my gums bled, until I vomited blood. I could taste blood, day and night: in my throat, on my lips, on my raw teeth. The very substance of me seemed to be blood, pushing ever outwards, as if to show the world what I truly was.

My twenty-second birthday fell in that August of 1833, but I was barely alive. I was not at all surprised to see the skin on my body flushing red, with mere islands of white remaining. Wasn't I a devil from hell? The ship was hell, and I wasn't yet out of it.

Once my tour had ended I quit my naval career with relief and resigned myself to going back to Massachusetts to practise medicine with my father on the dilapidated widows and nervous virgins of New England, as the old man had long been urging me to do.

I am one of the Boston Carvers, the only son of the eminent physician Austin Otis Carver, a man of terrifying energy: co-founder of our city's General Hospital, Emeritus Professor of Anatomy and Surgery at Harvard College, inventor of the extendable scalpel, and all-round indefatigable civic buttress.

I wasn't speaking idly when I told Captain Barnard that Papa could be of help in the Borden case. The Carvers of Boston didn't just know anyone who was anyone. We were that anyone.

Our family tree boasts two Puritan divines, four *Mayflower* passengers (twin sisters, who married a pair of fellow Pilgrims and spawned devoutly for the next twenty years), a governor of Massachusetts, a brace of commodores, and at least one liquidator of witches. My mother was a Cabot; my father's mother, one of the Newport Ellerys (the Ellery signature on the Declaration of Independence – those noosed, onomatopoeic Ls! – is that document's chief ornament).

We lived in Mount Vernon Street on Beacon Hill, in a fine flat-fronted mansion set well back from the sidewalk, with a trim grass plot and iron fence, an entablature of white marble above the doorway and Grecian pillars set into the brick; a soaring aspect, picturesque balcony, and four stone wreaths along the cornice. Being domiciled anywhere else, in any other style of property, with any other type of fence or aspect or number of wreaths, was unthinkable.

When he wasn't at the college or the hospital, Papa ran a family practice from the upper story of our home. That is, he occasionally bled a vein or administered a laxative; it was a family practice strictly in the sense that we existed on family money.

On most days my father took his midday meal at Julien's in town. He spent the evenings toiling at his memoirs. His study, sandbagged by bronzes, oils and other Carver heirlooms against incursions by the present, occupied two entire apartments on the top floor, for, as Papa was fond of saying, he 'could not create a large work in a small room'.

In this labor the old bloodsucker used only the finest paper. Although we were forbidden to touch the pile of foolscap on his writing table, I made up my mind, one afternoon when I was about twelve, to disobey him. Turning the watermarked pages over with anxious fingers, I read: 'Chapter One: Birth of My Paternal Great-Grandfather', 'Chapter Two: Birth of My Paternal Great-Grandmother',

'Chapter Three: Birth of My Maternal Great-Grandfather', 'Chapter Four: Birth of My Maternal Great-Grandmother', 'Chapter Five: Birth of My Paternal Grandfather', 'Chapter Six: Birth of My Paternal Grandmother', 'Chapter Seven: Birth of My Maternal Grandfather', 'Chapter Eight: Birth of My Maternal Grandmother', 'Chapter Nine: Birth of My Father', 'Chapter Ten: Birth of My Mother'.

Presumably my father reached an obstetrical climax with his own birth in Chapter Eleven, but this must remain conjecture, as I'd lost any desire to read on.

My mother. Ah, my mother was languid and vague, qualities which, in certain lights, could pass for easy-going charm. I think I intuited even as a child that her affableness had a splinter of ice in it. I felt that I made no lasting impression on her; that she had no real sense of me from one moment to the next.

I recall, when I was seven or eight, meeting Mama at the top of the stairs on my way to fetch a book from the nursery. She was standing quite still at the dormer window overlooking the elm that grew on the street outside our house, with her hand pressed to her heart. A large pale aquamarine glinted on her middle finger. Improbable as it now seems, she appeared to be communing with that damn tree. My slipper collided with the banister and she turned towards me with a puzzled and slightly irritated air, as if she'd never seen me before. I was an impressionable boy, and it took me several days to get over the vacantness, the utter lack of recognition, in her stare.

Mama left the running of the household to my sister Caroline, my senior by five years, a lanky, dutiful, narrow-faced girl with red hair and eyes the color of scullery soap. In an attempt to offset her natural palette Caro always wore shades of green or cinnamon. She did a great quantity of light sewing, knitting, and other fancy work, most of it without any utilitarian value at all, as far as I could tell, since her dresses and their trimmings all came from a dressmaker and haberdasher's in Chapman Place. Perched at her needle among the potted ferns in the parlor, she reminded me of a large, fantastically tinted bird of paradise, head cocked, lying in wait.

Caro has never married. (Nor, as it happens, have I.) Barring one brief, sad entanglement, which I will come to shortly, no likely mate ever strayed within range of being snapped up by her. She continues to keep house for me today in what used to be our childhood home. She is a stalwart attender of Trinity Church in Summer Street, a twice-weekly volunteer at the Lying-in Hospital, and a mettlesome member of her embroidery circle, the 'Boston Maiden Ladies'.

When she was still a young woman my sister once confided in me that she admired the poetry of Byron. Byron! She proceeded, her sharp nose turning as red as her hair, to quote some lines from *Don Juan* about love being of man's life a thing apart, but woman's whole existence.

It strikes me that Caro's has been a life of prolonged bathos.

At the high point of a fruitful career such as mine, it would be easy to ascribe the rewards of hard work to the heft of family connections. But the truth is that my apparently advantageous start in life was anything but.

Papa decided early on that I should study medicine. Custom decreed that I had first to enter Harvard College to take a degree in general science, fine dining, and intoxicating liquors. This was the prelude to three hardly less dispiriting years at the Medical College in

Mason Street. There were no laboratories and few experiments. New ideas weren't nurtured, but hoofed out and left to die of exposure.

What's more, the cutlets at Forster's Coffee House around the corner were overcooked. I wrote my graduation thesis on the benefits to digestion of a vegetarian diet.

And then, just as my father began to press me to join him in his eyrie on the third floor in Mount Vernon Street, I ran away to sea. I was aided and abetted by an acquaintance of the Cabots whom Papa didn't much care for, an old relic of the *Chesapeake*, with influence in the remoter reaches of the navy.

In spite of this, I couldn't escape my heritage. The most fibrous admirals went as weak at the knees as any Boston debutante at the first mention of the Carver name. Even Spalding turned out to have been a beau, in his distant youth, of my mother's Aunt Lavinia (known to us all as Bunny). I learned within half an hour of boarding the *Orbis* that as a girl my own mother had to sit on his lap and endure being chucked under the chin by him.

It was almost too much to be borne.

WHEN I CAME HOME to Boston in the New Year of 1834 my father studied my distempered face and informed me coolly that I was suffering the aftereffects of Dengue Fever, which Spalding had referred to as 'the Breakbone'.

In the weeks that followed my return I no longer burned, but I still had intermittent and severe joint pain. Worst of all was a corrosive fatigue that never seemed to leave me. The acuteness and duration of my symptoms, and how weak I became afterwards, was frightening, and unlike any illness I'd experienced before. Once back in Mount Vernon Street I kept to my bed all day, sleeping or pretending to be asleep. I was in hiding from Papa, and his scalpels, which he was daily urging me to submit to, and his even more cutting advice. Whenever he knocked at my door with his tireless rat-a-tat-tat, I felt the blood drain into my feet, as though he'd already started slicing into me.

Caro often sat at my bedside during those deadened afternoons, stabbing at her embroidery hoop or carding her silks. Sunshine dithered through the window while I dozed. Fitful puffs of snow, full of the cold of the season, breathed their last in the cobbled street outside.

Caro was restless. As she shifted, her skirts, warmed by my bedroom fire, gave off a fragile perfume. I watched her bent head with its bands of ruddy hair through my half-closed lids and was astonished at how soothed I felt.

'Caro, when I was ill I heard a voice calling me home. Was it you?'

She merely shrugged, pleating the folds of her dress in her speckled fingers. She looked absurdly bright, and in her own way absurdly desperate.

'Oh, Hiram. Why must it always be something or someone?'

For those weeks I forgot William Borden. No charges had been preferred against him after we docked in Boston. His obvious and advanced state of insanity ruled out any form of naval trial. I was told that when we came into harbor in mid-January he was met by friends and taken back to Nantucket. Buskirk, I heard, returned to the care of his family in New York. An infection had set in at the site of his badly stitched wound, spreading all the way into the tissues of his face, and for a while no one knew if he would pull through.

I only learned this later, via our mutual connections. At the time I was myself too weak and despondent to take note of anything.

At moments I wondered if I hadn't in fact died on the *Orbis* and been resurrected. Glad as I was to escape my imprisonment on that vessel, it had the peculiar effect of throwing a new and unreal light on the daily existence of our household. After more than a year at sea, so much appeared alien in Mount Vernon Street that I felt that I'd unwittingly arrived in another world. I was as good as the survivor of a shipwreck. My old life had vanished forever beneath the waves, and the ocean had spat me out on a foreign shore.

Released from the drab prison of the ship, I couldn't get used again to the high bright angles, the smells and flubdubs of home. The front door flanked by a whorled boot-scraper, the hall littered with walnut card tables and dribbly watercolors; the blue-papered parlor and the dining room hung with the sword my grandfather had carried at Fort Stanwix, from which you climbed ever upwards, ever vertically, to the drawing room with its japanned screen and Turkey rugs and bowls of forced hyacinths, the bedrooms with their marble-topped washstands and counterpanes sweetened with lavender, the beeswaxed acres of Papa's study, and the shrouded nursery, drowsing in its quiet bubble under the eaves – all of it was exotic and utterly irrelevant to the posthumous person I now was.

In the kitchen a lusty fire burned in the range, and no one ever complained that it was about to go out, or had already done so, or blew a whistle to have it relit. Into the oven of that range went sections of sheep, calf and pig of so impressive a size that the mere sight of them would have given Ole Henry a conniption fit. Doors led from the kitchen to sundry compartments dedicated to the storing of dry goods and vegetables, of eggs, milk, meat, wine, and other things that could be drunk or eaten.

For oh, how we ate. There was strong Hyson and Souchong steeped for ten minutes and poured into the best cups, each with a fat pink tulip on the side; raisin bread and butter and pellucid grape preserve; fissured loaf cake and crumbly drop cakes and macaroons valved like seashells. Stinging ginger beer and lemonade. Clouded cherry cordial and clear cider cup. Chocolate spiced with nutmeg, and coffee, burned and ground every morning and brewed in a biggin, rather than a common coffee-pot. Buttermilk-fried chicken and salad greens. Peppered veal soup and skimmed lamb bouillon. Goose liver pie with a pastry roof soldered onto solid pastry walls. Crab fritters and cod chowder latticed with pork and coarsely chopped marjoram. Broiled parsley shad and salted haddock left overnight to soften in scalding molasses water. Roast duck stuffed with capers, dressed in a cream sauce studded with oysters. Six-egg batter puddings soaked with lemon-brandy. Boiled beet-tops and squashes and kettle-baked beans and savory catsups and mixed pickles with vitreous chips of watermelon rind.

Or rather, how they ate.

I refused all of it. Food seemed unnecessary to my new, reduced life. I had no wants. All I wanted was to be left in peace. I lay as still as I could, beached on twisted sheets, willing myself to disappear. I saw the sunlight come and go across my wasted legs and knew that I was finished, done with it all.

My skin was dry and garishly veined. In spite of the fire in my room I was always cold.

You can't help your coldness.

That's what wanting is. The looking for what you cannot have.

Angry tears spilled from my eyelids and dripped down my cheeks into my hair.

Every minute was threadbare. Every breath felt provisional. I no longer felt hungry, or even empty. I'd tried so hard to be something else, something other than who I was, and I'd failed.

ONE EVENING IN FEBRUARY my father told me that I had to get up whether I liked it or not and present myself for dinner. Dinner on land, unlike at sea, was a meal consumed after dark.

'You can't stay in bed any longer, Hiram,' he said, studying the dish on my lap tray. 'What's this?' He brought the bowl to his nose before discarding it pooh-poohingly. 'Arrow-root jelly? You take only nursery food. Your sister has indulged you enough. If you lie here another day she'll have you winding her wool for her. Stop behaving like a child. You'll come downstairs and sit with the rest of the family tonight, sir, like a grown man.'

At just after eight o'clock I entered the dining room shakily, aware that my trousers were too big for me and might end up around my knees at any moment. The floor was tilting in a way that it sometimes did since I'd left the *Orbis*.

They were already there when I arrived, seated at the monstrous mahogany expanse of the dining table: my father, all cleft chin and tubular brows, the tip of his heavy shoe tapping against the table's claw foot; Caro goggling at me in turquoise velvet, mottled shoulders tensed; and my mother, her celestial eyes locked on nothing in particular (the very features which are most earthbound and awkward in Caro seemed moonstruck in Mama).

Grandpapa's sword shone luridly on the wall above them. On the surface of the polished table, which had the sickly luster of marmalade, bits of silver and china were laid out in dimly familiar runes: the letters of a language which I'd once spoken but long since forgotten.

'Ah, my son,' said Papa. 'The seasick sailor. Welcome back to the land of the living, sir.'

Mama crooned, 'My darling! You're *far* too thin. We need to put some flesh on your bones or you'll be taken for one of those Hindoos in loincloths. You know the ones.' She fluttered her jeweled fingers in an easterly direction. 'The Yogis.'

'Don't worry, Mother,' I said, hitching up my trousers and finding my old place on her right, beneath the sword. 'I'm still an Episcopalian.'

'Are you, Hissy?' she asked absently. 'You don't go to church now.'

'That's thoroughly in line with the best Episcopalian practice, Mama. And please don't *call* me that.'

'My dear, he doesn't go anywhere,' said my father, signaling to the servant to fill my glass with Zinfandel. 'Perhaps he's finally traveled enough.'

I chugged the wine down my gullet and waited for indifference to arrive. Instead I was swamped by dread: dry mouth, ringing ears, plummeting heart. All my defeated hopes promised to well up and choke me.

My mother lapsed back into her reverie. As my father started to itemize the day's doings in his ruthlessly cheerful tones, I concentrated on smearing a cucumber mousse around on its saucer. Across the table Caro gave me an encouraging wave. She was intent on the gears and levers of the meal, gauging the stations and the temperature of various dishes with an alert air, and – did I imagine this? – never once truly enjoying it.

'Now then, Hiram,' said my father after a while, 'I saw Mansfield at our board meeting this afternoon.'

In 1832, when I bolted on the *Orbis*, Papa had recently been appointed as one of the trustees of the Asylum for the Insane at Charlestown. The place was run by a superintendent, Richard Mansfield, whom I had no particular interest in meeting.

He was on the point of saying something further, but just then Caro called in half a dozen stunted fowl, diapered in pastry. I looked on in horror as one of these fetal carcasses was eased onto my plate. My father was temporarily deflected by the mechanics of dissecting his. Though he set about it with surgeonly gusto, I sensed that the moist lilac bones, scraped into a pile, repelled him.

'Caroline,' drawled my mother, letting her napkin stray to her mouth, 'please explain to us what we are eating.'

'This is pigeon *en feuilleté*, Mama. It's French.'

'Well yes, darling, but how did these French pigeons end up on our plain little Boston table?'

'I got the recipe from the Winthrops' cook.' Caro's twanging gaze met mine. 'I thought it might tempt Hiram's appetite.'

'My, is there no end to your cleverness?' Mama frowned, as if on the brink of a momentous observation. 'Don't we usually have ours – *potted*?'

'*C'est délicieux*,' I said, flattening a scrap of pigeon skin with my fork.

'*Ah, bien*. In that case . . .' Mama, amiably aloof again, dropped her sparkling hand onto my arm. 'But is the dessert American at least, darling? I do like our American desserts.'

'It's custard pie,' conceded Caro.

'Hmm,' breathed Mama, dabbing at her lips. 'Thank goodness.'

'Have some more wine, Hiram,' said my father. 'You haven't eaten a bite but I see you're not teetotal, at least.' He took a sip of his own, averting his eyes from the charnel heap in front of him. 'Mansfield is about to admit a new patient. Someone you know.'

'Fancy that, sir. Another unfortunate whom Boston society has driven mad.'

My father contemplated me grimly. 'In fact, you served with this man.'

I felt an acid wavelet of apprehension. 'Did I?'

'Yes. I am referring to William Borden.'

I was assailed by a sudden hammering of blood in my ears. 'He's to be sent to the asylum?'

'He is. Next month. I believe it was you who suggested it.'

The hammering gave way to a vertiginous sensation, as if I were falling from a high ledge. I raised my glass and drank so deeply that I began to cough.

'Oh, that poor creature,' sighed Mama.

'His former commanding officer is very concerned that Mr Borden should be well looked after,' said my father. 'Until this crisis overtook him he had a most promising career.'

'Oh no,' said Mama, giving up on her pigeon. 'I don't mean him. I meant the other one – Gussy's child, the one who was attacked. The Buskirk boy. And how frightful that Uncle Toppy was hurt, too.'

'Spalding?' I wheezed. 'I'd have bitten him myself.'

'Hiram,' said my father, aligning his knife and fork with an emphatic clink, 'I would like to ask you something. Did anything out of the ordinary happen on board ship around the time Lieutenant Borden became ill? Was anything amiss? Please be straight with me.'

I had an inrush of memory: the weird calm, Fryar's spidering blood, a storm wind rising.

My father waited.

'We flogged one of the hands that day,' I offered.

'Is that unusual? Flogging on the high seas is sanctioned by our maritime laws. In your opinion, was something wrong? Wasn't it properly done?'

'Oh, it was properly done, sir. We made sure to do it properly. We did it by the book. Because, you see, we were as terrified as the man we flogged.' I forced out a laugh. 'Or at least I was. And we knew that we had to disguise what we were about, not just from him but from each other, and even from ourselves. We had to make ourselves into the administrators of the most careful ideal of the law in order to do it at all.'

'These laws have been passed by our legislators. Are we wiser and better than they are?' Papa sat back and swilled the wine about in his glass.

'Shouldn't we be? Our legislators have been elected by us.'

Caro bit her lip. My father was intent on rearranging the remaining silverware around his plate. 'You are quite the philosopher, Hiram,' he said. 'Or at least, you are when you're awake.'

'Oh, Austin, please don't,' murmured my mother, stifling a yawn. 'We were having such a stimulating discussion.'

'But Father, I hardly think it was this flogging that precipitated Lieutenant Borden's mental collapse.'

'No?'

I looked hard at the old vampire. 'No. The way we did it was insane. But then the whole ship was already insane. Every rule on her. Every regulation. All those rules that we pride ourselves on having passed! It seems to me that the entire civilized world itself is insane, and that it's only through a fit of insanity such as William Borden's that we can ever hope to stand in any sort of true relation to things.'

My father returned my stare. 'Well, Hiram, insane or not, this is the world we have to live in. It is heartening to see you taking an interest in it after all. Have you given any thought to what you might like to do next?'

'No, sir. At the moment I'm still mulling things over.'

'Ah. I see. Let me help you with that. I've fixed up an appointment for you with Mansfield on Monday. He's looking for a new medical assistant. I'm sure he'd be very interested to hear your reflections on our collective insanity.'

'Father, I am twenty-two years old!' I had a rabid desire to hold my breath and kick the table, to grab the sword from the wall above me and swing it around my head. 'I don't need you to fix up anything for me! And what's more, I don't want you to!'

'Yes, Hissy,' said my father crisply. 'You are twenty-two. And soon you will be twenty-three, and still in your dressing gown.'

'Be careful, Papa, or Hissy won't ever speak to you again,' smiled Caro.

'Well, my girl. If your brother intends to lie in bed all day for the rest of his life, then we won't have much to speak about anyway.'

*

'IT'S INTOLERABLE,' I COMPLAINED to Caro while she was arranging cut flowers in the kitchen the next morning. My eyeballs stung from the wine I'd drunk the night before. The winterberry and amaryllis heaped on the table in inflamed mounds irritated my vision like a retinal disease. 'Being set up like this with his cronies. When am I going to be allowed to do things for myself?'

Caro gave a snip to the end of a hectically beaded rod and placed it, still drizzling sap, onto a newspaper which she'd spread out for this purpose. Her face was stern with effort. After clipping another four branches she gathered them up and laid them in a basin of cold water.

'Papa is right, you know. It's time you found something to occupy you.'

'Is it? What do you suppose it's like, always being pushed to prove yourself, to excel? Always being called on to buff up the family name?'

'Ah, I wouldn't know,' Caro replied. 'I've never been asked.'

I slumped in my chair and blinked glumly at the oilcloth floor. Swept and washed under Caro's direction, it had the patina of alabaster.

'I'm full of good resolutions, Caro,' I stammered. 'I just don't seem able to carry them out.'

Caro put aside her secateurs. 'Listen to me. Many people are stuffed so full of resolutions that they don't know what they want. Don't you want to live a useful life?'

'Useful? I want change. Liberty. Most of all, I want a real purpose!'

'Gracious,' said Caro lightly. 'All those things at once?'

'Laugh if you like. For things to stay as they are is unbearable.'

'I'm not laughing.' She wasn't. Her green eyes were pensive. 'This is one way of getting what you want. Please at least consider it.'

I thought over what she'd said. Then I went round the table to where she stood, up to her wrists in water, and wrapped my arms about her waist. I touched my nose to the top of her head. The parting in her hair smelled of violets and gravy.

'What would I do without you? If only all girls were like you.'

'Oh, hush up now, Hiram,' said my sister, pushing me away with a wet hand. She picked out another bough and commenced ripping off its lower twigs with quick downward strokes. Angry berries cascaded onto the newspaper. 'I'm not a girl any more. I don't know why, but of all your smart remarks, your compliments hurt the most.'

SIX

I LEFT TOWN THE FOLLOWING Monday for my appointment
with Mansfield in Charlestown. At Lechmere Point on the other
side of Craigie's Bridge, a few miles out of town, the high road ran
back to Boston in the south-east, and a narrower, more primitive
track led northwards, via a footbridge spanning the open water of
the Charles River, all the way up Pleasant Hill. I could see the arc
of the hill above Miller's Creek, laid out on the horizon like a cup
placed upside down to dry. The asylum buildings bestriding the
summit were half hidden by a poplar grove that fanned out almost
to the base.

I had no choice but to start walking to the top.

There were bleak clouds drawing together and once I gained the
densely branched poplars it felt like dusk, even though it was not yet
mid-afternoon. In places, as I climbed, I came to gaps in the trees
from which it was possible to glimpse stretches of river dotted with
boats and barges, and beyond them the granite mass of the General
Hospital and the spires of the city. But I walked without stopping, my
head bent low. In my right ear as I walked I could hear the Charles,
running sluggishly over its bed of mud. All I could think of was how
much I resented being on that hill, that I had a stitch in my side, and

that I would soon have to rest. As the path rose deeper and deeper into the poplars, I began to fear that I would never find my way out.

I was still thinking this when I rounded a clump of poplars and emerged, breathing hard, onto the lower level of a tiered lawn. Above it was a broad terrace whose steps descended past ornate fountains and tumbling gardens all the way to a distant wharf. On the top flight of the terrace, glowing apricot in the dim light, stood a bow-fronted mansion built in the style of nearly half a century earlier, with a curved portico and two wings that reached down the hill like arms. The air was filled with a mysterious warbling noise.

I have walked or driven up that hill more times than I can count in the intervening years, but this is always how I remember the house: the cusp of the wood unveiling glowing brick, those broadly beckoning arms. I'd never been there in my life, but it was instantly familiar to me. I felt as if I had, in some indefinable sense, come home.

There seemed to be no one about. Without knowing it I had approached the building from the back, rather than the front, and on trying the only entrance in sight I found that it was unlocked. (When is our real home ever locked?)

I walked straight in. I found myself in an oval hall, from the opposite ends of which a double staircase led to a platform supported on fluted columns. Further flights ran from this to a gallery, up into unseen spaces. A tall-case clock crested with three round finials ticked loudly in the silence.

As I stood listening to the clock I became aware of footsteps and raised voices coming from the top of the house. Far away a door slammed, followed by the sound of scurrying.

The clock struck three. A set of footsteps detached themselves from the hubbub overhead and clopped, in a staccato counterpoint to its throaty chime, down the farthest set of stairs. By inches a uniformed and very flustered woman, whom I took to be an attendant, arrived above a pair of sturdy boots.

'Why, Dr Carver,' she exclaimed. 'You're right on time.' Her astringent tone implied that she'd been looking forward to reprimanding me for being late. 'Dr Mansfield is having some slight trouble with a patient. Would you mind waiting in his study for a little while?'

The apartment into which she drove me before hurrying off was long and ungarnished, and bore the traces of once having been a gentleman's library. Two of its walls – painted a dreary muffin color that might have started off as white – were covered from floor to ceiling with bookcases bracketing an islet of tapestried chairs. The floorboards, scuffed and deeply scored, appeared to be of an age with the house. High windows with pinned-back shutters looked out onto the terraced garden. An unlit wood-stove, whose squat utilitarian bulk was comically out of keeping with the airy lines of the mantel, occupied the fireplace, near which sprawled a battered desk where ledgers and books lay tumbled.

I turned over a volume: Shakespeare. *Julius Caesar.*

The place was cold, and very quiet. I could hear the measured ticking of the clock in the hall, and beyond it, that far-off, arrhythmical thudding, like a shoal of feet dragging from room to room. Within minutes the thudding stopped, giving way to silence.

I took a seat and prepared to wait. Through the open shutters I made out a triangle of grass, the fork of a poplar. Behind an adjacent

roof drifts of high cloud combined and recombined.

Again I had the uncanny sensation that all this was not alien, but in an essential way known to me. I felt my head fall against the chair back: the walk had tired me out. I had a strong desire to nod off, and as the seconds passed, and still nobody came, my eyes grew heavier. The silence rose up, lapping at my lids.

I was almost asleep when a change in the temperature of the room, some movement of the air, brought me back to full consciousness. I sat up with a start and saw that the study door was open. An old lady wearing an antiquated high-cut gown and cap hovered on the threshold, regarding me tenderly.

'I beg your pardon, child,' she said. 'I've gone and disturbed your rest. I didn't think there was anybody here.'

'No, please, do come in. I was just – sitting.'

'Why, thank you. May I sit with you?' she asked companionably. 'I am waiting for the doctor.'

'Of course. So am I. We can wait together.'

She wriggled into the chair next to mine with a comfortable sigh, loosened the neck of her bodice, and pulled out a wad of knitting.

The clock ticked. The sound of scurrying began afresh somewhere up above. Watching my elderly acquaintance shake out her wool and begin her work, I again felt at peace.

'Is it often such a long wait?' I asked, for the pleasure of hearing her whispery voice.

'No,' she answered thoughtfully, 'I would not say *often*. Dr Mansfield is usually very quick. But perhaps you are not a frequent visitor?'

I smiled wryly. 'I have never been here before.'

'I hope you won't think me a silly old woman. But it did cross my mind that you might be a new admission. You don't look quite as hale, somehow, as a young man should.'

'Hale? No. I suppose I don't.'

She went on knitting, between sideways peeps at me.

There was something consoling about the movement of her hands. 'My sister likes to knit,' I murmured.

'Ah, so does mine. It's her I've come to see. Poor dear Eliza. She has been here for years and years.' She added, with some feeling, 'They don't let *her* knit, you know. Ever.'

'I am sorry to hear it.'

'Well, it's a pitiful place nowadays. Eliza and I used to visit the house as girls, when it still belonged to the Bartletts. What parties we had back then! The carriages lining the drive – the midnight suppers! We even had rum shrub! You can imagine what it must be like for Eliza, wandering through these echoing halls.'

She drew herself up with a shimmy of concern. 'Oh, child. You are shivering, and here I am, prattling on.' Taking a rug from the back of her own chair, she tucked it around my legs. 'There. That's better. Now you'll be warmer.'

'Oh I will, yes. You are tremendously kind. Thank you.'

The commotion above us was becoming more obtrusive, and seemed to be traveling down the stairs. My guardian closed her eyes.

'It is the noise. One never gets used to it. Tramp, tramp, tramp. All day. Sometimes one just longs for a little peace. But the world simply won't leave one alone – don't you find?'

'I do. Absolutely.'

'Your rug is slipping.' She gave it an attentive pat, and as she did so her sleeve fell open to her elbow. I saw for the first time that her dress was torn and that there was a deep wet scratch on her inner arm. I glanced up and found her assessing me slyly.

At that moment the door flew open. Two wild-looking men burst in, one fat and youngish and the other in his vigorous middle years, with a tussock of graying hair and a face that would have inspired immediate confidence but for the fact that it was bleeding rakishly from a gash under the left eye. They were trailed by a crush of uniformed women, among whom I recognized the attendant who had greeted me.

'So, Miss Todd,' gulped the man with the bleeding face. 'There you are! You've given us a great deal of trouble by running off like that. Dr Carver, please don't move.'

While speaking he kept his eyes trained on my aged companion, who was pressing her knitting to her bosom. She gave me a conspiratorial wink and laid her finger against her lips.

'Now, ma'am,' he continued sternly. 'Kindly put away your needles and come with me. I am watching you, mind.'

My friend whipped one of the needles from its wool. Holding the pointed end in front of her like a dagger, she stuck out her cracked tongue at him.

'I'm sorry I had to hurt you, Dr Mansfield,' she parried, 'but you *would* go on so. And then –' she spat out the words as if they were coals – 'I HAVE ALREADY WASTED YEARS IN THIS DAMNED TRAMP DEN OF OLD WOMEN AND HAGS.'

'Miss Todd,' said the bleeding man, 'either you put that knitting down or Dr Goodwin and I will be obliged to carry you upstairs by your arms and legs and give you a shower bath. The choice is yours.'

'Really, Doctor,' she replied tartly, 'that is no choice at all.'

Getting up with a bound that made both men take a step back, she faced me. She hesitated for a moment, then rolled up her knitting and laid it in my lap. 'Would you be a dear boy and look after this?'

'Gladly. As if it's my very own.'

Miss Todd gave a snarl of relief. 'Dr Carver, it was delightful to make your acquaintance. I do hope we will have the opportunity to converse again soon. Dr Mansfield, I have nothing further to say to *you*.' Dismissing him with a flick of her wrist, she squared up to the fat young man. 'Very well, Dr Goodwin. I am ready. Your arm, please.'

'Will you manage alone, Frank?' asked Mansfield.

Goodwin nodded uncertainly. He crooked his arm and crossed the room. Miss Todd took it and, without deigning to look around, was led out.

'I had no idea,' I said faintly.

'You'll get to know the signs,' exhaled Mansfield, sinking down into the chair recently vacated by Miss Todd and digging in the pocket of his coat for a handkerchief, with which he dashed at his cheek. 'Oof. Better get some iodine on this in a minute. I was most favorably impressed, by the way. You showed no fear. A remarkable set of responses all round, really.'

'I didn't know that there *was* anything to fear! She said she'd come to see her sister!'

'Eliza Todd doesn't have a sister. She has no surviving relatives. She's been a patient here for longer than anyone can remember. She wants to knit and sew and whatever else ladies do, but –' he turned over the palm of his left hand to display a puncture that was just scabbing – 'much as I'd like to, I can't let her. Knitting needles.

Embroidery needles. Sewing scissors. Crochet hooks. She can't be allowed them. When she doesn't have her implements, she's quite tranquil. But if she manages to lay hold of any – well! God knows where she's been hiding *that*.' He indicated the roll of grubby wool in my crotch, with its projecting wooden spikes. 'She tried to take out my eye with those half an hour ago. I was very glad to find her here with you. I thought she'd eloped.'

'*Eloped?*'

'Ah.' His lips tightened. 'That's our word for "escaped". We have developed our own language here.'

'She seemed tranquil enough while we were keeping each other company.'

'So I noticed. Hmm. Interesting.'

'And she told me that she used to visit this house as a girl.'

'Yes. That's true. Her father knew old Bartlett – Jacob Bartlett. They were in business together, before Bartlett lost his fortune. That's how we got this place. I often think it must be the most beautiful country house in all New England. You should see our dovecotes.'

'I think I may have heard them.'

Wincing, he started to massage his forehead in gradually expanding circles. 'That's the way it is with the insane. There's always a grain of rationality in their madness. I'm Richard Mansfield, by the way.' He held out his uninjured hand, and I shook it. 'Miss Joy told me that you were here. I apologize for the chaotic delay in seeing you. Oh, and – thank you for your help.' He winced again.

'You have a headache, I think. Shall I come back at a time that suits you better?'

Mansfield regarded me with interest. 'I was right. You *are* intuitive.

No, let's have our interview now.' He laughed wearily. 'The truth is, Dr Carver, that it's never a good time. We have seventy-nine patients here, with another arriving, and only a handful of attendants. Goodwin is a diligent fellow, but I'm understaffed. I won't beat about the bush. You have the – well, shall we say, the enthusiastic endorsement of the trustees. Normally I'd resist being strong-armed in this way. But if you're willing to join us, I'd be grateful to sign you up.'

'This new patient of yours, Dr Mansfield. William Borden. Possibly you're aware – that is, my father may have mentioned . . . Well – I've met him before.'

'Yes. It did come up at the board meeting last week.' He raised an ironic eyebrow. 'I understood that he's being sent to us on your father's recommendation. Dr Carver was very persuasive.'

'He can be. I'm sorry.' I stared wanly at Mansfield's good-humored face with its squiggle of blood, and had an irrepressible urge to confide in him. 'I have no experience in mind-doctoring. As long as you know that. I've only ever worked on a ship.'

'A ship.' His thoughts seemed to stray for a moment. 'Good Lord. What a piece of work is a man. So many forms of confinement. You'd think we'd have had our fill of them by now.' He hauled his attention back to me. 'You must tell me about it some time.' Then he said puckishly, 'You're not at all what I expected.'

'Well, Dr Mansfield, if I may say so, neither are you.'

'It's Richard, since we're to work together. And to distinguish you from your father, I think I'll call you Cassius.'

'Cassius?'

'You have a lean and hungry look.' He grinned, then sighed a heavy sigh. 'I had no experience in treating the mad either, till I came here. In fact, even after more than ten years I'm not really sure what I'm about.'

It was difficult to know if he was joking, then or at any time. He slapped his knee and got up. 'Shall I show you around?'

His cheek was glowing like a lighthouse. 'Didn't you want to stop for some iodine first?'

'Oh, to hell with the iodine. We could begin in the men's ward, if you like, and then proceed to the hydropathy room, the conservatory, the dining hall, the airing courts, and the ballroom, et cetera.'

'Ballroom? Surely you don't still hold *balls* here?'

'Well, not balls, no. But dancing lessons for our boarders, yes.'

'Boarders?'

'Our patients. Do you dance?' He surveyed me with mellow amusement from under his tufted hair. 'I imagine you do.'

'I can waltz, in my own way. And I'm pretty good at the polka.'

'Aha, just as I thought! Your own way, indeed! You'll fit in beautifully. Welcome to the Charlestown Asylum for the Insane, Cassius.'

This is how I came to enter the institution which, like so many of its inmates, I have yet to leave.

SEVEN

A WEEK LATER, HAVING PACKED up a few clothes and books and (a gift from my father, inscribed with his menacing flourish) my new copy of Rush's *Medical Inquiries and Observations upon the Diseases of the Mind*, I moved into the rooms set aside for the asylum's assistant physician. I had just over a month to get used to my position before William Borden was to arrive.

And so I began to exist on intimate terms with all that is pitiful, misshapen, and unresolved in the human heart.

Nothing about the arrangements at the Charlestown asylum corresponded to my expectations. Its metaphysical architecture was one of enclosure. But there were no fences, no gates, no grilles. The doors were seldom locked. The interior – apart from the constant smell of day-old boiled carrots, and a certain shabbiness in the details, as if, like its inmates, the place had worn itself out by the effort of presenting a shining face to the world – resembled that of any fashionable house on Beacon Hill in having carpets, mirrors, engravings of fruit and flowers, and sherry-brown furniture wherever you looked. There was a Chickering pianoforte and a Spanish cedarwood billiard table. I swear the china the insane ate off was better than my mother's own (it was certainly more lavishly scabbed with gilt, and still bore the

Bartlett monogram, a long curling J held in a stranglehold by the B). It was exactly like being in a country residence, whose aristocratic inhabitants were identical to the denizens of the world I knew in every respect except that they were free to give expression to those ugly and inconvenient passions which the rest of us had to suppress.

'We give shelter to a better class of sufferer,' Mansfield explained on one of our rounds during my first week there. 'You have to remember that our patients come from a section of society whose artificial wants are many. They've become accustomed to a thousand minor comforts and attentions, which they particularly need when their minds are enfeebled by disease.'

That morning I'd helped Frank Goodwin, who doubled as the asylum apothecary, to mix up a tonic of castor oil and strychnine for distribution to the enervated and bored. Now Richard and I were supervising the fossils of the men's wing as they hirpled woozily through a game of bowls on the thawing terrace.

Sixty feet below us, beyond the shoulder of the hill, flowed the wide river with its traffic. Wagons and carriages rumbled over Craigie's Bridge and were lost in the haze rising from the estuary's salt flats. Up here, though, there was no sense of urgency, hardly a mechanized sound. In the crystalline air of the summit the cries of the bargemen calling from boat to boat seemed as trivial as the tinkling of a glockenspiel.

An old lunatic with a jumping eye and a military air limped up to the center line and played a drawing shot. Goodwin, who had joined in the game, was next. He delivered a dead bowl, which sheered well clear of the jack and ended up in the ditch. Pretending to be crushed, Goodwin struck his forehead with a pudgy hand and declared that he couldn't continue as he was certain to get a thrashing. Eleven scrappily haired heads immediately surrounded him and tweedled encouragement. This pantomime – the plump young doctor shaking his head and tugging at the roots of his hair, the wizened madmen hobbling and twitching and uttering papery cries – went on for some time.

I thought Goodwin's high jinks ridiculous, but Mansfield smiled approvingly.

'Well played, Major Bradlee! That was nearly a toucher!' he called out. 'Occasionally, you see, Cassius, to encourage them to trust us, it is necessary for us to feign less understanding than we have.'

Our male and female boarders were housed separately in the asylum's two wings, in which the rooms were ranged along double-loaded corridors.

The separation of the sexes was the first division on which Mansfield insisted.

'Next, we divide the quiet from the noisy, the clean from the dirty, the clothed from the naked.'

'And the latter from each other, surely?'

'Yes.' He looked at me with a flicker of merriment. 'Very good. The idea is that one patient should in the least possible way disturb or offend another. Each division should form a little family, where habits and tastes align – just like our own.'

'Richard, you may be basing this on your own experience. I'm not sure if you've ever met my family.'

'Hmmph. We should have them over for dinner. Your father has written to me to ask how you're getting on.'

'Oh God no, don't!' To my dismay my upper lip had begun to

sweat. 'Please,' I said more reasonably. 'Not yet. This is the only refuge I have.'

'Very well. For now I'll simply tell him that you're settling in, shall I? But you know –' his tired eyes, hazed with creases, brightened as if at an unexpected intuition – 'our primary purpose is to give shelter to our patients, not their doctors.'

I blushed. 'What do you mean?'

He gave me a genial dig in the ribs. 'I mean – physician, heal thyself.'

THERE WERE VERY FEW violent patients at the asylum. Bed straps and restraints were rarely used: Mansfield insisted that they should be a last resort. Some of our more excited inmates seemed to benefit from being gently steamed in long tubs with canvas covers, or swaddled in hot cloths in the hydropathy room, where they were rolled out onto benches like loaves of bread being left to prove. Hours later we unwrapped them again, pearled and damply placid.

The real ragers, mostly male, were isolated in a purpose-built lodge or 'cottage', a low structure containing four strong rooms built as islands, separated by a corridor with unglazed windows. The rooms had inclined floors, heated by subterranean flues; an ingenious design which Mansfield had borrowed from the Romans.

He forgot to take into account that the Romans didn't shit on theirs.

Frank Goodwin and I sluiced these cells down every morning, and always found them caked in feces. In the final weeks of February, cell number one was occupied by an attorney-at-law called Mr Wigglesworth, who was a prodigious manurer.

'It's a nasty job, but we must try to be stoical about it,' said Frank in his jovial way as we went in the first time. His eyes widened. They were thickly lashed, like a calf's.

We hesitated on the threshold with our buckets of lime-water, regarding the sloping cement. It was crusted with baked crap.

'Yes, well,' I demurred. 'I'll bet Marcus Aurelius's floors never looked like this.'

Wigglesworth, trousers still rucked about his ankles, was being removed by two attendants. He did not struggle but merely hung there, suspended by the armpits, smiling forbearingly at us as a loamy turd tumbled from his buttocks.

'Oh, Cassius,' muttered Frank, clapping his hand to his nose. 'You're right. Don't tell Richard I said so, but – what a filthy bastard.'

He went white with the shock of having spoken so freely.

'He's a lawyer, Frank,' I laughed. 'Of course he's full of shit.'

Frank favored me with his most veal-like stare. 'We shouldn't make light of a patient's suffering.'

'It wasn't *his* suffering I was trying to make light of.'

'I take your point, I really do. But – um.' He studied the floor again, and, crumbling a little, began to gnaw his thumb. 'Lord alone knows how we're going to get it all off.' A guilty scowl flitted over his brows as he seized the handle of his pail. 'Come on, I'll go first.' Then, bashfully, bravely, Frank tried a joke of his own. 'I have to tell you, I've never felt so grateful for a gradient.'

'Grateful for a gradient. Ha, ha! Yes.'

Christ, how dull he was.

The female ragers were confined to a second cottage in the grounds which differed from the male lodge only in that it had muslin curtains over the windows. Our female patients didn't soil their floors. They hurt themselves instead. They were ingenious and determined in their agony. If they couldn't cut or harm their bodies in any other way, they beat their heads against the walls.

Soon after I started at the asylum I was sent to the women's cottage to put some mittens on Miss Todd, who was shut up in one of its rooms, attempting to pick out her eyes with her fingers. The 'mittens' were made of leather and looked like stuffed gloves, laced at the cuffs like a boxer's.

Eliza Todd was a mystery to me. No one ever inquired after her. She was one of the very first patients to have been admitted, sixteen years ago, before Mansfield himself had joined the staff. In those days the asylum's record keeping was even more rudimentary than it was during Mansfield's superintendency. In the case-book her age on admission was given as forty-nine; her symptoms as 'forgetfulness of who she is, and given to fits of violence towards herself and others'. No change there. Her board was paid annually, without fail, but there was no mention of where she'd lived prior to coming to us. It wasn't unheard of for the friends and family of the insane to vanish once we'd taken a patient off their hands, while continuing to settle the asylum bills. We enforced a policy of forbidding visits, which effectively encouraged abandonment.

Beside Miss Todd's name, in the column where the details of the admitting person or persons were recorded, there was just one word: Bartlett.

Several minutes passed before I felt able to address the tented figure pressed up beneath the far wall. Save for the jerking of its elbows it was motionless.

'Miss Todd,' I said. 'It's me. Dr Carver. May I come in? Are you well, ma'am?'

In my sorrow and confusion at finding her there I didn't know what else to say.

'Oh!' she shouted, at once stopping her clawing. Her face, which was strangely rigid, turned my way, although the rest of her remained immobile. Her eyes, in their blood-streaked lids, had the bright density of gelatine. 'Oh, child! Are you my sister's child? You are come back to her, are you? Sit here by me.'

I lowered myself down next to her on the bare floor, convulsed with fear. Her reed-like arm under its dark sleeve lay against my side. Her fingernails were rimmed with pus.

The grotesque mittens still dangled from my hands.

'Are you going to put those on me?' she asked.

'No,' I said. I was quite clear on this. 'Not now. Not ever.'

Miss Todd shuddered happily and closed her bruised eyelids. I shut mine. Within minutes my fear left me and I was filled with the inexplicable peace I'd previously known in her company.

'Rest your head on my shoulder, my darling,' she said.

I did so, not wanting to see the pus. I could feel the beating of her heart through my entire body.

'Don't tell him,' she said. 'Don't tell him, or he will try to take you away again.'

'I won't,' I promised. I meant it as much as I've ever meant anything in my life.

I sat with her that whole morning. She was released back to the women's wing in the evening, much improved.

OH, MUCH IMPROVED. THE asylum case-book noted that some patients were discharged once 'much improved'. Others were simply 'improved'. These terms were obviously mere expressions of opinion.

Mansfield was hesitant when I asked him to define what they meant.

'But what's your theory of insanity, Richard?'

'I have no theory on the subject. Everything we do here is based on observation alone.'

'Doesn't Rush tell us that insanity is the result of an inflammation of the blood vessels of the brain? That it's an arterial disease like any other?'

'You've been reading that blood-letter, have you? Well, I've performed post mortems on the brains of mentally ill patients, and the tissues I've examined usually show no anomalies at all.'

'No lesions? No deformities?'

'None.'

'I'm surprised. Rush says unequivocally that madness affects the part of the brain which is the seat of the mind.'

'Oho! And that part is – which, exactly? We are dealing with a functional disturbance, Cassius, not a structural one. That's the devil of it. There is no earthly use in purgatives and emetics and Rush's infernal blisters. We need a psychological remedy for a psychological illness.'

'Then what's the cure? How do we treat it?'

'There is no treatment for insanity *per se*. I don't like the word "cure". That implies an outside medicinal agent, and quite truthfully, we haven't found any that works. All we do is assist Nature in performing her own cure. I prefer to talk about recovery, not cure.'

'But how do we get our patients to . . . recover?'

'Sadly, we don't always get it right. The trouble is that there are so few institutions like this one. We have no reliable model to follow. Since we can't profit from the mistakes of others, we have to make mistakes of our own.'

'So what *do* we do?'

'We create a wholesome environment. We encourage order and regularity in whatever our patients undertake. We are kind and respectful. Wherever practicable, we avoid coercion and unnecessary physical restraint. We provide a judicious moral management of the problem. And we do not – we absolutely *do not* – engage with our residents' disordered mental processes.'

'Hallucinations, phobias, delusions – ?'

'Precisely. Absolutely no advantage can arise from reasoning with the insane. We try to break up their irrational thoughts. We don't give these thoughts any credence. We afford them no room whatsoever in which to frolic.'

'So they expire from sheer lack of exercise, so to speak?'

'If you like.' He chuckled. 'Lack of excercise. Yes! I like that.'

'I didn't realize that it was all quite so hit and miss.'

'I'm sorry if you're disappointed. The fact is that we still don't know much about the mind. Our science is mostly the topography of ignorance. It would be wrong of me to pretend that I am different to any other alienist in this respect.'

'What do *you* believe, Richard? You speak mostly in negatives

– we don't do this, we don't do that, we don't know much. But what do you *think*? I'm sure you must think something.'

'I think that almost all of what we need to know concerning the human mind and its affections has already been written long ago. And can be found here.' He stroked the book at his elbow.

'In *Shakespeare*?'

'Yes.'

'Forgive me, Richard, but . . . isn't it time, then, for a new science of insanity? For – oh, I don't know – *research* based on the records of the cases we admit?'

'Possibly. But until the veil of darkness is withdrawn from the functions of the mind, we can hardly expect that arbitrary facts lying around the distant periphery of the circle will help us solve the obscurity of its center.'

'But aren't you tempted at least to try to plumb the mystery? Doesn't Hamlet say that there are more things –'

'Please don't lob *Hamlet* at me. Do you want to know what I really think?'

'I do. More than anything.'

'Well, it's this, and you may not like it. I think that when a man once becomes insane, he is about used up for this world.'

TO MY UNTRAINED EYE it seemed that insanity was not an absolute requisite to become a tenant of the asylum. Money, however, was necessary to remain so. Some of our patients were so civilized, and so well-to-do, that their eccentricities might easily have been put down to the deranging effects of extreme wealth.

Indeed, during my years at the asylum, I have sometimes wondered if wealth itself – and its first cousin, social importance – shouldn't be recognized as infectious agents, so productive are they of distorted cognition, particularly of delusional feelings of merit.

Those patients of ours who displayed exceptional lucidity or good behavior were eligible for special permissions which exempted them from the usual asylum rules. These exemptions were recorded in the permissions book. There was an especially long list of permissions for a Miss Sarah Clayborn, a handsome lady of fifty-one years whom I'd seen strolling about the grounds without an attendant, whacking the ornamental shrubs with an ivory-handled cane. Miss Clayborn not only had her own bedroom in the women's wing, but also a parlor and bath.

Miss Clayborn goes in and out of the house to the terrace and garden frequently.

Miss Clayborn goes to bed and gets up freely as she feels the need, within reason, and has cocoa when she feels like it – night or day.

Miss Clayborn has baths once or twice a day and shampoos her hair to suit herself.

Miss Clayborn may have visits from her dressmaker.

Miss Clayborn may order toilet articles.

Miss Clayborn has permission to have confectionery delivered to her room.

Miss Clayborn's notes in the asylum case-book indicated that she was the daughter of a pious Hingham family. Her father was Professor of Pulpit Eloquence and Pastoral Care at Harvard Divinity School; her two younger brothers were both Unitarian ministers.

'What's wrong with her?' I asked Mansfield. 'She seems perfectly normal.'

'She believes she is a messenger from God, sent to announce the Second Coming. The Prophet Isaiah. Or John. It varies.'

'John the *Baptist*?'

'Yes.'

'I take it that this is a revelation for which Hingham isn't quite prepared?'

'Not quite yet, no.'

'I can imagine the embarrassment to her father and brothers.'

'Just so. She is practically a Trinitarian.' Mansfield massaged his forehead in an anticlockwise gesture I'd come to know well. 'Miss Clayborn is otherwise quite conversable and in no way a danger to anyone. You're not to question her in regard to her beliefs, Cassius. Talking to her about them will only incite her to greater delusions. Pay them no heed and behave towards her exactly as you would to any lady of good family. Of all the manias, religious mania is the most contagious.'

'Really, Richard. I think I'm immune.'

Mansfield smiled. 'I wasn't referring to you. I was thinking of the other ladies in the women's wing. We don't want an outbreak of Old Testament prophets if we can help it. Especially if they all have a taste for licorice laces.'

A few days later Miss Clayborn approached me when I was out on the lower terrace. One of our two fountains had inexplicably stopped spouting and I was rooting in it, clearing away ribbons of slime, when I saw her striding up to me with her mannish walk.

The fluted branches of the poplars, tipped with hairy buds after a long frost, rippled in the breeze. An early March sun shone bravely. Behind us stood the house, discreet and solid and safe.

'Good afternoon, Miss Clayborn,' I offered. 'Are you enjoying this bright day?'

'Good afternoon, young man. Yes, thank you. Fountain packed up?'

'It would appear so. We may need to call in a plumber.'

'A plumber – pffft! You may dispense with your plumbers.' She gave the greenish spout a tap with her cane. She wore a severe jacket which encased her upper body like armor, and accentuated her considerable muscular strength. 'These waters are choked by sin and despair. They are waiting to announce the arrival of the Son of Man. They will not flow again until He is come.'

'Well, thank you for your diagnosis.'

'It's no trouble,' she replied magnanimously. 'I have been appointed by Yahweh, the Eternal Lord God, to bring His prophecy to all.'

I was genuinely surprised by her supercilious tone, and a little irritated. 'Is that so, ma'am?' I remembered Mansfield's injunction not to engage her on the subject of her monomania, but I ignored it. 'What are we to call you today? John? Or Isaiah?'

'Don't be ridiculous, Doctor. You know perfectly well that my name is Sarah Clayborn.'

'Exactly. You say you are a Judean prophet. But you are female. How do you explain the contradiction?'

'Goodness, Dr Carver,' she answered with a combative sparkle in her eye, 'you claim to be a physician with jurisdiction over grown men and women. But anyone can see that you're just a boy who should properly be in short trousers. Explain *that*, if you please.'

'I have completed three years' medical training, Miss Clayborn,' I bridled. 'I am fully qualified in my field.'

'Oh yes, you whippersnapper? Since you are so well qualified, why don't you recognize that the Son of Man will soon be coming, eh?'

A flare of exasperation went through me. 'There's the thing, Miss Clayborn. Coming where? *Where to?*'

'To this hospital, for a start,' she said victoriously.

'I look forward to it,' I said, suddenly feeling dreadfully tired. I sat down on the rim of the dead fountain and put my face in my hands.

Mansfield was right, and I was an idiot.

'I can help you,' whispered Miss Clayborn. Through my fingers her blackened teeth swam into view. Her breath smelled mightily of aniseed.

'Indeed? How?'

She placed her hands on my head. 'I have come to baptize you with Love and with the Word, Dr Carver.'

'I feel no different,' I remarked.

'Oh, but you will,' said Miss Clayborn.

PART TWO:

Eddies

EIGHT

MY JOINTS HAVE BEEN troubling me again, as they frequently do when the weather is cold. Ever since I contracted Dengue Fever two decades ago my bones have remained sensitive to the slightest change in temperature: I feel it right in my marrow. After the illness that struck me down on Nantucket last month the problem has got worse, and I have to be particularly careful. Probably I'm still not completely over that episode: at forty-three my powers of recovery aren't what they once were. I have lit the stove – not the old stove, but the newest anthracite-burning model with dolphin flues that coughs out heat like a boiler in Hades – in what used to be Mansfield's office (it is now mine) and closed the drapes. We still use the original wooden shutters throughout the building, but in recent years I've updated the soft furnishings; repaired the scrapes and chips left by time; replastered and repainted.

Mansfield wasn't very good at attending to such details. By the time I took over from him – it's been a good eleven years now – the place was becoming shabby. It looked all too much like what it was: a parvenu merchant's house fallen on hard times. Under my auspices it has acquired an elegance, a finish, it perhaps never had. I've paid attention to chandeliers and cornices, to wallpaper patterns and shallow porcelain bowls filled with rose petals. We have gas lighting these days, of course, and one has to be careful.

Everything is visible in a way it wasn't before, every rip, every blemish and fright.

Every terror.

Unlike Mansfield, who lived in for the whole of his superintendency, I prefer to spend four nights a week in Charlestown and the remainder, from Friday through to Sunday, at home. Five years back I appointed a very able assistant super called Benjamin Schultz – a Midwesterner, no less, from Illinois, which has, gratifyingly, caused quite a stir among the trustees – and having him permanently on the premises (he occupies the rooms here which I had as assistant physician) has made it possible for me to enjoy a degree of peace, and a distance from my work, which was never available to Mansfield. What happened to poor Richard is a sad example of the dangers of allowing one's calling to become all-consuming.

And besides, the mad are exhausting.

Last night my legs ached so much that I couldn't sleep, and I went down to the asylum parlor to look out onto the Charles from its bow windows. The window panes (I have preserved Bartlett's thick glass) were misted with cold, and I was dressed only in my nightshirt and robe. But I wanted, for reasons I couldn't really understand, to see the river. I had a strange notion that it might soothe me.

I rubbed at the pane until I'd cleared a patch. Standing there with my naked shins sticking out I could just about make out the watery elbow of Miller's Creek, now crowded by railway sidings and metal-working factories. This is no longer the bucolic spot it once was. While I have been building up and harmonizing within, outside the opposite has been going on. By day the thundering and chugging of iron and the stink of waste is inescapable. The second half of this century has arrived at the foot of our hill, with all its noise and confusion. There is even talk of a hog slaughterhouse moving into the neighborhood. But the railway is my biggest headache. Apart from its ugliness, I live in constant fear that an eloped patient might throw himself (it is rarely, if ever, *her*self – why is that, with all the perfectly good reasons we give our womenfolk to put an end to their existence?) onto the rails.

As I squinted out at the darkness I thought I heard a rustle, or a pawing, coming from behind me, near the door. Was it a feeble attempt at knocking? A patient, trying to get in? I wanted to cry, 'Enter! Don't be afraid!'

But when I wheeled around with the words still on my lips, there was no one there.

WILLIAM BORDEN ARRIVED AT the asylum on a gusty day in late March 1834.

Throughout that month Mansfield had corresponded with the young woman who was to have been Borden's wife. Miss Macy wrote from an excellent address on Nantucket. It appeared that she had means – her family, I discovered, were Quaker whaleship owners on the island, as well as being the proprietors of a candle and oil factory and several other commercial concerns – and was used to managing her own affairs. She and Borden would be accompanied to New Bedford on the ferry by a Macy agent, after which the pair would make the sixty-mile journey on to Charlestown alone.

'Alone? Is she in charge of him now? Her behavior seems rather conjugal.'

Mansfield and I were in his office, going over the week's business. Since Goodwin didn't have much of a head for lists, the finer points of any practical arrangements usually fell to me. I was startled to hear that Miss Macy was proposing to pay for the whole of Borden's board at the asylum, which included a substantial set of rooms in the men's wing.

'She has no father or brothers,' said Mansfield. 'She's heir to a small fortune.' He tapped his fingers on his paper-strewn table, tried to make a note with the stub of a pencil, which broke under the pressure; at last located his pen. He was always in a hurry, always beset. 'Borden's career is finished, you know. He's without any other form of support. And fortunately for us, Miss Macy has chosen to invest her money in our enterprise.'

'If she's a businesswoman, Richard, then she'll expect a return on her investment. Does Mr Borden – ah – understand this? Is he coming to us willingly?'

'Entirely willingly. The lady makes it very clear that his admission is voluntary.' He shuffled the mess of papers and filleted out a sheet ribbed all over with black ink. 'She writes a good letter. This is her latest. Would you like to read it?'

I took a chary look at the letter. It didn't contain any of the usual Quaker mannerisms, no *thee*s or *thy*s: Miss Macy could write as the world wrote.

'. . . *That he will be in such skilled hands is my consolation – that you will, in time, restore to me the man I have known, my audacious hope*,' I read.

Audacious. A hatch opened in my gut. 'If you don't mind,' I said, thrusting the paper back at Mansfield, 'I'd rather form an impression of her once Mr Borden's here.'

I wanted to see Borden, and I did not. There were moments in that tranquil hospital, surrounded by the mad, with no one but Mansfield and Goodwin for company, when I believed myself under a spell, delivered from everything that had pressed so heavily on me. The memories I had of my sojourn on the *Orbis* were slippery, like scenes from a submerged world, or the fragments of an earlier, more turbulent self. When they rose to the surface they did so in a tumble, throwing off serpentine glints before being carried away.

At those times I thought of Borden and grew agitated.

I tried not to think of him. I didn't want my hours in that orderly place to be disturbed by anything or anyone that would remind me of my humiliating months on board ship. I learned to follow directions without resisting; I made myself – as Caro had urged me – useful; I developed the knack of biting my tongue and concealing my true feelings when it was politic to do so. For whole days I went about my business – I was perpetually busy; we began our rounds at seven in the morning and didn't finish until every patient had been put to bed – like the detached, efficient, cheerful physician I was training myself to impersonate, attending only to the appearances of things and looking away from the depths.

And then the sun would light up the back of the Charles River snaking below us, or the breeze would carry over a waft of salt from the flats, and I would think of him again.

*

THAT MARCH THE PEWTER sky, long sheeted by dirty clouds, turned riotously blue. As the spring nor'easter tore at them a felted sheen came and went across the lawns, whose cropped acres unfurled in the sun like newly laid baize.

On the afternoon Borden was due it blew so violently that I left Mansfield and Goodwin waiting in the parlor while I raced around the main building, fastening the banging shutters. I was upstairs in the gallery when I heard the shirring of wheels at the front of the house. Instead of going down at once I stayed at the window, where I had a view of the sandy drive that extended all the way up the north side of the hill, ending in a circular parterre at the main door.

From above I saw a woman in a gray dress and bonnet alighting from a chaise. Something about her comportment, the agility and quickness of it, suggested not just youth but another, more disturbing property – determination. She wasn't simply resigned to being here; she was zealous, and in her zeal she performed a rapid rotation as she took it all in: the swept drive, the long poplar-girt avenue, the brilliant lawns and the distant summer house in its tangle of rose trees.

Her head turned to the right, then the left, but she didn't look up. She hesitated only briefly at the carriage step before holding out her hand to whomever still sat inside. A stooped figure, sheathed in a coat and wearing a hat that hid its face, extended a skeletal leg, then another, and slid haltingly to the ground. The two stood close together, swaying a little.

I held my breath. The house seemed to be lying in wait: buffeted by wind outside, unchanging within. Then a hinge moaned downstairs. I could hear a commanding voice, blunted steps. Mansfield strode out onto the porch, confident, energetic, full of self-effacing reassurances, with Goodwin clumping behind.

For a moment I saw us all: the magus, the fat fool; the lovers. And myself, watching.

The moment passed. The woman in gray shook Mansfield's hand with the merest touch of the fingertips, and the skeleton, now clutching her by the sleeve, was bundled indoors.

For the next hour I occupied myself in the women's ward. There was some difficulty between Miss Joy and a patient who would not remain in her room while the corridor floors were being washed, and for once I was grateful for the disruption. I didn't want to see Borden. And I didn't want to meet this Quaker heiress who wrote good letters and thought nothing of traveling a hundred miles out of her natural sphere in the *audacious hope* that the world – contrary to all probability; the temerity of it! – would put aside its true nature, and show her mercy.

I WENT DOWN TO Mansfield's office at four o'clock, as our patients were being shepherded into the conservatory for their afternoon cocoa. The wind had quietened but the shutters still hung wide open. The stove, in a rare concession to comfort, was lit, and the study was full of piercing light. When I entered it I had an irresistible impression of thorny brilliance, of a prickle passing back and forth along the floor to the far corner where two people sat, outlined against the glowing stove door, exchanging murmurs.

Mansfield got up and beckoned me over.

'Cassius, where have you been? I've wanted you.' I noted that he spoke with difficulty, as if his real focus were elsewhere. He didn't wait for a reply. 'Miss Macy will be leaving us soon.'

Miss Macy rose as I came towards her. In the glare of the window, backed by the stove's vibrating heat, she struck me as almost transparent. Her cheeks were pale; her hair, just visible under its bonnet, blonde as ash. She was slender and upright, and though her eyes glittered as if her whole being were on fire, her hand, when it took mine, was cold. In her narrow gray dress, and with those shining eyes, she was as dazzling as a burning icicle.

She sat down again and smoothed the column of her skirt. Contrary to what Mansfield had said, she showed no signs of being about to go. I sat down opposite her, aware of a terrible crackle in the air. The sounds of an ordinary afternoon — the clinking of cocoa cups and the bumping of chairs — drifted into the room.

Miss Macy cleared her throat. 'Dr Carver, I've longed to thank you.'

Her voice was refined and surprisingly low. She glanced at Mansfield, and then back at me. As her hand went to her neck I saw that a modest silver band encircled her ring finger. She wore no other jewels or ornaments.

My first impression of her was that she was far too inflexible a body to lay claim to anything as elastic as longing. (How wrong I was!) Then in the next moment I noticed that she was not as young as I'd first thought her: she was at least Caro's age, possibly a little older. And she was afraid.

'William has mentioned your name,' she said levelly. 'You were there with him, on board — you looked after him — you knew him.'

Miss Macy could speak as the world spoke.

'I think I knew him, yes. We were friends,' I lied, and felt myself flushing under her gaze. 'He was good to me,' I ventured more truthfully. 'He was . . . someone I looked up to.'

'Of course you looked up to him!' she returned with a jarring smack of her ring against her breastbone. 'How couldn't you? *You* knew him before –' She tilted her icy chin at Mansfield, but did not go on.

Mansfield made no reply. His eyes had a skewed look. I knew, all at once, that the afternoon must have been trying; he had one of his migraines.

We stared at the stove until silence enveloped us. Just as the stillness promised to take on a settled quality, Miss Macy turned to me.

'I'm glad you've come, Dr Carver. Dr Mansfield and I were talking over the arrangements for William's treatment.'

She made it sound, somehow, as if he had been consulting her, not the other way around. Wasn't this what was understood by Quaker forthrightness, this effrontery masquerading as a lack of guile?

'How is Mr Borden now?' I asked.

'He is asleep,' interpolated Mansfield, blinking furiously. 'Miss Macy has impressed on me that he is often, indeed usually, lucid. And I've explained to her that, once a patient has been settled here, it is hospital policy not to admit visits from friends or family, however rational that patient might seem.'

'No visits at all, Doctor?' returned Miss Macy in a flash. 'Really – *never?*'

Mansfield rubbed his forehead. 'Forbidding the visits and correspondence of loved ones is one of the severest trials we have to face. But long experience has taught me that it is crucial to the wellbeing of the patient.'

'How can it hurt him to speak with those of us who remember him as he was?' A radiant tear kindled in her eye. 'As he really is?'

'Nevertheless, ma'am, it will,' said Mansfield. 'You must trust me in this. Everything and everyone in Mr Borden's environment influences his condition of mind and therefore has therapeutic or destructive potential. What he needs now is absolute seclusion and absolute routine. No deviations, Miss Macy. No surprises.'

'If you say so, Dr Mansfield.' Her eyes continued to hold me in their febrile grip. 'But since I am forbidden even to write to Mr Borden, I know you won't object if I correspond with Dr Carver instead. As someone who will see him every day. As a friend – a friend of William's.'

A shiver went through her. I could see her readying herself.

Mansfield opened the stove door and threw a piece of wood onto the fire. In the sudden guttering of the light Miss Macy's small figure flared out, immense.

'Please,' she said, breathing shallowly, twisting her ring. 'I must have something. I must.'

Mansfield's reply was guarded. 'Here at the hospital Dr Carver will be Mr Borden's physician, not his friend.'

'Yes. But there is friendship in your treatment, Doctor. Isn't there friendship and great kindness in it, as you've explained it to me?'

Oh, she was a clever woman. I could sense Mansfield's resistance to that stainless, nimbly wielded will disintegrating.

'Yes, ma'am, there is.' Mansfield sighed. His fingertips stroked his forehead in urgent circles. Inside the stove a chip of wood, stoked to white heat, exploded with a pop.

'Richard.'

They both looked at me.

'I can do this, if you agree. If it would help Miss Macy to feel — to feel confidence in us, and in our care of Mr Borden, then I will undertake to send her regular reports of his condition, and to answer her questions as they arise. As his physician, naturally.'

Mansfield got up and took me to one side. His brow was seeded with sweat. 'We don't do this for our other patients,' he whispered. 'If we were to start —'

'Oh, stuff, Richard! Just because we don't do it for the others doesn't mean that we can't do it in this case.'

He laughed scratchily out of the corner of his mouth. Then he flinched. 'All right. If anyone can manage her, it's you. Now let's get her on her way before my head splits in two.'

'I'll do it. You just sit.'

I left him and walked Miss Macy back to her carriage in silence. (Stillness seemed to be her natural mode.) As I assisted her into her seat, she surprised me by pressing my hand.

'Thee's a good man, Hiram Carver.'

It was if she had breathed her hot breath on me. I was so startled to hear her slipping into Quaker speech that my fingers closed around hers in a pinch.

'I'm not sure about that, ma'am. A conscientious one, maybe.'

'Is there a difference?' She scanned my face cautiously. She was still holding on to my palm. 'Thee will help me, won't thee?' she said.

'I will. We both want the same thing. We want Mr Borden to be himself again.'

Standing there on that hill with her chilled hand in mine, I knew that it was true.

The tear that had threatened to fall from Miss Macy's eye for the last hour splashed down her cheek, and was overtaken by another and another. She sat and cried in a way I'd never yet seen a woman cry, bearing the full brunt of my scrutiny without once covering her face, her eyes wide open, her spine erect.

'Can thee do that?' she asked. 'Can thee give me that?'

'I don't know. But you want it above all else, I think – and so do I.'

Her tears stopped as abruptly as they'd begun. A moment later she resumed her worldly mask and smiled an austere smile. 'Dr Mansfield is angry with me.'

'It may not be necessary for Dr Mansfield to be privy to every detail of our correspondence.'

Freeing her hand from my grasp, Miss Macy drew in the hem of her dress. 'I'll be guided by thee – completely.' Her pale eyes appeared to float before me in the twilit carriage. 'Why does the doctor call thee by that queer name?'

'It's a whim of his, I guess.'

'Friend, I believe thee deserves a better one.'

I found Mansfield doubled over in his chair. He raised his head blearily. 'Good Lord. What a tenacious woman. Though she be but little, she is fierce.'

'I thought her rather fine.'

'Don't be fooled by that Quaker simplicity. Wives and relatives. Fiancées. Why do they always think they know better?'

'Perhaps she does know him better than we do, Richard,' I said, tossing him a cushion to put behind his neck.

'Yes. But can she make him well?'

'Can we?'

'Oh God.' Mansfield shunted the cushion aside and lowered his forehead to his knees.

'Shall I fetch you your morphine?'

'I'm trying to do without. And in any case, Frank's busy.'

'I can mix it up for you. I've watched him often enough.'

'Thank you, Cassius. Will you visit him tonight? I think I may have to lie down.'

'I take it you mean Borden?'

'Yes. Borden.' His face puckered in pain. Keeping one eye closed, he shot me a wobbling look through the other. 'I know you a little by now. You haven't said a word, but you've been waiting for this moment.' He passed his hand over his eyes. 'Lord. I can see two of you.'

'There's only one of me.'

'Ah, pity. I'm starting to find you indispensable, you know.'

AFTER SUPPER AND MY early evening rounds, when the building was beginning to sink into its nightly blue-black slumber, I went to find Borden. He was housed in one of the larger sets of rooms at the back of the men's wing, overlooking the fountains and the poplar grove. From here, by day, you could see the busy river with its boats where it ebbed into the salt marsh at the foot of the hill. I wondered if this would be a consolation to him.

I carried a candle that splurted unsteady light down the corridor. When I opened the door my hand trembled so much that hot wax shawled the stick. I was aware of the tripping of my heart, and the beating of my pulse in every part of my body. I could feel it in my groin, my neck, in the crook of my arm.

I did not know what to expect.

Like that of all the better apartments, Borden's door led first into a short vestibule or interconnecting passage, which gave way in turn to a parlor. The bedroom door, at the far end, was ajar. Crossing over to it with my heart still drumming, I went in.

The room was bathed in the green river-light peculiar to that part of the ward. As I entered it a gull sent up its concentric cry from the flats and flew off in a dolorous clatter. In its wake the quiet had deepened, so that I could hear my breath coming and going. I set my candle down on a table and only then dared look up.

In the middle of the floor stood a bed, and there, under a welter of blankets, laid out like a corpse on a bier, was the body of a man. I could make out the shape of the legs, stretched out in a flattened lath, and a declivity where the hips and stomach should have been. The rest was too shallow, surely, too attenuated, to be human. The hollow chest – hollow though blankets were heaped on it – rose and fell irregularly. Beyond it arched an endless neck, topped by an enormous head resting on a pillow. The jaw was canted towards me and at that angle, in the sepulchral light, I had an overwhelming impression of bone, shadowed by a jutting nose and tunneled nostrils.

I drew nearer. A memory swam into my mind: of a quiet midnight at sea; Borden on the silvered deck of the *Orbis*, unaware, or so I thought, that I was observing him.

Then, as now, I'd wanted to kneel. Approaching the bed, I went down on one knee.

'William.' My own voice, rebounding in that enclosed space, accused me as if I were defiling the peace of a crypt.

No movement or sign of recognition came from the face on the pillow. The wide-set eyes in their pools of bone were shut. Perhaps, between my entering the room and kneeling before him, he really had died. I leaned forwards, until my cheek brushed his. Below his vaulted nostrils I felt rather than heard a faint agitation of the air.

Then, inches from mine, a yellow eye opened, steady and vital.

I reared back.

A scraggy arm appeared from the blankets and jackknifed itself against the mattress. The other crept out and attempted, with a painful effort, to do the same. The torso half rolled to one side. The great head blundered upwards, swung loose, surged upwards once more.

Slowly, jerkily, the being on the bed raised itself onto its elbows and turned to me.

'Hiram. Your hand.'

His voice was the same as I remembered it: deep, plangent, ripe with authority. Coming from that shriveled frame it seemed, by contrast, to have grown in richness and power.

'Will. Is that really you?'

But I knew from his voice – by the leonine rumble of it, which struck up an answering vibration in some deep cavity in me – that it was.

His oddly colored eyes were looking directly into mine while his rake-like fingers combed the air. 'Your hand. I can't sit without your help.'

It was as if I had woken from a protracted swoon. In that moment I became aware of a rending emotion that wasn't made of memory, hardly even of sense, but was more brutal and final than that – a realignment of all my inner self, as if my heart leaped out of its cage and my mind, suddenly alive, began to move again.

Giving Borden my right hand, I slipped my other arm behind his shoulders and lifted him until he was propped against the bedhead. It was like lifting a specter. His flesh felt diaphanous, his body like vapor wrapped around a brittleness.

His breath was coming fast now. 'Aye, it's me,' he rattled. 'But is this you?' His fingers encircled my wrist. 'You've grown thin.' Baring his teeth in a grimace, he corrected himself: 'Thinner.'

'You're a fine one to talk.'

I tightened my hold on his shoulders. I was alarmed to find myself shaking uncontrollably. Then I realized that he was shaking too, in spasms that seemed about to tear his body apart.

Not shaking – weeping.

I watched him cry, as I had watched him many months ago, and as I'd so recently watched her. His crying was completely dry, as if there were no moisture left in him.

'Why are you crying?'

'I am afraid.'

'Do not be afraid. You have nothing to fear here.'

'Don't I? There is the truth, Hiram. Don't you fear it?'

I didn't know what to say. He rested in my arms for a long time, until his knobby head started to sag and his chin to hurt my collarbone. My candle, which had almost burned to a stub, was smoking. Gradually Borden's eyes closed, their lids translucent in the uncertain light. I could see the veins beneath them, the patchwork of red capillaries. His breath filed, rasping, at my skin. Cell by cell, he was slipping back into sleep.

Still shaking like a sail in the wind, I laid him down again and covered him up.

ONCE I WAS ALONE in my own room, I sought out my little writing table. The wind had died away, leaving an utter absence of sound. Featureless night filled the window.

I sat in the silence for some time with my eyes shut, listening to my pulse thudding in my eardrums. After a while it slowed, and my hands became steadier. I took up my pen, dipped it into the inkwell, and tried out its steel in the margin of my blotter. A liquid mole swelled from the nib and tentacled towards the edge.

Squaring a sheet of paper, I began a letter to Ruth Macy.

'My dear Miss Macy,' I wrote.

I have this evening spoken with Mr Borden. I found him weak, and physically much reduced, but in his essential self, in that grace, that strength, that – I cannot think of a better word – *virtue* which radiated from him when he served on the *Orbis* and which compelled my respect and the respect of everyone who knew him, still recognizable. I hope this gives you courage.

I dare to believe that we will be able to open a crack in the darkness now surrounding him through which this light may again shine.

I signed my letter, 'Your friend, Hiram Carver.'

Who was I tonight? I wondered. What was this strange sympathy he drew from me? He never asked for anything, made no demands.

His former self-sufficiency, and now his weakness, roused me as no challenge in my life ever had before. Had I really been changed by my contact with him – or was it that I was being slowly revealed as I really was?

And she, with her transparent beauty, her piercing devotion and her artlessness (was it artlessness? Even then, I didn't quite know) – what was her role in my translation?

For at that time, you see, I still thought of it all – every tremor, every look, each desperate appeal – as being somehow about me.

I blotted the letter, folded it, and set it aside for the morning's post. How tired I felt! A single, importunate star had risen in the sky and now semaphored across the void.

I got up to close my curtains. As I did so I caught sight of my own distorted image, a crazed shadow of me, looming from the black glass.

NINE

I N MY FIRST WEEKS among the mad, the thrilling thought often
occurred to me that they were just like us. They gibbered, and sulked,
and raged, and pursued their fixed ideas, but what stayed with me was
this sense of their similarity to us – an impression of their affinity with
those who were supposedly sane. Or of our affinity with them.

I was never – am never – sure which it was. Is.

Though I knew I was breaking asylum rules, I found it almost
impossible to remain disengaged from their mental processes. There
was Borden. But before Borden, there was Miss Clayborn.

Once I'd taken the misstep of speaking to her about her delusions,
Miss Clayborn developed a trick of luring me into further debate. I
tried to cut her off, but she was most persistent.

Eventually I resorted to invoking a higher authority.

'I'm sorry, ma'am, but I can't discuss this with you any more. Dr
Mansfield himself has forbidden it.'

'Why is Miss Joy allowed to worship her God openly every day
when I am not allowed to proclaim mine?'

'Miss Joy? Do you mean our attendant? As far as I can tell Miss
Joy isn't especially observant.'

'Oh but she is! She worships her God daily, *without fail*, in the showiest way! And Dr Mansfield says nothing about it, and nor do you!'

I wiped my eyes on the back of my wrist. 'You're going to have to explain this to me in very simple words.'

Miss Clayborn brought her heel down hard on the sailcloth floor. 'This floor, Dr Carver. *This floor* is Miss Joy's God!'

She was right. Every afternoon without exception Felicity Joy (who was, by the way, a gloom-spreading bitch; never was anyone less aptly named) insisted on having the floor in the women's wing mopped, and then dried with chamois cloths. If any of the boarders risked putting a foot on it they were reprimanded and confined to their rooms, as Miss Joy lived in fear that someone might leave a mark on its virgin surface.

After this conversation I knew, whenever I saw Miss Joy contemplating that shriven corridor with the rapt absorption of a fanatic, that she was lost to us in the grip of an essentially private ritual.

And yet, she passed as sane.

I began to suspect that what we called madness was just this — terror, a very proper holy terror at the soiled and intractable nature of the world.

'Richard, isn't the distinction between the mad and the sane simply that *they* admit openly to the true fragility of things?'

But Mansfield refused to understand me. 'Fragility?'

'Yes. Consider all these obsessions of theirs – their little fads, even their acts of self-harm, and the ferocity with which they defend them – why, the very deviousness they show in carrying on with these when we try to stop them! It may seem crazy to us, but what if they see this – this hocus pocus as a perfectly reasonable defense against chaos?'

'What chaos? We run a very orderly place here.'

I meant the chaos that presses in on all of us from every side – that void I'd sensed at the back of things ever since I was a boy, and again, most horribly, when I was sailing on the indifferent face of the ocean in the *Orbis*; chaos that is no less appalling for being nameless, undefined.

This sense of a hidden affinity with our patients visited me at the oddest moments; so much so, that I started seeing a shadow meaning in many of our own ostensibly innocent habits. I noticed that Frank Goodwin, for instance, had to have his mouth occupied at all times. When not snacking he was always chewing at his finger ends; his nails were nibbled down to fleshy pincushions. He was fat because he ate too much, that was plain, but after a while I wondered if a desire for food was really at the bottom of his constant gobbling, or if he wasn't soothed, on some level of his being, by the mere action of putting something in his mush.

One day I decided to test my theory. Frank kept a tin of caramels on his work table, and in the spirit of empiricism I hid them. I just went ahead and palmed the tin into my pocket when his back was turned. On glancing round and finding it gone, he took off on a frantic search of the tabletop, lifting order books and shifting cartons of magnesium sulphate and nearly upsetting a bottle of rubbing alcohol. And then, at last, stumped, he picked out a marble from the detritus on his pen tray, *dropped it onto his tongue as if this were the most normal thing in the world, and sucked on it.*

Ha. Vindicated.

And Mansfield, of course, had his morphine.

The one person whom I couldn't make out clearly, on whom I

could fix no enduring perspective, was William Borden. He eluded me utterly. It was not only that there was less of him – less flesh, less substance, less *man* – to get hold of, that his body was so ethereal, his physical being so tenuous, that it seemed almost to flicker. No – it wasn't this, though this was frightening enough. It was something even more alarming. The core of him was submerged, sunk, buried leagues beneath a cold darkness that was apparently eternal. It still gave off the faint heat of its old charge, but the treasure was lodged so far down in the splintered depths that I doubted – whatever I may have written to Miss Macy – that it could in fact be salvaged, that I would ever see it whole.

He was never violent. After that first evening he was seldom, if ever, distressed. Most of the time he was simply not there, lost in fathomless black water where I couldn't follow.

Mansfield prescribed a regime of exercise and regular meals for Borden which I oversaw. Every afternoon I took him out for a walk on the hill, but we never crept very far before he asked to sit. He was so emaciated that I believed I could see his heart straining through his chest. He wore well-cut, expensive clothes; a gentleman's clothes, evidently chosen for him with great care: cambric shirts, woolen trousers, a napless coat. Draped from his gaunt frame, however, they looked unfashionable, even quaint, like priestly robes. His entire appearance was alien; cursed, or charmed. In full sunlight he resembled a changeling, a creature barely human. His jaundiced skin was gauzy, with the sheer luster of beaten gold. His bronze hair had grown long and fell to his shoulders in unkempt waves.

We sat on a faux rustic seat on the middle terrace, our shadows blue on the ripening grass. The brown film of winter still lay on the lower slopes of the garden, whose eighteen acres, ponds and espaliered fig trees stretched ahead of us like an enchanted kingdom.

What were Borden's thoughts? They were impossible for me to imagine. He behaved as if he remembered nothing. He never asked after Miss Macy. He never asked after anyone. What explanation he gave himself for the divorce between his old life and his new one, and his presence in Charlestown, I didn't know. Perhaps he didn't have one. Perhaps he was beyond such explanations.

Borden's silence had a completely unpredicted effect on me. First it pricked my clinical interest, then it provoked feelings of dismay, and in due course I became unnerved. It was as if his wordlessness were slowly absorbing me; as if, while spending those mute hours with him, I was becoming gradually separated out from myself. I resisted the urge to fill them with talk, as I had when I'd shared his prison below decks. Still, I longed for him to speak: my very being was focused on it. He spoke so rarely that every word of his, waiting for it as I did, seemed to carry the stamp of a great truth.

Late one afternoon, as we rested on our bench, Borden finally drew an etiolated breath. I leaned towards him greedily.

'So. Here we are, Hiram.' He shrugged his scalpel-like shoulders. 'Two scarecrows in a garden.'

Yes, there it was again: when he did speak I felt it again, the sparking to life of my own pulse, that flash of a hidden kinship with the mad. On we, the sane, went, cajoling and exhorting and chivvying them, and all the time I wondered if we didn't recognize, deep down, that there was little to choose between us; that if they, whose hungers and illusions we found so disturbing, were once like us, then we could easily – oh, in a heartbeat! – turn into them.

I HAVE USED THE word 'hungers'. I saw already in Borden's earliest days at the asylum that the question of hunger was going to be vexatious. Our meals were served in Jacob Bartlett's dining room, at two long tables arranged in parallel. The tables were swathed in clean linen and set with crystal and bone-handled cutlery. A crumb cloth placed underneath them protected Bartlett's valuable old carpet from spills.

Mansfield presided over the first table, Goodwin and I over the second, as though the two of us were somehow equivalent to one of him, which seemed right and fitting to me then. The implication was that we were a family, a civilized family: father, favored older sons, occasionally unruly but nevertheless cherished minor children, all breakfasting or dining together. But the scene had a smudged, disjointed air: several of the diners performed the same actions in a loop, as if keeping a ship's watches, or emitted weird chirrups and bleeps, or stared; the conversation snagged, and swirled off in irrecoverable directions. It was like being seated at the mess of a sunken galleon, some ghostly and vaguely disreputable old barque of legend, trapped in a dumb-show of eating and drinking at the bottom of the ocean. The porters glided into view with our food – suppurating lamb stews and cuts of blackened pork; bread and cheese and vegetables boiled down into a tan glue – and drifted out, leaving us to sway aimlessly in the currents of insanity.

I put Borden near me so that I could monitor his diet. Once in a while he took a sip of milk and crumbled a piece of bread. I never saw him touch meat. He didn't object to being there, but he had an exasperating way of emptying his features of all expression and staring trance-like at the tablecloth with his amber eyes that managed to convey his totemic indifference to the meal. He was part of the mass but aloof from it, an idol that was made of a different substance to the human life around him, and would outlast us.

After a week of this, I went to Mansfield.

'He won't eat.'

'Well, neither will you.'

'Yes, but I'm not insane. Or shut up here. Or engaged to a demanding woman.' I looked at Mansfield in exasperation. 'What are you trying to say?'

'I'm trying to say, Cassius, that if you're going to treat him you might start by leading from the front.'

'I hate those mashed parsnips we have on Wednesdays.'

'Yes. So do I. But if we don't eat them, how can we expect our patients to?'

'You make it all sound so easy.'

'It's not easy, exactly. But maybe it's easier than you think.'

'Richard, he was on the *Providence*. The damn thing was taken over by mutineers. He starved for two months on open water. You'd have thought he'd appreciate the value of food. He ate on the *Orbis*. Why isn't he eating now?'

'I don't know. All I know is that he's not exempt from the laws of human biology. He needs nourishment. So do you. Why don't you set him an example?'

'I can't, Richard. When I was on that blasted ship I felt so seasick

– I felt as if I'd vomit up my soul. And then afterwards, once I was home, that feeling stayed with me. The endless meals, the teas, the dinners and suppers – I just couldn't. It was as if . . . Oh, this will sound ridiculous.'

'Go on.'

'Well, it was as if I'd be consuming *myself* somehow, or – or letting them devour me, if I shared their food.'

Mansfield was thoughtful.

'I heard a voice once,' I blurted. 'I've never told you this.'

'What sort of voice?'

'It was when I was on board ship. I was ill, though I didn't realize it. It spoke to me very clearly.'

'Hallucinations during severe illness are common. You know that.'

'Yes but this was so distinct. I was – looking after Borden at the time. At first I thought it was his voice. But then, later, I wasn't sure – I began to feel differently. I thought it might be a woman's voice. Or the voice of someone, something, that was neither male nor female.'

'What did it say?'

'I was feverish. Dreaming, I think. But I wasn't asleep. I had a sort of waking vision that I was outside the ship and that someone was calling me home.'

'*Outside* the ship?'

'Yes. In the water. On the water. Walking on the water.'

Mansfield folded his arms and smiled at me with mock concern. 'Fasting. Walking on water. How long have you believed that you are the Messiah?'

'Richard, be serious. It was the closest I've ever come to a – to an otherworldly experience. It was as if something alive, as real as I am, were summoning me. Later I thought – ah.'

'What did you think?'

'You'll think I'm mad.'

'An interesting choice of phrase. Try me.'

'Well, I thought – it seemed to me – that the spirit of the ocean itself had spoken to me. Some ancient thing, at any rate. There. Am I insane?'

'Oh, Cassius. On balance, I think not. You can call spirits from the vasty deep. Why, so can I, or so can any man. But will they come when you do call for them? I'm not about to consume you. Please, just eat the goddamned parsnips.'

IF I AM GOING to be absolutely truthful in these recollections of my early days at the asylum then I must admit that I was sometimes puzzled by the presentation of things. Take our dancing lessons. They weren't called balls, but they seemed so much like balls that it made no difference. Mansfield arranged these sessions on a spontaneous basis, whenever he felt that the asylum inmates, sane and insane, needed stimulation, or perhaps just cheering up. Those patients who hadn't recently made use of the hydropathy facilities were washed and toweled. Everyone wore his or her best clothes (I had to ask Caro to send me my pumps – how stupid they looked, grinning around my thin feet).

One evening not long after Borden's arrival we all shuffled down to the ballroom for a 'lesson'. The moire curtains had been drawn against the arrival of dusk and every candle in the great chandelier lit, giving the room an air of vitality and warmth. The worn gilt chairs and side tables had an attentive air, as if living, breathing Bartletts had lately passed among them; even the flaking ceiling above us appeared to have regained the lofty altitude of a bygone age. Gawking at it, I collided with Goodwin wheeling in a trolley loaded with plates of shortbread and jugs of lemonade.

'Oh I beg your pardon, Cassius. These things send me into such a funk. I wish we had more notice.'

'Richard likes to keep us on our toes.'

I waited for his appreciative laugh, but it didn't come.

'*Toes*, Frank.' I mimed an instructive jig.

'Toes?' He was fussing with the lemonade. A sticky wave splashed over the side of the trolley, puddling its wheels. 'Oh, yes, I see! I'm awfully stupid tonight. Toes, as in dancing!' He went on fussing. 'Darn it. I'm a jug short. I may have left it in the kitchen.'

'Don't cudgel your brains, Frank.' We'd become so friendly that I was emboldened to feign a punch to his chubby gut. 'Let me see if I can hunt it down for you.'

I was almost at the door when Miss Clayborn intercepted me. 'Aha,' she said, flicking imaginary fluff from my collar, 'the Infant Prodigy. Very elegant. Your mother dresses you most respectably.' She herself was dressed in men's trousers and one of her formidable armored jackets, which proved, on closer inspection, to be corduroy. 'You'll do. About turn, my boy.'

'I'm needed in the kitchen, ma'am.'

'You're needed more here. We have a plague of flies due north. Go on, sir. About turn. Exercise your skill.'

I turned and saw Miss Joy's narrow back, stooped over a female patient of whom only a varicosed ankle and a tatty silk shoe were visible.

I'd developed a savage dislike of Felicity Joy. I hated her fastidiousness, and I particularly hated the way she hid her pinched nature under the veneer of duty. The intensity of my antipathy toward her bothered me for weeks, until it dawned on me that she reminded me of Fryar. That rigidity, that dainty meanness – she was probably at it now, stinging some wretch into submission over a trifling infringement of the rules.

Miss Joy straightened up, disclosing Eliza Todd. Miss Todd's shoulders were loosely bandaged by a yellowish muslin of an antique design. Diamonds dangled from the withered lobes of her ears. Her cheeks were streaked with tears.

'He hasn't come,' she said in a shrunken voice as Miss Clayborn and I approached. 'He gave me his promise. Oh, where is he?'

I knelt at her feet. 'Whom do you wish to see, ma'am? Is it Dr Mansfield? He is just fetching his music.'

Miss Clayborn gave me a thump on the back. 'She is awaiting the bridegroom, you noodle.'

'Dr Carver. Miss Joy.' Mansfield, who had come in and taken his seat at the pianoforte, rapped on the lid for silence. 'Dr Goodwin? That shortbread is meant to be a refreshment for our interval.'

'Oops.' Goodwin, sputtering pastry crumbs, swallowed gluily. 'Sorry. Yes, all set, Richard.'

Mansfield rotated his wrists. 'Excellent. Ladies and gentlemen, we will begin with a quadrille. Those who are familiar with this step may lead the others by example. Those who are uncertain should do their best. Since we are unequally matched as to gender the ladies may feel free to dance with the ladies. Got that? Off you go.'

'I doubt that Miss Todd will know this dance.' Miss Joy started to work at Miss Todd's bare old forearms. 'Come along, ma'am. No more mischief. It's upstairs with you.'

But Miss Todd had risen. 'On the contrary. I have often danced it. I am ready to dance it now.' Her hatched breast heaved; her blistered face was lifted to someone behind us. I looked round and saw William Borden standing alone on the margin of the room: tall, fleshless, his geometry draped in black, like an awful totem pole.

The thought washed over me: he is alive. He may be mad, but he lives. He is the most alive thing in this room.

Miss Todd took a pace or two towards him. 'You have kept me waiting, sir,' she pouted with hideous coquetry. 'But you have,' she continued sadly, extending her hand, 'my forgiveness.'

The words seemed to recall Borden to himself from an inhuman distance. What would he say, this skeletal veteran of the seas, this angelic hero, this would-be murderer?

He answered her with as much kindness as I'd always seen him answering any weaker creature. 'Thank you,' he said evenly, folding her fingers into his carved fist. Together they went out into the middle of the room and began a broken progress up and down it. I had the strangest sense that I was peering through the back end of a tunnel, at the origins of something; but of what – creation or catastrophe – I couldn't tell.

'Dr Carver, please *stop* her,' Miss Joy seethed. 'She will excite herself.'

'Then she's a lucky woman,' retorted Sarah Clayborn. 'Let her alone. Tonight the beams of our house are cedar, and our rafters of fir. Come to mention it, *you* look particularly comely, ma'am.'

Implausibly, unbelievably, the corrugated slab of her arm stole round Felicity Joy's waist. 'May I?'

In the next few moments this already outlandish evening became even stranger. Miss Joy made no protest. Patting her hair-net, she glanced warily at me. I nodded.

Down and across they went, up and around, the mad and the sane, in a jittery human chain. When Mansfield announced a waltz, Borden delivered Miss Todd back to me before retreating to the shadows. I saw him sitting there, his legs limp, as if whatever force had briefly animated him had now departed. I danced with Miss Todd and felt my knees jam; the angled parts of me sliding in on themselves. It scarcely mattered. By some weird magic her elderly bones had become pliant. She bore me up, her face aflame with tenderness.

As I poured myself a glass of lemonade Miss Clayborn, whom I'd very much hoped not to encounter again for the rest of the evening, appeared at my side. 'You there! It's nearly seven. Should you still be awake?'

'My working day isn't finished yet.'

She strode over to the piano, where Richard was flicking through his sheet music. 'Dr Mansfield,' she hooted, 'this Infant ought to be abed.'

'I assure you, ma'am –' he smiled drily, selecting a polka – 'that Dr Carver has a dispensation to be up.'

'Very well, sir, but you will have no one but yourself to blame if he overtires himself and becomes fractious.'

'I'll take that chance, ma'am, if you'd be good enough to put him through his paces in the next dance. He needs to work off some of his enthusiasm. He'll sleep the better for it.'

'Very true.' Taking my arm, she gathered me to her plated bosom. It was like being tucked into the armpit of a rhinoceros. 'Come, Doctor, what are you waiting for? This is a wedding, after all. Look lively, sir.'

Mansfield struck a few cautious chords. 'All right, Cassius?'

'Oh yes, Richard. Never better. Play on.'

AFTERWARDS, AS I HELPED Mansfield to set the chairs back against the wall, I felt dazed. A miasma of bromides and stale feet hung over the room.

'I think that went well, Cassius, don't you?'

'Did it?'

'Absolutely. It was a success. Everybody danced. You were marvelous.'

'I *was*?'

He inclined his head, suddenly grave. 'Yes. Though you lied to me.'

'Lied? Lied about what?'

In the month I'd been working at the asylum I'd already lied about a couple of things.

He twinkled. 'You waltz beautifully.'

'Richard,' I confided in a rush of gratitude and relief, 'I don't know. Is this – are these dancing lessons – really a good idea?'

'What's your reservation?'

'It occurs to me that we weren't *ourselves*, somehow. Oh, I can hardly say. I felt odd for some of the time. And I think a few others did, too.'

'My dear boy.' Mansfield passed his fingers through his hair till it stood up in peaks like beaten egg whites. 'You are a constant damn tonic. I want to hug you. Some of the time! If you feel odd for only *some of the time*, then you're doing extremely well. A few others! We're treating the *insane*. Remember?'

'Thank you for the reminder.' I shrugged sheepishly. 'In that case.'

'In that case, what?'

'I found the experience –'

'Yes?'

I took a step back, half wondering if he was going to make good on his desire. 'Well, then. I'd have to say that I found it – transformative.'

TEN

SHORTLY AFTER EASTER I received a reply to my note from Miss Macy. I have kept it all these years because I knew in some part of me that I'd never again get a letter quite like this; at least, not from a woman. It was made up of elements so unfamiliar and ingenuous, so free and unpretending, that subsequently I couldn't work out, even once I'd read it several times, if its absence of inhibition constituted a barefaced challenge or a straightforward cry from the heart.

An unabashed appeal is certainly what it appeared to be. Mostly, when I reread it today (I have it in my hands now, and it retains the power to disturb me) I still feel that's what it is.

It was only later – much later; I must repeat that I had none of these doubts at first – that I thought, why did she send me this? Were her actions calculated, or was she merely shining her beam out into the dark, in the hope that she might somehow, by any means possible, steer herself away from the cliffs? Ruth Macy had an unaffectedness that was so confusing to me that it might as well have been cunning. For a start, she was so unlike the few women I knew in Boston; so different to my mother and sister, with their social airs and gewgaws. In spite of her wealth Miss Macy was not just unworldly – in her frankness and want of outward display, it was as if she lacked materiality. I'd told Mansfield I found her fine, and her pale face and ice-bright hair, her limpid eyes, were to me merely a reflection of this fineness. During our parting conversation in the dusk, she'd seemed almost to vanish under my gaze: I had to stop myself from reaching out and taking hold of her.

I didn't then, of course. But at the last, rashly, fatally –

I am reluctant to remember this. This is the boulder in the current, the crisis in the way, the shipwreck, among so much other wreckage, that still lies ahead.

Miss Macy began her letter without elaboration. 'Your note,' she wrote simply, 'has indeed given me courage.'

I closed the shutters to my bedroom window and trimmed the wick of my lamp. Once my work was done, I had those spring nights – full of the sounds of river birds: flocks of wild ducks taking wing, herons and the stray gull – to myself, and as I sat down to read I surrendered to the sensation of being alone with the swoop and dive of Miss Macy's voice.

I feel I should apologize for crying in front of you as I did on the day we met. You may have wondered why I, a silly spinster no longer in the first flush of youth, should be making such a spectacle of herself. Such a show.

My family has been settled here on Nantucket for many generations. I am an only child. My father was a wealthy man. He died sixteen months ago. I don't remember my mother – she didn't live past my first birthday. My father made his fortune from fat. Candles. Oil. The sort of things the world needs, and declines to mention in polite company. But this money has given me a freedom in arranging my own life I am aware most women do not possess. If I sometimes appear to be unwomanly, Dr Carver, perhaps this is why.

The Starbucks and the Macys and the Folgers and the Coffins have occupied this island since time began. We have all married each other. They say we all look alike. I don't know. I do know that, in this busy town, we have made a very small life for ourselves. Some may not think it small. I did, and do.

My father knew just about everything there was to know about oil. That was his business: not just any oil, but whale oil, which is called spermaceti by us. Since I have no brothers, he raised me, from an early age, to understand how a factory is run; about profit and loss. And risk. He saw that it would be an advantage if I was acquainted with the ways of the world, and he encouraged me to take an interest in every detail of his work. He taught me about the refining of the spermaceti, how the wax is extracted by heating in kettles, and the big black cakes are pressed and re-pressed until the oil is strained off, and then heated again in coppers and purified with potash to yield the white smokeless candles which we prize so much here. There's some skill involved in this clarifying work. It is a mistake to expose the boiling wax that goes into those candles to anything impure in the atmosphere because the fumes produced by that unknown combination can smother you.

In fall of the year before last I was asked to an 'At Home' by the Chadwicks, Congregationalist neighbors of ours in India Row. I hadn't previously been invited to such a thing, and my father insisted that I go. The Chadwicks are bankers; they've long managed our money. They had asked most of the north side of town, and they didn't hesitate to advertise the fact that their chief guest, the haul of the evening, was going to be the man no one could ever lure away from his own fireside on his brief visits to shore, the Hero of the *Providence*: William Borden. His bravery was the stuff of legend, matched only by his reputation for aloofness. He didn't walk or dine out; he never paid calls, and seldom even went to church. It was whispered that he would be on his way to the Pacific to rejoin his squadron before the winter came, but for now he dwelled among us, unseen and unsociable.

I'd never met him. I was a girl of fifteen when the few survivors of that disaster returned to home waters years ago. What did I know or care about the suffering of men? I was tired of our island stories, of our self-congratulatory epics about hardship and endurance. There are other kinds of endurance, it seems to me, more domestic kinds, which aren't even acknowledged. I didn't want to attend this party; didn't want to sit about in an overheated parlor exchanging pleasantries with the nabobs of the North Shore, but I saw that I had no choice. I wanted to please my father. We'd reached the stage where we would argue, and these arguments gave me pain: an aging man and his unmarried, crabby daughter.

My father was set on getting me a new dress for the occasion. He made a great to-do of picking a suitable fabric, calling in bolts of tussore and having them unrolled to display their quality, but the selection was only between different shades of brown. As a last-minute concession he presented me with a lace collar and told me to put it on. When I did, its two points dangled down the front of that dingy bodice like a signpost to my deficiencies.

On the morning of the party I'd woken up suffering from a familiar indisposition, and was out of sorts. I knew as soon as I set foot in the Chadwicks' house that the dress was all wrong. Why do we always feel, on entering a room, that everyone is looking at us? Except this time it wasn't a feeling, Dr Carver, but the simple truth. Mrs Chadwick saw me and came straight over. I watched her approach with envy. Certain women have a way of gliding rather than walking that I've never managed. She wore a gown of scalloped jade, like the scales of a mythical beast, a dragon or a sea serpent, which, low as it was, barely left room for her necklaces.

'My dear!' she said knowingly. 'What a charming silk. But you're the color of paste. Being a woman can be a trial, can't it?'

She gave me some wine punch and sailed right off again. I didn't know what to do with the punch, and must have wandered about the hall with the glass in my hand for several minutes. I wanted to abandon it on a side table, but was afraid that I might be observed. At last I slipped into Mr Chadwick's darkened office – I guessed it was his office by its general masculine disorder and the smell of stale tobacco; my father had just such an office – and placed it on the mantel. But then, in my haste as I turned to go, I clipped the glass with my shoulder. I could feel it bump down the back of my skirt: the wetness, the warmth. It left a bright red stain.

Anyone seeing me would think that I'd been bleeding.

I was examining the stain when I heard a stifled intake of

breath. I wasn't alone. Someone had been watching me. A man was planted beside the secretary near the door, partly concealed by the papers and other rubbish spilling from it. He was tall, and when he stepped forwards into the light that shone from the hall I caught my breath in turn. He gave an impression of shocking strength, as if he were made of some unbreakable substance, marble or bronze, instead of muscle and bone. I remember this especially because his physical vigor contrasted so surprisingly with the expression on his face. He looked pathetically unhappy. He looked unhappier than anyone I'd ever met. His coat was stretched across his sad shoulders, and his fingers were clenched around an untasted glass of wine.

'You can stare at me all you like, sir,' I mumbled, 'but I'm leaving now, before anyone else comes in to see me make a fool of myself.'

I had to pass close to him to get to the door, and as I did I caught his odor. I recall that he smelled of rust, or wood smoke; a heavy, almost non-human smell quite different to the smell of the room. I couldn't place it then. Afterwards I realized it was sweat.

'Please don't go,' he said. 'Unless you are hurrying away to meet the Hero of the *Providence*?'

'No,' said I. 'I have no desire to meet him. I'm only here because my father wanted me to come.'

He smiled regretfully. 'Ah. That's good, then. In any case,' he added, 'you've spoiled your dress.'

'There was nothing to spoil,' I said. 'See?' And then, because I felt a scratchy irritation with that dress, and with myself and, in a way I didn't understand at the time, with those preposterous shoulders of his, I took the glass from him and threw its contents over my skirt.

I stood there with wine dripping down its ugly folds.

When I did this, something remarkable happened. That unhappy man laughed, as if I'd pulled off the most wonderful trick. He swept his palm over his eyes and nose, laughing, and held out his hand for the empty glass. I gave it to him.

'Thank you,' he said. 'I didn't know how to get shot of that. Are you always so efficient?'

'Oh, always.' I laughed back.

'At least let me see if the coast is clear,' he said.

'No need,' I replied, still laughing. 'Good night.'

I ran out of the door, straight into Mrs Chadwick and her necklaces. She thrust me to one side, darted her chained head into the room and hallooed, 'Mr Borden! Why are you hiding in here, sir?'

'Well, ma'am,' he said, his great square face brimming, 'I seem to have spilled my wine on one of your guests and now I don't dare come out.'

So this was William Borden.

She looked at him in puzzlement, and she looked at me, and I could see her deciding that I was no threat to the success of her evening and that I could safely be humored. 'Oh, Miss Macy!' she cried reproachfully. 'Your lovely little frock! These men are so terribly clumsy, they have no idea what trouble we go to, just to please them,' and so on.

Really? I wondered. I'd never thought to go to any trouble to please a man. Was this what my father had had in mind, by buying me this dress – that I should *please*? Poor Papa.

I began to see many things that evening. I saw that I was a wealthy woman who was there on sufferance. I saw that I wore the wrong clothes and couldn't drink wine, and didn't know how to walk well or how to flirt. I saw that I wasn't young any more, or not young enough, and that I'd soon be older, and that there was nothing I could do about it. And I saw William Borden looking at me. Whenever I glanced round, or raised my head, his eyes were on the stain disfiguring my skirt.

I also saw that they were afraid of him. They fawned over him, and made much of him, but they feared him too. He alarmed them because he did not fit, this hero who had escaped death and returned from the sea. They adored his looks, and they adored his courage, and they were thrilled by his story, which had come to them in snatches, through newspaper reports and hearsay. And yet – there was something wrong, something slant, in the way he spoke and moved, as if he'd perfectly mastered the outward forms of their customs without really understanding or even caring what they meant. They wanted to gather him up, and make him one of their own, but he had an out-of-plumb set that resisted them.

That night I dreamed of him. He came to me dressed in a punch-colored coat. I asked him, in my dream, if he meant me harm, but he only laughed.

When William started to court me I didn't tell my father. He called on me one morning when Papa was at the factory. He called again a week later, and the next week. After that, I knew to await him regularly. I don't know if anyone remarked on his visits; maybe people assumed, since he was known not to go into society, that he arrived to do business with the hard-nosed Quaker spinster. News of his appearances at our house did not reach Papa.

These visits were very strange. Sometimes I doubted that William was courting me at all. He never talked love to me. He never paid me a compliment. He seldom said much about himself – but then, that he had no fortune and that I was rich, that we were divided by deep differences of faith and custom, hardly needed to be said. I learned, as much by what he chose not to say as by what he did, that his father had been a fisherman but that William had shipped with the navy at the urging of his mother, an off-islander. He never talked about the *Providence*. He sat on one of Papa's chairs, with his shoulders straining at the cloth of his coat and his hands smothering a teacup, and talked about almost anything else.

He talked to me as if I were a man, like him.

Mostly he would ask me questions, unexceptional everyday questions – what did I like to have for my breakfast? What did I like to read? Where did I like to walk; what did I do at the factory when I went? Which papers did I take? What did I think about the governor's recent speech? About the last state budget? The state budget! – and he always stared at me with the same directness as on the evening we'd first met. No one had ever looked at me like that. I found that I didn't mind. I found myself answering his unloverlike questions more freely than I would have replied to flattery or attempts at persuasion. I found myself chattering. Weeks went by. I wished that he would speak, that he would tell me what he wanted from me. At times I felt that I was lost; that I'd swum too far out and would never now get back – to what? To the tight-lipped woman I'd been before?

One day, when he'd parted from me and had gone out of the house, I went over to the parlor window. I hadn't yet done this. I wanted to see what he did, how he appeared, once he'd left me. Did he walk away lightly after these meetings? Was he unmoved, unconcerned?

I could hear the front door close. It had rained heavily in the night and out-of-doors the world was trickling, as if the solid earth beyond our walls had ceased to exist. I drew the curtain aside and peeped out. He was still there, standing on the bottom step in the wet, staring around him with a slow swaying movement of his head. Have you ever seen a creature, a cat or a snake, glance up after drinking its fill? It was exactly like that. He seemed *satiated*. Then he gathered himself, took a few steps forwards, and plunged down the street. He didn't look back.

But I knew, now, that I was necessary to him. I just didn't know in what way.

This went on all through that fall. I was aware that William would be sailing for the Pacific soon. I waited because I did not know what else to do. I had no plan, Dr Carver.

Then my father died. He came home from the refinery one November afternoon, complaining of a numbness in his shoulder. At supper later, when he tried to take a dish from my hand, it crashed to the floor. I stooped to pick up the pieces and when I raised my eyes they were met by a frightful sight. Papa was still sitting in his chair, his arm resting along the table, but the left side of his face had run together like hot wax. That night he suffered two further seizures. He never spoke a whole sentence or left his bed again. Though I nursed him hour by hour, and tried every remedy prescribed by the doctor, it made no difference. In little over a week he was dead. I did not communicate with William in this time. I buried my father, and then – I did nothing. That is, I went to the factory the next morning as my father would have done, and I went on with my life.

The day before he was due to leave for Boston, William came to see me. I didn't expect him. I felt my father's death as a barrier between us where earlier, despite the many differences that might have kept us apart, I had felt none. He wore his uniform, and seeing him in it made his departure real to me in a way it hadn't been till that moment. I thought he'd come to say goodbye. Instead, he asked me to marry him. I accepted immediately. I knew that I'd never gain the consent of our Meeting for this marriage, even if I were to wait years.

You must understand that in engaging myself to William Borden outside our Meeting, and so soon after my father's death, I have risked the disapprobation of my entire world. I am under dealings. We were to have been married this spring. Now William is in Charlestown and I – well, I am here. I still consider myself engaged to him.

Dr Mansfield encouraged me not to hold myself responsible for what must be. But I tell you that I can't follow this advice. I do not want to be absolved of responsibility. I want to be held accountable for everything that happens to William from here on, and I warn you that I will hold you accountable also, as I would myself. I will help you in any way I can.

I am sending you some papers that touch on those long-ago events on the *Providence*, in the hope that they may show you – as if you, of all people, need showing! – what sort of man William was; and will, I believe, be again. I *must* hope.

I live for any news that he remembers me.

I sat quite still as the room intruded itself on my consciousness: my single bed with its smoothed cover, tomorrow's shirt hanging on the wardrobe door, the lonely towel stiffening on my washstand. The night seemed to slacken, moving insensibly towards the dissolution of dawn and the springing back to wakefulness of a hundred harried minds, when the whole mad round in that madhouse would start up. Sleep was overdue, but I'd never felt more awake, or more receptive. Something new, something tremendous, was happening to me. I had made my first contact with a naked female soul, and the revelation sent a corresponding trill along my nerves.

Ruth Macy was ardent. She was ill at ease in her world. She was in search of the thing that would make her existence feel substantial. She thought she'd found it in William Borden, only to have it inexplicably snatched away. Didn't I know, perhaps better than most, how painful that search could be? She was, in her ardor and her discontentment and her quest for answers, not unlike me.

I laugh now at my discovery, at the bumptious age of twenty-two, that women aren't so very different from men in their essential humanity, but back then the shock of it was all the more immense for being completely unforeseen.

Enclosed with Miss Macy's letter, wrapped in a plain sheet, were two documents. Topmost was a clipping from a newspaper, and beneath that lay a pamphlet. I ran my eye over its cinched columns: it was a published legal record of some kind. But then I let the thing fall from my hand. For, written on the reverse of the docket in which it was enfolded were three lines which sent a prong of lightning straight to my heart:

'Friend, I would speak to thee of something else. I could not do it when I brought William to thee. If thee will call on me here, I will tell thee more. R. M.'

ELEVEN

As my sister has aged the greens and pinks of her wardrobe have become deeper, more essential. Today is a Sunday, and as usual I am spending it at home, in Mount Vernon Street. A quarter of an hour ago Caro came into the drawing room while I was at the bureau, writing this. She was dressed for worship in a skirt like the puddle on a butcher's block and a matching pelisse girded with chartreuse braid (she is always running off to church, to her sewing circle, or to her Lying-in Hospital – if I didn't know better, I'd think she was avoiding me). Her hair, her single beauty, was completely hidden under a bonnet the hue of ox-blood. She was a perfect agony of red.

'How do I look?'

'Very colorful.'

Caro decided to take this as a compliment, gave her skirt a twitch, and picked up her prayer book from the mantelpiece. Then she stopped, giving me an entreating glance that was at odds with what she said next.

'You know, I almost forgot to tell you. Yesterday Molly Pratt delivered herself while alone in the water-closet.'

'That should please those who believe in the virtue of early baptism.'

'Oh, Hiram. You mock our faith, and the work we do. But the fact is that half the women at the hospital when we first started were unmarried.'

'I'm not surprised. They were mostly either ignorant immigrant girls, trulls or trollops like Molly.'

'In the last five years only two per cent have been unwed.' She paused warmly, holding the prayer book out like a nurse trying to coax an infant to take its porridge. 'What does that tell us, Hiram?'

'A simple arithmetical calculation will convince us that Boston women of the present day are twenty-five times more moral than their mothers were.'

Caro pursed her lips and turned away to adjust her pelisse, but I could see that she wasn't really cross. She is used to me. Is there anyone else in the world of whom I can say this? 'You are awful. I don't know why I put up with you.' And then, offered lightly, as an afterthought, she arrived at the real point of this exchange. 'Please come to church with me today.'

'No, Caro, no. I have my arms too firmly about the world again to let go of it now.'

'Are you really feeling better? You gave me a scare at Christmas, you know.'

'Oh, much better, old girl. You'll be pleased to hear that I'm making steady progress on my memoir.'

'Well, try not to overdo it. You know you must be careful.' She left, with a final humping of her mouth. I watched her from the drawing-room window as she waited, a hectic blur on the steeply cobbled street, for the brougham to be brought round. I was suffused with a sudden rush of love.

And to think that, through my own carelessness, I very nearly lost her!

BEFORE I BEGAN TO read the papers Miss Macy had sent me, it was to her letter – and to its mysterious postscript in particular – that I returned again and again. All this talk of heroes was a distraction. William Borden was sick, he was mad; he was a man of flesh and blood. He'd been an extraordinarily impressive sailor and officer, but whatever he'd once been, he no longer was. She knew it, and I knew it. And not only did we both know it, but here, issued to me by the one other person who grasped the real extent of his fall, the woman who was determined to raise him back up, was a summons. She'd summoned me to see her; but over and above that, she'd summoned me to action. She'd promised to reveal more. What was this *more*? It was a more which, understandably, she hadn't been able to divulge in Mansfield's presence.

The fact that she'd chosen me to be the recipient of her confidence, to the lengths of calling me to her from a hundred miles across land and ocean, stirred me deeply – it left me idiotically breathless. She trusted me to help her where no one else could. She believed in me. She saw something in me – an expansiveness, a boldness, was that it? – that even I couldn't, at that point, quite see in myself. But I would honor her vision, I'd repay her faith. Wasn't it (oh, my silly egotism makes me howl now) in fact *me*, Hiram Carver, my true self, that she was uncovering to me?

I would go, of course I would. I just didn't know how, yet.

These thoughts went around ceaselessly in my head. I was still revolving them days later as I headed up to the dispensary to go through the medications list with Goodwin, when Mansfield stopped me on the staircase.

'You can make a start on all that this afternoon. You have someone waiting for you downstairs.'

'I do?'

'Yes. A lady. In the parlor.' He laughed. 'Don't look so flustered. It's only your sister. Take an hour off.'

My sister! I'd been remiss in writing to Caro, and was indefinably displeased by this visitation. She belonged to home, and the part of me I was trying hard to leave behind. Finding her at the asylum was as upsetting as an encounter with a ghost: it hadn't crossed my mind that she might arrive, of her own volition and uninvited, from the realm to which I'd committed her.

'I'm sorry to keep you waiting, Caro. I wasn't expecting you.'

Caro's stringy body was angled towards the parlor window facing the garden, nose beveled against the glass. Her cloak, an absurdly girlish thing with a rosy hood in the latest French style, was still tied about her shoulders. She took no notice of me, but simply went on staring, so I sauntered over and gave her a shove.

'Move up. What's so interesting?'

I put my head next to hers and wiped my sleeve across the pane. Behind it Miss Clayborn roamed the hyacinth beds, stamping down the clods with her boots.

'That woman is bored,' said Caro.

'Bored?'

'Yes. Remember what that feels like? Hello, Hiram. It's nice to see you too.' She rocked back on her heels. Reaching out as if to clasp me to her, she gave my upper arms a squeeze. 'Just as I thought. You're not eating, are you? Here, I've brought you something.' She had a wicker trug with her, covered with a napkin which she stripped away – ta-da! – to expose a clutch of tumescent dumplings pimpled with maple butter. 'Johnnycakes. These were your favorite when you were small.'

'Caro*line*. I'm a grown man now.'

Before Caro could reply, Frank's fat fingers appeared around the door, heralding his grinning mug. 'Yoo-hoo, Cassius. I'm about to begin without you.' Seeing her, he blushed. 'Oh Lord. I didn't know you had company.' His head swiveled in the direction of the basket. 'Or – or food. I'll just wait for you in the dispensary, yes?'

Instead of leaving, though, he loitered. He was a risible sight: round-faced, offal-eyed, and now starting to dribble – yet at the same time impossible to loathe entirely.

'Who's Cassius?' asked Caro.

'Um. I am. Frank, this is my sister.' I made a violent chopping motion behind my back with my hand. 'Dr Goodwin and I work together.'

Ignoring me, Caro flicked up her napkin at Goodwin. 'Will you have a cake?'

'Oh my, are you sure?'

'Yes, quite sure. I fear Hiram won't eat *any*. And I spent a half-hour this morning making them.'

Frank crammed a johnnycake into his mouth. 'Really?' His lower lip was glazed with oil. 'You made all of these in just half an hour?'

'I did. Give me a whole hour and I'll roast you a pork loin and chitterlings to go with them.'

'Never! Do tell. How d'you get them so moist, Miss Carver? Do you use milk?'

'No, I use a generous foundation of lard in the bottom of my skillet.'

I waited until this performance had played itself out before clearing my throat. 'May I speak to my sister alone, Frank?'

'What? Oh, certainly.'

But Caro got there first. 'Don't go without having another cake, Dr Goodwin.'

He rammed his paw into her basket, still blushing.

Caro turned on me once he'd crashed his way out. 'Was that necessary? He seems rather congenial.'

'Yes, if you have a high tolerance for eructacious flatulence.'

'Speak English, Hiram.'

'Wind, Caro.'

She took a few steps round the room, twirling her cloak and pretending to admire the crackled pictures on the walls. 'So, Hiram, how have you been? Or should I call you Cassius now?'

'No, of course not. I've been busy.'

'Don't you miss us at all? We've hoped for a visit from you.'

'I thought you'd be pleased for me.'

Caro stopped her perambulation and threw me an earnest look. 'Well, have you found it?'

'Found what?'

'Your purpose.'

'Oh, I have! I really think I have. But there's so much more to do.' Taking her buttery hands in mine, I pulled her to my side. 'Caro, I didn't mean to be rude. The thing is this. I've so many ideas, and so little time in the day.' I nibbled at her thumb. 'I want more than an abstract understanding of my subject. In this place we only see our patients in isolation. We cut them off from all their closest, their most human ties.'

'Ah, that's why you're so happy here.' She sighed.

'Don't be a goose. I want to know everything about them, and what shaped them. I want to meet their families. If their families aren't allowed to come to us, then I want to observe them in their own homes.'

'Will they let you into their homes, do you think?' asked my sister doubtfully.

'Caro, you're being no help. Why are you so discouraging?'

'I'm worried about you, Hissy. You don't visit, you don't answer my letters. You still look awfully thin. Mama worries about you too.'

I gave a bark of laughter.

'All right. But Papa is ready to schedule a special inspection by the asylum trustees, just to get a glimpse of you.'

I let go of her fingers. So *this* was why she had come. She didn't really give a goddamn about me. 'Do you know what?' The words were out there between us before I could stop them. 'You're a fraud. Who do you think you are? Helen of Hoecakes? Little Red Riding Hood?' I gave her stupid Frenchified cloak a tweak. 'Madame Boun-tiful?' My ears were filled with a noisy twittering. 'You're nothing but a low-down, common spy.'

Caro put her palm to her face as if I'd slapped her. 'Oh, you're a fool.' She stood in front of me, shrinking with shock, strawberry clouds blotching her cheeks. 'You have no idea how pompous you sound.'

'No, *you're* the fool. Coming here with your – your *fried goods* and flirting with the medical staff. As if anybody cares! I'm tired of having you tell me what to do.'

She drew herself up to her full height. 'I know you, Hissy. I've known you since you were in your napkins. Always so self-righteous. Hiss, hiss, hiss.' Her meager frame shuddered with anger. 'I was much happier before you ever arrived to disturb my life. I'm going now.'

'That suits me just fine. Get out! And take your traitor's cakes with you.'

But she didn't; she left them right there, like unlobbed grenades, and when Goodwin came into the parlor after lunch he saw them at once and snaffled up another.

'Your sister is a charmer, you know,' he said, his mouth full of cornmeal.

Caro, with her carroty hair and beaky nose, her silly clothes, her vatic pronouncements?

'My sister is damnably irritating,' I snapped, and threw the cakes into the wastebasket, where they couldn't cause me any more anguish.

THAT SAME NIGHT I started to read the documents Miss Macy had sent me. The newspaper clipping, from the *Nantucket Inquirer* of 5 July 1821, was as brown as old pastry.

'MUTINY!' the headline ran. 'SIXTY-FIVE DAYS IN AN OPEN BOAT!'

From the Pacific we bring news that is as dreadful as it is astonishing, of the loss through MUTINY of USS *Providence* and the miraculous survival, despite diabolical odds, of five of her men, including her Captain. We receive word from Chile that this vessel, under the command of Captain Morton de Kay Fitzgibbon of Norfolk County, Massachusetts, was on New Year's Day perfidiously commandeered by her crew, led by one Daniel Small, and Captain Fitzgibbon put out to sea in an open boat with seven loyal men to face inescapable Death.

But the demonic schemes of this Imp of the Ocean could not prevail against the stout heart of the American Tar. Cometh the hour, cometh the man. There had arisen out of the depths of the ship, like Orpheus from the bowels of Hades, a Hero who was equal to the worst trials that Satan himself could inflict on suffering human souls.

The following may be taken to be a fair summary of the details.

Our Consul at Valparaiso reports that on the Wednesday marking the beginning of Lent, as the population of the town was preparing to withdraw to the solemn observance of its devotions, a seemingly unmanned dinghy was apprehended off the coast of Chile by a humble *bote* or fisherman's smack. The earnest salutations of the crew going unanswered, they hove to alongside the vessel, and there discovered such a scene as would strike pity into even the most hardened of hearts.

In the boat lay five bodies, so wasted as to be nearly unrecognizable as human. Most were naked or almost entirely so, their cinder-gray flesh cratered with suppurating sores. Two still wore tatters of the blue cloth that distinguished them as officers of the United States Navy. The pilot of the *bote* discerned with horror that the shredded jacket of one of these figures, which was curled in the stern with its gums bared, partly hidden by a tarpaulin, bore the traces of a Captain's insignia.

Taking the poor wretches for dead, and unable to account for their presence in those waters, he prepared to tow their craft to shore. Then, to his amazement, the tallest of the cadavers, a mere leathery shell of a man that had its arms still locked around an oar, raised its salt-caked head — and spoke! Its lips were as black as jerky, and at first its voice was so feeble it seemed to blow away in the wind. But after some moments the fisherman could make out a single word: 'Mercy'. 'Mercy,' whispered this husk, its grating syllables rising in an awful petition. And then the other bodies in the bottom of the boat began to squirm and writhe and to pick up the rippling cry, 'Mercy, mercy,' until the kind-hearted Chilean fell to his knees and wept.

The tale that has reached us is terrible in the extreme. While afloat on the waves this unhappy Band of Brothers endured sixty-five days of privation and near despair, and would surely have perished, but for the resourcefulness of one among their number. One man among them — the very cadaver who had so pitifully appealed to his rescuers from the Brink of Death! — hewed out a route across the trackless Pacific that would carry their frail boat to safety. One man induced that heartless ocean to yield up the scraps of its bounty, procuring sufficient nourishment from the perilous deep to keep his fellows alive until they gained the Succor of Civilization. One man, through the simple exercise of his skill as a sailor, guided their vessel onwards to the verdant safety of South America and, when all hope seemed forever extinguished, taught them, by his example, how to overcome.

This man is Ordinary Seaman William Borden of NANTUCKET. We are proud to claim him as our own.

We are advised that Consul Slocum has written to the Secretary of State to apprise him of this heinous act of mutiny on the *Providence*, and the truly providential recovery of her faithful officers and men. USS *Hylas* has been dispatched to capture the vessel and to bring Small and his Nest of Fiends to justice, and we now await the authoritative verdict of THE UNITED STATES LAW on this case.

Post Scriptum. When these unfortunate souls were raised from the waters there was, *mirabile dictu*, one among them who proved to be a son of that cruel ocean. The Captain's boy is a bona fide Scion of the South Seas who goes by the appellation of John Canacka. He hails from the rock-bound coasts and wooded slopes of the Pacific isles of the Marquesas. The Marquesas! What strange visions of outlandish things does the very name spirit up! Naked houris – groves of cocoa-nut – coral reefs – tattooed chiefs and bamboo temples; sunny valleys planted with bread-fruit trees – carved canoes dancing on the blue waters – savage woodlands guarded by horrible idols – Heathenish Rites! It is a pitiful indictment of our civilized nation that this Savage Youth, having shipped with the United States Navy in order to escape the barbarism of his native islands, should have met with worse contempt for the sacredness of human life on one of her

vessels than he could have expected to encounter even
on those godless shores.

Post Post Scriptum. It is our immeasurably sad duty to
report that Captain Fitzgibbon, despite so valiantly with-
standing this Villainous Ordeal, has since succumbed to
a resulting bodily weakness. He died peacefully in Christ
on Good Friday at the Consul's residence in Valparaiso.

The bound pamphlet, published towards the end of the following
year, was less effusive, consisting of a verbatim transcript of the
proceedings of the court of inquiry appointed to investigate the
affair. I reproduce it here with minor annotations.

This court convened on board USS *Refulgence* at the Charlestown Navy Yard in February 1822, shortly after the *Providence* was
brought back to dock. The surviving castaways had returned some
months earlier.

When the ship was recovered by the *Hylas* off the coast of Peru
with a rag-tag crew of only six aboard, Small wasn't on her. These
remnants of the mutiny were themselves by then half starved because
they didn't dare risk setting foot in any port. The hold was full of
specie, but they couldn't eat that. All insisted that they'd mutinied
for the highest motives, after intolerable provocation by a captain
who'd kept them as slaves to his avarice. That they'd simply wanted
their cut, as Captain Barnard had intimated to me, and would have
kept quiet if they'd got it, was apparent to everyone.

Yet who'd have thought that this money, once prised out of the
clutches of the law, would prove so worthless? Where was Small?
Nobody knew. It was said that he had jumped ship and turned
plain old pirate (as opposed to United States Pirate) on another

vessel. Or that he'd been wounded in a skirmish. Or that he'd fallen overboard and been swept away by a wave. Or had repented of his crime and asked to be set ashore on the South American continent, and was last seen wading through the surf, headed for the rainforests of the interior. He had vanished like the ghost of an idea of liberty, like ocean foam. Nevertheless, specter though he was, he was tried in absentia, with the remaining six skeletons. A skeleton crew, indeed.

The court was ordered to investigate the circumstances attending the mutiny. The president was Captain James Allen (vice commander of the newly formed Pacific Squadron), assisted by Commodore Robert ap Hywel Evans, retired (veteran of the Revolutionary War, formerly commander of all vessels at Boston, and now eighty-two years old). The judge advocate was the Honorable Rupert Shaw, US attorney for the district of Massachusetts. At the insistence of Captain Fitzgibbon's family, who feared for his reputation, the navy had appointed Martin Van Tassel, a New York lawyer, to cross-examine the witnesses. The captain should have had the privilege of conducting this cross-examination himself, but of course he was dead.

Next came brief details of the crew now in irons, and then the names of the four survivors from the boat, who would all be called as witnesses: Oliver Lenox (third lieutenant), Michael Duggan (boatswain), William Borden (ordinary seaman), and John Canacka (captain's boy).

The *Refulgence* was the flagship of Captain Allen, who was so heavily decorated that he must have appeared, presiding from a railed table set under the main cabin porthole, to be an extension of her splendid brass work. The commodore, Evans, who had lost an eye to the British at Valcour Island and an arm to the French in the Pacific, sat with his head bowed, empty socket snugly patched, maimed torso supported by strategically placed cushions. It was impossible to know if he was asleep or awake. Save for the judge advocate himself, Van Tassel was the only civilian there. He was a rising star of the New York legal circuit, and by the time the Articles relating to mutiny had been read, and Shaw had subjected the six prisoners to preliminary questioning, he was eager to begin his cross-examination.

First on the stand was Caleb Scholes, seaman.

Van Tassel: If we consider all the mutinies that are on record, it is immediately evident that they were occasioned by gross tyranny on the part of the commanding officers. The mutiny on board the British frigate *Hermione* during the French wars some twenty-five years ago sprang from no disloyalty on the part of the mutineers, but was provoked by a long course of grievances, and although the principal offenders were executed, their complaints were afterwards redressed by the action of the proper court. The mutiny on board the British frigate *Bounty* grew out of the brutality of the captain and directly out of an insult to one of the officers. That which arose among the crew of the French frigate *Medusa* —

Shaw: Yes, yes, Mr Van Tassel. What is your argument?

Van Tassel: My argument, sir, is that no such circumstances existed in this case. We must bear in mind that there was on board the *Providence* no cruelty, no disregard of the dignity of any of the crew, no weakness, no incapacity in her captain which could provoke or encourage any of her men to this act of mutiny.

Shaw: You have yet to put a question to the prisoner, Mr Van Tassel.

Van Tassel: Well, Scholes. I put it to you. Do you deny the truth of what I have just said?

Scholes: I wasn't doing what I joined this man's navy to do. I wasn't serving my country on that ship. I was only lining the pockets of Captain Fitzgibbon.

Van Tassel: And you thought that this was grounds enough to try to overthrow your betters? Captain Fitzgibbon was acting within the law. Did you think that setting yourself against your lawful captain and your country could ever lead to anything other than this? That you could escape justice? Did Daniel Small believe it?

Scholes: Well, sir, I don't rightly know. You'd have to ask him. You see, sir [*Making a great show of looking around the courtroom.*], it may have escaped your notice, but – he ain't here.

Van Tassel: You can be certain, Mr Scholes, that though he may not be answering to his superiors now, he soon will be.

After a full day of this the prisoners were ordered to stand down. On the second day, as soon as the court reconvened at ten o'clock, Michael Duggan, boatswain, was called as a witness.

Van Tassel: Mr Duggan, you served twice as boatswain under Captain Fitzgibbon's command, once on USS *Stella* and again on the *Providence*. Yesterday we heard the basest imputations against his character from mutineers and chained felons. I ask you now, as a patriotic servant of our great navy and an honest son of America: what sort of man was he?

Duggan: He was my captain, sir. Begging your pardon, I never thought to ask what sort of man he was.

Van Tassel: A worthy answer! The court will please take note of this worthy and fair response.

Shaw: We do, Mr Van Tassel. Our court reporter is taking note of everything, as you know. Please continue.

Van Tassel: Forgive my rhetorical enthusiasm, Mr Judge Advocate. I will. Mr Duggan, I ask you next: what manner of man was Daniel Small?

Duggan: He was an able seaman, sir.

Van Tassel: Able? In what way *able*?

Allen: Mr Duggan is referring to Small's rank, Mr Van Tassel.

Duggan: Aye, sir. There is the rank of ordinary seaman, like Will Borden there [*Nodding at the settle where the witnesses were seated.*], or able seaman. Like Dan Small. Able seaman is the longer service.

Van Tassel: I see. And apart from his rank? What was Small like, as a man?

Duggan: Well now, sir. Ah. As a man. I'm trying to think.

Van Tassel: His distinguishing characteristics will do, Mr Duggan.

Duggan: Characteristics?

Van Tassel: Yes. His features.

Duggan: His eyebrows met in the middle, sir.

Van Tassel: What about his *moral* qualities?

Duggan: That's harder, sir. He had very few. There ain't much call for being moral on a ship. Not like at church, now.

[*Laughter in the court.*]

Van Tassel: Let me try again, Mr Duggan. Was Small an honest sailor?

Duggan: Well, no, sir. That seems pretty clear. He was a mutineer.

Shaw: You are chasing your own tail, Mr Van Tassel. Please ask Mr Duggan a straightforward question.

Van Tassel: Indeed, sir. Mr Duggan, please just give me one word to describe the sort of man Small was. Just one, if you will.

Duggan: Sir, he was a coward.

Van Tassel: A coward?

Duggan: Aye. He shirked his duty. He shirked following his captain's orders. And when he called on the men to mutiny he shirked seeing the business through.

Van Tassel [*dubiously*]: Thank you. We have heard from this good man that Captain Fitzgibbon was a most proper captain, and that Daniel Small was a coward – as if we needed proof of his cowardice beyond the reprehensible and bloody act of mutiny itself. I will now ask you, Mr Duggan, to recount the events of that fateful night of the first of January. Where was the *Providence*?

Duggan: We were cruising at one hundred and eight degrees west, sir, and well to the southward of the equinoctial line.

About twelve or thirteen degrees south. I ain't certain now of the exact latitude. We were outside our usual bearings. That day we had met with a foreign craft on the open sea and taken a heap of specie on board. The men weren't happy, sir. There was muttering about the money, and the way we were straying from –

Van Tassel: Yes, thank you. What time was it when you went on deck?

Duggan: It was eight bells, sir. Start of the middle watch.

Van Tassel: What o'clock would that be on land?

Duggan: Midnight, sir. Captain Fitzgibbon had gone below for the night. Lieutenant Monroe was officer on deck, but he wasn't always visible.

Van Tassel: 'Wasn't always visible'? Do you mean that it was dark?

Duggan: No, sir, the deck was as light as a stage that night. I mean that he kept appearing and disappearing below again. I was keeping an eye on the mainsail. We were wandering in alien waters, not following our proper course. All was strange. It was as if the stars had slipped their moorings. We weren't drawing right. We were listing to starboard, and I fancied – see, I fancied that we were being pulled awry by the dead weight of the treasure in our hold.

Van Tassel: Never mind your fancies. Was anyone else with you?

Duggan: Will Borden and some of the hands were on the quarterdeck with me. Lemuel Price was at the helm.

Van Tassel: How long were you there?

Duggan: We were there for nearly the whole of that watch but not all. Three hours. Lieutenant Monroe came to me and told me to keep the sails drawing. He cursed me several times because I had the ship in the wind. We were all out of temper, sir. There was a queerness in the air that night, a brightness that wasn't natural. The moon was as big as a wagon wheel and she lit us up and made everything look hollow, as if we were a ship of phantoms instead of men —

Van Tassel: This court is not interested in your temper at the time, or the stars or the moon, or in any other metaphysical speculations, Mr Duggan, only in the facts.

Duggan: Well, sir, no matter. Will — Mr Borden — was not out of temper. He advised us to keep true to our course as Lieutenant Monroe had determined it.

Van Tassel: Good gracious, Boatswain. Did you often take advice from — let me see now — from *ordinary seamen*?

Duggan: From Mr Borden, sir, aye. I would gladly have had him as my mate in place of that damned Owen Jones. Will was a 'cute sailor, though he hadn't many years on him. He could hand, reef, and steer, and he could make a dead reckoning as well as any officer. I'd heard reports that there was a treacherous mess of coral about in those parts and I misdoubted Lieutenant Monroe's calculations. And, sir, if you'll pardon me, Lieutenant Monroe was drunk.

Van Tassel: Drunk?

Duggan: Yes, sir. He had taken a great deal of drink. At dinner, and — and after.

Van Tassel: Surely he'd imbibed no more than was usual for any officer?

Duggan: Yes, sir. As I say, he was drunk. But Will — Mr Borden — was sober.

Shaw: Please go on with your testimony, Mr Duggan. We know that the hypothetical coral, and Mr Monroe's sobriety or otherwise, proved to be the least of your troubles. What happened then?

Duggan: We were ambling along towards God knows what part of the ocean, sir. The wind was blowing from the east, but not hard. We were listing, and I was trying to bring us round to leeward. Then when six bells struck — that's an hour short of the start of the morning watch, sir — Small came up with Jones, my mate.

Van Tassel: Aha. Was Jones due to relieve you?

Duggan: Yes, sir, but only at eight bells. I thought it mighty strange that he should appear so early.

Van Tassel: And then?

Duggan: And then, sir, I saw that Small had a knife in one hand and a pistol in the other. I said, 'What have you there, Dan, my boy?' And he came right up to me and said, 'Stand clear, Mr Duggan. Stand clear, Lem. Owen here will take the helm. And if you make the least damned bit of noise, Mr Duggan, I'll send you to hell.' And then out from behind the rigging there came Sam Gallagher, Caleb Scholes, Peter Olson, David Souza and Patrick Ballou. All had muskets and pistols. I said, 'What are you doing, boys?' Small said, 'We are freeing this ship from greed and tyranny. We are overthrowing Captain Fitzgibbon.' And I said, 'Is this a mutiny, lads?' And they said, 'Yes. Are you with us, Mickey, or against us? Think carefully now because your life depends on it.'

Van Tassel: What did you reply?

Duggan: God and His angels help me, sir, I didn't know what to reply. I was that afraid of dying. All I could think of was death.

Van Tassel: What then?

Duggan: Mr Borden came up and stood in front of me and said, 'I am relieving Mr Duggan, and it's to me you must address yourself. Mr Duggan, if you will, go below and see to the captain. He is in danger of his life.' And then Small said, 'You are too late, my boys are already at him. He will be brought up shortly and his sots with him.'

Van Tassel: And then, Mr Duggan?

Duggan: Oh God, and then, sir, the first I knew of them having begun their work was the sound of a hatchet, which I distinctly heard on deck, and was afterwards informed was their striking at the captain's door, and the screaming of his boy. And then this child ran out naked and came and crouched by the helm, a great cut on his head –

Van Tassel: He was wounded?

Duggan: Yes, sir, he was all over blood. They had struck at his head and cut the top of his ear clean off. Mr Borden called out to him to keep near me. Then up out of the companionways, hugging their jackets, half dressed and forced by a man with a pistol on each side, came the second lieutenant Mr Perry, and Mr Monroe, and behind them Captain Fitzgibbon. Mr Monroe was sober now, out of sheer terror. When he saw Small he cried, 'Dan, don't kill me! Haven't I always been fair to you? Didn't I say I would share anything I got with you if you would be patient?' Small said, 'You damned bastard, you are all words and I am out of patience. It's a damned good time to beg now – you are too late!' And he hit him on the temple with his pistol, so that Mr Monroe fell to the deck.

Van Tassel: What happened next?

Duggan: The second lieutenant made to defend the captain, sir, by drawing his sword.

Van Tassel: Very proper, too. That must have struck fear into the hearts of those wicked rogues.

Duggan: No, sir, Small felled him with a shot to the head before he could take a step.

Van Tassel: Good God. Where was the third lieutenant, Mr Lenox?

Duggan: Well, sir, they'd already given Lieutenant Lenox an anointing by this time. He couldn't hardly see to move. The poor bastard was wearing full mourning.

Van Tassel: I'm not sure I understand what you mean.

Allen: Mr Duggan means that Mr Lenox had been beaten and that he had sustained two black eyes, Mr Van Tassel.

Van Tassel: I see. Thank you, sir. Continue, Mr Duggan.

Duggan: By now there was a crowd on deck, summoned by the shot. The middies and the warrant officers were all put under guard. Then Small said, 'If you'll come over to

us, Billy, you'll not regret it. You are a brave boy and we
mean you no harm.'

Van Tassel: He was addressing Mr Borden?

Duggan: Aye, sir.

Van Tassel: Was Mr Borden friendly with Small?

Duggan: Will was friendly with everyone, sir.

Van Tassel: What was Mr Borden's reply to this solicitation?

Duggan: Will said, 'You have killed one officer and as good as
murdered two more. You are covered in blood. You will
all hang.' Then he told them that their only hope now was
to spare the captain. He said that if they hurt a hair on the
captain's head they might as well go ahead and slit their
own throats at the same time.

Van Tassel: Where was the captain just then?

Duggan: Sitting on the deck, sir. His legs had given way.

Van Tassel: Mr Borden didn't seek to defend Captain Fitzgibbon
by a show of force?

Duggan: No, sir. He knew, begging your pardon, sir, that it'd
be no goddamn use. They'd have cut him down the way
they'd done Mr Perry, and the captain with him.

Van Tassel: And what were the other officers doing at that
moment?

Duggan: Begging your pardon again, sir, they were wailing
like banshees and pissing themselves.

Van Tassel: Please keep a mind to your language, Mr Duggan.
What took place after that?

Duggan: Small said, 'That may be, Billy, but I am in blood
now so deep I might as well wade on.'

Van Tassel: What did Mr Borden say?

Duggan: He said, 'Dan, I see a way out for you. It is the only way. Put a boat out to sea with the wounded in it and the captain too. And any of the officers and men who will not take your part. Then you will be doing right by them. Then your mutiny will be just. Otherwise it's straight murder and you know it.' To which Small replied, 'If I put them out to sea in an open boat, that would be murder indeed.'

Van Tassel: Did Mr Borden have an answer to this?

Duggan: Will replied, 'No, it would not, for you'll give them such provisions as may secure their survival, God willing. If they live, then they will give a fair report of you, and if God does not choose to spare them, then it is providence that they die, and not murder.' And Small said, 'A boat. And one cask of water.' Will said, 'One cask of water, and one of bread. A piece of pork. And they must have a barrel to keep it dry.' Then Small said, 'Oh Jesus, Billy, I am a marked man, and I fear this will not save me. But I no longer care, I mean to be free or die. Will you help me?' And Will said, 'I will help you to get the boat ready, yes.'

Van Tassel: Have I understood you right? Did Mr Borden tell this mutineer, this murderer, that he would help him?

Duggan: To ready the boat, sir. He did not promise more.

Van Tassel: Is that what Daniel Small understood by his words, do you think?

Duggan: I don't know, sir. Maybe not. I didn't much care, sir. I was kneeling in Johnny Canacka's blood.

Shaw: Mr Van Tassel, what Mr Borden did or did not mean Small to make of his words is immaterial. It is what he did that matters. Please proceed with your testimony, Mr Duggan.

Duggan: Sir, there was an evil half-hour as the dinghy began to be lowered. The grinding of the davits sounded like the opening of the gates of hell. Dawn was just breaking and all had come on deck to see off the damned. When asked, only one other man offered to go with us, and that was Joseph Webb, the purser. He'd been in charge of the money and he reckoned they'd kill him anyway. It was all done very orderly. Will saw to the shipping of the casks and Small gave him leave to pass freely between decks. He got us all in the boat. When the time came, Mr Monroe and Mr Perry were lowered in first.

Van Tassel: Wasn't Mr Perry, ah, deceased?

Duggan: No, sir. He was dying, but not dead yet. Then we lowered in the captain's boy, who lay in a faint. Then we did the same with Mr Lenox. Joe Webb climbed down after. Then I went in. At the very last Will advanced to the rail, keeping Captain Fitzgibbon behind him all the time.

Van Tassel: He shielded the captain with his own body?

Duggan: Yes, sir. Though the captain wasn't volunteering to come out, if you catch my drift. He was shaking like a wart on a whore's backside.

Shaw: Language, Mr Duggan. Please tell us what happened next, without the profanities.

Duggan: Well, then Will pushed Captain Fitzgibbon to the rail and said, 'Now you, sir.' It took him a couple of shoves to get the old – to get Captain Fitzgibbon to go over.

Van Tassel: He pushed the captain? Do you mean that he *threw* his commanding officer over the rail?

Duggan: Well, sir, he used his hands to pitch the great boo— to pitch him over. He hooked him under the armpits and gave him the old heave-ho. You see he had to, sir. Captain Fitzgibbon was clinging to the rail like a blue-bummed baboon.

Van Tassel: Language, Mr Duggan!

Allen: Yes, yes, Mr Van Tassel. We are all sailors here. Or most of us are. Mr Duggan, you have established that Mr Borden had no choice but to use bodily force in order to save Captain Fitzgibbon's life. Go on.

Duggan: Well, sir, once the captain had flopped into the boat and lay there blubbing, Will turned to Dan Small and said, 'And now me.' Small shrieked that he was a fool, and would he leave him alone on that ocean, and asked him again to go with them.

Van Tassel: What did Mr Borden answer?

Duggan: He said that it was Small who was the fool, and that he'd soon be a dead fool, but that, as to himself, he meant to live.

Van Tassel: And then?

Duggan: And then he jumped into the boat. [*The court was silent for a moment.*] Then Will gave the order to row —

Van Tassel: Mr Borden gave the order? Don't you mean that Captain Fitzgibbon gave the order?

Duggan: No, sir. It was Mr Borden gave it.

Van Tassel: But Captain Fitzgibbon was the commanding officer in the dinghy.

Duggan: No, sir. Begging your pardon, sir – he wasn't. When the ship is gone, the captain's command is gone with it.

Van Tassel: The ship wasn't gone. It was stolen.

Duggan [*patiently*]: Yes, sir. And now we'd fetched up in the dinghy. Will shouted, 'Row, Mick! Row, boys, row! And I rowed, sir, I rowed. Joe and me pulled like we never pulled before. The lieutenants were all heaped one on top of the other at our feet. Canacka looked like he was near death, so slippery with blood was he. The captain was half crazed, laughing and hugging himself. Will himself seized two oars, and by God we rowed. And all that time Small was firing at us from the deck, and shrieking and begging Will not to go. But we went, sir, and into such suffering as I can hardly describe. And but for Will –

Van Tassel: Yes, Mr Duggan. This court humbly acknowledges your suffering. Nevertheless, Captain Fitzgibbon was your senior officer. And in that boat, in the weeks that followed, did Captain Fitzgibbon's comfort take precedence over that of the others?

Duggan: No, sir. Mr Borden treated us all exactly the same.

Van Tassel: Mr Duggan, I must ask you to desist from answering as if Mr Borden was in charge of that vessel when he wasn't.

Duggan: I'm sorry, sir. You're right, sir. But even so, sir. He was.

On the third day, William Borden was called.

Van Tassel: Mr Borden, you had the honor of serving with Captain Fitzgibbon on the *Providence* as an ordinary seaman. Was he a fair captain, according to ship's law?

Borden: According to ship's law, sir, yes.

Van Tassel: Did you ever see him strike, mistreat, or otherwise punish one of the crew unduly?

Borden: No, sir. I never saw it.

Van Tassel: Did he ever deprive the crew of proper rest or leisure?

Borden: Not that I knew of, sir.

Van Tassel: Of rations? Salt beef? Biscuit?

Borden: No, sir.

Van Tassel: Of water or grog?

Borden: No, sir.

Shaw: Thank you, Mr Van Tassel. You have established your point. You needn't give us a grocery list. Please proceed to another substantive question.

Van Tassel: Mr Borden, do you believe that a commanding officer should be obeyed, whatever his conduct may be?

Borden: I do, sir.

Van Tassel [*surprised*]: You do? Even in the case of flagrant cruelty?

Borden: Yes, sir. There ain't no other way of running a ship. If every man on her is master, then she's unmastered, and that's worse.

Van Tassel: I see. But you agree that where Captain Fitzgibbon was concerned there was no cause for any such dissatisfaction among the men?

Borden: Not according to ship's law, sir, no.

Van Tassel: And was he a good captain to you?

Borden: Captain Fitzgibbon was always a good captain to me.

Van Tassel: Thank you, my man. Now. It would seem that you assumed a certain, ah, position of importance among your unfortunate fellow shipmates once you were cast out to sea, did you not?

Borden: Yes, sir.

Van Tassel: Have you any idea why?

Borden: Perhaps it was because I fished, sir.

Van Tassel: Fished?

Borden: Yes, sir. For food. We were starving.

Van Tassel: Indeed, yes. So you, ah, fished.

Borden: Yes, sir. We caught a turtle first. And then later we trawled a line –

Van Tassel: I know what fishing is, thank you, Mr Borden. But Captain Fitzgibbon didn't lead the men in this enterprise?

Borden: No, sir. He was too weak. And he didn't know how to fish with a hand-line. See, some gentlemen – yourself excepted of course, sir – don't.

[*There was irreverent snickering among the prisoners in the dock at this.*]

Van Tassel: Ah. Quite. And you had such a line about you?

Borden: Yes, sir. I had a roll of sail thread and a needle in my jacket.

Van Tassel: A needle?

Borden: A sailmaker's needle. To fashion a hook with. Maybe you've sometimes done the same, sir, when fishing.

Van Tassel: Heh. So. So you were deputized – deputized to fish.

Borden: You could put it that way, sir.

Shaw: Mr Van Tassel, where is this line of questioning – if you'll excuse the expression [*Smirks from on the bench.*] – leading?

Van Tassel: To sum up, sir – [*Here the president was heard to murmur, 'Please do.'*] It was not that Captain Fitzgibbon was neglecting his duty to command, even after he'd been thrown out upon the waves. He was incapacitated by starvation. [*At this juncture the proceedings were interrupted by one of the prisoners calling out, 'He was a greedy bugger and a flaming meater,' and having to be removed by the guard, which precipitated a scuffle. Once the cabin was quiet again, Van Tassel continued.*] Incapacitated, as I say, by starvation. And of course, we know all too well what effects this starvation had. Although, according to this honest man's testimony, Captain Fitzgibbon did his best – his very best – by his crew to the last, he is no longer with us. [*Addressing the president.*] Sir, I put it to you that he was murdered by these conscienceless mutineers as surely as if they'd shot or stabbed him on board ship. I appeal to the court not to allow his good name to be murdered also.

Allen: Thank you, Mr Van Tassel. I would like to put a few more questions to Mr Borden about his dealings with Daniel Small.

Van Tassel: Sir, I do not see how this is germane to the case. I have another witness to call. We have already established that Captain Fitzgibbon –

Allen: I will decide what is germane here, Mr Van Tassel, not you. Be seated for a moment, please. You may call your witness by and by. Mr Borden, in your parley with Small, did he tell you where he was to cruise after taking the ship?

Borden: Aye, sir. He said he would cruise wherever he could pick up the most prizes. And that he would then strike out for the Marquesas and go to ground there.

Allen: In your estimation, was there a reasonable probability that the *Providence*, commandeered as she now was, would be able to reach those islands?

Borden: Entirely reasonable, sir. Dan Small knew well enough how to sail a ship. He had the chronometer. He had a sextant. If you will look for him on Nukuheva, you will find him there.

[*A hum went around the room at this. The judge advocate called for silence.*]

Shaw: Is this your considered opinion?

Borden: It is. I would have staked my life on it, and the life of my men. That was why we didn't set out for the Marquesas, but turned south-east.

[*Now Van Tassel got to his feet.*]

Van Tassel: Sir, the court will record the fact that these were not Mr Borden's men. The captain was alive and well when —

Allen: Yes, yes, Mr Van Tassel. Please sit down. Mr Borden, in your desperate state in the weeks to come, how did you know with any certainty which way was south-east?

Borden: When I took the pork, sir, I also took the precaution of putting a compass and a quadrant in the barrel.

[*Here a 'heugh heugh heugh' was heard from the bench. All were amazed to realize that the commodore, who hadn't said a word up to this point, had raised his saurian head and was making a sound somewhere between a cough and a laugh. He seemed to look around. His lone eye was marbled, its socket florid with some antediluvian growth. Could he even see? His whole sea-scarred body appeared to waver. His single turnipy arm shook as he propped himself up on the table. A hush descended on the cabin.*]

Evans: I ask the indulgence of the court. If I may put. If I may just. A question.

Allen: Of course, sir.

[*The old man began to speak. I imagined him uttering the next words in a chapped voice, a voice so thin and dry that it was like dead skin flaking into the stillness.*]

Evans: I am talking to you now as a fellow sailor, Mr Borden. As an old, old sailor to a young one. You undertook to sail halfway across the Pacific Ocean to the coast of South America, with a cask each of bread and water, a bit of pork, a line, a compass and quadrant, your knowledge of the stars, and – well. I have exhausted my inventory of the resources at your disposal. I sailed that ocean for sixty years. Sixty years, and I cannot conceive it. No man in his right mind could conceive it. It is quite marvelous. Quite, quite marvelous. How did you think you could live?

Borden: How could we not, sir? We had to live.

Evans: Were you not afraid?

Borden: Yes, sir. I ain't ever been more afraid in my life. But

186

also I ain't ever been clearer in my own mind than I was
then. And now.

Evans: And now?

Borden: And now I am here. And I live.

Evans: You live. Yes. You live. [*The commodore leaned forwards,
smiling broadly, toothlessly, and slapped his taloned old hand
on the table top in delight.*] Life – that is the thing, is it not?
Dear life.

[*They were startled into a long moment of mutual recognition,
these two survivors. Then at last, Borden spoke.*]

Borden: Yes, sir. It is.

TWELVE

'Look at this, cassius. I've been sent an advertisement for a design patented by your Dr Rush.' After reading into the night I'd got up at six the next morning to look in on Miss Todd in the women's wing, and had skipped breakfast. When I stopped by Mansfield's office later I found him sitting at his desk. He flapped a piece of paper at me. 'The Tranquilizer. Guaranteed to lower the pulse by locking the sufferer into a sitting position. Bound to work a treat.'

I took it gingerly. I was fagged and nervous from lack of sleep, and Mansfield's flippancy made me querulous. 'Dr Rush's Tranquilizing Chair'. the paper said. 'Restores proper blood flow to the ORGANS OF THE BODY and the BRAIN and thereby calms the MIND, reducing AGITATION and the symptoms of DERANGEMENT. Only seven dollars. Limited stock. Early subscription essential.'

Below these words was a picture of a man strapped to a wooden chair. His ankles, wrists, and chest were bound by restraints. His hands, palms down on the arms of the chair, gripped the rests. His head, save for an aperture for the nose, was entirely encased in a hefty hardwood block, bolted to a staff protruding from the back.

'Now that's a nice solid jaw harness,' remarked Mansfield. 'Not being able to move one's head is always incredibly calming. What do you think?'

'Richard, please. He's not *my* Dr Rush. Since coming here and getting some experience in mind-doctoring I've realized how ludicrous his circulatory theories are.'

'So you don't think we should invest in this?'

'Of course I don't.' He was about to go off on his rounds, but I stopped him. 'That doesn't mean that I don't think we should invest in *something.*'

'I smell a manifesto coming. Make it quick, please.'

'Well, to take a random instance – Miss Clayborn. I don't believe we're doing enough for her.'

'Count on you to suggest the least likely example. Tell me, what more could we possibly be doing for Sarah Clayborn? She has absolutely everything she has ever asked for.'

'I don't think she does. Materially, yes. But what of – of – the things of the spirit?'

'The spirit? Have you been talking to her about her delusions?'

'No,' I dissembled. 'But it occurs to me that she might have an understandable, perhaps even an ordinary, desire for mental stimulation. Have you never wondered if our patients might be trying to tell us something through their madness?'

'Tell us? Tell us what? She is not an ordinary woman, however she might appear to you. It is vitally important to recognize that there are certain symptoms peculiar to the insane.'

'Yes, Richard. But from what I've seen here, it's considered even more peculiar to do much about them.'

'I keep saying this. We are not in the business of curing our patients. Our task is to give them safe harbor.'

'Why do we only aim at giving them safe harbor, as you call it? Why don't we try to do more?'

'Madness is like the ocean. It's a shattering force. We can't control it. We can't plumb its depths. We can only try to manage it. We can divert it and domesticate it, and hope that it expends some of its energy in the process. If you begin to play Prospero you will be stirring up a storm.'

'I've heard from Miss Macy.'

'Ah.' He stared at me closely. 'Did you write to her first, or was this a reply to a missive of yours, by any chance?'

'Well, yes, it was a letter in answer to one of mine. Look, I understand her concern, her – her –'

'Her desire for results?'

'Exactly. Is that so terrible?'

Mansfield laughed and shook his head. Then he became serious. 'Does he ever mention her?'

'No. Never.' I felt a twinge of gratification at this. 'She says she is "under dealings". What does that mean?'

'It means that you must be very careful.'

'I can't make sense of it.'

'It's not your job to make sense of anything. I can't condone you haring off in these directions while you are at work. Your role here is to care for our patients along the therapeutic lines we have laid down.'

'To play bowls. To take strolls. And to dance.'

'Where is this heading?'

'Miss Macy isn't a patient of ours. And I'm due a holiday from dancing. If I decided to spend one of my vacation days on Nantucket, you wouldn't object?'

'It's not my place to object to whatever you may choose to do in your vacations.' He subjected me to another searching look. 'I'm not your father.'

'You certainly aren't, thank God.'

IT WAS MID-AFTERNOON BEFORE I returned to the trial transcript. While Miss Joy and the other attendants were busy doling out cocoa in the conservatory I excused myself on the pretext of having to finish off that morning's notes, and slipped up to my room.

On the fourth and final day of the inquiry the third lieutenant of the *Providence* was called on to testify. Oliver Lenox was a Bostonian of the kind I knew well – articulate, educated to within an inch of his life, urbane and obliging – and he was Van Tassel's key witness. But his testimony did not go according to plan.

Van Tassel: Mr Lenox, please state your position on the *Providence* to the court.

Lenox: I was third lieutenant on board the *Providence*.

Van Tassel: You sustained grievous injuries when you were beaten while attempting to protect your captain, did you not?

Lenox: I was only doing my duty.

Van Tassel: Quite right, and your country thanks you for it. I won't insult you by asking you if your lawfully appointed captain was deserving of the duty you owed him. Were conditions on board ship, and later in the dinghy, as Mr Duggan and Mr Borden have described them?

Lenox: Pretty much. The captain was very ill by the time we'd been out on the open ocean some weeks, as Mr Borden has noted. Mr Monroe had been struck hard on the temple and never regained full consciousness. Mr Borden bound Canacka's ear as best he could after bathing it in whiskey –

Van Tassel: Mr Borden had whiskey?

Lenox: Yes. Mr Monroe had a flask about his person, and thank heaven for it, it was our only medicine. Captain Fitzgibbon relied on it heavily for the first few days, God help him. We were unable to do anything for Mr Perry. He was dying in front of our eyes. The pistol shot had gone right through his face and shattered his jaw. His mouth was hanging open, full of blood. He couldn't speak but he could still make a noise, and a chirping came from that bloody mouth all day and all night, a chirping like a bird or a mouse that's been hurt, over and over until I could hardly bear it. It took him five days to die.

Van Tassel [*taken aback*]: Five days.

Lenox: Yes. When he did, I think we were all glad. I know I was. We said a prayer over Perry's body and then we threw it out to sea. We were fearfully low by that time, but Mr Borden rallied us. We had already determined that we would not strike out for the Marquesas as Small had threatened to land there. Dog-leg winds and currents would beat us back from the Galapagos. Our only hope was to head for South America, and pray that we would meet a ship along the way.

Van Tassel: That must have been dispiriting in the extreme. But surely Captain Fitzgibbon—

Lenox: Mr Borden kept us at it. The dinghy was rigged for sail but when we unfurled the jib on our second day at sea we found that it was worn, and the first thing he did was to urge us to give up our shirts that he and Mr Duggan might repair it. Then he set all those who were fit enough to do so to keep watches.

Van Tassel: Mr Lenox, how did Mr Borden come to be in charge, with two senior officers in passable bodily health on board?

Lenox: The captain was distracted, and I was still in considerable pain. But other than that, I can't really say. It seemed natural that Mr Borden should lead us. He thought to do things that, in our tormented state, did not occur to the rest of us, and the way he presented them left no room for argument.

Van Tassel: What manner of things?

Lenox: Well, I've never repaired a sail, for one.

[*'A-course you fucking ain't!' a voice in the dock sang out.*]

Shaw: Order! Proceed please, Mr Lenox.

Lenox: Once we were clear of the *Providence* and satisfied that Small was not pursuing us, and our sail had been mended, Mr Borden took an observation and decided that we should try to head south. He calculated that after thirteen or fourteen days' sail in this direction we should be able to catch the variable breezes blowing towards the South American coast, and that if all went well, the rest of our journey might take another month. He also rationed our food from that very day, and he wouldn't be budged on this.

Van Tassel: Oh, come, Mr Lenox. Your modesty is out of place. Rationing the distribution of food in such circumstances is the obvious thing to do. As an officer, injured or not, and whatever your skills at patching sails might or might not be, you would have known that.

Lenox: Indeed, but if it had been left to me to distribute them, I am quite certain that I should have been overrun and that we would have consumed all our supplies within a week. Or I would have been too lenient, and killed us that way. Mr Borden was – well. He's bigger than I am. [*Gesturing to the witnesses' bench.*] As you can see.

[*Laughter from the prisoners, and jeers of 'pollywog' and 'runty little scut', at which the president banged his fist several times on the table.*]

Allen: Silence, I say! Silence in my court, or I'll damn well have you all keelhauled! Go on, Lieutenant.

Lenox: Aye, sir. Mr Borden gave us half a pint of water and about six ounces of bread every morning, with a mouthful of pork. And we were grateful for it.

Van Tassel: That was a diet that would guarantee your starvation!

Lenox: Yes. We knew it. But we did it because Mr Borden said so. He estimated the number of days it would take us to reach South America if we stayed on course and he divided our food accordingly. We had no glass, but Mr Borden was able to calculate our heading using the quadrant, and by dead reckoning.

Van Tassel: How did he do that?

Lenox: There was a supply of rope in the dinghy and he used it to make his own log line using wood salvaged from one of the benches.

Van Tassel: Kindly explain to – to the court what a log line is, Mr Lenox.

Lenox [*with a disbelieving look at the judge advocate*]: Really, sir?

Shaw: Go ahead, please, Mr Lenox. I myself would very much like to know.

Lenox [*in the best naval academy style*]: Certainly. It is a tool for determining how far a craft has traveled in any set period. Usually one uses a custom-made line with a piece of wood at the end. The line, which is knotted at intervals, is run out into the water. One records the number of knots thus run out with one's sandglass – that tells one the speed of one's vessel. Then one estimates one's north–south position from one's speed and direction.

Van Tassel: But one – but you *had* no sandglass!

Lenox: Indeed. We had no log line either, until Mr Borden made us one. I could not see how this would work. But then – [*wryly*] Mr Borden got us to count the seconds aloud as we ran the rope out.

Van Tassel [*fascinated in spite of himself*]: Most ingenious.

Lenox: Yes. Mr Borden always seemed to know precisely what he was about, and his certainty gave us confidence. After a week on rations we were already very hungry. Famished, in fact. Mr Webb became – became insistent, but Mr Borden refused to give way. And then it was as if heaven rewarded our obedience. A great turtle came swimming by on our larboard side and Mr Borden seized it by the fins. It came aboard as light as skating. Mr Borden slit its neck with his clasp knife and we drank its blood.

Van Tassel [*drawn in now*]: How did you contrive to do that?

Lenox: Mr Borden showed us how to suck at its neck while it was still living. We each took our turn and when we had drunk we waited to take it again. I have never tasted anything so good in my life. While I was drinking, the beast's eye was pressed up close to mine, wide open and still. It was as if I were taking its spirit directly into my body. It was terrible and wonderful at the same time. I felt remade. Reborn.

Van Tassel: Reborn?

Lenox: Yes. Called to life again. It was the most marvelous experience of my entire existence up to that point. Once the turtle was dead Mr Borden cracked the shell and cut the flesh into strips which we hung about the boat. We ate them slowly, chewing on the bones and the skin. But it was not the same. It was hot and the meat started to rot. And there was so much fat on it that it stank – it stank like a charnel house. The smell was so vile that we had to throw the remains overboard. And then – oh God oh God oh God.

Van Tassel: What is it, Mr Lenox?

Shaw: Please take your time, Lieutenant. Would you like to stop for a moment?

Lenox: No, thank you, sir. I'm – I'm all right. We'd been making fairly good headway southwards when, after about nine days at sea, we entered rough waters. The waves threatened to flood our dinghy faster than we could bale. Mr Borden cried out that we had to head her into the ocean or we'd drown. He strapped up a sea anchor from whatever planks we could spare and threw it over the bow. For two days we did nothing but bend, bale, bend, bale, as the water crashed onto our backs. Then the waves sank as if a plug had been pulled in the ocean floor and we saw how desperate our state was. We floated on that lifeless water like flies in milk. We floated for more than two weeks without a breath of wind as the sun rolled overhead. By day we burned and at night we froze. The seemingly impossible had happened – Mr Borden's plan of getting us into the variables had foundered.

At first we tried to row to regain our course, but we were pushing against the current. We were too weak and had to give it up. All we could do was drift. We'd been at sea close to a month and our remaining clothes had rotted on our backs. Our hunger was unspeakable. But our thirst was worse. Our lips and tongues were black like the turtle's. My feet and legs swelled up so that I was convinced they were going to split. I was bleeding all over like a leper. Sometimes the clouds gathered and we would watch them in a fever, wanting to suck the moisture out of that sky, but then they would disperse and leave us in agony. When a man is that hungry and thirsty he will either lash out, or sink into apathy and wait for the end – it doesn't much matter which. The end will come.

[*Lenox stopped speaking. All sat expectantly. At length the judge advocate broke the silence.*]

Shaw: Go on with your testimony, please, Mr Lenox, if you are able.

Lenox: I'm sorry. Yes, sir. Eventually we all came near to failing. I slipped into a torpor. In that hour dreams become your solace. Oh, I dreamed that I was whole, and drinking at life, and slicing through the ocean wave with my fins, swimming up and down through the spume. I was happy, happy. I didn't want to be anywhere else. I wouldn't have exchanged that boat for the world. And then Mr Monroe began to die.

Van Tassel: He died? How did he die?

Lenox: His wits had been sent flying by the blow he'd received from Small's pistol and he never got 'em back. We all kept away from him. But when Mr Borden saw how things were he went over to Monroe's corner of the boat and took his head in his lap. Monroe's head was resting on Mr Borden's knees and he was gabbling 'Billy Billy' again and again, 'Billy Billy Billy', until I thought I would go mad. I wanted to be back in my dream. Mr Borden said be quiet now, be quiet. Hold still. I was quiet. Very quiet. Monroe died. He hardly made a sound. And then Mr Borden started to fish.

Van Tassel: To fish?

Lenox: Yes. We had enough to eat for a while, I don't know how long for. But he fished and we ate then. And the wind – oh God. The wind came at last. It came the night Monroe died as a breeze pouring out from the starlit sky, the lightest brush of a wing on our upturned faces, and by the following morning it had shifted into the west and was blowing steadily. The gods had answered our prayers. Our sails filled and we began to tack towards South America, exactly as Mr Borden had predicted. And then, as we drew closer and closer to safety, Webb died –

Van Tassel: How? Was he unwell?

Lenox: Oh yes, we were all unwell. We were so skeletal that you could not tell one of us apart from the other. Our skull faces all looked alike. All the time there was a preternatural high-pitched whistling circling about the boat. I heard it quite clearly. The captain's boy was folded in on himself in the bow. I remember looking at his arm, fretted with burst boils like the stops on a pipe, and wondering if it was the wind making that noise, playing him like a flute . . . Or maybe it was my own spirit trying to leave my body. I wasn't certain if it was he or I who was dying. But it wasn't either of us. It was Webb. He was feeble and he gave up after a short struggle for his life. After this death Captain Fitzgibbon begged to die. But Mr Borden said, 'No, sir. You are our lodestar. You are our figurehead. You are crucial to our cause.'

Van Tassel: And rightly so.

Lenox: Yes. God help the poor foolish old man. [*There was silence in the court.*] And so we came back.

Van Tassel: Thank you, Mr Lenox.

Lenox: I want to add something, if I may.

Van Tassel [*caught off guard*]: Please do.

Lenox: We endured great suffering in that boat. But without him we would all have died. Every last man of us.

Van Tassel: Your sentiments do you credit, and your loyalty is duly recorded.

Lenox: He speaks as if it were nothing. But he looked after us. He kept us alive. He sacrificed himself so we might live.

[*Here the president leaned forwards and interrupted.*]

Allen: I'm not sure I understand you, Mr Lenox. 'He speaks'? Captain Fitzgibbon isn't here to speak for himself.

Lenox: I don't mean the captain, sir. I mean Mr Borden.

Towards midday the final witness, John Canacka, was called.

Van Tassel: You, Mr Canacka, served as Captain Fitzgibbon's boy.

[*The witness did not respond.*]

Shaw: Answer Mr Van Tassel's question, Mr Canacka.

Canacka: What question, sir?

Shaw: Did you serve as Captain Fitzgibbon's boy?

Canacka: He says so, sir.

Shaw: Yes or no, Mr Canacka?

Canacka: Aye.

Allen [*interrupting*]: We must make allowances for this young man, gentlemen. He is not well.

Van Tassel: Indeed, sir. I can see that.

Shaw: Please proceed, Mr Van Tassel.

Van Tassel: What duties did you have, Mr Canacka, when you served the captain?

Canacka: I kept his cabin tidy. I fixed his clothes neat. I cleaned his pot.

Van Tassel: Was he a fair captain?

Canacka: The captain was a man. Couldn't help shitting like any other man.

Van Tassel: Answer the ques—

Shaw: Mr Van Tassel, we are nearly out of time. It is our dinner hour. Kindly advance to your main line of questioning.

Van Tassel: Sir, that is what I am trying to do. Mr Canacka, either during his command of the *Providence* or when you were marooned in that boat, did Captain Fitzgibbon ever fail in his duty to you? Did he ever fail in his protection? [*But the witness had sunk down against the panels of the settle.*] Answer me, Mr Canacka. Did he ever sacrifice you to his own interests?

Canacka: Sacrifice, sir.

Van Tassel: Answer the question, you goddamned savage, don't repeat it. Did Captain Fitzgibbon –

Shaw: Enough, Mr Van Tassel. The boy is ill. Mr Canacka, if you are able, reply to Mr Van Tassel. Clearly, now.

Canacka: The captain never had no real care for me. I reckon he used me 'bout the same as anyone else. No better. No worse. World don't care for us.

Shaw: That's a harsh philosophy for one so young, Mr Canacka.

Canacka: I ain't young.

Shaw: How old are you?

Canacka: Fourteen.

[*Laughter in the court.*]

Allen: Silence, please! Silence! This boy has done a man's work. Mr Canacka, we are making an inquiry into a very serious matter. Mutiny is a reprehensible crime that tears at the fabric of our world. Men have suffered and died in the course of this calamity on the *Providence*. The lives and reputations of several more hang in the balance. But mutiny does violence to every one of us who trusts his life to that little kingdom at sea that is a ship. We are all bound up in the meaning of it. If you have anything to say – anything at all – that can help us to make sense of this awful and unnatural event, then you must say it now.

Canacka: *Ika.*

Shaw [*looking at his fellow judges*]: We do not follow you. Please speak a language we can all comprehend.

Canacka [*pulling himself up with great effort, and turning to the president*]: Thee's strong, sir. Every man here is strong. Thee never shakes in the night. Thee never hungers. Thee never fears. So thee thinks hunger and fear and shaking ain't natural. But it is. If a man is weak it is. Mebbe thee's a king but I ain't. On that ship I weren't no king. I was nothing. We was all nothing. Tell me what's natural and what ain't natural. When we got in the boat Will said, 'Be easy, Johnny, ain't nothing gonna hurt thee no more now. That all over now.' We was alone on that ocean and starving and 'bout to die but I weren't afraid. I was already dead before. I was already weak and nothing could weaken me more. The strong live, sir.

Allen: And the weak?

Canacka: *Ika*.

Allen: What is this *'ika'*? Was that you?

Canacka [*his voice splintering*]: No, sir. Will kept me safe.

Allen: I don't understand you, Mr Canacka.

Canacka [*sobbing freely now*]: Nor do I understand myself neither, sir.

Allen [*appealing to Evans*]: Do you understand the boy, Commodore?

[*But the commodore had fallen asleep. His desiccated breath could be heard rising and falling in the cabin, which had gradually filled with the smell of beef and suet.*]

Shaw: Well. The lad is distressed. There is nothing coherent in any of this. Gentlemen, it is time to break for dinner. I move that we draw today's proceedings to a close. Mr Canacka, do you have anything further to say?

Canacka [*between sobs*]: No, sir. I ain't got nothing more to say.

After the court had dined, the verdict was handed down. Captain Fitzgibbon was exonerated of any conduct unbefitting his command. The prisoners were condemned to hang. Small was sentenced to death in absentia. Neither he nor the remaining mutineers were ever apprehended: a note at the end of the transcript recorded that a party of whalers landing on Nukuheva many months later, penetrating as far as the valleys, found only the remains of a hut, its mud walls washed away by the Pacific rains; a rusted ship's chronometer, and a cairn of stones.

Feeling oddly perturbed, I let the pamphlet fall from my hands and wandered out onto the hill. The two asylum fountains were splashing and gurgling in unison as if no fallen leaf or human hand had ever interfered with them.

The strong live. And the weak?

As I reached the summer house I saw that the rose trees were in bud, pushing forth tight buttons of pink and white. Sarah Clayborn sheltered on a step under the trellis, skirts tucked around her brawny calves, a paper bag in her lap.

'Hello, Infant,' she said. 'Glad to see you've been let out of the schoolroom. All work and no play, eh?'

'Miss Clayborn, I've been thinking things over and I wonder if you mightn't like some . . . some occupation.'

'What did you have in mind?'

'Well, I thought the choice could be yours.'

Miss Clayborn drew a piece of candy out of her bag, popped it between her lips, and began to grind away at it. Her eyes narrowed in challenge. 'But a suggestion, sir.'

'Ah, let's see now.' I thought of Miss Todd and her needles. 'How about knitting?'

Miss Clayborn went on grinding.

'If not knitting, then, maybe – quilting? Tapestry work? Or,' I offered wildly, when no answer seemed to be forthcoming, 'painting in watercolors?'

She looked at me with the bemused skepticism of a large mammal: a bull elephant, say, regarding a spear-toting tribesman on a plain. Her cheek bulged as her tongue probed for shards. 'Why on earth,' she said at last, 'would I wish to do any of those things?'

'I don't know. I really don't know! I wouldn't want to, either. But perhaps, ma'am, you would like to read a book?'

'I don't need books, Infant. All nature is my book. Look.'

She directed my gaze to the mass of flowering branches above us. Far off, the fountains spouted merrily. I sat down beside her and we skulked in our thicket with our heads together, like two spies. There was an aura about her of toffee and toothpowder.

'The desert shall rejoice, and blossom as the rose,' she pronounced in her bass rumble. 'In the wilderness shall waters break out. What do *you* see?'

'I see, ma'am, that the broken fountain is working again, without divine intervention.'

She gave her paper bag a forceful shake. 'Humbug, Dr Carver.'

'No, thank you.'

'I am not offering you a peppermint. I am trying to tell you that you have it all ass-backwards, as always.'

'Admit it, ma'am. The fountain *is* working, isn't it?'

'Oh, yes.'

'And the Son of Man –' I spoke with firm finality – 'hasn't come.'

'That is where you are mistaken.' Her voice was round and cracked, like a devilish tocsin, a primitive bell called back to life. 'He is already here.'

THIRTEEN

O N THE FIRST SATURDAY in May I took a day's holiday, and set off for the island of Nantucket. I'd never been there before. The Carvers traditionally summered at Newport, venturing as far as the edge of the Atlantic without ever putting a toe off the continent of America. We were strangers to that swatch of sand lying thirty miles offshore. Just how strange the place was (or how strange I would prove, in relation to it), I was about to discover.

In those days there was, of course, no ferry from Hyannis, so I had to take the New Bedford steamer. Since being carried bodily off the *Orbis* I hadn't gone near a ship, or felt the slightest desire to board one ever again, and I was relieved to find that the steam boat was a long and low-slung one like a gravy boat, with a homely chimney and an engine. I found a seat on the upper bow deck in the shade of the pilot house, facing the open Atlantic. Soon we were making our way into that great body of water, and when she'd rumbled past the cliffs of Martha's Vineyard the steamer hove eastward with a growl and struck out for the horizon.

This is where a sense of caution should have made itself felt in me, but I was young, I was nicely warmed, after that hard Boston winter, by the generous May sun, and I was very glad not to be seasick. A couple of hours later I spied land, stretched gray over a thin smile of sand, rising up out of the ocean. At our approach the gray took on mass and definition, assumed the guise of peaked steeples, houses, roofs and turning windmills, hills and winking ponds, and then, as we rounded a swell and swung, past a stubby lighthouse astride a promontory, towards the mouth of the harbor, I smelled it: the insinuating stink of a hundred refineries and candle factories, sloughing off their smoke into the clammy air.

I could hear the wharf before I could see it. Once the steamer had crossed the bar it reached me as a low buzz, unscrolling to become the whoosh and slop of waves breaking along the pier, the slamming of barrels and the cries of men: of coopers and ropemakers and boatbuilders and pie sellers, of blacksmiths and fishmongers and lumber merchants, riddled with the ack-ack of gulls and the creaking of what seemed like a fleet of ships jostling for position on the tide.

When I stepped off the boat onto the quay at midday, it was into an alien roar. The din! It appeared that every single person who got off every single vessel to Nantucket came here. The place was a maze of warehouses, inns and oyster stalls, overlooked by higgledy-piggledy shingled buildings. Carts piled with cod trundled through unpaved alleys in which oil spills shone like loose change.

From out of the heart of this hubbub a church bell began to stutter the hour. Two Indians squatting on a coil of hemp, mending a net, leered at me while I picked my way through the scales and grease. One gave a low whistle and the other laughed, causing me to trip and crick my ankle.

I leaned against the wall of a warehouse with as much sangfroid as I could muster and tried to get my bearings.

At the head of the wharf there was a sandy road lined with wooden shops that extended uphill. I got to it, limping, and found that the stink of the harbor was overlaid here with the stink of new timber and paint. This had to be Main Street. I checked my paper with the address: Miss Macy lived near the very end. At the top the street ran up to a brick bank, where it narrowed almost imperceptibly and veered off into a hush. Beyond there were no more shops, only large houses set in spacious plots, separated by sunny avenues and tethering posts, and I waded gratefully into this promised seclusion. The upper part of Main Street was virtually treeless, its sandy verges sprinkled with the furled heads of pea and willow herb. It was as quiet as a village. I walked on under a shy blue sky with a scribble of cloud, like a child's drawing, pleased to be away from that foul harbor, listening to the drip of water from the eaves and marveling at the light-rinsed air, the caulked white chasteness of the buildings. Occasionally a figure, dressed in sober black or brown, opened a door and glided down to the dirt before going about its silent business.

I plowed through deepening sand until at last, flush with the street and surrounded by a scatter of block-like houses, I found number 99. It was five-bayed, neat and flat, with facing boards of pure white, so smooth that they might have been painted yesterday, into which were set windows and trim of a dark green. Along the façade ran a fence that curved up at the step to form a balustrade, and above it, topped by a fan, was an austere front door. I approached the house cautiously, aware of an anxious tremor in my knees. I was sweating from every pore and my shoes were ruined. As I raised my fist to the knocker, I heard a scraping coming from behind it.

My knocking produced a maidservant with a harried air. A dustpan and brush lay at her feet: she'd evidently just got up from sweeping the hall.

'Yes?' She tossed her head in an attempt to dislodge the bangs that clung to her eyebrows.

I drew out my card. Since she carried no salver, I thrust it into her hand. 'Dr Hiram Carver. I have an appointment with your mistress.'

A puff of air blown through compressed lips sent the girl's hair flying upwards. 'Thee'd better come in. She's waiting on thee in the front sitting room.' She looked equivocally at the floor. 'It's this way.'

I crunched after her down the passage, mortified to realize that my trouser hems left a trail of sand on the boards. The skivvy glared at me as if I had the Sinai desert hidden in my pockets, gabbled something about a blessed blamed broom, and opened the sitting-room door with a blow of her elbow.

Miss Macy was bent over a work table, gazing unseeingly at some tatting. Sunlight lay in bars across her shoulders and picked out, here and there around the room, a subdued opulence that suggested generations of quiet prosperity: the gleam of wood and ivory, an inlaid candle stand, an ebony chessboard with a set of polished chessmen. She wore, I was certain, the same gray gown she had worn in Charlestown; either she had several cut to the same pattern, or she hadn't troubled herself to dress for me.

'Gentleman from off-island, marm,' announced the maid, and disappeared.

Miss Macy registered my gritty shoes and hot face with a complicit wince. 'Dr Carver. There you are. You'd care for coffee, I expect.'

'Well, not unless. Only if.'

But she'd already gone out of the room. I could hear her footsteps receding, and the low sound of her voice in the hall.

I stood about, at a loss, until I thought I would combust from the strain. I picked up a mother-of-pearl snuffbox from a side table; remembered that I'd never tried snuff before, and put it back. Clownish sweat plopped from my nose.

'I'm sorry to run off like that,' murmured Miss Macy on her return. 'I've sent Patience in and out three times this morning. I don't like to keep interrupting her at her work. Please sit.'

I sat. There was a stiff silence that continued for some minutes. It was broken by the sudden entry of the alliterative young woman with the bangs who had shown me in earlier, now carrying a tray with a coffee pot, cream jug, and two bone china cups.

'Thank you, Patience,' said Miss Macy. 'No cake?'

'No, marm.' Patience's hair achieved the perpendicular. 'Thee didn't say *cake*.'

Miss Macy capitulated. 'Coffee will do.'

She handed a cup to me. I sipped in fear of breaking a handle and incurring the wrath of all the ghosts of Macys past who seemed palpably to inhabit the south rooms. Presently she lifted her eyes. I was struck by their colorlessness – their impenetrably nude cast. Her whole head, offset by the severe collar of her dress, was like a head made of Parian marble. When I saw her last, at the asylum, she'd wept in front of me without any defense. In her letter she had been frank to the point of boldness. But here, in this foreign parlor, redolent of ancestral household pieties, she seemed as far removed from me as a statue on a plinth.

Then she smiled apologetically, and I again glimpsed the living woman of the letter. 'What a poor welcome. I seem to manage the business of my factory quite well, while letting the business of my own house go all to pieces.' Her skin had the faintest flush, as of ice held over a candle flame. It deepened with her next question. 'How is he?'

'He is calm. Peaceful.'

'Does he ever refer to – ?' She faltered. Her fingers touched her breast; returned, burrowing, to the folds of her skirt.

I said nothing. Miss Macy tried again. 'Does he ever ask after – ?'

'No.' Her knuckles went to her mouth, so that I was moved to add, 'He will. You must be patient.'

'He is so changed.' The heat in her face had mounted to form coins of pink on her cheekbones. 'It's not just that he's so reduced, so frail. I feel, sometimes, that he's found the – the taste of me abhorrent. That he's spat me out.'

I felt a shiver of compunction. 'Dear God, Miss Macy, please don't blame yourself.'

'He is a hero, of course. The world sees him that way. But I still remember him as he was when he sat with me here in this room, before he sailed on that ship. He was clumsy. He was helpless. He was – in need. May I tell you something?'

I nodded dumbly.

'There are days, as I'm leaving the factory and going out into the crowds on the wharf, when I imagine they'll part at any second to reveal him. Do you know that air of – of difference people you love have, when you see them in a crowd?'

While Miss Macy spoke I felt the whisper of a steady fire. Was this what Borden had felt, this promise of heat under the ice?

'I'm not sure I do.'

Her reserve had vanished completely. She was reddening like any common servant girl. 'Well, that will be the only difference between before and now. It will take me a moment to recognize him, but only a moment. And then he'll walk towards me, just as he was.'

She seemed about to weep. But in the next instant she brought her palms briskly together. 'So, Dr Carver, let's not sit here like two clams.' She started to gather up the coffee cups, spilling my half-drunk coffee over her hand, which she wiped across her lap. That plain dress was stitched from a lustrous fabric: I could see the marks left by her wet fingers on the convexity where her thighs must be. I was struck by how unconcerned she was with her own appearance. It had clearly never crossed her mind that I might, during this visit, be subjecting her to scrutiny – either that, or she no longer cared about the impression she made.

'Miss Macy, I have a question for you. In your letter to me you wrote that you were "under dealings". I didn't understand your meaning, ma'am.'

'To be under dealings is a very serious matter, Hiram Carver. You should speak of it under your breath, in a whisper,' she said with an angry laugh. And then, whispering, 'Like this.'

I did my best to mimic her, making my voice as small as Caro's at its most disapproving. 'Like this?'

Miss Macy laughed again, surprised. It was a real laugh this time, and like her crying all those weeks ago, it was done without disguise or visible effort. 'Yes! That's it, exactly.' Her gaze, charged and defiant, challenged mine. 'It means, sir, that our Meeting is debating the wisdom of disowning me. Oh, well. *Debating*. They will, of course. Unless I break my engagement.'

'And will you?'

'Oh, no.'

'You are giving up a great deal.'

'Abandoning one's faith, the faith of one's fathers, is a terrible thing. It's an awful fear and a sorrow. But I know that I'm in search, not in error.'

Though she spoke quietly, her ferocity couldn't be overlooked. She seemed, slight as she was, to fill out the contours of herself so fully.

'Miss Macy, I don't care what anyone else thinks. I know all too well what it is like to carry the weight of others' expectations, when one only wants to find one's own way. My own father demands. That is, he has always –' I stopped. 'I don't know what I am trying to say.'

'It must be a burden to you to know that you are already a marked man, whether you do anything worthy of mark or not. You want something more,' she urged. 'You want the truth. You want, I think, to know what is real.'

'I want the truth, yes. Reality – yes!' It was astonishing that she'd so precisely intuited my hopes and fears in the brief time we'd spent together. 'But more than that – I want not to be a slave.' I made a little moue of disparagement at myself, at how nonsensical this sounded. 'You may ask, how is he a slave, this privileged young man, this son of a free city and a free society, this pampered child of affluent parents, this *male* child –' she smiled palely at that – 'in what way can he possibly believe himself unfree? But I can't be happy, I can't think myself truly free, if I simply follow the way that's been laid down for me. This is what we all do; what we've always done. Well, at least –' I grimaced – 'we Carvers have always done it. We do it and we pretend that it's enough, that we've made sense of the world; that there's an automatic end to uncertainty in behaving just as our forebears have behaved. We call it tradition, or wisdom, or family, or society. I've tried to go along with it, but I can't. Beyond it all I sense chaos.'

'Chaos?'

'Yes. Chaos.' She looked at me steadily. Her watchful eyes were alight with intelligence and understanding. 'Ma'am, I sense terror in the everyday. And I don't believe that we've solved the problem of how to live, that we've made that terror safe, merely by going along with the old ways and the old forms. We should be free to question, we should be free to reinvent, we should be free to feel that terror, the terrible freedom of *being uncertain* – but we aren't; we cling to our false certainty and call it freedom, and we can't see that what we've really created out of freedom is a prison.' I stopped again, short of breath, my heart racing. I'd never yet spoken like this to anyone, let alone to someone of the opposite sex.

'You are eloquent.'

'Thank you.'

'I don't doubt that you'll do well. This is a world in which words count for more than deeds.'

I didn't know whether to feel flattered, or reprimanded. She had William Borden's own knack of hiding a bruising truth in plain sight.

'But you, ma'am –'

'Oh, I am a woman. For the most part we're supposed to know all sorts of women's work, and the result is that we spend our lives learning this, while the universe of truth remains unentered.'

We sat without speaking for a moment. Miss Macy folded her

bloodless hands; her eyes became unfixed. I was filled with a head-long fear that she would retreat from me and turn back into an effigy of herself, and so I spoke recklessly, not fully knowing what I was saying.

'I've read everything you sent me, ma'am. *Everything*.' I shifted towards her, wanting, but not daring, to touch her fingertips and call her back to me. 'And I have to admit that – that there are things that puzzle me in those papers. It is only a feeling. I can't define it. A confusion – but whether it's a confusion in the facts, in the way they are presented, or a confusion in *me*, of understanding, I can't decide. Take that word – the word in the trial record, the term the boy used – *ika*. What did he mean? The littlest thing I've read seems to imply more than it says. What is *ika*?'

The two syllables trembled between us like the oscillations of a cymbal.

'You saw it. I knew you would. Oh, I knew!' It was as if she were undergoing some transformation, some change of substance. She appeared to melt under my eyes, to become exposed, as if some real and essential connection were being laid down between us. 'I don't know. But I have wondered, often, if there was something else – something that still troubles William, which he can't speak about –'

'He hasn't talked to you?'

'Ah, no.' She let her palms fall open in her lap in a gesture of such helpless dispossession that I felt intensely sorry for her. 'But maybe he will – to you.'

'You know that I will do all that's in my power to do. But I don't think you asked me here today just to tell me that.'

'No. It's this. Every word you've said convinces me that I am right to turn to you. The boy –' She looked at me imploringly. A vein had begun to throb in her temple.

'Do you mean Fitzgibbon's boy? The savage?'

'The newspapers called him that. He's no more a savage than you or I.'

'Then who or what is he?'

'You will have read that William was his protector. In that boat.' The heat in her face had mantled again: only her throat was still chill and white, as if her heart would allow no commerce with her head. 'But the newspaper report doesn't say that they knew each other before.'

'Before?' The last word had dropped almost inaudibly from her lips.

'Johnny Canacka was born here, on Nantucket. His father came to us from the Marquesas on one of our whaleships. His mother was the cook in a boarding house for sailors down town. When she went to live with Canacka her kin cast her off.'

'It sounds rather as if she cast them off.'

'Dr Carver, that is no light thing. This is a small place. It's not as easy to defy convention here as it is in Boston.'

'It's not easy there either, ma'am.'

Miss Macy scrutinized me: sharp now, appraising. 'Canacka's father hired himself out as a fisherman. For a time he worked a boat with William's father. William knew Johnny Canacka from a child. They fished together. They were – well, perhaps you know how it is, between boys.'

'No ma'am, I don't.'

'They were knit like –' She picked up her tatting, set it down:

useless simile, since I knew even less about whatever bond had existed between them than she did. 'He still lives on the island. I wonder if you would, now that you are here. In – in a medical capacity. I wonder if –'

'I will speak to him.'

'Oh, I hoped that this is what you would say!' Again, that peculiar note of commonness, or commonality, as if all forms and ceremonies between us were redundant. 'But I must warn you that he doesn't live in the town. He keeps to himself. His dwelling is remote. It's all the way to the east of the island, at Sconset.'

'All the way?' I remembered the paring of land I'd glimpsed from the ferry. 'How far is that?'

'Seven miles. If you are willing, I know someone who can take you there.'

By now I was utterly mesmerized by her pale forehead with its animated vein, the intent bulge of her brow.

'I'll go at once.'

AN HOUR LATER I was jouncing in a cart down a rutted moorland road. An insidious breeze blew inshore, cooling the nervous sweat on my body. On leaving Miss Macy I'd gone directly, as per her instructions, to the Pacific Reading Room, housed in a building at the foot of Main Street Square, to find a Captain Bunker. This captain would take me to Sconset and back in time to catch the evening ferry, after which, I promised, I would write to her immediately.

I look back now at my arrogance with mingled astonishment and shame. All I can say in my own defense is that I felt strangely dejected when I realized that she was dismissing me – it was managed with such naturalness, and with such candid expressions of dependence on my help, that it took me a few moments to understand that this was what she was doing – and that I wouldn't see her again. I was elated but obscurely unhappy, full of high purpose but needled by an anxious excitement I couldn't account for, as I set off back down Main Street.

When I located the place, a high-ceilinged chamber with engravings of ships nailed to the dado rail, I found three old men hunched around a stove, smoking pipes. To this day I don't know why it was called a reading room since there wasn't a book to be seen; in fact it was hard to see anything at all above a certain height, so dense was the fug of tobacco rolling from the bowls of those pipes. Everything was dyed yellow by smoke: the smidgen of rug on the floor, the walls, even the sails of the engraved ships hanging from the kippered rail.

The yellowest of the three old sea devils admitted grudgingly to being Captain Bunker. On receiving the note that Miss Macy had given me, however, he knocked the ashes from his pipe without demur and led me silently into a yard where a light cart was parked under an awning. A horse was produced to go with the cart, and having shooed away my offer of payment with his yellow hand, the fellow took the reins and indicated the bare plank next to him. We were off, up through the town, out into unfenced fields, along a wide sandy road of parallel ruts, over flat land dusted with clumps of wind-twisted gorse. All about lay moors, tan as scrubbed deal, with water pooled in their hollows.

My driver neither spoke nor looked my way, and after a quarter of an hour those seven miles, punctuated only by the odd straggling milestone, began to seem very long.

'Will it be easy to find this Mr Canacka?' I burbled.

'Mebbe.'

'I believe that he is a private man.'

'Mebbe he is.'

'What does he do?'

'Same as his father did.'

We bumped on in silence for another half-mile. 'Will he speak to me?'

'Mebbe. And mebbe not.' Captain Bunker gave me a lapidary stare. 'Depends on what thee has to say.'

I decided to pounce. 'Well, sir. Do you, by any chance, know Mr Borden – the Hero of the *Providence*?'

'Knew him as a nipper,' replied the old Sphinx as we passed an outpost of stunted pines. 'Don't know him so much now.'

With this unanswerable aperçu he turned the cart into an avenue so sandy that it seemed half beach, bordered on either side by low fishermen's cottages, some with smoke shuddering up out of their roofs. At the very end of the sketchy road, where the sand threatened to spill over the cliff into the abyss, the captain stopped and, leaning back in his seat, pointed to the mist and spume erasing the horizon.

'Thee'll want to start walking here.'

'*Here?* But there's nothing beyond here.'

'Follow the path along the bluff. I will wait on thee.'

That was, apparently, all he was going to volunteer. I wanted to ask him if I should do it by flying, since I couldn't make out anything solid enough to stand on, but he'd already taken out his pipe, curved his shoulders against the wind, and begun to stoke a concealing cloud of tobacco.

I got out and walked blindly into the mist, like a fool in a fairy tale, until I came to the rim of the cliff. It was covered in a scrawl of bayberry. Directly ahead the churn of cloud and spray was split by a shaft of sun. There was the ocean again, stretching from side to side, heaving and bucking with its own life. A billion particles of salt and dissolved gas, a billion prisms of refracted light, hung suspended in every cubic foot. It surged and broke in a glassy rhythm.

I was skewered by a return of my old fear of the sea. It was as if I had come to the edge of the world, and could go neither forwards nor back. I stood there, my soft parts flinching helplessly, looking at the white saucer of the horizon, at the ledge of rock and the cantering lights on the water, until a nearby voice said,

'Have a care, friend. It's a long way down. Has thee lost thy way?'

A stranger had stolen up unnoticed by me on the coastal track that rose from the scrub and planted himself directly behind me. Save for a piece of cloth tied around his chest he was bare from the waist up, like a man from another time, and inked all over in fantastical patterns. His knotted blue-brown arms supported two creels; his head was a mass of filthy ringlets. A wiry beard skirted his chin – the beard, I thought confusedly, of an ancient chieftain, or a Roman emperor. He might have belonged to any civilization, and been any age from twenty to a hundred, so weather-beaten and discolored was his face.

'Yes,' I said. 'I'm looking for a John Canacka. Do you know where I might find him?'

'I am Canacka,' said the stranger, lowering the dark fins of his eyes. 'What's thy business with me?'

'I'm the friend of a man you know,' I began. 'I have come on his behalf. I am, in fact, his doctor. He is very ill. I believe you would speak to me if you knew how ill he was.' Why was I explaining myself to this disconcertingly self-possessed primitive? 'I am trying to make him well,' I went on automatically. There was a pleading quaver in my voice, a note that irked me.

'What is this man's name?'

'William Borden.'

'Well,' declared the ageless stranger, 'I am going home.' He hitched up his creels. Before I could protest he had walked away, tattered toga flapping dismissively. Just as he reached the end of the bluff, where the path dove into the scrub, he stopped and addressed me over his shoulder. 'Come.'

I staggered behind him along a narrow path that led through hoops of overarching spruce. Neither of us spoke. His back, I remember, was covered with knolls of muscle, crossed by a mad scripture of indigo stitching which I had no hope of deciphering. I perused that back fruitlessly as we walked. The sole of my right shoe had peeled away and made a fatuous slapping noise. When it felt as if we had tramped for miles the canopy gave way in a spurt of green onto a dune overlooking the sound. Set aslant to it, fringed with grasses and broom, sat a shanty built from scrap lumber with a sloping roof and a slit for a window. An overturned fishing smack lay a little way off. The wind was blowing in a frenzy from across the shingle a hundred feet below, sweeping upwards into the tangle of scoured roots that curtained the scarp.

I glanced back at the diminutive cluster of houses making up the village of Sconset. From here they resembled a patch of salt works.

In the distant west I could distinguish the outline of Nantucket town with its steeples and windmills, hemmed by swamp and plain, and the dark harbor studded with sails. Suddenly I yearned to be back there. This was a deathly place: dry, sand-choked. From time to time a gaunt sea-bird rose from the cliff with a screech and plummeted down to the strand. Above it all, mingling with the roar of the wind, came the thump of the ocean, *boom, boom, boom*, like the beating of a giant heart.

'This can't be where you live,' I burst out.

Canacka turned and looked at me for the first time since we'd set off. 'It is,' he said. And then, tilting his head at the shack, which was barely large enough to accommodate one man, let alone two, 'Get along inside.'

I squeezed after him through the batten door into an airless hole that stank of fish. The whole place – no more than a single room – seemed to have been put together from the remains of a shipwreck. There wasn't a level surface or a flush joint anywhere, and the wind sliced at us through the cracks. At the end of the room was a place for fire, a slab of stone raised over a crude hearth, giving way to a brick chimney. Three gutted flounder were hung up to dry from a brace. On the opposite side a ladder, above which a frayed rope dangled as a handrail, led to a loft. Except for a solitary chair there was no furniture at all.

Sliding his baskets down next to the hearth, my host went to the nearest wall and worried away at the panel. A fold-down tabletop made of common boards descended with an almighty squeal. He pulled the chair up to it, indicating that I was to sit here, and began to poke and blow at the embers in the fireplace. Heat rolled through the murk. Within minutes the warming stone set up a hiss as it met with the salt water draining from the creels. Canacka lowered his hands into a creel and raised a handful of something alive and legged and resisting, which he tossed into a blackened pot. After a moment he reached into a gap in the chimney breast, drew out a wedge of bread and broke it in half. Putting one chunk on the table, he started to chew on the other.

There was a whistling scream as whatever was in the pot came to the boil. He hooked it away and poured a share of its contents into a bowl set next to my untouched bread. Just then his hair, brushing past me, parted over his right ear. I saw that the auricle was a stub.

'Eat.'

There lay a crab with opaque eye stalks, claws still scissoring.

'I can't. Thank you. But, please – you. You eat.'

I crouched on the sandy hearth. He took the chair without a word and went about cracking the shells with his bare hands, tearing off the legs and sucking out the flesh, bending low at his work. The light of the fire threw the hinged shadow of his jaw across the wall. When there was only a heap of broken shells left he turned to me.

'What is thy question?'

In that stinking hut, faced with his hunger, I hardly knew.

'William Borden.'

'Aye.'

'Why is he ill? Why?'

He looked at me impassively. *Boom, boom, boom.*

'Ain't thee the doctor?'

'You sailed with him on the *Providence*.'

'I did.'

'You were very young. You were only a child. Your captain – Captain Fitzgibbon – was an indifferent captain.'

'Aye.'

'Did he – ah. Did he leave you to shift for yourself?'

'He was the captain. It was my work. To shift for myself, and for him.'

'But you were a boy. I've served on a ship. I know what it is like, that drudgery. It must've been hard on a boy. Those hours and hours of pointless toil. That never-ending round – until you feel as if you are going to part company with your reason.'

Canacka picked at his teeth. 'Aye. That's a ship, pretty much.'

I tried another tack. 'Was William Borden good to you?'

'He was.'

'He knew you before you went to sea together, I believe.'

'Who told thee this?'

'I've heard it said.'

'Many things are said. Many and many.'

'What things?'

'That I am a half-breed, and not a Friend, and don't belong here. That Will was a half-breed, like me, because his mama weren't from this island. But he was a true friend to me.'

'When you were boys together?'

'Aye. My daddy was a Taipi. He came to this island by fire. The papalangi landed their ships on Nukuheva and burned the valley of the Taipi. Every house. Every holy place. When my daddy shipped here he was called Canacka, but what was he? My mama raised me as a Friend of the Light. That was what she was before she knew my daddy. Then she ain't nothing nor no one neither.' Just when I thought he was done with this riddling speech, he tipped his frizzed head to one side and, with as much coy propriety as any Beacon Hill society lady adjusting the 'false front' of her hair-piece, inquired, 'Who is thy mama?'

'My mother is Mrs Austin Carver of Boston.'

'My mama was Miss Amity Chase of Nan-Tucket.' He pronounced the name as two distinct words. 'I am an American. An American, as Will is an American.'

He was one of the most self-contained people I have ever met. He spoke without gestures, his hands resting on his thighs; almost without inflection. But when he said *I am an American* he raised his left arm a fraction. My stomach swirled with an indefinable horror. Canacka's side was tattooed with the same fish-like torque, devouring its own tail, which I'd seen on Borden's body when he lay in the sick bay of the *Orbis*.

'What's that – that mark under your ribs?' I cried.

For a moment he didn't answer. His stillness was so complete that the thundering of the waves could be heard above the wind outside. Then his stippled lips opened in a smile. 'It was set there as a covenant between Will and me. Will had a hungry spirit, see. Couldn't be bound by this place. This place is only rocks and sand and women's tittle-tattle. Could be thee thinks Will joined the navy to serve his country. Could be thee thinks he joined up for glory. But I tell thee he joined 'cause his spirit was famished.'

'And you – why did you go?'

'I went 'cause I feared he would never come back. I feared the sea would swallow him up and that he'd go out of my sight forever.'

'And afterwards –' the feeling of horror, nameless and oily, was still coiling through me – 'Mr Borden kept you safe.'

'Aye,' said Canacka. 'Far as he was able.'

The wind chivvied and dartled at us, shaking that pitiful room. 'There is something I must ask you,' I ventured. 'At the court of inquiry you said very little. It was of course because you were in extreme distress. But I have read over what you said and there is a word, a word which puzzles me very much. The word is "*ika*". You repeated it. What is *ika*?'

Canacka stretched across that cramped space and touched his fingers to the grinning belly of one of the flounder above the hearth. 'This is *ika*.'

'This? *Fish?*'

The thing spun in the firelight.

'Aye.'

'Is that all?'

'It is everything.'

'All is not the same as everything.'

'Aye, friend. It is. It is life and death. *Ika* is an offering to the gods. It's a sacrifice.'

'A sacrifice?' The rustling word struck me dumb. His lids had dropped again, partly obscuring his gaze, yet I knew that he was still looking at me, noting every hesitation of mine – and that imperial gaze contained so much silent condescension, hinted at such a deep knowledge of my inadequacies, that I cringed. I wanted to say something penetrating, to nail him to the spot. Instead I found myself squaring my shoulders just like my father, and speaking in my father's hectoring, petty voice. 'Mr Canacka. Was there anything that happened, in those months at sea – anything at all – that you can – that you would like – to tell me?'

He shucked a crab shell into the fire and pushed his bowl away, then leaned towards me, wiping his mouth. 'What is thee? Is thee a priest?'

'No. No. A doctor. Only a doctor.'

'Thee has the look of a priest. There was a priest in Valparaiso who was as hungered as thee, as close to being a spirit as thee, ain't never a time he came near me but I kept looking to see if he ain't gonna float off the floor. And he was a cold fish, with his thin hands, always praying over me when we fetched up there. Will told him be gone, this boy ain't sick in his soul, get thee gone, thee bugger, thee'll not have him. He's blood of my blood, he is my brother.'

'I am not trying to convert you. I know you are not – not the foreigner you have been painted.'

'Ain't thee?' He seemed to sniff at me, disdainfully, as if sensing the rot within. 'Ain't thee a foreigner?'

'No. No, I am just – just an American, like you, just a doctor. Just a man,' I finished up inanely, 'in pursuit of the truth. And I don't believe in the supernatural.'

'Then thee's a fool.'

'Fool, or not, Mr Borden is very sick and I merely wish –'

The inked creature cocked his maimed ear. 'How is he sick?'

'He won't eat. He won't speak. He is very, very sad. He is not himself.'

'He ain't sick. He is sorrowful in his nature. Every hurt thing draws him. Every wounded thing. He goes to it like a shark to blood.'

I stared at his wild head with its furze of beard. In that moment he seemed to me, despite the traces of civilization in him, like the impervious messenger of a force far outside my experience; something at once unknown and impersonal.

'That I cannot believe. He was a well man, a whole man, when I first knew him. And a kind man, one of the kindest men I've ever met. I've thought long and hard about this, Mr Canacka –'

'Thinking too much on one thing is a sickness, Doctor. It's a sickness I ain't got. I won't be sick for any priest. I won't be sick for thee. And if thee loves Will Borden thee will let him go.'

I was angry now. 'For what? To come back to *you*, here? To sit in this hut?'

'Let him sit anywhere he likes. He has lost his courage. Don't matter what he does now.' He got up, a crazy mandala of patterns in the dusk of that room, swimming at me all blue legs and arms. 'I have eaten. I guess I am done here. Now go. Go.'

I STUMBLED BACK ALONG the cliff in a rage. As I hopped through the spruce my shoe came apart entirely and I flung its two halves, with my sodden sock, at the undergrowth, hoping that they would land in the sea. Damn the tattooed Quaker savage. Damn the old lump of scrimshaw who sat waiting for me in his tail-breaking cart, not troubling to hide his gratification at the way my self-control was falling to pieces.

I was shaken through and through by my interview with Canacka. A covenant! The suggestion that William Borden should have been in any way bound to this barbarous being was grotesque. But I had time and opportunity, as the cart rucked back down the road to Nantucket town and my mind began to clear slightly, to think over what I'd heard.

He is sorrowful in his nature. I'd denied it. But wasn't this exactly what I'd noticed on the *Orbis*: that Borden had a deep-rooted melancholy whose origins were mysterious to me? I wasn't telling a deliberate untruth when I'd insisted on his wholeness, any more than Borden himself had been when he presented this face to the world. Weren't we all, we civilized men and women, as I'd told Miss Macy, ready to live in unfreedom, to embrace our imprisonment in lies of habit and tradition? It came to me with a jolt (which was, in that cart, physical as much as intellectual) that we live by lying to ourselves daily about every last thing, by denying the truth not just about what we do and think, but about our very fears themselves.

All at once I felt a rush of terror – terror at my own civilized duplicitousness, my own fragility. I recalled Lenox's final remarks regarding Borden at the inquiry. *He speaks as if it were nothing. But he looked after us. He kept us alive. He sacrificed himself so we might live.* If Borden no longer appeared whole, if the mask had cracked, then was it because he was now insane, or because there was a self-immolating insanity in trying to wear such masks in the first place? Seen from this angle, his heroism was perhaps the maddest mask of all. Canacka had spoken of offerings to the gods, of sacrifices. But there were no gods outside ourselves. We *were* the gods. We were all guilty of perpetuating the myth of our immortality.

I have wondered, often, if there was something else – something that still troubles William, which he can't speak about. Sarah Clayborn, as thrusting as any man, turning herself into a New Testament prophet. Eliza Todd, who'd become her own sister. Borden, with his starved body, his muteness. But weren't they all mute? What if what we called their madness was a way of speaking without words? What were they trying to tell us – to tell me – that they couldn't tell us in any other way? What if I were to ask Borden the right questions, lead him towards speech, translate this broken attempt at communication back into its proper medium, the medium of language – wouldn't this bring him relief, wouldn't this break the spell that now bound him fast?

What if I could help him to *remember?*

There was a thread to be followed here, a way into the labyrinth, if I could only grasp it. I felt that I had the end between my fingers, that it was live with possibility, that the path would be shown to me.

Captain Bunker put me down at the basin on Easy Street as the afternoon was waning. I had struck out for Nantucket as a civilized man, a man in control of himself, and I was returning from it shook up and nauseated – when had I last eaten? After seeing Canacka eat, would I care if I never ate again? – a man who was more than a little in love; a man, what's more, with one bare and very dirty foot.

In front of me was the harbor with its tangle of boats, in which stray lights had begun to appear. The tide was coming in, and as I hurried to the wharf to catch my ferry the sun, sitting low behind the masts, set the waves a-glitter. They seemed to clatter together with a sigh. Above the horizon the reddening sky made an endlessly receding tunnel.

My breath was coming quickly now, forcing me to stop for a minute. A passing woman holding the hand of a small boy came up to me, cast a concerned glance at my face, and hurried away with her child. The day – ah, what was happening? – the day appeared to telescope inside out, until the glare of the water shrank to a circle the size of a pin head, liquid and infinitely far away. The briny air lay heavily on my lungs. As I stood gasping, a gull floated across the meniscus of the ocean, its wing raised like a hand extended in greeting.

How dazzling the blackly flashing waves were, at once transparent and occluded, bright and dark. It seemed to me just then as if I were staring straight into William Borden's heart. Or was it my own? The enormity of what I was going to undertake shook me. I knew that I had come to the brink of something, that I couldn't look away.

There is the truth, Hiram. Don't you fear it?

Behind me lay the jigsaw of factories, shops and inns, and beyond it, like an old print seen long ago – had I really been there only that morning? In my memory it was already tinged with nostalgia – the ghostly spine of Main Street. Ahead was the ocean, with its obscene heft and its steadily beating pulse; all the pressure of its hidden life. I leaned as far over the edge of the pier as I dared. Yes, I was afraid.

I couldn't have been more afraid if I'd been about to walk straight into that dark water.

FOURTEEN

O N GETTING BACK TO Charlestown in the early hours of
Sunday morning I went straight to my desk to write to Miss
Macy. I was aware, while writing, of choosing my words with deliberate care. The memory of her intelligent sympathy was like a refining
crucible. She made me want to be better and to *do* better. Isn't this
what all men feel about the woman they are falling in love with?

I wanted to impress her.

My interview with Johnny Canacka was — I was going to say,
unrevealing, but it was hardly that. I can't make out if he is
a civilized man, a half-civilized man, or a savage. Although
he professes a great attachment, still, to Mr Borden, he was
unwilling —

I crossed this out, and wrote 'unable' —

to shed any light on Mr Borden's illness. Nevertheless, I am
left with many new intuitions as a result of our meeting.

Canacka said something that angered me at first. He said that
Mr Borden has lost his courage. I didn't want to accept this, or

what it implied. To say that someone has lost his courage is to say that he is a coward, unable to act in the face of fear. It seems to me that the ultimate measure of courage is how we behave when the thing we fear most, death, is near. Mr Borden didn't fear death on the *Providence*, and I saw no sign of any such fear in him on the *Orbis*. Indeed more recently he seems to be indifferent to preserving his own life. I really don't believe that he has ever been afraid of dying.

How, then, does he lack courage now? What is he afraid of? I wanted to reject this imputation of his failure of courage completely. But then it came to me that he *is* afraid. He is afraid, not of dying, but of living.

I paused for a moment, absorbing the stillness of the night. The old commodore's words at the court of inquiry seemed to breathe through the silence. *Life – that is the thing, is it not? Dear life.* But wasn't life itself precisely the difficulty? Wasn't I surrounded, every day, by people who proved the precariousness of the whole human endeavor? I dipped my pen into my inkwell again.

That he is a true hero I don't doubt. But my dear Miss Macy, I begin to wonder if we don't do our heroes a great injustice. It must be as terrible to be a god as it is to be a slave. To be a hero one has, I think, to have an immense capacity for illusion, in order to be able to lead men, to ignore impossibilities, to laugh at our natural human fears, to give ideas precedence over reality. It sounds not a little like madness! But it occurs to me that we ask our heroes to live exactly such a life for us. We ask them to make the sacrifice on our behalf. The person such a hero has to persuade, first and foremost, is himself, or no one else will be persuaded. What happens when this capacity for self-persuasion fails? What does one do when one has lost the illusions that have made life bearable? Isn't one then in touch, at last, with what is real – in touch with uncertainty and terror, just like the rest of us ordinary men?

We say that men and women who have lost touch with reality have gone mad. But is a life without illusions bearable at all? Isn't that what true madness is?

THE FOLLOWING TUESDAY AFTERNOON Goodwin and I were working our way through the men's wing, dispensing postprandial soda powders, when we heard the sound of running.

'Cassius, Frank.' Mansfield put his head – bright-eyed, vulpine, artificially perky; the measure of morphine I'd given him after lunch had been a large one – into the room. 'Follow me, at the double.' I scarcely had a chance to look up before he was off again. 'We're about to take delivery of a Mr Adam Thornton,' he panted as he and I galloped (and Goodwin trotted) down the stairs. 'From Salem. Merchant. Shipping and navy provisions.' He gave me a tight smile. 'Should be right up your alley, Cassius. You can swap anecdotes of the high seas.'

I didn't reply. Richard had been perversely disapproving when he discovered that I'd carried out my plan of visiting Nantucket, and I was finding his little jokes increasingly tiresome.

'I've called in three attendants for this one,' he threw out as we reached the front door, which was being held open for us by Miss Joy. Through it we could see a burly middle-aged gentleman in a smartly cut jacket being manhandled from a chaise. One of the arms of the jacket had been torn almost right off. Two similarly attired, prosperous-looking men stood well out of the way of any stray limbs. 'Thornton's business partners have brought him in,' said Richard, dipping his head at them. 'He's been raging all morning.'

'Would you like Mr Thornton to rest up in the cottage, Richard?' wheezed Goodwin. He was folded over, clutching his side. 'Resting up in the cottage' meant being locked up in one of the strong rooms.

'No. Let's start him off gently. Two white pills and an afternoon of hydropathy, I think. His wife is here too. I don't want to frighten her.'

He nodded encouragingly at a tiny woman with a stricken expression, who flitted behind the others as Thornton was hauled up the steps. When he passed us, Thornton kicked out twice. The first kick nearly caught Goodwin on the shins; the second took a gay streamer of paint off the door.

Miss Joy sucked at her lips. 'Must you deal with this, Dr Mansfield? You know you felt poorly earlier. And now you've had to race about, on top of it all.'

'Once more unto the breach, Felicity. You might bring me a fortifying cup of tea after Dr Carver and I have spoken to Mrs Thornton.' He looked around for me, as was his habit. 'Coming, Cassius?'

Yes, I thought. And no doubt you'll need another fortifying dose of morphine to go with that tea.

'Of course,' I said.

*

ON FINISHING MY ROUNDS I went to the record room to write up Thornton's admission notes.

Our interview with Mrs Thornton had been distressing. She tried her hardest to cry quietly, surreptitiously wiping away her tears, and to answer Mansfield's questions with dignity, but her confusion was extreme. I couldn't help feeling that her husband's madness, if that's what it was, had caused her to suffer intensely – almost as much as he did, and to the point of making her ill too. In her case one might say that the marriage itself was pathogenetic, and that by removing him from the family home we were treating not merely one, but two afflicted people.

Adam Thornton had long been subject to alternating spells of exaltation and depression of the spirits. His wife told us that in his states of depression he talked little, scarcely answered questions, went to bed early and rose late; that he neglected his clothes, refused to walk, ride, or even attend church, wrote no letters, read no newspapers, and took no interest in his business. This would continue from two to three weeks, after which he typically became more active and cheerful.

I looked over what I'd just written.

As a first sign he begins to smile again, and to answer his wife's questions; then he sits up later, sleeps less, rises earlier, and takes exercise when asked. In a few days he starts to converse freely, follows the newspapers, and plays at chess. Next he calls for his best clothes – is anxious to attend church, visit everywhere, and see everybody – is full of business – writes letters to his associates and creditors – then to the editors of the newspapers to express his opinion on what he has read that day – then to all parts of the United States, to the president himself, and to the governments of England, France, Holland, Germany – becomes merry – dances – sings – is irascible, and offended when opposed – passionate and violent – tears his clothes, swears, strikes, kicks, and breaks windows. After his exaltation has reached its peak he collapses swiftly back into depression once more.

Yet the change from Thornton's depressed to his exalted state was always gradual. In the initial stages his business letters were well-written, his plans shrewd, and his judgment sound: during this phase, which would last for up to a month at a time, he would appear quite well, and was, Mrs Thornton insisted, a kind-hearted, intelligent, agreeable man.

I was flummoxed. This didn't fit any pattern I'd observed among our other patients so far. There seemed to be no amnesia or loss of identity in this case. Adam Thornton knew who he was; and judging by the bellowing that had come from his room all afternoon, he knew that he didn't want to be here.

'WILL, I'D LIKE TO talk to you about – about ships.'

It was a day or two later. Borden, who was getting ready for his usual walk, waited obediently for me to help him into his coat. I laid it across the back of his parlor sofa and settled myself in a chair.

'Ships?' He stared at me as if I'd asked him about butterfly collecting, or the rings of Saturn.

'Yes. About your career. About the sea.'

I'd had enough of these walks: their geriatric hesitations, their silences. It was time to enter the labyrinth, to start coaxing him towards recollection – towards speech.

'Ships.' He sat down on the sofa. Was there the vestige of a familiar response, a wryness, in his expression? 'You have no interest in ships.'

'Well, let's begin with our time together on the *Orbis*.'

'I've told you, Hiram. I don't remember much about it.'

'But you do remember some things. You remember that I dislike the sea. You've just admitted it.'

A slight but unmistakable tremor of the muscles hedging the mouth. 'Yes, I remember that. Satisfied? Are we going to walk now?'

'No. Do you remember the way it was piled up all around the ship like – like snow?'

'*Snow?*'

'Yes, snow. Great big glistering banks of snow. Or pitched like sheet metal?'

His smile was as open and undefended as it was before, in that earlier time. My heart jumped at it. 'Snow. If you like. Yes. Why not.'

'And the Galapagos? And those goddamn tortoises? That evil stew? Being ill with dysentery? Do you remember that?'

'Yes.'

'And then we were becalmed.'

The smile vanished. A hesitant nod, so hesitant that it was barely there.

'And then – Fryar. Fryar was flogged at the mast. There was a storm brewing, the sky was full of black cloud –'

Borden got to his feet, his hands held out in a bizarre gesture of supplication. 'I can't see it,' he said. And then he said again, 'No, I can't.'

'We were on deck. You were *there*. You spoke to me.'

'I don't remember.'

But I did: I saw that strange sky, its arterial purple, the light creeping along the horizon; felt the gleeful pressure of the breeze, so longed for and now suddenly dreadful, the heave of the ship, and the spatter of blood on my body, and as I spoke I became aware of a slow, twisting ribbon of sound, a moaning, that seemed at first to be flowing from the heart of this memory like a rising gale, as if the storm had escaped the bounds of time.

I returned to myself with a contraction of terror. Then I realized that the source of the sound wasn't in me, or even in the room. It was coming from the corridor outside.

'What is it, Hiram?'

'The new patient. Adam Thornton. The one – well, you've probably seen him. And heard him. Listen.'

We could both hear it quite clearly now: an endless chant of grief, rising and falling like plainsong.

Borden hung over me, towering, sharp-boned. 'Adam Thornton ain't mad.'

'Are *you* mad, William?'

'No.'

'Ah. Then why are you here?'

His voice, issuing from that withered frame, was as dead and dry as the voice of a judge. 'I am here because I have no refuge from myself.'

*

ON SATURDAY MORNING I was alone in Mansfield's study, dealing with the asylum correspondence while he paid a visit to our medical suppliers in town, when I heard loud voices outside the door. Miss Joy was spread in front of it, barring the way to the very last person I'd expected to see: Adam Thornton's wife.

'Mrs Thornton! May I help you?'

'I must speak to Dr Mansfield.' She stood before me in an uneasy, resentful attitude, her head bent. 'I made a mistake.'

'It's out of the question.' Miss Joy smiled. Countermanding something was guaranteed to make her dolefully happy. 'The doctors aren't at leisure to meet with you now.'

'Thank you, Miss Joy, that will be all. Dr Mansfield may be out, but I have a few minutes to spare.' I was amused at her expression – she was as startled as a sniper who finds herself on the wrong end of the firing squad. 'Mrs Thornton, please come in and sit down.'

I took hold of Mrs Thornton's shoulder and maneuvered her into the room. Once over the threshold, with the door shut behind us, she continued to stand around in that curiously belligerent way.

'I should never have let them take him. They said he was worse than ever. But I'm used to him. He didn't seem any worse to me. I let them tell me what to do and I shouldn't have. He's *my* husband. Mine!'

I led her to an armchair near Mansfield's bookshelves. They were full of novels and works of poetry and it was brought home to me, not for the first time, that we really didn't have the least idea of what we were doing.

Mrs Thornton sat down heavily, but still did not look up. I could tell, however, by the quivering of her neck that she was weeping.

'Ma'am, I think you did right.'

'Right? It can't be right for him to be here while we are at home without him, can it?' She sobbed. 'Oh, Doctor, may I see him?'

'I'm sorry, ma'am. You can't. Hospital rules. You used the plural just now. Do you have children?'

'Yes, two. A little boy and a girl. Seven and nine.'

'They must be your first care now – your children. And you yourself.'

'But who will care for Adam?'

'Mrs Thornton, I can't put this emphatically enough. You must think of *yourself*. You're worn out by living with him, aren't you?'

She raised her eyes at last. 'Oh, Dr Carver, I am. God help me. I am.'

'Go home. Look after your children. Let us look after your husband. I promise you that I will visit him this afternoon.' An uncomfortable thought occurred to me. 'Do you – do you have sufficient means for the present?'

Her head flew right up. 'Yes,' she said proudly – and then, hitting away her tears with the back of her hand, added with a trace of asperity, 'Adam has always provided for us. Always.' Her red-rinded lids stopped their beating; her lips drew down to a thread. She spoke the words that followed without any apparent sense of paradox. 'He has been the best of husbands to me.'

AFTER LUNCH I ASKED Miss Joy to report back to me in Mansfield's office. It was coming up to two o'clock, when she normally oversaw the washing of the floors in the women's wing, and I had to summon her from the broom cupboard. She came downstairs wielding a mop.

I reviewed my case notes without any particular hurry. 'How is Mr Thornton today?'

'He's been complaining of cramps in his legs.'

'Perhaps he's suffering from a lack of exercise?'

Miss Joy lowered the mop to the ground as if it were a regimental ensign, and we two heralds negotiating on the field of battle. 'He shouldn't be. When he's not raving he's been traipsing up and down his room since he got here, morning and night.'

'Has he had scheduled shower baths? Wet packs?'

'Yes, daily. It's the only way to get him to rest.'

'Is he eating? Drinking?'

'Eating, yes. He won't drink our ale.'

The asylum 'ale' was a filthy brew of dilute small beer and molasses. A mere sip made me bilious. 'An eminently sensible decision. Please give him unadulterated water in future, Miss Joy.'

Miss Joy smiled gamely. Her face was damp, either from strain or the cold cream she routinely used. 'Dr Carver, if I could –'

'We're almost through, Miss Joy. Just a few more questions. Now what was it I was about to . . . ? Ah, yes. Here we are. Sleeping?'

'I've already mentioned that.'

'Have you? Oh, so you have. The pacing. Morning and night. So that means no sleeping?'

She stood a little straighter. 'No.'

'One last one. Bowel movements?'

'As far as I know, Mr Thornton's bowel movements are perfectly regular.'

'As far as you know. So they're not being – recorded?'

'Not at the moment.' Spoken through her teeth.

'Please record them. We need to rule out any physiological irregularities. There have been some cases – not many, it's true, but some – where a breakdown in mental functioning has been one of the sequelae of an underlying somatic condition. There are examples, for instance, of sufferers who –'

'Of course, Dr Carver.' By now she was willing herself not to break ranks. It took considerable effort on her part.

'Thank you, Miss Joy. I know I can rely on you to be thorough. Punctilious. Devout, even, in the smallest details; such details as might *floor* others.' Bull's eye. Her gaze flew upwards. I followed its trajectory. It was fastened on the ceiling, as if its plaster were permeable to her. 'Is anything wrong? You look somewhat agitated.'

'I've a lot to do. If that's all, Doctor, I really must see to the washing of the upstairs corridor now.'

Poor woman. It was unfair to play with her any longer. Though she had thoroughly deserved it, I felt dirtied.

'Why, certainly. I'll see you at tea-time.' I held my notebook pregnantly aloft. 'Oh, and Miss Joy.'

She picked up her mop. She seemed ready to impale me on it. 'Yes, Doctor?'

I shut the book with a snap. 'Bowels, remember.'

I watched Miss Joy decamp before going up myself to the men's wing and knocking on Thornton's door.

He was on his feet, pacing, his shirt unfastened at the collar and darkened from the neck down by a V of sweat. He sported nearly

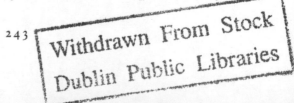

a week's beard growth, which gave him the jauntily vicious look of an assassin.

'So, Mr Thornton. How are you feeling?'

'I remember you. You're the beanstalk from the day I was brought in. Where's the other one?'

'If you mean Dr Mansfield, he's out on business. I am to be your physician this afternoon.' I sat down on his bed. 'Please take a seat.'

'I'd rather stand.'

'How are the cramps?'

'Crampy.'

I sighed. He was going to be one of those.

'Thank you for not saying "we", anyhow.'

'"We"?'

'Dr Mansfield always says, "How are we feeling?" As if he and I are just two old lunatics chewing the fat together.'

I suppressed a smile. 'Do you think you're a lunatic?'

'Is that a trick question?'

'Is Dr Mansfield's?'

'Very canny, Doctor. No. I reckon he's just being a hoity-toity bastard.'

'Well, I don't mean to be condescending. Even though *you've* called *me* a beanstalk. I really do want to know what you think.'

'Truly?'

'Yes.'

'I ain't any crazier than you are.'

'Hmm, I'm not sure that's answered the question.'

Thornton laughed. 'Well, I apologize for my remark, Doctor. You're a rum 'un, and no mistake.' He shook his locks dazedly. 'I think I will sit for just a moment, if it's all the same to you.'

'Of course.' I pulled up the bedside chair and he swerved down onto it. Now we were almost face to face. At close range I could see that the skin above the line of his beard was fiery and dry. 'How *do* you feel?'

'I'm troubled. I've been expecting my wife to come. She'll soon set Dr Mansfield straight about this supposed madness of mine. But she ain't been to see me.' A crooked look darted across his eyes. 'I wonder if I can beg a favor of you.' He leaned forwards confidingly, pulling at his hair. 'I've been robbed.'

'*Robbed?*'

'Yes. They've taken away my pocket book, my money, my gold watch. My knife, rule, pencil, my hair comb! I'd like a comb. I don't like Lucy to see me like this.'

'Those things were taken for your own safety.'

'What can I do to myself with a comb, Doctor? I must comb my hair before Lucy comes.'

'You mustn't expect her, Mr Thornton.'

'Oh, but I know her. She can't be parted from me. She won't stay away. She'll tell Dr Mansfield I'm sane.'

'Mr Thornton, she has come. But we can't let her see you. It's against our regulations here. Hasn't this been explained to you?'

'No. No one told me this.' He lowered his head and rubbed the flat of his hand slowly over his chin. In an instant his entire face had turned to shale: crumbling, gray. The slippage of his despair was so precipitous that it was like witnessing the opening up of a sink-hole. 'Oh, Lucy,' he moaned. 'Oh my poor girl. Oh, Lucy.'

'Mr Thornton, you must bear up.'

'I can't. Oh God, oh Jesus, I can't.'

As I crouched down beside him I felt unexpectedly out of my depth. 'Mr Thornton, I will get you that comb.'

'There ain't no need now. No need.' Hauling himself over to the bed, he crawled onto it, still moaning. 'No. No. No. Oh, Lucy.'

FIFTEEN

I BROUGHT THORNTON A COMB the very next morning. He was still in bed at ten o'clock, sleeping as if drugged, though he'd had no pills since his admission. I left the comb on his washstand and noticed, when I paid him a visit later that day, that he had straightened his hair. He seemed very downcast, and barely acknowledged me. But from what Mrs Thornton had told us I predicted an end to his pacing, and a return to a state resembling normality, and I was right. In the next few days he became meek; biddable. He took no further trouble over his appearance, but he ate whatever was given to him, used his chamber pot every morning, and continued to sleep deeply. I spoke with him in the afternoons and he was always polite, though he didn't say much. His only continued sign of resistance – if it could be called that – was that he persisted in asking if his wife had come, and if he could see her.

'Richard, I've observed him carefully for a week now and I don't believe that he is insane. Apart from his initial agitation he has otherwise been perfectly calm and reasonable.'

'Aha. But you don't deny that he was raging for the first four days of his confinement?'

'No. But that could be ascribed to his distress at being taken from his family and brought here against his wishes.'

'Thornton's own friends brought him to us, Cassius.'

'I'm sure that no man is ever sent here except by persons who call themselves his friends. It's still my belief that he's no more insane than you or I. He is particularly sad since he thought Mrs Thornton might come and see him, only to discover that she is sent away whenever she calls – she has a number of times now, you know – on the grounds that he might be injured by her visits.'

'And how the devil does Thornton know that she comes and is sent away?'

'Well, he asked me, and I took it upon myself to tell him.'

'You know full well that it is our considered policy not to communicate facts to our patients which might distress them! Is it any wonder that his spirits are depressed? You are to blame – you are very much to blame! I've a good mind to remove you from this case, and if I didn't already have eighty others to attend to I would do so at once.'

'Richard, if I broke with asylum policy it was for very specific diagnostic reasons.'

'Diagnostic? In what way *diagnostic*?'

'You see, quite simply, I believe that Mr Thornton's resulting state of depression – which, by the by, I anticipated – is further evidence of his essential soundness of mind.'

'What on earth do you mean?'

'Well, deception might satisfy an insane man, but it will just tip a rational one into despair. By this test Mr Thornton is quite demonstrably sane.'

'Cassius. Please. I knew when you came here that you needed scope – more scope for your intelligence and ambition than you'd yet been given. Indeed I think you know that I applaud these qualities in you.'

'Thank you, Richard.'

We regarded each other in silence.

'But?' I hazarded.

'But you go too far. You seem never to know when to stop. If I give instructions that something is not to happen, then I expect you to adhere to those instructions. Do you understand me?'

'I'm very sorry, Richard. I do understand.'

'Very well, then. Let's get on with our work. Who's next on your list this afternoon?'

'William Borden. Before I go – may I confirm that you did give me permission, as Mr Borden's physician, to keep Miss Macy informed about his progress?'

Mansfield scrubbed his scalp vigorously with both hands. 'You see. This. *This* is what I was referring to. It's push, push, push with you.'

'I don't know what to say, Richard. You were so obviously upset. I merely wanted to make sure that I didn't do the wrong thing again and upset you further.'

'Oh good Lord. "Do the wrong thing"? "*Upset*"? You really don't have the most basic idea of how rules work, do you?'

He was truly angry now. 'I'm not asking you to obey my instructions as a personal favor to me. This is how institutions *function*. If everyone behaved like you, we'd have mayhem. I can only imagine what merry hell you must have created on that ship of yours.'

'Talking of which –'

'Oh, for pity's sake. Yes, write to her. I said you could and I can't, at present, see the harm. God knows it will occupy some of those excessive energies of yours. But watch out, please.'

'You can't seriously think she's a risk to him, Richard. She's utterly devoted. She's – she's selfless!'

Mansfield's ill-temper subsided as quickly as it had arisen. His crinkled face was ivory with fatigue. 'Not a risk to *him*, no. I know that you admire her selflessness. But I fear that like all truly selfless people, she might just turn out to be a despot.'

AT THE END OF May I had another communication from Ruth Macy. My hands shook as I opened it.

'Your letter has moved me a great deal,' she began.

You say that it is we, we others, we ordinary men and women, who break extraordinary men like William – men of courage and action – by demanding that they suffer on our behalf. If this is true then it's indeed an unforgivable thing. I've asked myself if I'm guilty of this. Did I forget, like those others, that he is a man? Did I take what I wasn't entitled to?

If I did, then why do I feel so cheated? So dispossessed?

I have often wondered why he chose me, you see. His life has been so varied, so full of event, whereas mine – but you've seen a little of my life. I'm an unremarkable woman, Hiram Carver. I fear I may have nothing to offer a man like William Borden. When I met him I became interesting to myself for a while, and now that he's gone I can't go back to being the person I used to be. I feel I am somehow *less* than I was.

If Johnny Canacka can't help us to see into William's suffering, then there is only one person who can, and that is William himself. I know that he will speak to you, that there are bonds between men, former comrades, that a woman can't enter into. I have perfect trust in your perspicacity. In your eloquence. I hope you won't object if I tell you that I've given you a new name. Dr Mansfield may call you Cassius, but he has mistaken his Roman in you. In my private thoughts you are Cicero.

While I was still taking this in she seemed to step right up and, casting off all wordly formalities, to whisper her conclusion in my ear.

I have told myself that I must not ask thee this, but I cannot help it. Does he remember me?

I was grossly flattered by this letter. Cicero! Without meaning to, she'd hit home. When you've been called Hissy all your life, to be renamed in this way is intoxicating. And then – I was in her private thoughts . . .

I have often wondered why he chose me. How could anyone not have lost his heart to that single-minded little woman? It was perfectly clear to me (yes, I reflected, Miss Macy was right, I *was* perspicacious) that Borden had chosen her because she alone, of everyone he had met, hadn't the slightest interest in how his world worked. She'd ignored him, she'd turned her back on him, she didn't want to hear about his heroism or his silly importance. Ships? The sea? She may have made her money from them, but she cared for them even less than I did. She couldn't see him for the colossus he was. She saw a man hidden in the shadows, who asked her about herself – and what she herself was, she didn't yet know.

But she knew me. She'd recognized *me*. Though there were times when I believed that I would never carry this journey off, she was drawing me, through the force of her candor and her conviction, the firmness of her hand on the thread, directly to the heart of the mystery.

Oh, Cicero, indeed. When I look back now at the young man who received this note, and kept it in his coat pocket with the page folded back to that particular blandishment, and reread it every day in order to nerve himself to his task, I can hardly believe that I didn't appreciate what was staring me in my dull Ciceronian face all the time: that her last thought, then and always, was of him.

I CAN SAY THIS now. He was just as much a fabrication to me as she was, back then. I can see that I invented him, filled in the gaps, to satisfy myself – my own hollows, my own starved sensibilities.

'William. You said that you have no refuge from yourself. But what if the answer to – to your suffering, lies in you?'

'In me?'

'Yes.'

'There's nothing in me, Hiram, except confusion.'

I sat on the only hard chair in Borden's parlor, with my hands resting on its wooden arms. Though my whole attention was locked on him, I felt, strangely, as if I were the one who was pinioned.

'What about you?' he said. 'What's in you?'

'Is that what you want? Me first?'

'Yes. You first.'

'Well. I am a doctor. I was a sailor, for a while. No – I tried to be a sailor. I failed. And now I'm trying to be a doctor. Is this right? Is this what you want to hear?'

'Yes. I don't know. Yes.'

'A sailor – a sailor. That's what I tried to be. But. The incessant talk of *lines* – which any right-thinking person would call ropes. And rank. And glory. And ropes! Always ropes! All the splicing and hauling and tying and untying of ropes! Halyards and lanyards and clew lines and sheet lines and bobstays and braces. I didn't under-stand the slightest thing about it. Not the glory. Not the ropes.' I felt, shamelessly, like giggling. 'Can I tell you something?'

'Go on.'

'I still don't know how to tie a goddamned bowline knot.'

'I can teach you.'

'Don't you damn well *dare*. I wished every day on that blasted ship that the blasted ropes were around my neck. Remember Fryar's knots?'

Borden did not reply. His face took on what I'd come to think of as its idol's look: polished, venerable, aloof.

'Oh, come along, Will. Try. If I'm going to do this then so must you.'

'I'll try, Hiram. I'm trying – I am.'

'Fryar. All that tying and untying. *No, no, no, boys. Smaller in the hole. Ease it round. Pull the ears now. Pull, pull, pull! Pull that rabbit! Close it up tight! If it ain't right we'll begin again. Turn it over and break its back*.' As if from nowhere fury surged in me, rising and cresting and rising anew. 'I hated him.'

'Maybe. But you feared him more.'

'*Feared* him? I didn't fear that slicked-up kiss-ass. I *loathed* him.'

'Aye. You feared him for the same reason you hated him. Because he was as weak as you.'

I was ready to roar at him that he was wrong, wrong, when I realized that it was true. My anger drained away, and where it had been a sense of dread seeped up. Wasn't this second sight, this sense of the transcendent, what I longed for from William Borden? Why, when it arrived, did it terrify me? It alarmed me almost as much as the tenuousness of his wasted body. Weak. I was weak. And Fryar was weak –

'That day, William. *That day*. We flogged Fryar.'

'Yes. And then the wind rose.'

'So you do remember.'

'I remember indistinctly. I can see dark shapes without any clear form. It's like looking into a room through a dirty window. Sometimes there's light, part of a face, an eye, a staring eye. I don't understand it. Behind it all, or *inside* it, there's noise, a roaring noise, as if there's an – some animal trying to get out.'

'There was no noise. It was perfectly still. That noise was inside your head.'

'What about the eye, Hiram?'

'That eye was Fryar's.'

'Aie, aie, aie.' A keening sound, like a savage chant. His skull-like head lolled sideways. Again he made that awful sound. 'Aie, aie, aie.'

I grasped his wrists. My heart hopped beneath my ribs, but I drove on, willing myself to remain calm. 'What happened that day, Will? *What happened to Fryar?*'

'Don't you know, Hiram? He was the sacrifice.'

'What do you mean? We had to punish him. Fryar was violent – he'd attacked another man. You said it yourself. There has to be discipline. There has to be control.' I stared at him, at his brambly legs and riveted arms, with a sudden misgiving. 'Doesn't there?'

'Aye. But ain't there violence in you, Hiram? Ain't it there in me? We can't flog it out of each and every one of us. We fix it so we sacrifice the weakest. That's the way it's always done. And you see –' his head lunged towards me, his teeth clacking – 'our sacrifice was accepted. It raised the wind.'

I quailed instinctively, as if at a rain of blood. *Our sacrifice was accepted.*

Then I recovered myself. Second sight? What a delusion.

He was mad. Quite mad.

SIXTEEN

WHEN I WENT TO Borden's rooms the following afternoon, intending to go on with our give-and-take, I found that he'd retreated back into himself. He was sitting at his window with his face turned to the river. A full summer moon had already risen and hung on the edge of the sky, diffusing its ghostly light over the estuary below. The parlor was filled with green shadows, against which Borden's figure stood out like a dark relief. The water sounded so close: the murmur of its passage could be heard in the silence.

'How are you now, William?'

He didn't reply or look around. The man was gone and the idol had taken his place. He'd become a thing of bronze.

'HE'S STOPPED SPEAKING, RICHARD. He won't say a word to me.'

'Is he eating?'

'Not really. A little bread. Milk, sometimes. He won't touch meat.'

'Do you know what might have caused this?'

'No. I've no idea.'

Mansfield scrutinized me somberly. 'That is not good news.'

'I've – I've seen him like this once. On board ship, when he first fell ill. He wouldn't take anything at all, unless I fed him. And he refused to speak then too –'

'Don't fret about that for the moment, Cassius. No one has ever died of silence. But we must persuade him to eat something more.' He paused, considering. 'I'm going to arrange to have his meals sent up to his room. Sit with him, please. Cut up his meat for him. Spoon it in, do whatever it takes. I want you to get food into his stomach.'

'What if I can't?'

'You will. You've done it before.' Mansfield's eyes dwelled on me. 'I've been meaning to ask you this. You've been distracted lately. Is something wrong?'

'Oh no, no. Nothing.'

'Good. That's all right, then. Other than –' He pointed at my ribs, mimed lifting a fork to his lips. 'Please. While you're feeding Borden. I won't state the obvious.'

MISS MACY NOW BEGAN to write to me several times a week. At first I welcomed these letters. Then, as the days wore on and Borden still refused to speak, or take proper food, my sense of guilt was mixed with a swelling panic. I started to see the truth of Mansfield's warning: I found it impossible to temper her expectations. Because she was so willing to sacrifice herself to her lover's cause, there was no solid ground on which to oppose her. What was more, her faith in his recovery was of one substance with her faith in me. There were moments when I felt this faith, which was presented by her as an unalloyed tribute to my skill, as a heavy weight. As I held her letters in my useless hands I could almost believe, to my shame, that her love might have been an equally troublesome thing to carry about the world; a prize, yes, but an unmanageable one, like an amulet that had the power to take on a life of its own.

Though I didn't admit this to Richard, I *was* distracted. Since Borden's arrival the asylum no longer seemed like the shelter it once was. I felt the tug of the insane, heard the clamor of their affliction, in a way I hadn't before. It was like standing in the center of a conflagration while shouts went up all around me, until to my scorched senses they became a single howl of bewildered human grief.

Are you my sister's child?
Does my wife come?
Do you feel a change?
Does he remember me?
Aie, aie, aie. Aie, aie, aie.

In the evenings before my final rounds began I sometimes took refuge in the summer house at the top of the hill, where I sat on the ground with my head bowed, miserably inhaling the smoky odor of the roses. I was stunned to realize that I missed Caro. After our falling-out, though she no longer visited, she continued to write to me: beautifully crafted, polite letters that appeared to say one thing and mean another. Once she sent me a doily which she'd crocheted 'for you to use on your tea tray', as though it were a matter of course that everyone should own such a thing. I held its silky web in my hands for many anxious moments, like a coded message on which the safety of nations depended.

I had no tray and I seldom drank the asylum tea.

I couldn't entirely avoid my father. He arrived in the women's wing one June day on a board inspection, just as I was brushing Miss Todd's hair. This brushing was something I'd begun to do spontaneously during my morning visits to her. She was still only partly dressed when we made our early rounds, and being so dishevelled caused her great anguish. It was easier to help her than to scold her (which Felicity Joy did at the least opportunity). We became complicit in dodging that harridan, and making sure that Miss Todd's cap was properly pinned by breakfast time. My spirits were usually low, and this simple ceremony buoyed me as much as it calmed her. Whenever I felt the ridges of her skull under my fingers I was again filled with a strange tender hope – hopefulness for myself and for my own life, for my work, and for those in my care.

But we hadn't anticipated Papa, who opened the door a stealthy inch as a prelude to rudely flinging it wide.

He surveyed us with thinned lips. 'What in God's name are you doing, Hiram?'

'Good morning, Papa. I am assisting a patient.'

'Is this part of your normal routine here?'

'Of course. We support a practical approach in all our treatments. Occupational therapy, if you will.'

'Occupational therapy? For whom – for you, or for this old crone?'

I placed my hands firmly on Miss Todd's shoulders. A soft rumble was building in her throat. 'Papa, will you step outside, please?' I knew the warning signs by now, and I wanted to get him out of the room. 'Thirty strokes,' I said, putting the brush in her hand, 'and no cheating, mind, or I'll know when I get back.'

'Oh, that man is Satan,' she whispered. 'He wants to chew on your living bones and drink your blood. Be careful, my darling.'

'Good God,' said my father, once we were in the corridor. 'Does Mansfield know how you spend your time?'

'Naturally. Dr Mansfield approves every one of our therapeutic programs.' This was, strictly speaking, untrue. Richard was so busy that I sometimes spared him by giving him the outline of my methods, but not the details.

'Well, I'm relieved to see that you're up and dressed and hard at it, though it's not even eight o'clock yet. That's something, I suppose.' He eyed me narrowly. 'Mansfield has given me a good report of you.'

'Father, is it the asylum you've come to inspect, or me?'

I was treated to his frostbitten smile. 'Both.'

'Then please set down this in your report. I won't have anyone speaking about my patients in front of them as though they had no ears. As if they can't hear, or understand. Or feel insulted.'

'Do you mean that witch in there with the undone hair? She's crazed. Anyone but you would recognize that she's beyond help.'

'Crazed or not, you might have said good morning to her.'

'Well, well, Hiram. You certainly *have* woken up. You'll have to wish her good morning on my behalf. I'm due in the men's wing in five minutes.' He half turned, stopped, faced me again. 'Your sister warned me that you were like a man possessed. Let me give you some advice. In our profession there is such a thing as dedication. And then there's the sort of excessive enthusiasm that is unhelpful to the patient. I hope you can remember the difference.'

If he hadn't left, I might well have killed him then.

I see that I have inadvertently included Ruth Macy in that chorus of the mad. Let it stand.

IF I WAS OVERWORKED, Mansfield was hardly less so. He and I made no distinction between weekdays and weekends. Frank Goodwin, on the other hand, was frequently missing that summer. I'd stroll into the dispensary during my free hour on a Saturday, hoping to perk myself up by chaffing him for a few minutes, and find that he wasn't there. *Poof!* Vanished. The medicines book would be cracked open on the counter, receipts wedged in any old how between its pages, which were greasy with fingerprints. I'd turn a page or two in disgust, and within moments I'd be overtaken by an urge to parse and sift –

'I've finished copying out these medication receipts, Richard. I've taken the liberty of arranging everything alphabetically. Should make looking up a particular preparation much easier. Where would you like the originals?'

'Splendid. Thank you.' Mansfield went on reading the trustees' inspection report and massaging his head. 'Would you mind filing them in the dispensary? Not filing, *flinging* – I don't think we've ever had much of a system there. Frank was going to get to it, but – you know how it is.'

'I'd be glad to file them properly. Where *is* Frank?'

'Hmm? Oh . . . in town. He said he was going out for tea.'

'What, is he propping up the counter in that pastry shop *again*? That's three Saturdays in a row now.'

'I hadn't noticed. You could go too, you know. Take a break. See a little of the outside world.'

'The last time I decided to see a little of the outside world you weren't too pleased, as I recall.'

'Hem. Just try to stay away from Nantucket.' He made a few swift underlinings in the report and skimmed it my way. 'Take a look at this. There are some nice remarks by our boarders regarding you. Mr Coolidge says you're the only worthy opponent he's ever had. High praise indeed.'

Mr Coolidge was a securities broker who'd defrauded several of New York's biggest tycoons on the grounds that their cash was poisoning the air around Manhattan with its metallic fumes. We played the occasional game of poker together. As I was an indifferent tactician, and he a monomaniac skilled in deception, he invariably won.

'Quite seriously,' mused Richard. 'You work far too hard. Go to town with Frank some Saturday. Buy yourself a sugared bun.'

'D'you know, Richard, you *do* sound rather like my father at times.'

'I've figured out enough about your relationship with your father by now to realize that you don't mean that as a compliment. But — at the risk of being a busybody — I think you should go into Boston once in a while. Go home, while you're at it. The thing we fear is often so much worse in imagination than it is in reality.'

'Oh, the reality's bad enough, believe me.'

'Then that's the more reason to confront it. This asylum is full of people who try to avoid reality at all costs, Cassius. Don't let that be you.'

But I didn't go then, or the month after that, or even the following one. It was Christmas-time before I paid a call at Mount Vernon

Street again, and when I did I discovered something that threatened to alter the pattern of my whole life.

THE SIGNS OF FUTURE disaster were already there, lying all about me, if only I'd known how to interpret them.

By mid-June Adam Thornton had a beard so full that I could have stuck my pen into it. Why did we give some of our boarders leave to groom themselves, I wondered, while denying others access to those toiletries that are considered essential to a civilized existence? I consulted the permissions book and found that Mansfield had made a cursory entry against Thornton's name: 'Severe depression of spirits. No sharp implements permitted.'

I had an unworthy hunch that this ban had nothing to do with the state of Thornton's spirits and everything to do with his social position. Being a politician or a professor, however gloomy, got you access to a pair of nail scissors. The grimmest army general was at liberty to trim his own whiskers. A crazy lady of undisputed gentility like Miss Clayborn could crimp her hair daily with heated tongs in her own suite – though there was little Miss Clayborn couldn't do, other than live a life that was meaningful to her on her own terms.

As a mere chandler in a single room, Adam Thornton had to remain hirsute. And more to the point, he was no longer depressed. He was animated, extravagantly talkative. During my visits to him he exuded a fizzing energy which his four modest walls were barely able to contain. And he was even better at poker than Mr Coolidge, perhaps because he was playing for higher stakes.

'I'd like to shave.'

'I can't allow you to have a razor.'

'Why not?'

'You know why not.'

'Listen, Doctor. There ain't a single blessed bar on these windows. There's no grating to this fire. If I'd wanted to kill myself I could've jumped to my death or gone up in smoke long before now.'

Backed into a hand. 'True.'

'I just want to look decent for Lucy. She won't know me, seeing me with a beard.'

'She won't be seeing you, Mr Thornton.'

'No, of course not. But if she might. If she just might, now. Would I want her to see me like this, if she *did*?'

Straight flush. 'I suppose not.'

It was madness, arguing with them! And yet I succumbed to it, every time. An illusory visit. A real razor, for a real beard. What was the difference? Where did the distinction lie? Talking to Adam Thornton I felt worse than ever to be a Carver, with my money, my family money, my family connections and – it's there in all of our family portraits; I'm looking at our distinctive mandibular cleft as I write, in my father's picture above the bureau in Mount Vernon Street – my genteelly bifurcating, expensively barbered Carver chin, which now seemed to me like the very badge and seal of privilege itself. All Thornton was asking for was a cheap old straight razor.

I let him shave.

SEVENTEEN

Towards the end of June there was an incident to which I should have paid more attention.

I was in the men's wing at about five o'clock one afternoon when I was stopped dead in my tracks by a hideous noise coming from Adam Thornton's room. It sounded uncannily like a child being chastised by a furious parent. *Wha, wha, wha.* And again: *Wha, wha, wha.*

And then an indignant howl, like a child being struck.

I opened the door. Thornton was holding Goodwin by the elbows and was slinging him around. Flakes of paper floated through the air like the smuts of a bonfire. Frank was covered in ink: welts of blue daubed his trousers, his shirt, his jiggling face. With each stumble a different part of his anatomy struck the furniture. *Wha, wha, wha.* That dreadful sound was spilling from his blue lips.

'Mr Thornton! Let Dr Goodwin go.'

'Fuck you,' said Thornton, and went on slinging.

I put my head outside the door and roared. Four attendants came barreling down the corridor, Mansfield behind them. Within minutes Goodwin had been prised free and Thornton was hauled off to the showers.

'Oh, for goodness' sake, Frank,' Richard snapped, 'grow a back-bone. You're not seriously hurt, are you?'

'I think my thumb might be sprained.' He held it up for our inspection.

'Cassius will put a bandage on it for you. Lie down and take a nap. Cassius, come downstairs and see me in an hour or so, after you've fixed Frank up.'

'Come on, stop hollering,' I said, once Mansfield had left us.

Goodwin cut a sorry figure: inky, flabby, dripping with sweat and self-pity. 'Cassius, would you please look at my feet and tell me – tell me if they're all right?'

'Your feet look the same as always.'

'Are you sure? Even the left?'

'Yes. Even the left.'

'Not the one on *your* left. The other one.'

'Yes, Frank. Your other left foot looks quite all right too. Let's see this thumb of yours, then. Indeed, that's a first-class sprain. What happened?'

'I tried to take Mr Thornton's paper and pen away. He was getting wilder and wilder. He was writing letters all day – letters to Congress, to the White House – he said he had to inform the authorities about the deplorable state of the Salem–Boston road.'

'Well, it's high time that somebody does.' I began to wind gauze around and over Frank's doughy hand.

'I didn't mean to cause any trouble. *Wha!* Gently! You're pulling too tight. I just wanted him to calm down.'

'Why didn't you call me?'

'I just – I wanted to manage *something* on my own, just something, just once.'

'And how did that turn out for you?'

'I know! I've spoiled it all.' A great big salty drop hung from his eye. Even his tears were fat. 'And now Richard is – is – is – disappointed in me. I need his good opinion, Cassius – I need it particularly at this time. I wasn't going to mention this yet, but the thing is – the thing is –'

I cut him short before the waterworks could begin in earnest. 'Don't worry about Richard. I'll put in a good word for you. I'd better go down, or his head will be coming off his shoulders.' Tucking in the end of the bandage, I searched for a pin. 'There. That'll teach you to poke your thumb into every pie you can find. Please don't meddle in Mr Thornton's care again without consulting me first. Got that?'

'Yes, Cassius. Thank you. Oh, I won't!'

'See here, the only person you've harmed in this instance is Mr Thornton himself. He's to be shut up in the hydropathy room for the rest of the afternoon.' I stuck the pin in with as much compassion as I could bring to the operation. 'And you're going to get the evening off. Doesn't seem fair, somehow.'

'HOW IS FRANK?' ASKED Mansfield when I entered his study an hour later.

'He's guilty of a stupid error, but no real harm's been done. What about Mr Thornton?'

'We've made him safe. He should be asleep.'

'Oh God. "*Safe*". Is he in the cottage?'

'No. He's in bed. He's had a shower bath. With luck he'll be out like a light. If you'll excuse me, I'm going to go to bed myself.'

'Do. You look shocking. But let me get you a dose first.'

'Would you? I can hardly see straight. Oh, and Cassius –' He stayed me with a touch to my elbow. 'Thank you. It seems I'm always thanking you these days. Felicity is on hand if you need help.'

'I think I'll absent me from Felicity awhile. It's no trouble. I'll get you that morphine. Go to bed, Richard.'

The usual effect of the shower baths was to drain agitated patients of their aggression and to leave them deeply relaxed. Many fell asleep. Thornton was stretched out in bed, but his eyes were wide open.

'Good evening, Mr Thornton. After your exertions this afternoon I'd hoped to find you in the Land of Nod.'

'You're a brave man, Doctor, to come in here.' His upper body gave an ineffective jerk. Of course: bed straps. 'I have you in my power. If you kill me, you'll be hanged. But I can kill you with safety, for I am crazy, and so not responsible.'

'I'll take that chance, Mr Thornton. I don't think either of us is about to kill anybody.' I sat down next to him, undid the buckle across his chest, and felt his pulse. It was alarmingly rapid. I palpated the fold beneath the palm. 'What's this? You have cuts on your arm.'

'I hurt myself shaving this morning.'

'Really? Three times, in the same place? On the *wrist*?'

'The razor snagged and I dropped it. It's a bad blade. Blunt. I need a better one.'

I let go of his hand. 'Mr Thornton, don't play games with me. You won't get any permissions, indeed you won't get any*thing* or any*where* here, unless you show that you mean to co-operate.'

'You seem to speak from experience, Doctor.'

'Perhaps I do.'

'Co-operate with whom? With you?'

'Well, with all of us. All of us who care for you. Above all, with Dr Mansfield. He wants to make you better.'

'Why, that's just it. He's decided that I'm insane. So I must be. *I must be insane before I can get better.*' Thornton raised himself to a sitting position. 'But if I ain't insane – if this is Adam Thornton in his right mind – then where does that leave me?'

'Well, so far you're giving him plenty of confidence in his diagnosis. Listen –' I tried to guide his shoulders back to the mattress. 'Please stop this. Please stop *raving* at the staff and demonstrate an improvement. I know you're capable of restraining yourself. Consider how sensibly you speak to me.'

'You're different. You know I ain't crazy.'

'Either way, if you ever want to go back to your old life, this is your best – your *only* chance.'

Thornton fell back despairingly. 'I'm finished, Doctor. I may as well be truly mad. Who will do business with me now, after I've been in here?'

I sat in silence for some minutes. There seemed to be so much common sense in this that I didn't know how to answer him.

'Has my wife come again?' The bleak radiance of the evening made his newly shaved face look pitted and disturbingly raw. 'I'm concerned about that road. She's risking her life driving over those ruts. I don't like the thought of her traveling on it.'

'I can't speak to you about her. I shouldn't have, to begin with. I'm sorry.'

He surged up at me so quickly that his spittle landed on my cheek. '*Sorry?* How in hell's name are you sorry?'

But I'd already ducked away, leaping to my feet and holding my empty chair between us. 'Mr Thornton, you must control yourself or I'll have to call an attendant.'

'And then what will you do? *Dragoon* me into self-control? Don't you see the lunacy in that, *Doctor?*'

'We don't use physical violence or coercion here. You know that.' I set the chair back in its place by his bedside, feeling slightly foolish. 'That's not what I'm proposing.'

He subsided with a laughing groan. 'Dr Carver, now I'm *really* starting to fear for your sanity. I know exactly what you're proposing. Another of your little baths, I'm guessing. Or maybe a swell old wet sheet pack?'

'Hydropathy is not a form of coercion.'

'Ain't it? What do you call being tied up in a fucking six-foot sheet? Have *you* ever tried sitting in one of those shower baths?'

'No, of course not.'

'Well, you can't sit. There's a canvas covering right up to your neck, in case you ain't noticed. You can't bend your knees, you can't move your arms. You have to *lie down* for however long Dr Mansfield says you're going to be in there. And when he's bory-eyed and goes off in one of his stupors that can be for *up to two hours*. I've counted every minute. And then at last he comes to and tells the attendant to bring you round and the cold shower is turned on and the fucking jet hits your head and it's like suffocating, Dr Carver, it's like drowning in your own –'

'All right, Mr Thornton. Enough.' I dropped into the chair,

flattening my fingers against my temples. 'Dr Mansfield does *not* drink.'

'Well, ain't that just so? Dr Mansfield don't drink, and you don't eat, and Dr Goodwin don't know his ballocks from his beam end, and – oh yes – *I'm* the crazy one.'

'All right, all right.' Though Thornton appeared to have plenty of fight left in him, I was spent. 'I'll do my best to arrange for you to see her. God knows how I'll do it, but I will. I won't send you to the showers again tonight. And I won't sedate you.'

'Do I have your word? Are you signing on the dotted line?'

'You do. I am. I promise. Just give me some time.' I stood up and settled the blanket around him. 'I want you to sleep now.'

Thornton took hold of my hand and pressed it to his mouth in a fierce kiss. 'Thank you. Thank you.'

'*Sleep*, do you hear me?'

BEFORE STARTING MY EVENING rounds I paid Goodwin a visit. He was lying on his cot, fully dressed, with the coverlet pulled over his feet. I saw within seconds that his earlier self-pity had given way to self-reproach, which was going to be even more tedious.

'How are you bearing up, Frank? You had quite a turn earlier. Recovered a bit?'

'What good are we to them, Cassius? I feel more and more that I can't help them. I am as lost as they are.'

'Well, *Solamen miseris socios habuisse doloris*. It is a comfort to the wretched to have companions in misery.'

Goodwin smiled wanly. 'Is that all?'

'Look. I've brought you crackers and warm milk. Drink up. Doctor's orders.'

'I'm not hungry or thirsty.'

'Really? This is serious indeed.' Recalling a jingle that Caro used to sing to me when I was a boy, I dipped a spoon into the cup. 'Come on. Lap, lap, lap, said little puss. Show us your tongue.' I waved the milk under his nostrils. 'There's honey in it.'

'You are a dear, good friend.' A painful rearrangement was going on behind the slack pudding of his face. 'But I can't manage anything tonight.'

'Get some rest, Frank. We'll all feel better in the morning.'

I hoped against hope that I was right.

EIGHTEEN

THOUGH I HATED TO admit it, I agreed with Frank. *Some slight trouble with a patient. Rest up in the cottage. Made safe. Excited. Eloped.* I despised this institutional language, which we had only evolved, as far as I could see, to hide the suffering of our patients from ourselves.

While Goodwin soon regained both his bland good spirits and his appetite, I couldn't settle back into my usual routine. I was filled with a rising sense of unease. I'd begun to dread Ruth Macy's letters: those apparently harmless vessels, brimming with self-immolating fire. She seemed to loom over the intervening ocean like the figure-head of a ship, the flame of her yearning ready to gallop across the distance and burn me to ash.

For I was getting nowhere with Borden. Our daily meetings were torture. All around me, the whole of creation was feeding: tearing, grinding, chewing, sucking, swallowing, ingesting, excreting. The smallest mosquito gorging itself on blood, the lowliest fish pursuing other fish in the river, the very maggots mouthing the earth – every blessed thing was taking into itself whatever was necessary for life. But William Borden, though a fully grown man, an engine of tendon and bone, designed by nature to be one of her most rapacious creatures, still refused to eat more than a helpless infant would eat. I believed that what Mansfield had predicted would come to pass: if Borden didn't consume proper food, and soon, he would die.

Why didn't he speak? Why had he started, only to stop? I was convinced that his refusal to eat and his refusal to speak were one and the same thing, sprung from the same place. It was unbearable to be in the same room with him, bumping a silly spoon against his rigid lips, while he pretended that I didn't exist. I was tormented by the impulse to confront him, to fling the spoon away and – and then what? I was more certain than ever before that the wellspring of the mystery that enveloped him like a fog was lodged deep within, and I cursed my inability to follow it to its source. It was especially awful since his entire manner was, surely – because I was, by now, certain of this also – an inarticulate plea for intervention, for help. I *knew* that I could help him, and that, on some sunken level of his being, he knew it too. But in order for me to help him, he would have to speak. And asking for my help was the thing he couldn't do. I would have to go down into those depths without a pilot, without a light, without any invitation . . .

Oh, it was an insoluble problem.

And Mansfield's stubbornness, his refusal to entertain any sort of therapeutic approach to our patients that didn't involve healthful walks and games and square meals, his almost pathological refusal to engage with their affliction, was as much of a problem. In his attempts to be provoking, Thornton had unintentionally touched on a real worry of mine. I was more and more disturbed by Richard's reliance on morphine to relieve his headaches, and I wondered, at times, if it affected his general judgment.

In my frustration I decided to take Goodwin into my confidence.

'Frank, I'm in an impossible situation. Richard expects me to overcome William Borden's reluctance to eat. But I can't manage it unaided.'

'What are you asking me to do?'

'I need to spend time alone with Mr Borden occasionally so I can try to get to the bottom of his affliction. I want you to – not to lie for me, no, not that, never that, but to divert Richard's attention, if need be, so that he isn't troubled by this.'

'Richard won't like it.'

'Oh, I know. Richard insists that we're not to talk with our patients about what ails them. In fact *we're not supposed to examine their symptoms*. But just name one other branch of medicine in which this would be acceptable! Can you? Can you imagine trying to treat a man who is dying of a tumor without ever once opening him up, and attempting to find the location of his disease?'

'Well, if you put it that way –'

'Oh, Frank.' I laughed bitterly. 'I do.'

'But Cassius, it's dangerous! You saw what happened with Mr Thornton. And anyhow we hear of cases all the time where patients die under the knife. I don't – I don't want that on my conscience. I don't think I could bear it.'

'Listen, Frank! The art of healing men is a little like that of destroying them.'

'I don't know. It all sounds very fine, but I don't know.'

'Sometimes timid actions gain – well, nothing. Doesn't victory follow the audacity of brave soldiers? It seems to me that success can also crown the efforts of enterprising surgeons.'

'Yes, but are we surgeons?'

'Why, of course. We are soul-surgeons.'

He bit his pulpy thumbnail. 'You're the soldier, Cassius. You've been in the navy. I don't know anything about war. But I often feel that Mr Borden is hiding from us, somehow, and wants us to leave him in peace.'

'He isn't hiding from us, Frank, he's hiding from himself. I think he can be helped, if I can ask him the right questions. In fact I'm convinced that he will improve if he can only be made to *remember* —'

'Don't ask me to go against what Richard's decided. It doesn't seem right.'

'Frank. Aren't we friends? Aren't we —' I groped for the mystical word Miss Macy had used — '*comrades?*'

'We are. Of course we are.'

'Then don't be such a ninny. Do this for me, please.'

'I want to, Cassius. I really do. But I just can't.'

Comrades, indeed. Why did I ever think there was any help to be had from that quarter?

IT WAS COMING UP to ten o'clock at night. I went into the parlor, hoping to sit down with the newspaper for a minute, but was immediately put off by the exhaustion in my limbs, the dismaying sight of the cold cinders on the hearth, and a craving for warmth. I also had a strong desire to urinate. I went upstairs to my room, where I searched in the dark for the chamber pot. The sharp stink of my own piss offended me, and I averted my face.

The day's post lay on my table, unread. Among the circulars and requests for subscriptions there was, as usual, a letter from Miss

Macy. I hesitated to open it and to accede to the tug of her will, the implacable force of her exhortations, which had come to feel to me as inescapable as weather, or the tides. But the message it contained was short.

What if you are unable to help him? What if he never gets well? I have tried, in these last months, to imagine what my future without William might be, but whoever I was is gone. I've arrived at the floor of the ocean, Hiram, and I am looking up at the surface. Everything comes to me in fragments. Everything is altered. The world has become alien to me, and myself most of all.

I may be a woman. I am sure there is much about his illness that I do not understand. But don't I have a claim? Don't I have a claim on him?

'Oh good God, woman,' I wanted to scream. 'For the love of God, let me be. Leave me alone.' But then, as I dropped the still half-folded sheet onto the table, something slipped from it and fell at my feet. It was a smaller oblong of paper. When I'd straightened it out, I saw that it was a second letter, written in a firm dark hand.

It was dated '*May 8th, 1833, Hood Island, Galapagos*'.

'*My darling Ruth,*' I read. The top of the page was foggy, as though it had once met with damp. The words '*we sail into that great ocean tomorrow*' swam out of a cauliflower-shaped stain, and then '*many fears*' and '*until I see you again*' and then there stood out, boldly and blackly, an utterance so strange that I had to read it several times before the shock of it wore off.

I long to speak the truth to you. I don't know if it's ever possible to speak the truth in love. But with you – I long for it.

I want your lips. I want your cheeks. I want your nostrils. I want your neck, the sinews of it, and the down on your neck. I want your feet and your ankles, your hands, all their small bones. I want your eyebrows and your hair, the hair on your head, and the hair on your arms, and in all the places of your body. I want your ears and your ear lobes, I want your mouth with every tooth. I want your ribs, I want your wrists. I want your elbows and your knees, the whole smooth map of your skin – oh I want all of it. I want your spit, I want the deep note of your voice, its flow, its roundness, your eyes, and to see what they see.

You are the clearest person I know.

I wonder what you'd say if you could be here, and had sight of this island. It's like a reverse world. The lizards are larger than men and the birds flightless. The earth is dry and hard and the night sky sown with dewed stars. The trees are white and the ponds crusty with green salt. But I'm already a traveler from myself, turned inside out and about and about by you. There ain't a single thing here as rare or new as you are. I see the cormorant swimming upside down on wings that don't know air, right the way to the sea-bed, the fearless mockingbird with its dainty awl of a beak – and I see that they should love you too.

I'm going far away from you but it is part of our contract, yours with me and mine with you, that we can never stray too far out of one another's orbit, that we can never forget each other entirely.

I am nearly asleep – and that ain't very usual in writing love letters, but you know mine are all love letters that I write to you.

Whether sleeping or waking, love with me is still the same – W. B.

I refolded the sheet along its creases, and sat for a moment with my face resting in my hands, breathing shallowly.

I found to my distress both that I was aroused, and that I was unable to pinpoint the object of my yearning. Was she its target? Was he? I wished I hadn't seen this letter. I wished it was I who'd written it. At the same time I wished that I, and not Ruth Macy, had been the recipient of this naked outpouring of intimacy.

Enough. Enough of this.

I felt exhausted, worn out by the struggle of the last weeks and my failure to make any headway. William Borden wasn't the problem, I suddenly saw. Miss Macy wasn't the problem. Mansfield wasn't the problem, Goodwin wasn't the problem. I, I alone, was the problem. Oh, Hiram Carver had fine theories all right. He talked and talked, but what did he actually *do*? I felt like a stranger to myself, someone I had only just met, someone more decisive, more *ruthless* than I'd ever been, whose actions might yet surprise me. Why should I argue with this stranger? Why should I resist him?

Still holding Borden's letter, I left the main house, crossed the starlit hill, and stepped into the darkened hallway of the men's wing.

Upstairs, Borden's corridor gaped in front of me. I hurried down it and entered his rooms without knocking. The parlor was arid and badly lit by a wavering candle. It smelled of vegetable soap, and, more troublingly, of stale roast fat. In the middle of the table, like a burnt offering left on an altar, was the joint of lamb I hadn't been able to get him to eat that evening.

Borden was still awake, seated in his usual chair at the window. The shutters were open, and though I couldn't see his features, I could distinguish the ashen outline of his head and shoulders against the scythe of the moon.

'This won't be pleasant, William, but you will feel better afterwards. I know it.' I fumbled for the oil lamp and lit it. As it spluttered into life it scarcely seemed to make a dent in the darkness. Then Borden's face leaped out, as vivid as the face on a medallion.

I held the letter before me like a charm, keeping it in the light as I drew nearer. 'Do you remember this? *I long to speak the truth to you,*' I read out loud. '*I don't know if it's ever possible to speak the truth in love. But with you — I long for it.*'

Borden rose slowly to his feet. 'She gave you this?'

'You've regained the power of speech. Not only that, but you appear to remember her. Yes, Will, she did.'

'May I have it?' He held out his hand. I stared at him, waiting for some expression of shame. But none came. 'Give it to me, Hiram.'

'Not until you speak to me.'

His fingers closed. His voice was defiant. 'I can't recall the things you want me to recall.'

'I don't want to ask you about Buskirk tonight. I want to know what happened in the boat.'

Borden swallowed with great effort, as if his throat had hardened.

'Thirteen years ago. When you were put out to sea from the *Providence*.'

'Don't make me talk about that.'

'But you remember.'

'I remember such things as I'd rather forget.'

'You owe it to her, William. What you write here is – is a promise.' I slipped the letter into my shirt, noting that Borden followed it with his eyes. 'As clear as any promise ever made.'

'Why must I talk about it?'

'Because it's the key to you.'

Borden stared at my breast as if he could see, not merely through the cloth to the vanished self who had written those things, but all the way through me. 'Have you never felt desire for a woman? That hunger?'

'No – that is, yes.' I felt myself reddening. In that moment, I'd thought of her. 'No. I'm not sure.'

'Hunger for food begins in the mind. Just like desire. Long before you feel it in your belly.'

'Words, Will. I want the words. *Tell* me.'

'We had no words. We were hungry. When you are that hungry there ain't words for it.'

'Is that how you felt about – her?'

'Yes. When I first met her, when I . . . When I . . .'

'Courted her, pursued her?'

'Yes.'

'And afterwards – at sea – once we'd set sail on the *Orbis*?'

'Afterwards. I couldn't see her face.'

'Why not?'

'It was the ocean. Being there again, on that water. I knew that everything on the land was a lie.'

'What was a lie?'

'Kin. Love. Safety. The promises I'd made her. To eat with her. Sleep with her. To live with her in common humanity. I couldn't do

281

it. All of it was a lie.' He acknowledged the lamb on the parlor table at last. 'This meat – the meat was a lie. I was defiled.'

'Defiled by what? By *what*?'

'By my hunger. You don't know what that hunger was like.'

'In the boat.'

'In the boat, yes.'

A taut silence stretched between us. I said carefully, 'Why are you so certain that I don't know?'

We'd both been standing during this exchange, but now he sat down on the sofa with an abrupt contortion. 'Hiram. What you've done to yourself you've done freely. You've *chosen* this death in life. But I. But we. We never chose.' He lowered his head, and again uttered that strange cry, like the unspooling of some savage chant: *Aie, aie, aie.*

I dropped to the floor and gripped the blades of his arms. I felt my knees striking the boards; heard words pouring from me in a swirl of urgency and tenderness that sounded nothing like my usual voice. 'Haven't you chosen it now? You must speak about it, William. If you don't speak, it will kill you. You *will* have chosen death.'

'I can't.'

'You can. Please speak. Oh, please speak to me.' The force of my desire swept through me like a tempest, but I lashed myself to the mast. 'I know that you suffered terrible things, things that the rest of us can only guess at. But don't you see how much better it would be – better for you, yourself, *for no one else* – to speak the truth about them?'

He lifted his head wonderingly. 'The truth.'

'Yes! It doesn't matter what the world wants to hear, or whatever name the world might give to what you felt. There is the truth – still alive – here –' I placed my hand over his heart.

'You want to know the truth about the *Providence*.' His face was ghastly in the lamplight, riven with shadows and blanks. 'The truth is that our captain was *insane*, Hiram.'

We were approaching it now, the dark form under the water, the shadow that lay on the bottom. Every artery in my body was quickening. I was afraid that he would feel the force of my craving surging through my fingers, into which my whole self seemed to be concentrated. 'Your captain? Captain Fitzgibbon?'

'Aye, Fitzgibbon. He didn't ration us. He didn't use the cat over-much. He never broke ship's law. But there was no sense of measure in his appetites. You could see it in the smallest thing he did. When he ate he packed himself to bursting. When he drank he was always drunk. And he could never get enough money. He wanted more, always more, and he dragged us up and down that ocean to get it. Being on that ship was like being trapped with an ape. A civilized ape. An ape with refined tastes. But still a creature all belly and teeth. It don't matter how smooth the face or manners of such a man are. His wildness is all on the inside. He will devour everything. Once a ship feels like that it ain't safe. No one is safe.' He tried, weakly, to withdraw his arms from my grasp. 'Don't make me go on. I don't want to go on.'

I moved closer, without relinquishing my hold. 'You must. There's no way back. If you stop now it will only be worse.'

Borden fixed his sunken pupils on me. His lips opened. Behind them, as if paralyzed, lay the grained muscle of his tongue. After an agonizing interval I saw it jump at my call, and come haltingly to life –

When he spoke again it was in brittle phrases, as though he were searching for something behind the words. 'There was a child on that ship. That boy was Fitzgibbon's pet, his toy. But the rest of us, too – I knew we weren't safe. We were caged with this wild thing that was all mouth. Couldn't they see it, the others – the danger? They couldn't. They'd become as frenzied as that ape, waiting for any scraps it might throw them. We'd all become wild.'

'*You* hadn't. You saw it.'

'I was trapped too. I was *in* that cage! There were times I asked myself, am I wild now, or am I still a man? And I didn't know. Is it human to be so full of fear? That was what I was most afraid of – not being the man I was before.'

'Yes, I think it is human. I think it's the most human thing there is.'

His eyes rested on mine in a long moment of comprehension. After what seemed like many minutes he nodded faintly, as if yielding to an invisible pressure. 'One of the hands, a lad called Dan Small, was the worst touched by it of all of us. He saw the money pouring in and disappearing into Fitzgibbon's maw and it sent him into a fever. He was great pals with the first lieutenant, Monroe, and he plied him with grog and whiskey stolen from the stores. He'd reached some kind of understanding with him, that he would get his cut. But that was only because neither could see that there wasn't going to be anything. An ape-man like Fitzgibbon takes, he don't give. The other two, Perry and Lenox, were revolted by it all. They were the sort who can't stand to smell their own shit. And by now they were covered in it –

'Then Small broke. When he did I thought, aye. Aye, this is the thing my fear's been leading me to. But the boat, Hiram! The boat was an escape from the madness they'd made. Everyone said afterwards that I was brave, but it was *easy* to choose the boat. I didn't care if it cost me my life. That ship was sure death. If I stayed on it I knew I'd die long before my body did.'

'Yet – yet you took Fitzgibbon.'

'I had to. That was the price of our freedom – the Ape. And then we were in the boat with it. I saw, truly saw, how crazed it was, and how powerless. Now that we'd burst our cage it was afraid – it was afraid of all of us. I didn't know what it might do, in its fear, so I fed it Monroe's whiskey to keep it quiet. Webb was with us – the purser. And the bosun, Duggan. And Johnny Canacka, the boy. Perry's blood was all over the dinghy. He'd been shot. I remember the feel of it on my hands, the smell of it, the sound of his pain that sounded like all that blood crying out, the way blood would cry if it could talk. He died and when we tipped him into the sea his blood left a trail behind – like the tail of a comet—'

Borden had been speaking with a mesmeric intensity, but now his words dried up.

'Go on,' I whispered. 'Don't stop.'

'It was strange, Hiram. When I saw that blood streaking away in the waves I had a vision. It was as if we'd made an offering to the ocean, signed a pact with it on its dark page. I felt as if we could fly. I could feel the wind tearing at us, tearing at the boat, and I knew that we would live, that we would cross that water. Everything was suddenly bright. Oh, it was bright! It was as if we were flying directly into the sun, as if we didn't need a thing outside that bright blackness . . . And then I learned what conceit that was. We began to starve. We caught a sea turtle, and that was the only thing we ever caught. We were flying towards death. Not life.'

'But you fished. Didn't you fish with – with a line?'

'I did. I tried to fish with a line and a hook I'd made from our one needle, but what could I do with a goddamn needle, Hiram? A *needle?* Monroe died after Perry. He died with his head in my lap. And after he died his dead mouth opened and spoke to me. "There was all that blood in Perry," he said, "and you didn't touch it. You didn't taste it. All that life: you let it run out, into the sea . . . Ain't I enough? Ain't I good enough for you? *Wasn't I once a man?* I yearn to live again, to find my life in you." He was still warm, the blood in him whispering its message to me . . .

'So I took out my knife. I was the first to eat. Oh, they wanted to eat, but they didn't dare. I showed them how. I was their teacher. But it wasn't enough. We ate, and then we starved again. When Webb died his blood cried out to me and I did the same. We ate his flesh and we sucked at his bones. And then I knew. I knew I'd become wild too.' He had drawn nearer to me, so near that I could feel his breath against my face, and he was speaking slowly. 'So you see. I can't belong to her. She can't belong to me. I can never feel that she, or anyone else, is safe from me. Her blood could speak to me in that way.'

'But you love her.'

'I loved those men well enough.'

'If she'd been in the boat, and no longer living – would you – would you –'

'Yes. Her. You. Anyone. Anyone.'

'William. Monroe and Webb were *dead*. They *never spoke to you*.

You were delirious from hunger and thirst. You saw yourself as their protector. All your actions show that! You were never like the others. If you had to resort to such an expedient when those men were dead, and you were starving, then that is no shame.'

'No shame? Who are you to say what's shameful and what ain't?'

'I'm a man like you, William. And if *we* don't decide what we're going to call things, then who will? Who will decide for us? The Fitzgibbons of this world? Our fathers? God? *I* say it's no shame. I, Hiram Carver, say it. I say it!'

Borden let out a bellow of pain. Then, with a loosening of his whole face like a door swinging wide, he started to weep. 'You're mad.'

'Yes, perhaps! I'm as mad as any other man in this mad world, no more and no less. I'm as mad as you. And you, by the way, have assured me that you're sane.' I was speaking fast, my lips so close to his that I felt as if I were sending my vital spirit forth into his depleted body. Or was he drawing it out of me? 'Listen to me, William! You are sane, do you hear me? *You are sane.*'

He looked at me with those undone eyes. 'Hiram, there's something you must do.'

'Yes, anything. Anything.'

'Absolve me.'

'How do I do that? Tell me.'

'Just say the words. Just say, *I absolve you.*'

'Very well. I absolve you, William. I, as a mere *man*, absolve you of all of it.' I reached for the plate of lamb. 'Now eat this, goddamn you.'

'I will if you will.'

'You think I won't.'

'I know you won't.'

Holding his gaze, I took up the fork and plunged it rapidly into the heart of the joint. Then I cut off two thick slices, and carved through each again, once, twice, three times, until it lay in pieces. I speared the largest and lifted it to my lips, the fork shaking like a divining rod.

'No.'

'No?'

'With your hands. I want to see you eat with your hands.'

'Very well. I will.' I scraped the lamb from the tines with the knife and then, resting the knife on the rim of the plate, picked the meat up in my fingers. It felt slippery, alive. I hesitated.

'*Now* eat it.'

I rammed the entire piece into my mouth, and chewed. Fatty juices ran down my throat. I could feel it: the jolt of power, the call to live.

'Choke it down, Hiram.'

I did. 'Now you.'

'Another.'

'Another for me, and then one for you.'

We ate the whole of the lamb, slice by slice. We took it in turns, first carving it and then cramming it in with our fists. When it was all gone I was overcome by an awful sickness, as terrible as the worst seasickness I'd ever experienced. My stomach felt solid, my lips puffed up. Borden's were a devilish oily red. I bucked away from him. Our knees, which had been just touching while we were eating, knocked together. It took me a moment to realize that I was going to faint.

There was a susurration in my ears, a sighing that came from some inner sea heaving and crashing inside me.

A funny thing had happened to Borden. Although the corners of the room were by now completely dark, he pulsed with light. The brilliance emanating from his body was tremendous. He seemed to have broken into a million shimmering particles. I couldn't speak, could hardly look at him. His red mouth was still opening and closing. Was he saying something? I sensed my body falling forwards and barely managed to stop myself from toppling into his arms.

'Hiram. Get up.'

'I'm not well.'

'You're well enough. You just ain't used to food.'

'I want to lie down.'

'You may want to, but you can't. You'll vomit it all up.'

I felt his shoulder in my armpit, levering me upwards. 'Come on, we'll walk together.'

We hobbled to the window. My legs had turned into clubs but the rest of me felt like air. My eyes were gummed with humiliating tears. As he lifted the latch cold air flowed in. At length I looked around; saw the lamp burning brightly on the table, the plate dulled with grease. I could taste the meat in my mouth. It tasted like giving up, like surrender.

Borden still supported me. 'Better?'

'Yes. A little better.'

The blaze that had surrounded him was gone: he'd resumed his ordinary human shape. He was smiling at me through wet eyes – smiling with open affection.

I reached into my shirt. 'Here. Take your letter. Will, are you *laughing* at me?'

'Not at you. At you and me both.'

He threw the letter onto the soiled and empty plate. Then he put his hand to my head, drew my face to his and kissed my cheek.

I felt the youthfulness of my own flesh under his mouth, a yielding of muscle above resistant bone. 'What happens now?' I asked.

'For now, nothing. Then tomorrow we get up and do it all again.' He rested his forehead against the window pane. 'See there, Hiram.'

I fought off my nausea and looked out.

My breath stuck in my throat as a shaft of raw air lanced me. Dawn was breaking on the salt flats below and over the sprawling grid of Boston, over bridges and boats and a first stirring of carts, with a purity and violence I hadn't thought possible. One by one the fronts of the city's buildings – mansions, prisons, hospitals, colleges, all the edifices that men spend their lives erecting – shed their rime of darkness and began to glow shell gray and pink. The granite cubes of Boston jail and the General Hospital lay strewn on the far bank of the Charles like toy bricks. Ticking through it all was the river, a tin snake twitching this way and that. The awakening sky was so bright it appeared bled of color. Its bleached transparency reached upwards, higher and higher, ever more whitely, until its blindness promised to become permanent – and as it did, the sun rose into the void like a sanguine eye.

'What do you want me to see?'

'All that life.'

On the slope of the hill the poplars crackled with a shift in the summer wind, blowing towards the Charles, where the traffic of the distant world flowed on.

NINETEEN

I WORRY SOMETIMES THAT I have failed, that my life, in spite of its many professional accolades, has in fact been denuded, thick on work but thin on grace. Yet it's also true that work – except on that one occasion at the end of last year, after my illness – has sustained me. In my limited way I've tried, in these two intervening decades, to build on my early experiment with William Borden by developing some simple exercises in systematic recollection with our patients. I've had a few modest successes, but nothing has ever equaled the pace and brio of his recovery. It was so vivid and so complete that one thought, quite unavoidably, in terms of magic.

Richard had warned me not to play Prospero, but I felt it was I, as much as Borden, who was being transformed – made new.

Over the next weeks, his symptoms started to disappear. I thought at first that he was simply entering one of his lucid phases. He took food; he slept at night. He walked with me on the hill. I was glad to have been able to give him some relief. I feared that an improvement so hoped for, whose workings I myself didn't completely understand, would vanish at any moment. But this change didn't reverse itself.

Once Borden had spoken about the *Providence*, the waters of his confusion seemed miraculously to divide, as if at the primordial

Word. Slowly, at my prompting, and then with growing sureness, memories of the *Orbis* came back to him. It was a peculiarly tender catechism, with me leading while he followed, until we arrived together at the climax: Buskirk.

William rode it out without resisting. In fact his submission to me at that moment was entirely in keeping with the humility that had always been an essential part of his character.

Yes, he remembered the attack now. He remembered it with horror at himself, with a panicked revulsion which I had to command myself in the sternest terms not to pity. Though every instinct of mine shrank from probing his misery, I pressed on, and when we'd wrung the last drops from his recollections of that afternoon – the after-image, clouding his inner eye like vapor, of Fryar's wounded body; the fury that overwhelmed him at Buskirk's high-handedness; the knowledge that hunger was about to be imposed on that ship, and the shattering apprehension that he couldn't hold any of it in any more – we were both rewarded with a sense of release. He was unable to say what mechanism, precisely, in all of this had triggered his collapse, but he didn't need to.

It seemed pretty plain to me.

He'd starved for so long, on that very stretch of water, in that hellish circle of the Pacific – he'd endured all, suffered all, hoped all, and would probably have undergone it all again if it had only touched himself and no one else – but then that fool, that unspeakable cretin, had imposed *the very same sentence*, to starve without any right of appeal, not on him – but on his men! This he couldn't bear. This was the turn of the wheel that broke him. He flew at Buskirk – and then he took the punishment on himself and refused to eat.

But now he was free. Now he could eat.

And as for me – I was ravenous. Not just for food, for meat and drink: for life itself.

I was astonished at the world. That there should be air with the smell of wood smoke in it. That there should be a sun like a buxom pumpkin, trembling on the rim of the hill when I walked to the top in the late afternoons. That there should be a saffron lizard, flicking its saffron tail, on the seat in the rose arbor. That there should be a seat at all. That I should exist to see it and touch it and be in it, merely by virtue of breathing in and out. How simple it was! In. And. Out. You did this without thinking – you only needed to do it even moderately well – and the world persisted, claimed you as one of its own; held you securely in its creaturely embrace.

I laughed out loud.

Dear God, it was all beautiful. The bow of the sky, the satin slap of the fountains – beautiful. The calm of it – beautiful. The greenness of the hilltop – beautiful, beautiful. I could enfold it, swallow it up, suck it into my ravenous marrow. The rail was not supporting me, but tethering me to the curve of the earth. Without it I would rise up and float away. This must be what convalescents felt, this hunger for solid and palpable things.

When I wrote to Ruth Macy now, it was from the fullness of my newly awakened senses. I knew that my feelings for her had to recede, and settle in their proper place. We'd been jointly engaged in a great endeavor of liberation, and the final measure of its success would be the extent to which we would all – she, I and Borden – in our different ways, seize our freedom.

For my part, I was determined to put away illusion.

Can you imagine how he must have suffered, all these years, in trying to reconcile the horrific truth of his experience with the role society had thrust on him? I don't blame him for a moment for attempting to maintain that insane deception. He would have had little say in the matter. He did well, well in excess of any sailor's craziest dreams, to get those four men to shore alive, but not, by society's reckoning, well enough. We expect our heroes to be without fault, Miss Macy. We won't allow them any weakness. When that boat came back the hero-worshippers wanted to welcome home a god, not a man of flesh and blood. We can't find our heroism in daily life; we need stories of superhuman trial and glory, of resurrection, we want to be rowed beyond the margins of what we know. If we can't find someone to play this part for us, then the history of mankind has shown us that we will find some other way of meeting our need, God help us; in conflict, in revolution, in war.

It says much about William that he couldn't sustain this lie. It tells us everything we need to know about him. He is an honest man, and most evidently a sane one, in a world whose lunacy consists of its dishonesty. Why do we lie to ourselves when it is as easy to tell the truth? Why do we pretend that we aren't all stumbling along the way? Why are we so cursed and stupid, so bewitched by our own fantasies? Why do we prefer what is unreal to what is real?

The only jarring note came from Richard.

'I'm not sure what to do with you, Cassius. No instruction of mine ever seems to make the slightest impression on you. You spoke to

Borden – you *interrogated* him – alone for weeks, months, without my knowing. The scale of the deception is staggering.'

'I kept quiet because I was afraid of what your reaction might be.'

'Ah, so – let me see if I understand this. All that time my possible *reaction* to your deception was the real problem, rather than the deception itself?'

'I was right though, Richard, wasn't I? Why call it deception? I thought of it as a moral enterprise. A quest – a quest for the truth. Not an exercise in falsehood. And it was hardly an interrogation. We simply spoke about what we could both remember. I've helped him, haven't I?'

'Dammit, you have. I should be furious, but I find that I can't be. I'm angry at the lie, but impressed, tremendously impressed, with the result.' He made a sound halfway between a laugh and a moan. 'You put me in a state of constant, maddening mental conflict. I don't know if I should discipline you, or promote you.'

'Oh, please don't promote me. There's only your job, and I don't want that.'

'Don't you?' His forehead was pleated in skepticism. 'You know I can't hang on to it for good. Every year in here is like two in the outside world. I doubt if I have much more than a decade of work left in me. Have you given any thought to what will happen later? When I go, you'd be the obvious choice as super.' Speculatively, he added, 'I'll bet your father would be pleased. This could solve some of your personal difficulties.'

'I don't want to think of you going, Richard. Why does anything have to change? Can't we continue as we are?'

He smiled, as if at a piece of childish folly. 'For how long?

Forever? No one has mastered the trick of that. From hour to hour we ripe and ripe – until at last, from hour to hour we rot and rot, no? Come, Cassius. You protest a little too much.'

AND THEN, AT THE start of October, just as life seemed most ripe, Eliza Todd died.

I went to her room one morning to help her dress and found her sunk in sleep, the bedsheet on the floor, her strong knitter's hands tucked under her chin. A lozenge of dusty light shone through the transom onto her face. It looked not merely old but abraded, like soap that has been used up; its waxy dullness offset by the silken hairs on their skullcap of bone. She didn't seem female; she didn't even seem human, and this struck me as such an affront, such a gratuitous humiliation on top of all the other humiliations she'd had to endure, that I rushed to cover her up. It took me several seconds – they felt like eons – to admit that this wasn't sleep, but death.

My father's diagnosis was correct: I no longer saw her with a physician's eyes, but through some quite other lens.

'I'm sorry,' said Richard kindly. 'I know you were fond of each other. I'll let her next of kin know.'

'Next of kin? But I thought she had none!' I was aware of a surging heat around my heart. 'You said that she had no surviving relatives!'

'None that want to be known as such. Still, Miss Todd's account has been settled reliably all these years. Doesn't that tell you something?'

'What? What should it tell me?'

'Well, Cassius. She has a son.'

'*A son?*' It made no sense. And at the same time, as the prickling in my chest began to kindle and spark, I knew that it did.

'Close the door, please.'

I got up to do so. I had a skew wish to run out, to lock Richard in and leave him there. Instead I sat down again and arranged my features in a suitable rictus of attention.

'Why didn't you share this with me?'

'There was no need. It's been a condition of her stay with us that this should be kept confidential. And it really wasn't relevant.'

'*Not relevant?* How was this *not relevant?*' I laughed spikily. 'Yes, I remember – safe harbor. Safe waters. Here we escape life's storms, we don't stir them up, et cetera. Am I right? And, oh my – weren't you lecturing *me* about transparency not too long ago?'

'There were good reasons for discretion. I haven't kept anything from you deliberately. But her son is a Bartlett. It's all there in the registers.'

'I saw. I looked.'

'Of course you did. Listen, please. Old Todd did a lot of business with Jacob Bartlett. This child was the result of an unfortunate indiscretion, over forty years ago now, between Eliza Todd and Bartlett's heir. He was already promised in marriage to someone else. The settlements were all drawn up. The disgrace to Miss Todd, if it had got out, would've been immense.'

'The disgrace was half his.'

'Oh yes, but she would have had to carry it forward alone. The boy was removed from her at birth and raised by his grandfather.'

'*Removed?* Did she agree to this?'

'She was sick with childbed fever. She wasn't in any position to refuse. And though she recovered her bodily health, she was never quite right in her mind afterwards. When the estate was acquired by the trustees it was considered best for her if she were given shelter here, and a chance to forget.'

'To *be* forgotten, you mean. Is this the origin of our famous ban on visitors?'

'Don't be ridiculous. And insolent. If there's nothing else, I'd like to get on with my correspondence now.'

'Richard, wait. I spoke imprudently, I know, but you see – I don't think she ever did forget. I think she retained the – the *imprint* of that loss for the rest of her life.'

'Do you?' He was listening to me with wary concentration. 'In what way?'

I gazed down at my fingers: the oval nails, the smooth unmarked skin of a physician who never got his hands dirty. 'This son of hers may not have wanted to acknowledge her, but she loved him. Her grief at having lost him colored everything she thought or did or felt – or saw. She saw him everywhere.' I remembered the span of her skull under my palms, its valleys and ridges, like a landscape which I'd recognized only imperfectly, and now wouldn't visit again. 'She saw him – well . . . She saw him in me.'

'You mustn't take this so much to heart.' He started to rearrange his papers: our interview was at an end. 'You're getting carried away as usual, probing where we have no business to probe.'

I shut my eyes, breathing in and out slowly against the outrageous blaze of pain in my breast. 'If you say so, Richard.'

'We have too many cases to become attached to each and every one. Stay on course, please. Don't overthink things. There's far too much work to be done.'

HE WAS RIGHT IN that, at least: the rhythms of the place, its unrelenting tide of human absurdity and suffering, bore me along and diverted reflection. This is something I later came to value about the asylum: the way that its crude crises forced you to live in the here and now, and made dwelling on the past and future almost impossible. In the world outside people were always going over yesterday's heartbreak, tomorrow's imminent rapture; no so-called sane person ever lives in the present at all. The life of the sane is just bookkeeping: an unremitting totting up of profits and losses. But in here the past was of no account because its places and people were a lost continent, a foreign shore, and the future – well, nobody dared talk of that.

Except for Ruth Macy. Her lover was well and she wanted him back. She wanted, naturally, to return their stalled relationship to the stream of time, to release him from the charmed sleep of our care. She wanted conclusions, beginnings, to move her story forwards. She wanted dailiness and domesticity.

Did Borden want this? He gave, I had to say, every impression of being willing to return to the world. He was more himself, more recognizable, with each week that passed. He was rapidly regaining mass and (this is how it appeared to me) definition. As he filled out and became substantial, the shape of him – not just of his body, but of his inner person – grew somehow clearer. How could this be, I wondered: that who he was depended on how much of him there was? And yet I couldn't find any other way of expressing the equation to myself. Perhaps it was a simple question of energy. He was *waxing*, exactly as fruit waxes, responsive to the force that drives all life. And I knew what this meant, because to accept life, to align yourself with that current, is also to accept life's ending.

Did I want this? Did I want him to become part of history again, subject to time and change? No, of course not. I didn't want it at all, any more than I wanted to step into those waters myself.

But for me, too, it was already too late.

He teased me about this. He was perpetually teasing me now. 'They won't know me back on Nantucket. I've grown so large, when my carcass rounds Brant Point it'll seem like an eclipse of the sun. How about you, Hiram? D'you think your folks will recognize the hulking fellow you've become?'

'Pshaw. I really don't care. This is my home, now.' The question gave me a bad case of the collywobbles. 'I should call on them, though. Next month. I'll go next month.'

'Next month? Is that the new word for "never"?'

'Ha, ha. Here, William.' I'd had another note from Nantucket that morning. They came in a daily flurry, like a foretaste of winter: October snow. 'Miss Macy is having the breakfast room repainted. She would like to know if you'd object to white.'

'Tell her white suits me as well as any other color.' We were sitting side by side on our usual bench, and, without warning, he reached out and put his hand on mine. 'I'll miss you, Hiram.'

We waited there, hand in hand, sixty feet above the darkly flowing river. 'Will. Is this what marriage is? This endless attention to *things*?'

'I guess.'

At first falteringly, then with increasing steadiness, I returned the pressure of his fingers. His proximity was suddenly unbearable. There was something I wanted to say, and the fear that I couldn't say it, would never be able to articulate it, reared like a black wave in my mind. But what was it I wanted to tell him? What *was* it? It seemed that, whatever it was, I couldn't allow myself to grasp it. 'I'll miss you too,' was all I could manage. Words failed me. Even the water below us seemed to have stopped its mumbling and to have fallen silent. 'I'll – I'll come and visit you both.'

'No, you won't. You like it too much here. And you don't like the sea. Remember?'

BORDEN'S RELEASE FROM THE asylum was accomplished very quietly. 'Discharge', I should say. Discharge – not release. He left us towards the end of that year, just as Advent began.

He went as he'd arrived, without a fanfare; without any struggle or fuss. Ruth Macy came for him in her hired carriage, its wheels slurring on the gravel drive, and again she came alone. She was so little as she waited in the hall in the winter dark, wrapped to her ankles in a black cloak, her shining hands clasped as if in prayer.

So little, so full of life, and so deadly.

She smiled the transparent smile I remembered so well, that shivered forever on the brink of melting. 'I'd like him back.' We'd discussed it all endlessly by letter; this was a piece of politeness, a courtesy offered by the victor to the vanquished. She'd taken hold of my wrist with both hands and now she rubbed my flesh with her cold thumbs. 'Oh, Cicero. Don't be sad.'

'I'm not sad.' I grazed her fingers with my lips. 'Not in the way you think.'

The most stupid thought occurred to me after he'd emerged from his rooms to meet her, after I'd said my goodbyes in a hollow imitation of Richard's bluff cordiality, after she'd taken his arm – stupid, because she scarcely came up to Borden's elbow; looked all of a sudden pitifully frail beside his resurrected bulk – and as the carriage turned back down the drive.

I thought: she'll kill him. She'll swallow him whole.

'All right, Cassius?' asked Richard once the last stone had spattered to a halt outside our doors.

'Oh, yes. I think I'll just drop in on one of my cases before tea.' Something stopped me as I was about to go upstairs. I stood with my foot on the bottom step, staring at the scarred old marble with its patches of shine, in which a hundred Hiram Carvers were reflected.

'Richard, do you know that I'll have been here a year come February?'

'Is that all? I thought it was longer.'

Borden's departure didn't leave a wrinkle on the uniform surface of the day. I climbed the stairs steadily: up, up, up. My fears were absurd. He hadn't gone to his death, he'd gone to a new life. He'd gone home.

Home, yes. Home. And what about me? I realized that what I had said to him was nothing other than the truth.

I was home.

TWENTY

'HIRAM, I'VE BEEN WONDERING. Since you have your own office at the asylum – and since you don't use Papa's old study – could I have it?'

'*You?*'

'Well, yes. That is – not for me to use, personally. For our women's hospital. As a consulting room. It's an awful lot of space going to waste.'

My sister, with impeccable timing, has chosen this moment to interrupt me. This very moment, just as I wrote *I was home.*

Well, I am home. Home in Mount Vernon Street. Where the sound of female chit-chat never stops, and the jangling of coal scuttles, and the clashing of carpet sweepers, and the rattling gunshot of female demands. I consider ordering her out. Then I restrain myself. She's a funny old thing, but infinitely dear to me.

'That's an interesting idea, Caro. I'll consider it.'

I mean this to be the end of the matter for tonight, but Caro doesn't go. She gives me a look of such naked pity that my stomach turns over. 'You were wrong about him, Hiram, altogether wrong. He loved us.'

For a minute, excruciatingly, her silhouette judders and swims before reassembling itself. 'Well, you, maybe.'

'Oh, my dear. Why were you always so jealous?'

'I have never been jealous, Caro. Never.'

'Oh, I think you have been.'

'Have I?'

'Yes. But it hardly matters now. You will give some thought to letting me have the study, won't you?'

'Of course, darling. Leave it with me.'

She stoops and drops a kiss on my temple. 'Good night, Hiram. Don't work too late.'

Jealous. Was that fair? Did I – do I – have a jealous nature? I'd been so preoccupied with William Borden in the summer and fall of 1834 that I completely failed to notice a development which, if fate hadn't intervened, would considerably have altered, if not the course, then at least the present comfort of my life. Even now I'm still not sure that I did anything intentional at all, or if in fact chance and character conspired to avert what should have been to me, in that year of obvious gains and subtler losses, a quite insupportable loss.

Truly the most unthinkable loss of all.

AT CHRISTMAS-TIME I FINALLY summoned up the courage to visit Beacon Hill.

In Charlestown we approached the Christmas festival with the seriousness of Carthaginian generals preparing to scale the Alps. Every knife was sharpened, every fork primed, every glass washed. Somewhere on a Massachusetts farm potatoes were being turned in a cellar; corn ground, milk churned, a flock of geese forcibly fattened for our dinner. In the meanwhile the asylum dining room was garlanded with boughs of spruce and wreaths of poinsettia, like the honors of war.

It must have been around that second Saturday in Advent. William Borden had left us (how lightly I write that). I was deployed at the top of a ladder all afternoon to skirmish with mistletoe while Miss Joy, helped by Miss Clayborn, aired the long damask tablecloths.

'Good job, Infant. What a cherub you make up there. Now come back to earth or you'll fall headfirst. Dr Mansfield, take hold of this corner for me while I lift our Prodigy down.' Before I knew it Sarah Clayborn had seized me by the waist and jolted me to the ground. 'There. A mistletoe kiss for you.' Her bristly chin scraped my cheek. 'And here's one for you, Fliss. Quit glowering.'

'It's good to see that those two have buried the hatchet,' said Richard as the women went off to the laundry room to take stock of napkins.

I straightened my clothing. 'Huh. You never know with Felicity. Are you ill?' For Richard had begun to cough, a dank morphine cough, all on a single reedy note. I noticed as he coughed how scrappy his arms were, ratcheting up in mid-convulsion to shield his crumpled chest. When had he begun to look so old? In just a few seasons, where Borden had bloomed, he'd wilted. 'Would you like to take forty winks?'

'No. Cassius, I can finish up here. I want you to go and stretch your legs. You haven't paid that visit to your family, have you? You can't keep putting it off indefinitely. The ladies seem to have everything in hand.'

'What about Frank?'

'He's gone into town. Call of the Copper Kettle.'

'In *this* weather?' It had been raining all day. But yes, I remembered seeing him slipping out, broken umbrella unfurled, an avid leer on his big ham of a face. '*Must* I? I'd rather see you comfortable.'

'You heard me. That's a direct order from your superintendent.' Steering me by the shoulders between coughs, Richard gave me a strengthless push towards the door. 'Go on, hop it. Don't make me tell you twice.'

I went.

It was still streaming with rain on the hill, and dark, though it was scarcely four o'clock; streaming for each step of the way across the river, streaming as I broached the outskirts of Boston, as if the Charles had broken free of its bed and, in defiance of every natural law, was running skywards . . . And I was soaked through, as I approached my family home, not simply by water but by the old obliterating feeling of being about to lose myself, of being drowned, of merging with that estuary named Carver in which I would no longer exist.

I still had my key, and rather than ringing the bell, I let myself in. I stopped and dripped in the hall, shaking my head like a dog. The noise of the rain, beating against the transom, was deafening.

And there it was. The silly umbrella, one spoke sticking out.

I picked it up. It yawned at the hinges, releasing a belch of rusty water. I closed it, turned it over. I turned it over again, and just as quickly put it down. From behind the parlor door not seven yards away, distinct from the percussion of the rain, came the unmistakable sounds of eating and drinking. *Tinkle plink* went a cup. *Gurgle gurgle glug* replied a pot. And then I heard Caro's wheedling murmur, and seconds later, a glutted, roundly satisfied male grunt which I would have known anywhere.

Goodwin's.

Of course. Frank was having his afternoon tea! This was why he came to town nearly every Saturday. This was where he'd been getting it — here, here *in my home*!

That Goodwin should be in our house; that Caro was entertaining a gentleman visitor — these things were violation enough of the order of things. It was surely unthinkable that my mother should be anywhere but in the drawing room, drinking her own tea, at four o'clock. I felt an incipient, swimming dread as I tiptoed up the stairs.

The drawing-room door stood partly open. Not a sound came from within, but a flash of cerulean behind its crack told me that she was there. I stopped, realizing with a thrill that I was going to observe her without her knowledge. What do the gods do when we aren't importuning them? I quaked like a swineherd spying on Juno.

My mother was seated on the sofa, her skirts spiraled around her in a stiff blue pool. She was utterly still, ringed fingers interlaced on her lap, her expression inhumanly serene, as if embalming fluid rather than blood ran through her veins. There were no signs of occupation anywhere nearby — no book, no newspaper, no needlework, no letters. She existed in the stillness like a giant star in the void, pulsing and impersonal. For a moment I was certain that the force radiating from her kept us all in our places, and that a break in her self-absorption would send us hurtling from the sky.

I knocked on the door and went in.

As I entered the room her head lifted a little. 'Darling, how lovely,' she murmured, without betraying the slightest surprise at seeing me. 'My, how you've grown. Were you always so big?'

I ignored this, kissing her obliquely offered cheek. For a fraction of a second I came into contact with her spicy scent, a smell like incense, like Christmas itself. I inhaled it hungrily. 'Mother, did you know that one of the asylum doctors, Frank Goodwin, is *talking*, alone, with Caro in the parlor?'

'Yes, darling.' She was at her most queenly, magnificently remote. Her ethereal regard alighted on me for a moment before flitting off again. 'What else would they be doing in the parlor but talking? Parlor, *parler*, *parlons*, we're quite French here now. And you know, my dear, if Caro is with him, then strictly speaking he isn't *alone* at all.'

'Oh good Lord, Mama.' I did some rapid mental arithmetic. 'How long has Goodwin been in the habit of visiting here?'

'Here?'

'Here – this house – that *parlor*!'

My mother addressed my kneecaps. 'Why this eccentric interest in rooms, Hissy? Sit down, pray. *Assieds-toi*. You're so elevated you're making me feel giddy.'

She smiled distantly, fluffing the sofa cushions as if inviting me to settle on an adjacent cloud. 'I don't believe one could call it a *habit*. He has been to tea here a couple of times. I'm sure I can't recall how many. More than you, certainly. They exchange recipes.'

'Mama. They don't just exchange *recipes*.'

'Oh, but they do. Dr Goodwin has given us such a choice one for honey-baked—'

'Mother, please! I don't want to know about Goodwin's baking.' I spluttered, spat into my sleeve. 'Oh God. Can't we, just for once, talk about what is *really* happening?'

'If you say so, darling.' A stray inspiration stirred the frigid calm of her brow. 'I think I'll ring for my own tea now. Will you join me?'

At her command our tea materialized in a nimbus of steam and silver. As ever I was agog to see my mother, who appeared to have no earthly needs, eating and drinking, as if this were a sleight-of-hand she performed for my benefit. Behind the implosions of her lips and the skreeking of her fork the mystery of her being continued to grow, until it seemed it would suck the air out of the room. While I nibbled at a macaroon I kept one ear open for noises from the parlor: the scatter of Caro's laugh, Goodwin's greedy assent, the slither of a chair leg . . .

What was Caro doing? Had she pulled her chair across to his? Was she sitting on his tubby lap, cooing about cups of currants or bags of sugar?

But more profoundly than that: *What was she doing?* Why was she letting this buffoon drool over her, why was she serving herself up to him on a plate? Wasn't her life here, her pleasant and orderly life, enough for her? Why did she need to do *this?*

At last it came: the crepitation of Caro's skirts in the downstairs hall, bungling *thunckety thuncks* as Goodwin retrieved his coat, his hat, his umbrella; a final grinding of locks, the quietus of the front door.

And then – nothing. I'd expected her to come upstairs, but she didn't. She'd gone back into the parlor to savor the memory of this meeting, to chew it all over in private.

Why, Caro? Why, why, *why?* Was this how all women felt? Were they all secretly discontented with their lot, however comfortable it was; all on the lookout for an escape?

The question that had been forming in my mind as my insides racked me and my mother took counterfeit bites of her bread-and-butter now threatened to tumble out and embarrass us both. But didn't I hope, still, that I would find the key to her? Didn't I dream, in my deepest recesses, that she would one day stop withholding what I needed to hear?

'Mama, may I ask you something?'

How supplicating my voice sounded, how tinny, in those stellar spaces! I knew that I couldn't ask what I most wanted to ask – do you love us, did you ever love us; were we ever enough for you?

'Of course, Hissy. You have always been such a *curious* boy.'

If there was a sting in this, I willed myself not to feel it. 'Do you ever wish for another sort of life? Are you ever – well, *bored*?'

My foolish question lay between us, gasping in the thin air of her disapproval. I saw in an instant that she had no intention of acknowledging it with a real answer. My mother studied me along her Olympian nose like the hardened immortal she was.

'Never, Hiram. A lady is never bored.'

I RESOLVED TO HAVE it out with Goodwin on Monday morning. The only time we were free to talk was over our work, and once the dispensary door was safely shut and we had our aprons on, I tackled him.

'I know you've been visiting my sister, Frank. I wish you'd confided in me. I thought we were friends.' We were making the day's tinctures, and at that moment Goodwin was measuring out antimony salts into a flask of filtered water. As soon as I'd spoken, his hands began to jog as if they were palsied. 'Whoa. You've put a double dose in that one. Here, I'll do it.'

'Cassius, I'm sorry! You are my friend – you are! And I wanted to tell you! But Carrie – but Miss Carver thought it best if we didn't say anything for a while. She felt that your – your connection, which is very precious to her, was too, uh, too fragile, too compromised, to support any further shocks to its –'

'*Carrie?* I'll thank you, and *Caro*, if you'll let me be the judge of what my feelings for her can and cannot bear. Shocks, indeed. You talk as if my relationship with her were some sort of suspension bridge! She's my sister, Frank, for heaven's sake. I'm her brother. It's not a question of *engineering*.'

'I'm so slow. What do you mean? She and I have reached an – an understanding. Are you saying that you don't mind?'

'Of course I don't mind.' Didn't I? Didn't I mind? I can say quite honestly that I didn't want to mind, didn't want to feel as abused and swindled as I did. (Goodwin – why *Goodwin?* Was this the best she could do? Was *this* what she was throwing us all over for?) 'I wish you both every happiness.' I grubbed about for the usual clichés one was supposed to offer in these circumstances. 'And *bonne chance*.' And then, since in his overstimulated state he was threatening to botch another tincture, 'Concentrate, for criminy sakes, will you? You've put three ounces into that flask instead of two. Have you spoken to my father yet?'

'Not yet. I haven't had the nerve. But I will now. You've been so awfully encouraging.'

Oh, better and better! There I was, greasing the hymeneal slope for Frankie and Carrie! 'I'm delighted to hear it.'

'Cassius, this may sound like temerity. But. I think I *can* make her happy. I'm gainfully employed here, and she's perfectly prepared to share the strains, as well as the rewards, of my career. But apart from that, I truly believe that she is uniquely fitted to me, and I to her. Never in my wildest dreams did I dare to hope that I would meet someone so sympathetic, so capable, so aligned with my deepest –'

Oh, blah, blah, blah. His deepest what? Cravings for pie and other flaky pastry? The delusional capacity of lovers astonished me. They'd feel a rumbling in their guts and mistake it for a reorganization of their souls. For a short time even I, in my dealings with Ruth Macy, had been susceptible to a belief in this sort of transubstantiation. But common sense, professionalism, and a hard-won awareness of my own true possibilities had prevailed. It was not real. It simply was not *real*.

I balk at writing this, but I must.

I was about to send Frank's career, with its 'strains' and 'rewards' – and with it, Caro's happiness – to the block.

TWENTY-ONE

AFTER THAT TÊTE-À-TÊTE GOODWIN was everywhere, scampering about on his fat legs, deferring profusely to my opinion, and seeking every opportunity to ingratiate himself with me. Even my hour with the weekly kitchen order, which he'd once treated as sacrosanct, was now fair game.

'*Ave*, Cassius.'

'*Ave atque vale*, chum. Can whatever it is wait two minutes? I have to add up this column.'

'I'll be extra quick.'

'One hundred and forty seven, one hundred and fifty-four, one hundred and sixty – what?' He was still there, slavering over me as if I were a chop. '*What?* I said *no*.'

'It's Mr Thornton.'

'One sixty-six. Sixty-seven. Damnation, Frank! Now you've made me lose count. Don't you *want* to eat this week?'

'He'd like a belt. He says he's ashamed to have his wife see him with his trousers falling down.'

'His wife . . . Oh, fuck.' I groaned. 'His wife.'

I was making no headway with Richard on this point. Whenever I broached the question of Mrs Thornton's visit his answer was always the same: no. No, and no. And not just a simple no, but *Absolutely not, Cassius. I won't give way on this. And believe me, if you defy me in this particular, I will find out. And this time I'll have no choice but to inform the trustees.*

'Don't be vulgar, please,' my future brother-in-law admonished me. 'I know he doesn't understand that he can't see her, but it's not an unreasonable request. He's lost so much flesh they won't stay up. I guess he has a point, regardless of this fantasy about her visiting –'

Thornton was subtle yet unrelenting in the pressure he put on me to fulfil my promise. I could see that he would once have made a formidable businessman. I rather admired both his doggedness and his diplomacy, and if I hadn't felt personally bound to honor my undertaking to him, I might have been interested to see how far these qualities would stretch. But I couldn't help thinking that Mansfield's stubbornness on the subject of Mrs Thornton was deeply irrational. That we shouldn't admit visits from relatives had become an article of faith with him; as unexamined as a belief in the Holy Ghost. Or at best it was a reflex, like a sneeze or a yawn – as automatic, and as empty. So much in Richard, admirable though he was, seemed a reflex or a matter of habit. His smug invocations of Shakespeare, his needling jokes, his bonhomie and his quasi-paternal way of putting me in my place while pretending to humor my ideas – did he even know, half the time, that this was what he was doing?

And I was disturbed by the amount of morphine he was taking each day. I was by now unpersuaded that the headaches really preceded the morphine. Wasn't it rather that the morphine had become the thing, the grail, the sacred cup in which every potential ill was tamed and transformed, the whole world diluted and magicked away? How could a man so removed from himself, so *drugged*, be left to make decisions concerning matters of daily protocol?

None of this, I reflected, would have been so trying if Richard hadn't been determined to deny others their props. It was only the hope of his wife's visit – no, the *vision* of her visit – that kept Adam Thornton in a state of equilibrium, harmonized the ragged elements of his inner life, and made the world we'd plunged him into bearable.

Because the asylum was a world: it was a world as vapidly comfortable and bereft of meaning as any other world ever created by the civilized human mind; as hamstrung, hedged, and frankly impossible to transcend in any lasting way without an overarching quest –

'Cassius, are you *listening* to me? I'm sorry to bother you with this, but I did promise that I'd run anything to do with Mr Thornton past you, you know.'

Jesus. Goodwin was still yammering on. 'Yes, Frank, yes. I can't deal with every tiny detail. He's had a razor for eight months without coming to any harm. Just use your discretion please, will you? Let him have a belt. For God's sake – it's Christmas, after all.'

ADAM THORNTON DID NOT come down to the dining room on Christmas Day. When I went to the men's wing to hurry him along, I found him dead.

After the hot-cold shock of the moment of discovery, after the wolfish howl that filled the house and was, I later realized, the sound of my own voice; after the pounding in the corridors and the press of bodies at the door, the snarl of arms and legs in which Mansfield's gray face sank and resurfaced, the bedlam of barks and wails and the sliding of bolts to contain the panic I'd let loose; the hirpling retreat of the mad and the horrible calm of that little room once we were alone with the corpse, this is what I remember.

The back of Thornton's head, higher, much higher, than any human head should be. The comb marks in his long hair, and his pigeon-toed feet, swinging above the braided rug which his wife had made him as a Christmas gift and I'd delivered to him as a charity, a pledge, a part-fulfilment of my promise. Hair, feet, the braided strips of the rug. The belt winched around the back of his neck. And when he turned, in a delayed revolution during which time itself seemed to split and gape, the swarthily swollen grin of his mouth.

'Richard, is he smiling? Can he be smiling? If he's smiling then he's alive, isn't he?'

'No, Cassius. He isn't alive. I'm going to give you a powder and then I want you to go to your room and go to sleep. I'll take care of this.'

If Adam Thornton wasn't mad when he came to us, we had driven him mad.

I went directly to my bed, got under the covers, and lay there intending never to move again.

That night I heard a knocking at my door. My face was mashed against the wall, but I knew who my visitor was by the vinegary aura of morphine that preceded him.

'Cassius, are you awake? May I speak to you?'

'I don't feel up to it, Richard. I feel like hell.'

'You can't afford to take this so personally. You were scrupulous in your care of Thornton.'

'Yes, Richard,' I rasped without turning around. The opiate he'd given me was still driving its muddy course through my blood. 'I was his *physician*. That's exactly it. He was in my care and he *died*.'

'It wasn't your doing. You were his advocate. His champion. You were all that you should have been.'

'Was I? Did I feel his agony as if it were my own? Did I watch with him when he couldn't sleep? Did I understand – *really* understand, to the point of feeling it in my pulses – that his pain was every bit as real as mine?'

Richard sighed. 'You describe a degree of empathy that lies outside our appointed role here.'

'Does it? Why does it? If we don't believe in the suffering of others, how can we believe in our own?'

'Ah.' He sat down on the edge of the bed: I felt his weight, the warmth of him, against the base of my spine. 'If we're running a competition for worst physician, then I fear the failure was partly mine.'

I shuffled onto my back. His head hung above me, his hair crazily bifurcated, his eyes gelid. 'Yours? How, by any reckoning, was it yours?'

'As superintendent, I didn't begin to appreciate the depth of Mr Thornton's despair.'

I hauled myself up through layers of mud. As always, Richard had managed to remind me both of his seniority and of his dependence on me. But wasn't that the role to which I'd *really* been appointed at the asylum: to shore up Richard Mansfield?

'You mean the business of his wife's visit, I suppose. Well, you have your preferred approach. And usually it doesn't lead to this. No, Richard. It was *my* fault.'

'Yes. But in Thornton's case I may have acted without due care.'
He coughed, and hawked several times to clear his throat – a new
tic. 'He seemed so certain that she would be admitted. It was such
a disastrously persistent delusion. I couldn't shift it with any of the
usual deflections or distractions. He insisted, absolutely insisted, that
she would soon be allowed to visit him, and that he had your word
for this. And I knew, after our many discussions of the subject, that
this couldn't possibly be true.'

I wanted to laugh. I wanted to explode in a shriek, to cry out,
Richard! *Don't you know me by now?* I put my hands over my face.
'No. Of course not.'

'Precisely. Yesterday I made this very clear to him – that it was
utterly contrary to our therapeutic principles, and that you knew this,
and would never condone it, whatever he thought you might have
promised. *I engaged with his delusion.* And now, you see, he is dead.'

'Oh God, Richard.' The shriek in me was gathering in volume
and force. What if I shrieked out loud? What if I threw my arms
around him and brought him down and had it out with him there and
then, two drugged madmen, rolling about on the floor? 'Oh Christ.
What a hash we have made of this.'

'The belt, though, Cassius. Cassius, look at me, please. This is the
worst aspect of it all. Poor Frank gave it to him. Without the belt . . .
Frank's been careless before. But a belt! What was he thinking? Why
didn't he see the risk?'

I lowered my hands. A glissade of sparks drizzled across my line
of vision. 'Have you asked him?'

'Yes. He can't account for it. He just doesn't appear to have
thought it through *in the least*. He says it seemed safe.'

'Is that all he says?' I asked miserably.

'That's all. It's exasperating.' His mackerel eyes tried to get a purchase on mine. 'Why, do you know more?'

What did it matter what I said now? The sparks had become an incandescent jet that threw everything into a negative image of itself. I was mad, and I was speaking to a madman.

'Richard, I didn't want to mention this, but Frank's been consistently careless. This wasn't an isolated incident.'

'No?'

'He's been heavy-handed with the antimony lately. Only the other day he nearly gave the men's wing an overdose. I've felt obliged to supervise him ever since. It's simply not an efficient use of my time, having to monitor him too.'

'Oh, good God. Yes . . . Yes, I can see that. I've sometimes felt that he's less of an asset than an extra responsibility, well-meaning fellow though he is.' He inhaled thickly and rubbed his forehead in silence. When he managed to retrace his thoughts minutes later, it was in the voice of a man for whom a crisis had been resolved. 'I'm fond of him, but it's no good. There's nothing else to be done.' He was gathering conviction to him with every word. 'I'm going to have to ask Frank to leave.'

Oh, mad! Mad! 'That seems rather drastic. Perhaps I shouldn't have said anything.'

'You did right to alert me. I know you're friends, but the safety of our patients has to be our chief concern. That must remain paramount.'

I bowed my head. 'I understand.'

'And for your sake, too – you'll find it less burdensome. Once a man starts to make mistakes like this his judgment can't be trusted. You're doing the work of two here. I can't have you carrying him any longer.' Again that hawking, as if he were trying to expel something from his gullet. 'You and I have to go on, you know. This place depends on us.' A piping wheeze; another cough. 'I want you to look after yourself, Cassius. You mustn't let this throw you off course. You're far too valuable a resource.'

'Thank you, Richard. It's kind of you to say so.'

'Kind? No, no. It's the plain truth.' His hand, with its chalky knuckles, sought my sleeve. 'I really don't know what I'd do without you.'

And so, between us, we stuck the knife into Frank Goodwin.

ON NEW YEAR'S EVE I was summoned to dinner in Mount Vernon Street.

After Thornton's death a brittle lassitude had settled over the asylum. In the days that followed, the roast geese which we'd failed to eat in the chaos attending my discovery of his body were served up, cold, to a silent dining room. The greenery was taken down, the candles snuffed. The place felt like glass, both fragile and dangerous, as if something might shatter at any moment.

I lingered over my rounds as long as I could that evening, leaving at the very last minute. I was full of a sick foreboding as I walked out onto the hill and started to make my descent through the poplar grove. After the recent rains the river was eerily full and still, ruffled by cat's paws of wind, the sky a bleak slate. The sick feeling grew as I crossed Craigie's Bridge and caught sight of the bulge of the

State House dome above the brown rooftops of Boston, the uneven elevation of Beacon Hill, the elm posted like a wagging finger at our fence; felt the airless swoosh of the front door sucking me across the threshold. When I went into the house, and heard my sister's footsteps on the landing above, I knew that the feeling in my stomach was terror.

'Hiram!' Caro ran down in a headlong rustle and snap of taffeta. 'You're late!' She grappled me to her in an embrace. 'How well you look!'

It was the first time we'd seen each other since our quarrel in the spring. 'So do you.'

In fact she looked better than merely well: she looked *juicy*, her freckles dissolved in a dewy flush (was that *sherry* on her breath?), her hair oiled, as sleek as a cat that's been feasting on stolen cream.

'I've been keeping dinner back till you got here. Go and have some Madeira while I let Cook know you've come.' She gave me another lush hug. 'I have so much to tell you.'

'Miss,' bassooned Papa's voice from the drawing room, 'is that your brother at last?'

'Go on up,' said Caro, as my sinews tightened under her hands. 'He won't bite. But wait – Hiram, wait.' She held me at arm's length for a second and lavished on me such a look of liquid, unadulterated love that I've never forgotten it. *Thank you*, she mouthed.

Once the gingerbread and the candies and the pecans and the muscat grapes had been consumed, and the coffee and the digestifs had been knocked back, my father's piggy eyes found me.

'Hiram, a word with you, if you will.' A frown notched the complacent gloss of his forehead. 'I've had rather unexpected news from

Richard Mansfield,' he began, after Caro and my mother had quit the table — Caro still with that molten look — and left us to our manly talk. 'Frank Goodwin is going to be given his notice — on grounds of gross negligence, apparently. I understand that there has been an unfortunate accident.'

Here it was. Oh, sick, sick.

'Well, sir, he killed a patient. Not much room for maneuver there.'

'*Killed a patient?* Mansfield said it was suicide.'

'Not with his own hands, it has to be said. But his carelessness led directly to the poor man's death.' I grasped the brandy decanter and poured myself a stiff one. 'Dr Mansfield will be submitting his report to the board tomorrow.'

'Mansfield tells me that he's acting partly on information provided by you. Do you have anything to say?'

I pushed the decanter in his direction. My mouth was so dry that I could hardly shape the necessary words. 'Father, if Dr Goodwin is incompetent, that's hardly my fault.'

My father toyed ruminatively with the brandy stopper. 'You do realize what this will mean for Caro, don't you? I've said nothing to her yet. Goodwin's been courting her for months. He asked me for my permission just a week ago. I thought him a promising young man — unpolished, it's true, but promising.' He stared into his empty snifter, then at me. 'He was competent enough before. It doesn't fit, Hiram. I can't put my finger on it, but something doesn't fit.'

I took a deep breath. 'Well, sir, if you still doubt the facts once you've read the report, then override Dr Mansfield and retain Goodwin, at whatever risk to your mortality rates. And since you seem to question my judgment, perhaps I'll go elsewhere.' Swallowing my fear, I lifted my glass. 'Your health.'

My father stared me down. 'Don't be absurd. If what you say is true, the trustees will never agree to retain him. The boy's errors are stacked against him now. And Mansfield thinks the world of you. You've done well at that place – I can see that.'

I set down my brandy so hard that urinous drops christened the table. 'Papa, you may not accept it, but I'm *good* at what I do. Dr Mansfield knows it. My patients know it. Aren't you the least bit proud of me?'

'I have always been proud of you, Hiram. You are my son. But I fear that you've done your sister an ill turn, sir. An ill turn.'

Oh, the shame of it – the shame. The shame and the terror, combined in a way that was age-old, as familiar as my own self, immutable. And mixed with them, the raw knowledge – gained in that very moment, and as crushing – that no matter what I did, he would never, ever be satisfied.

GOODWIN LEFT THE VERY next afternoon. He just packed up and left.

Richard waited until after lunch to deliver the *coup de grâce*. At a quarter past one I saw the two of them leaving his study, Richard unusually taciturn, Frank with his mouth in a queer twist, as if he'd eaten something putrid, and then Frank waddled upstairs alone, without meeting my eye.

What had he said, or not said?

Though there was no official timetable for Goodwin's departure,

I'd assumed that he would see out the week. When he didn't appear again after an hour I went to find him. The dispensary was empty, the only traces of him a muddle of unwashed flasks in the basin and a slick of spilled salts on the oilcloth.

I raced up to his room, which was across the corridor from my own set, taking the stairs two at a time. The door was ajar, his bed stripped. The striped ticking of his mattress, exposed like that, looked oddly boyish and bereft. An abandoned sock lay amid the dust and fluff on the floor.

Gone.

I steadied myself against the jamb, as winded as if an engine of destruction had passed me by: I could feel its backdraft on my face.

And that was that, or so I told myself.

Richard said nothing to me that day, or the next, or in the next weeks. Gradually, very gradually, the feeling of sickness in the pit of my stomach went away. But I slept badly, a difficulty I still have, and can trace back to that time.

And then I began to dream about Adam Thornton. It was always the same dream. In it I was standing on the threshold of Thornton's room, transfixed by shock as his dangling body performed its interminable revolution. But he was only half dead, only half hanged, his hands and face still warm, and I'd realize, with an exquisite access of joy, that there was a chance of my saving him, of reversing that entropy, if I could just find the right word. Night after night, it eluded me.

I made a point of stopping by at Mount Vernon Street on Saturdays, to keep an eye on Caro. Since Goodwin had lost his prospects he'd very properly withdrawn his offer of marriage, and after that brief and humiliating communication I don't believe she heard from him again. The rumor was that he'd left Boston and joined an aunt in Maine. My sister may have hoped for a reprieve; for his return from exile, like the disgraced Don Juan emerging victorious from the siege of Ismail. But unlike that Byronic hero Frank possessed a well-developed sense of shame – or what passes in our world as a sense of honor – and I didn't expect him to come back.

I own to feeling a craven sense of relief. For if he had –

I was equally relieved to see that Caro bore up well. She ran the house as capably as ever, baking and sudsing and polishing and needlepointing with a dauntlessness that was almost maniacal. She was made of stern stuff.

And yet. There was a flatness to her now, a stiltedness – I want to say a *stuntedness* – that hadn't been there previously. Did her voice really have that bladed edge? When she spoke she often sounded gruff, even brutish. It was as if she'd once been fluid, and had hardened, practically overnight, into some new and final and uncompromising shape. Her jaw had a calcified slant that I'd sometimes seen on the faces of our longer-term boarders. She was as upright and as spry as ever, but she was – no question about it – subtly diminished.

I didn't know that grief, simple grief, could do this – no, I didn't know. I yearned to comfort her, but I had no idea how. So I went to Mount Vernon Street every Saturday at dinner time, and ate the meals she continued, with faithful care, to plan and prepare: the meals that she would, if things had run their natural course, have made for him. Bedeviled by inarticulate remorse as I was, it seemed like the only thing I could do.

These evenings brought me a morsel of ease. I found myself

looking forward to them, and to the hour I'd spend with my sister beforehand in the parlor. Caro had taken to sitting there now, rather than upstairs with Mama, saying she needed time to think.

But she never again turned that look – the look I'd come to think of, with a fanciful sadness, as love's libation – on me.

I'd come across her there, screened by a drooping fern with a book open on her lap, not thinking but reading: sermons, devotional exercises, spiritual tracts. She appeared to have given up poetry. I now see that this was the phase in which Caro's religious convictions took root (if one can call a delusion that has lasted twenty years a phase). She would put her book away when I arrived and get up to embrace me, but on a day in August when I'd reasonably anticipated a warmer welcome than usual – it was, I remember, my twenty-fourth birthday – she drew away.

'This is supposed to be a happy occasion, old girl. Don't I get a kiss?'

'Well, Hiram,' she replied, scarcely above her breath, lifting her lips to my cheek. 'Many happy returns.'

She'd been crying. I couldn't remember seeing Caro cry before, except when she was a little girl, and I felt strangely frightened.

'Oh, my dear,' I pleaded. 'Are you *still* sad? Don't distress yourself like this.' I put my arm around her shoulders. 'He was nothing. A clown. A weakling. No Don Juan.'

'No what?'

'You know. *Love is of man's life a thing apart.*'

She gave me a sere smile.

'You deserve far better. Yes?'

'Yes.'

'Caro. You may quite naturally be worrying about the future.'

Her eyes darkened. Though I couldn't say why, it seemed to me all of a sudden that an unlit gulf had opened up between us and that we faced each other across it not as brother and sister, but as two adversaries.

'It may be premature of me to raise this now,' I continued. 'But. I'd like you to know that if you don't – well, if you never . . . That you'll be able to live here with me.'

'What if I don't want to live with you?'

'You may have no choice.' To my infinite horror, she'd begun to sob. My reassurances stuck in my craw. 'Caro,' I floundered, 'I'm sorry for your disappointment.'

She held up her hand to silence me. Her voice broke into an accusing cry. 'Hiram, are you happy? Are you satisfied?'

'Happy?'

'Yes. You have everything you want. Papa says Richard Mansfield won't so much as blow his nose without you. You've made short work of poor Mr Borden. And I – well, I'm here.'

And I – well, I am here. Where had I heard those very words before from a woman?

Ah, from Ruth Macy, of course. They spoke as if they were our victims. Only they weren't. Didn't they always get what *they* really wanted? Didn't they win out over us, each time? They asked everything, everything of us! They gave nothing tangible in return and yet they expected us to lay the world at their feet.

But my sister wasn't done with accusing me. 'Have you had enough, now? Is this enough for you?'

'I don't know what you mean. I haven't "made short work of"

William Borden, Caro, I've cured him. And I want to share everything I have, every success of mine, with you.'

'This house will be yours one day, Hiram. Not mine. What if you marry?'

'That makes no difference. It is your home too, Caro. There's no reason for you ever to have to leave it.'

'Oh God!' She threw her hands in the air, laughing and crying at the same time.

She never has left it.

THE WORST OF IT was that Caro was right.

I was twenty-four. Twenty-four! I was still young, and I had, as Richard had pointed out, already achieved a great deal. So much had happened. I was no longer the inexperienced boy I'd once been. Though I was troubled by regret at some of the things I'd done, there were so many reasons to feel satisfied. Replete.

Yet as that summer gave way to fall, and I continued to dine at Mount Vernon Street each week, and to pursue my tasks at the asylum, and it dawned on me that this would now be my life in perpetuity, for as far as I could see into the future, I felt, unaccountably – wasn't this what I'd gone out into the world in search of, this calling, this vocation, this *nourishment*? – like someone to whom nothing had happened at all.

I felt emptier, hungrier, than I ever had before.

PART THREE:

Dark Water

TWENTY-TWO

TODAY IS FRIDAY, THE end of another week of work, and I would normally have been due home by five. But Mrs Cushing, one of our hysterics, cut herself with the broken glass of her hand mirror as I was about to pack up for the day.

My assistant super, Benjamin Schultz, wrestled her to the ground as easily as I might settle my trouser seams. This is, I must confess, one of the reasons I appointed him, in the face of some opposition from the trustees (apart from the fact that he is only twenty-seven, and unlikely to have designs on my sister. Caro is now approaching fifty). Just look at him – those springy triceps, the gristle in his thighs. He has the strength of three men. I still find it hard to believe that he spent the first part of his career tending the sick in Illinois, rather than straddling steers. And yet he seldom exercises that strength with our boarders. He is invariably patient and persuasive. He is good at listening to their tales of woe with seeming interest while spooning oil of ricin into their mouths and assessing their vital signs, all at the same time. Occasionally he will utter soft *tchrcks* of encouragement. When he retreats, they come forwards. Maybe it *is* a little like herding cattle.

Mrs Cushing had succeeded in slicing her vena basilica – not deeply, but enough to send blood spurting in all directions. I fixed her up while Benjamin held her down. By the time I'd put away my needle, we were a gruesome sight.

'Time to wash up. After you, Ben.'

At the door of the storage room I stood back to allow Schultz to enter. It's a still unrefurbished wainscoted room with a chipped stone floor and teetering shelves, covered in grilles of wire mesh, where we keep boxes of glycerine soap and rolls of gauze, but it has the distinction of having been recently plumbed with a new sink. Schultz's cuffs were soaked with blood. He rolled back his sleeves and began to pump vigorously with his left hand while running water over his chunky wrist and arm with the right. Then he changed position. Water splashed onto the flags. He passed a cake of soap along his forearms and sluiced them down again, before applying more soap and water to his face and toweling himself off. When he lowered the towel I saw that his lids were sickled with mauve shadows.

'Are you going home this month?' I said. 'I hope so. You took no leave at Christmas.'

'Well, th-thank you, sir.' Ben always calls me 'sir'. It's a form of address I haven't discouraged among the staff. Richard's informality was well meant, but it set the wrong tone for an institution of this kind. 'I'm pretty tired. I guess I'm due a visit to Springfield. I d-didn't like to ask.'

Springfield, Illinois. That capital of mud and frame houses. 'Don't be a fool. You can ask me any time.'

I noted with interest that Ben, whose Midwestern drawl was normally unimpeded, started to stammer when the topic touched on something that held a particular significance for him. It's a phe-nomenon I've noticed previously among the sane, myself included. Though they may sometimes suffer from complete aphasia, the mad almost never stammer (nor did William Borden). One would have thought it much more likely to be the other way around. Since treating Borden I've often pondered what this suggests about the connection between language, or the higher-order control language demands of us, and powerful emotion. In those days I believed that the emotional charge of any experience, however damaging and even if initially lost to memory, could be defused, made safe, and the experience itself restored to its proper place in the sufferer's mental economy, by being translated into speech. Into words. Now I wonder. Could it be that language itself is a form of distortion, of repressive control, that our blazing inner self, when we are lucky enough to make contact with it, instinctively rejects? If the insane don't stammer, isn't it because they have discovered a way of bypassing this control completely? Their speech is a wire running straight to the red-hot core of who they are. Not for them the hypocrisies of polite intercourse. They are free, as we will never be.

'I'm g-grateful to you, sir. My mother will be glad to see me.'

Yes. I could imagine Benjamin caring for his mother with the same meticulous tenderness he showed in the care of his patients, and the washing of his arms. I rinsed my hands and gave them a swift pat with the towel. 'Very well, then. Take a week's holiday.'

He turned his bright face to me. 'Sir, if I may say something.' He wasn't stammering now. 'I know you have a reputation for – if you'll forgive me, for being a touch severe. But I also know that you're on the side of what's good.'

'*Good?*'

'Yes. Your work here. Your dedication. I've never seen a man work as hard as you. You're a champion of health. Of progress.' He hung back. 'Well, sir, I wouldn't be able to pull together with you, if you weren't.'

Pull together. Perhaps that was a ranching term. Still, my eyes prickled queerly. 'Heavens, Ben.' I managed to sound dry. 'You flatter me.'

Schultz gave a circumspect laugh. We stared at our feet. My shoes were striped with Mrs Cushing's blood. Rivers of it. Who'd have supposed the old woman had so much blood in her? I thought briefly of Mansfield, his well-thumbed Shakespeare, the years he'd given to this place. What did they amount to, when all was said and done? I turned the memory away.

It was nearly six o'clock by the time I got home to Mount Vernon Street. I was planning to work on this history, and hoped that Caro would let me slip in quietly, but she ambushed me at the door. Her hands were floury, and so was the collar of her house dress.

'Hiram, have you had a chance to think about my request?'

'Hmm, dearest?' A curiously formal word, 'request'. Ben – why, Ben had called me 'severe'. Is *this* how people see me now – as someone whom they are unable to approach freely? 'What request was that?'

'To use Papa's study. Just from time to time, you know.'

'Oh goodness, Caro. I'm such a simpleton. I'd completely forgotten that you asked me. The thing is that I've been going up there in the evenings to work on my manuscript. It's really the only perfectly quiet room in the whole house. I was rather thinking of turning it into my permanent writing room.'

334

'*Your* writing room?'

'Yes. You see, my dear, I'm still writing my memoir.' I drew my papers out of my bag and fanned them at her. 'In fact, I'm right in the thick of it. I was just on my way upstairs. I'm sorry, old girl. You know how I hate to disappoint you in anything.'

'I know.' She touched her hair, whitening its ginger. 'It doesn't matter.'

'What's for dinner tonight? I hope we're not going to have our digestions put through their paces by that eel pie?'

'No. It's beef.'

'Beef. Ah. Roast or boiled?'

'Roast. I know you can't abide boiled, Hissy.'

She'd deliberately used my loathed childhood nickname, but I let her have her little victory. 'I certainly can't. With pudding and gravy?'

'Yes. With pudding. And gravy.'

'Marvelous.' I patted the hillock of my stomach. 'You are making me quite fat, darling, but I'm not complaining. I'll be down shortly.'

'Will you change for dinner? You look an absolute fright. Is that *blood* on your shirt?'

'What? Oh. Yes. It might be. We had some slight trouble with a patient this afternoon. Very well, my dear, I'll change. Just to please you. Mercy, what a tyrant you are.'

I went up, lit the gas, saw the huge dusty room spring to life. I did try to write here a weekend ago – I believe I've never yet told Caro an outright untruth – but found it remarkably difficult. It was as if my father still had possession of the place, even though he's been in his grave these twelve years.

In any case, here I am now, trying again. I have settled myself at

Papa's desk, and tested the nib of my pen. (I write with a solid silver Gillott these days – a recent birthday gift from Caro.)

What did the last twenty years bring?

Though I planned to pick up my narrative where I stopped yesterday, I find that I'm bothered by thoughts of Richard Mansfield. The incident with Mrs Cushing, the struggle, the blood, has upset me. So let me write about him first.

When Richard left the asylum in 1844 it wasn't exactly in disgrace, but it was close to it. After some years I'd come to expect his departure. He was worn out, as an overwound spring can be worn out. He relied on morphine to get him through each day, but the days weren't long enough to accommodate the quantity of morphine he needed to take. He made a passable feint at being in command of the place until we did our rounds in the women's wing one morning and found that Miss Clayborn had eloped.

Her bed was neatly made, her windows shut fast. Her wardrobe was bare. She'd taken her corduroy jackets and her Bible and left by the front door.

'She's gone, Richard. She's damn well left us. How *could* she?'

'Cassius, we must get her back. Call Miss Joy.'

But Miss Joy was gone too. Her cold-cream pot and her hair-nets – spirited away into thin air.

Not 'eloped'; eloped.

'Those bitches. Those goddamned bitches.'

'Richard, stay calm.' I was staggered by the magnificence of their defiance of us. 'We could get them back, of course we could. Summon a police officer. Have them arrested. Have them dragged back in chains! But what for?' I asked, conscious of a whirling sense of disorientation. 'They're clever enough to know what they're doing, aren't they? Aren't we?'

'This is the end of me, Cassius. I'll be called on to resign if I don't get them back. A boarder and an *attendant*!' He turned to me thirstily, as if dredging for reassurance in a tried and tested well. But I was too spellbound by the new and startling fissure that had spread at our feet to answer him. 'Cassius? What shall I do?'

'They're free.' I was trying not to fall into that widening crevasse, unsure of where I'd be standing once the earth stopped shifting. 'We've never kept a jail here. Let's not start now.'

'Are you in earnest?'

'I'm sorry, Richard.' I suddenly saw it for what it was, this tectonic rearrangement – it wasn't a grin of destruction, but a smile of possibility. 'I am,' I said, my voice wobbling strangely. 'You know how much I admire you, and how deeply I value our friendship. Dare I say, our rivalry, at times! But you haven't been yourself lately. You've been – well, ailing.' I glanced up and met his eye. 'Maybe this is for the best.'

He said nothing. He was gazing out of the window of Felicity Joy's room. The river, burnished by the early morning sun, was topped with a sky like a ribbon of teal. Peace lay over the building that had been, for a decade, the arena of so many of our clashes. It was a long time before he spoke. 'The best for you.'

'The best for this asylum, and what we are trying to achieve here.'

'It appears to me that you and I have been trying to achieve different things.' He'd been staring hard at me. Now he drew back with an abrupt twitch. 'Good God. I've sheltered you, all these years. I've protected you. I've kept you close.'

'You've hardly *sheltered* me.' I was still battling to get my voice under control. 'We've been colleagues. More than that. You've been like a – a second father to me. And I don't mean to speak out of turn, but I really don't think you could've managed without my help all these years.'

'You cunning bastard.' His face was red and tight, alive with effort. 'I'm not sure which of us is the greater fool. I should have got free of you when I had the chance.'

At this my heart suffered a violent dilation. I knew that something dreadful was about to be uttered, something that couldn't be unsaid. 'Don't talk such rot. *Free* of me? What the hell do you mean?'

Richard spoke in spasms. 'When Adam Thornton killed himself, I suspected what you'd done. I didn't want to admit it to myself. But you let that stupid boy give him the belt, didn't you? Frank would never have risked such a thing on his own. He was completely under your thumb. I was so afraid of losing you that I looked the other way. Well, here's my reward. You're a goddamn serpent's tooth.' He seemed quite deranged. His thinning hair stood up in tusks, and even in the midst of my fright I noticed with disgust that some speck or crumb, the remnant of a distant meal, nestled in the corner of his mouth. 'Perhaps it's not too late. Your father isn't around to smooth your path any more. How would you like to give a full account of the circumstances of Thornton's death to the trustees?'

After an agonizing inner struggle I gained mastery of my voice. 'You misunderstand me. When I said "for the best", I meant not just for the asylum, but for *you*. It would be a terrible thing – much worse than this trifling matter of an elopement – if the trustees were to discover how much morphine you're taking. In fact, you were pretty well soaked in the stuff then too, as I recall.' I'd found my feet now, and was observing him from my full height. 'I never encouraged Frank to do anything in regard to Mr Thornton. I'd warned him off having any sort of dealings with him at all. Whatever you may have imagined was, I'm very much afraid, a by-product of your unfortunate habit. And that's exactly how I would have to present it to the board.'

'You wouldn't.'

'Oh, I would. I'm not a child.' Angry as I was, I wanted, maddeningly, to weep. 'I'm sick and tired of being threatened with the trustees. You're from Concord originally, aren't you? Why not go back there? Get yourself a cabin in the woods. Read Shakespeare from dawn till dusk, without any of these worrisome distractions. That's not such a bad life.'

'Oh, Hiram. You cold-blooded monster.' He made a frenetic outward motion with his palms, as if he were warding something off. 'You're ready to send me to the bottom as you kick your way to the top, aren't you?'

'Please don't say that.' Fighting a pulse of anguish, I edged forwards and placed my hand on his shoulder. I felt the torsion of his body, his old man's groaning humerus beneath my palm. 'That's not how I see it, and nor should you.' I bit back my tears. 'It would be – safe harbor, if you like.'

It was the first time he'd ever called me by my name. And the last.

I SHUDDER, NOW, TO remember that final scene with Richard Mansfield. My coolness was an act. The truth was that I still dreamed of Adam Thornton in the old way; had done so for years. Cruel dreams, beautiful dreams, in which, when trying to find the word that would resurrect him, I felt a power unavailable to me in waking life — and a degradation too, a frenzy of futile effort, as I sweated — oh, hopelessly! The word gave me the slip; try as I might, I couldn't find it — to bring the dead back to life. I recognized, of course, that these dreams were born of guilt. Behind Thornton, always, at the very moment when death would hog-tie him, and his mortal breath came retching from his grinning mouth, I'd see Frank watching from the shadows — and this was the instant in which the dream became unmanageable, and I'd wake.

For a while after Thornton's death I was convinced that it would mark a new epoch in my life, usher in a new order of being, a new self: humbler, not so cloven by ambition, forever grateful to have escaped punishment. More *whole*. And yet before long my sense of relief grew diffuse, my appetite for conquest returned, and I was back to the same old riven condition. Only the dreams, coming less frequently as the years passed, but never quite stopping entirely, remained as a reminder of that time.

In ousting Richard as I did I'd confronted — embraced, even — a hidden potential in my character. *Severe?* If I *am* severe then it's because I've had to develop this trait over the years, starting at that very moment. I'd had no choice but to save myself. It was him or me, and if I'd gone, all my work, whatever progress I'd brought about in that asylum, would have vanished as if it had never been. For if I'd failed in Adam Thornton's case, wasn't it also true that I'd succeeded, triumphantly, in William Borden's? I could live with my failure, I'd learn to put it behind me, if I could just have the opportunity to keep on working and building on the foundations I'd already laid down.

Or so I told myself.

I DON'T LIKE TO recall what happened immediately after Borden left us in 1834.

I'd corresponded with Ruth Macy a few times in the January and February of 1835. Her wedding plans were well under way; they were to be married quietly in the spring. The Society of Friends had, unsurprisingly, broken off with her, but she wrote that the ceremony would take place in Nantucket's First Congregational or North Church. 'Would you believe,' she wrote, 'that Mrs Chadwick, in whose house we first met, has proved a true friend to us both, and made all right? She has located William's name in the baptismal register, offered to act as our witness, and put everyone in their place.'

It was no surprise. And yet – there was something atrocious to me in the thought that he was now the Chadwicks' trophy, and would have to attend their 'At Homes' for evermore. Was this all his heroism had meant, in the end? I received an invitation from Miss Macy to visit them whenever my work allowed, which I politely deferred. Borden was right: Nantucket was too far, too drenched with remembered emotion, too *sea-bound* for me.

Good luck to her, and to the island of two that she was determined to create on that other island.

But then I didn't hear from her again. I wrote in the summer, congratulating them both on the event which I knew must, by that time, have taken place, and received no reply.

I'd made him well, she'd scooped him up and married him, they no longer thought of me. I'd seen this before, after a patient was discharged: this wish to deny or forget any connection with those who were associated with the period of illness. It was a common, even a necessary, part of rehabilitation; the last service the doctor could offer the sufferer – to disappear, and take that unhappy phase of life to the bottom of the ocean with him. *You've made short work of poor Mr Borden.* No, they'd made short work of me. I knew my role; I went beneath the waves, and whatever half-formed hopes I'd once had – not even half-formed; what had my coltish love for her amounted to, anyway? – finally went down too.

The days passed. Ben was right: I was nothing if not dedicated. I gave up my life to my duties. There were only my rending dreams of Thornton and Frank Goodwin to spoil that peace . . . But dreams are nothing, after all. What can dreams do?

The person I feared most, now – the sole person I feared – was my father. If he guessed that I'd played a part in Adam Thornton's death; if he knew, he never said a word. I lived in daily terror that he'd call me to account, that he'd rake over my transgressions, that he'd drag me before the ultimate seat of judgment: my sister. To lose her love, however squeezed and shrunken it now was, would be the end of me. But he never did.

I've no doubt he was protecting her, rather than me.

My father died in 1843. He had a fatal apoplexy while grafting an anterior cruciate ligament at Massachusetts General. The procedure involved extensive scalpel work: maybe the excitement of it turned out to be too much for him. Papa's left arm seized, and hey presto, the scalpel – one of his extendable models, with double the standard leverage – drove down, cutting the patient's hamstring in half. (Fortuitously it was a public case and the luckless man, who probably still walks with a limp, if he walks at all, wasn't in a position to sue the hospital.)

Overnight, I found myself the only Dr Carver in Boston. I knew that my secret was safe.

I don't know if I was a comfort to my mother after Papa went. That Caro hadn't ever been a comfort to her, and could never be one, was something that we all understood, though we didn't speak the words aloud. Caro was an indentured companion, a factotum. She and my mother had no choice but to put up with each other; it had always been that way, and my father's death made no difference to this fundamental truth. But I'd hoped that perhaps, one day, when the field was clear, I might, just possibly, capture Mama's attention. I might come home one day to Mount Vernon Street, throw off my hat and coat and, ascending the stairs, find her on the sofa in the drawing room, and she'd recognize me, really recognize me, and set down the teapot and – ah, well.

In the wake of my father's death the routine of my mother's life seemed to change very little. She wore black for a year, then shades of pepper, then a sort of stoat. I think that privately she was pleased – if she'd ever experienced anything focused enough to be called pleasure – to be allowed to sit in her widow's weeds, unaccosted, on that sofa for twelve months. Afterwards she went back to receiving the rare visitor, and paying the obligatory social calls, but her heart wasn't in it. She'd tasted oblivion.

She died unresistingly seven years ago, of complications from a ridiculously minor infection of the lungs, the sort of illness that wouldn't have killed a child. My own boyhood self, and all his foolish hopes, died with her.

To my surprise I started to feel, after Mama's death, that the house really was mine. I made no alterations, didn't meddle with Caro's running of it, didn't modify so much as a lamp-shade. But I came home more frequently to consume my sister's meals; then I returned each Saturday and Sunday as a matter of convenience, and in due course from every Friday evening through to the next working week. This is now my settled routine. Monday morning has been known to arrive and to find me still at the breakfast table at nine o'clock, filleting a kipper.

Caro may be a crotchety old thing, but I think she's glad, after all, to have me here. And she — well, she is my life. She is all I have of tenderness, and human warmth. But we are Carvers, and that means that I can't tell her what I truly feel.

So she feeds me, and I eat instead.

I WAS NEVER MUCH of a writer before, but after my father died, followed a year later by Mansfield's resignation — though it was a pity that Papa didn't see me appointed to the post of superintendent, at least no one could accuse me of having been unfairly favored by the trustees — I began to write up my cases. Not too long ago I decided to present, to the Massachusetts Medical Society, my notes on a young man whom we'd admitted for severe melancholia, issuing in fits of self-harm, occasioned by the death of his parents and two siblings in a house fire. The fire was the result of a freak accident when an oil lamp my patient had failed to extinguish on going to bed exploded in the night. This unfortunate fellow had seen the four people whom he loved most in the world burn to death, but he had no memory of the tragedy. It was my contention – quite correct, as it happened – that his apparently inevitable descent into madness could be reversed by applying those principles which I'd used to treat William Borden, and a few others since: namely, that he would stop turning his distress back onto himself if he could be helped to gain some recollection of the fire, and to accept that in any actual sense he wasn't to blame for it.

My lecture, which went better than expected, was issued as a monograph and circulated in three states. This was the paper in which I first used the term 'dark water' to characterize what was occluded, sunk deep in memory. One thing led to another, and I was soon publishing my successful case studies on an almost annual basis. Rather than exacerbating the symptoms of insanity, talking about any painful event seemed to bring the sufferer relief by robbing it of its power. Many of our recent patients, admittedly, had undergone experiences that were objectively less traumatic than that of my young man with the lamp – disappointments in love, frustrated ambitions, professional and domestic betrayals – but isn't a lack of objectivity precisely what is at play in mental illness?

'You're as regular as clockwork, Hiram,' quipped Caro when I'd penned three or four of these studies. I thought I detected an edge to this remark, but I couldn't be sure. 'You'll have to come up with a title for your series soon. How about "Carver's Cures"?'

'That sounds like a patent medicine for constipation. Can't you think of a better name?'

'What's wrong with it?' Yes, unmistakably an edge. 'Don't you unblock what's blocked? Free up all the – the – backed-up *waste* that the rest of us just call *everyday life* and send your patients purged into the world to gorge on more human folly and –'

'Don't be trying, my dear. You don't know the least thing about making people well.'

'Don't I? Haven't I made you well? It's taken longer than I thought it would, but – haven't I?'

Poor Caro. Was *this* what she thought she'd been doing by feeding me up, all these years that we'd been alone together? Making me *well*?

I certainly wasn't going to be put off by her sisterly teasing. She would've been a complete bully, if I'd let her. The weak always are. Oh, ask me how I knew. Borden – always, always I return to William Borden! – had said that I was weak. But *was* I weak? Hadn't I shown them all, in the end, that I was strong?

PERHAPS THIS CONVERSATION WITH Caro still rankled a little with me when I started to write up my notes on Borden last fall. Yes, quite possibly it did.

This was the case on which my entire career rested, the bedrock of everything. And yet I'd never had the courage to revisit it. The events of that time were still too personal, too spotted with regret. I realized, though, that I'd have to come to him sooner or later. His story was simply the most interesting and the most substantial of them all. Caro's insinuations of triviality wouldn't stand up here. And by now I surely had the maturity and the necessary distance on it to do it justice. I would have to make public his tragic secret, but wasn't that small betrayal of confidence the unavoidable price of enlightening this dark age of ours?

Once I began, my hesitations fell away. The paper was easier to write than I'd ever believed it could be, much easier than any of the others: the words, vital, urgent, gushed forth as if I were telling the story of my own self – which in a sense, of course, I was. Whoever and whatever I'd become – a professional success, a recognized authority on mental illness, a clinician, rather than a mere custodian of the mad – was anchored in the strata of those days. I found that I could remember them almost effortlessly, with all their attendant emotion and what I now recognized as their youthful distortions: my enthusiasms and resentments, my callowness and grandiosity; my admiration, verging on idolatry, of Borden. One after another, the scenes broke over me: it would just be a matter of getting them all down. Our first conversations on the *Orbis*. My disastrous mishandling of Fryar. William's shocking attack on Buskirk. Our incarceration together in the ship's stores; the afternoons we spent lingering on the charmed slope of the asylum garden. Ruth Macy, sitting in barred sunlight in her house on Nantucket, directing me to probe further; my meeting with Canacka – and later, the confluence towards which these living waters flowed, the triumphant conclusion, Borden's confession –

This, at last, was where I'd summarize my ideas, set out the essence of my work.

In the case of William Borden, it soon became evident that the patient's state of extreme physical and moral enervation sprang from a struggle to bury all memory of the incident that took place immediately before his collapse. The effort required had plunged him into a prolonged state of mental tension. It was abundantly clear to me that it was only by summoning this event back into the light that he could be given any relief.

But why was this memory so harrowing? *Why* did he have to make such an effort to sink it in the dark water of forgetfulness?

Could it be that the suffering of that moment sprang from the emotion surrounding a much earlier memory, a memory which, though lying well within the scope of his recollection, was so awful, so far beyond the realm of ordinary human experience, that he had never been able to speak of it?

It was going well. Flyers to all the medical societies went out; advertisements proliferated in the *Boston Herald* and *The New York Times*, announcing that Dr Carver's groundbreaking paper on 'The Astounding Cure of the Hero of the *Providence*, or, A New Theory of the Treatment of Moral Insanity' would be published in the New Year of 1855.

I'd been working on the manuscript steadily for a few weeks when I developed headaches. I struggled to think, or even focus my eyes. Was I taking on too much? The headaches were accompanied by an inexplicable sense of dread, with the usual physical and emotional symptoms: sweaty armpits, loose bowels, an overwhelming urge to dive for cover. Most distressing of all, my old dreams of Thornton, which had ebbed as I'd approached midlife, returned in full force – as ravishingly painful as before, and apparently deathless.

One Saturday at the start of November last year I woke up later than usual, and by breakfast time I had the distinct sense that something was amiss. That day it wasn't the angle of the cutlery (fork, knife, spoon, bread knife were all lined up correctly; the teaspoon lay at a diagonal to my place setting on the saucer of its cup, ready to stir my tea when it was poured) or the disposition, on the tabletop, of the morning's fare (porridge in its bowl, omelet and kidneys waiting under a silver dome in a separate dish, two pieces of bread, just touched by the griddle, pat of butter flaring its skirt of grease in the overheated room, a little loaf-shaped plum cake with jelly, one starched napkin) that triggered my sense of being out of kilter with the world. No, it was none of these things. They were the usual obstacles; I'd taken steps against them, I knew their scope. It was something else, poised perhaps in the day itself; in the dog barking in the yard behind the house next door, the clashing blades of light from the window, the sound of Caro and the servants beginning their daily scouring and taming of the house –

Whatever it was, the strain on my wrist of trying to read my old case notes while eating breakfast was suddenly unwontedly wearying. I severed an isosceles triangle of egg with my fork and transferred it to the bread on my plate, lifted the bread to my mouth (the slice was not an ideal size, it was too small to be cut into decent halves, so one had to eat it whole, like a barbarian), took a bite, put the bread down, turned another page.

My eye fell on a mark I'd made long ago beside a comment of Borden's. At the time I'd dismissed it as the babbling of a sick man. Now, coming across it again after all these years, I faltered. When I questioned him about Fryar's flogging, he'd replied, *He was the sacrifice. We fix it so we sacrifice the weakest. That's the way it's always done.*

The sacrifice.

A wave of bile swirled through my stomach. Was it the egg? It appeared to be properly cooked. I levered another triangle of omelet onto my bread. What was this queasiness? It had nothing at bottom to do with the food, I was certain of it. It was something particular to me, and it was deeply, arterially connected to the overwhelming mood of panic that was threatening to rise in my gullet and displace the egg I was chasing down it.

Nonsense, all nonsense. Nevertheless, I felt queasier, worse even than moments earlier. I gathered up my papers, left the table, and crept back to the drawing room, where I adopted a supine position on the sofa.

How strange it was . . .

'Rise and shine, Hiram.' Caro's rusty plaits, fixed with a malachite comb, hovered above me. 'I've brought you your morning mail.'

'Not now, old lady. I'm trying to think something through.'

'Why are you lying there?'

'My breakfast has disagreed with me. Bad stomach. Bad head. Bad everything.'

'Poor old dear. I'll fetch you some salts. Here, this will cheer you. Mr Schultz has sent along an advance subscription list for your lecture in January.' She hesitated, then said carefully, 'I've asked him to tea here next Sunday, by the way. I trust you approve.'

'Do whatever you think best. I really feel too out of sorts to be bothered by household matters now.'

'There's also this, from Cousin Con. Teddy says he's been asking after you.'

'From Cornelius *Buskirk*? Why ever – ?' If I hadn't felt so weak I would've fallen off the sofa. 'I haven't seen him in twenty years.

That idler didn't even come to Mama's funeral.' Buskirk's mother, the late Mrs Augusta (Gus) Buskirk, née Cabot, sister to Miss Theodora (Ted) Cabot of Fifth Avenue, New York, had been Mama's cousin once removed.

'Really, Hiram. That was uncalled for. You know he hardly leaves home.'

'Yes, but. Why would he be asking after me? Oh, good Lord. Don't look at me like that. You'd better let me have it. Now be a good girl and get me those salts, please.'

She surrendered my mail and went out, but not before giving me a hawkish backward glance.

The envelope from New York was watermarked and fragrantly expensive. My name slopped across the front (Buskirk always wrote a bad hand).

'Ahoy there, Carver,' his note ran.

Aunt Teddy descended on my humble abode this week with a copy of the *Times*. I see that you're limbering up to set the whole town on fire with your latest ponderings about our Hero. My, my. You never could leave that bastard alone, could you?

Do you know, old boy, I can't help feeling that you've rather neglected me since we sailed the old briny together. I haven't wanted to trouble you with a sight of my unlovely phiz. But now, it seems, from what Ted tells me, you're ready to rush in where angels fear to do the proverbial.

Lookee here, Carver. I won't beat about the bush. There's something you need to know concerning Billy Borden which – and I'm going entirely by the brave title of your talk, of course –

I rather fear you don't. Blood is thicker, etc., and I'd hate to see you make an ass of yourself.

Naturally it's your choice, old son, but I think it would be a wise move if you legged it over from that madhouse of yours for a chin-wag. I'm still in the old island domicile. I prefer not to venture abroad. Come next Friday. Come and stay the night.

I had no idea what this absurd letter signified, but my gorge rose even further as I read it.

What could Buskirk – who, as my sister had said, rarely left his colossally ugly house outside New York, and had made nothing of his life after his Glorious Calling was cut short – conceivably have to tell me in relation to William Borden that I, as Borden's former physician and friend, didn't already know? The self-regard of this purposeless man was laughable; his envy of my successful career, his bitterness at the marginal role he occupied in the world, all too obvious. I was intrigued to see, moreover, that after two decades his hatred of Borden appeared to be as strong as ever – if anything, stronger. To my trained eye it was clear that with long brooding it had ripened into obsession.

And yet something about the letter's insinuating tone spoke to my own brackish sense of uncertainty. Though I tossed the thing aside, and tried to get back to my work, I couldn't recapture my old self-belief.

By lunchtime, despite a double dose of Epsom salts and a half-hour spent in tortured communion with the lavatory bowl, my headache was worse than ever.

I gave in and started to look up the rail schedules to New York.

*

I MUST STOP. CARO came in moments ago and caught me still writing.

'Hiram, it's dinner time. Oh, look at you! You haven't even changed. The beef will be as dry as bone meal. Whatever is the matter with you this evening? You're not yourself at all.' She took a step towards me. 'Are you quite certain you're all right?'

'I'm perfectly well,' I hissed. Then I said, in a gentler voice, 'Nothing's the matter, old lady. Nothing in the slightest. If you'll excuse me, I'll go and tidy myself up. I won't be long.'

She paused at the door, raised her eyebrows significantly: *Get a move on.* I raised mine in return. I waited. It's so difficult, in this house – it always has been – to find a few minutes alone. And yet one is always alone.

'Caro, *please.*'

She left. Once she'd gone, I ran my fingertips over my face, feeling for cracks.

No more for tonight. No more.

TWENTY-THREE

Early one friday morning last November I caught the express train from Boston to New York.

Buskirk's mansion, which occupied an aloof fleck of land off the eastern shore of the Hudson, bore the improbably romantic name of Waterclyffe. It was a place of turrets, stained glass and secret staircases; opulent, granitic. I'd been taken to it once or twice as a child and disliked it intensely, it was so hideous. Now he and I were about to spring into renewed contact, like paired magnets. The very social forces which had made him repellent to me would bring us irresistibly together.

The fields of Connecticut, smeared behind the windows in a streak of red, gave way before Hartford to broad riverside, and then on each bank to blue hills that showed no sign of ending until they shaded with the declining day into gunmetal. We reached Canal Street at dusk. Buskirk's stretch of the Hudson lay two hours upriver on the central line. By the time I alighted, and glimpsed the Buskirk mansion looming across the water, it was black night.

Seeing it again I almost laughed, it was so exactly like a house of nightmare: a crooked mausoleum hidden away in a waste land of struggling trees, marooned on scant acres of blasted grass. The arched windows that faced me as I pulled myself over the current on the decaying chain-link ferry were all darkened, except for one that glowed along the edges. And then I was on the choked path to the forecourt, illuminated by sconces – I was at the peaked entrance, that looked like the helmet and visor of some ridiculous knight of old –

I was admitted by a manservant who took my bag and showed me discreetly up the maroon plush staircase to the drawing room. At the gargantuan double doors I dismissed him. I hesitated for several seconds, rehearsing what I might say. I was readying myself to knock when an indistinct voice addressed me from deep within.

'Is that you, Carver? Don't prance about out there, old boy. Advance.'

I could smell the room before entering it. The air was drenched with a cloying stench that was all the more unsettling for having no obvious source. The windows were shrouded in heavy brocade curtains. I saw, in the weak light of a mock-medieval lamp, a tenebrous gilt waste land, like an antechamber to Hades or some other realm of despair, littered with corpse-like sofas and high-backed tombstone chairs. As my eyes adjusted to the darkness I noticed that every flat surface bore vase upon vase of flowers – hothouse flowers: freckled lilies, gardenias, bearded and tendriled orchids, incensing the dimness with a funeral odor.

'Hello, old son.'

What I'd taken to be a glut of shadows detached itself from the depths of the room and began to skim towards me among the headstones, a spirit surprised by the living. Buskirk wore a velvet jacket and a voluminous and many-folded cravat that cataracted over the length and breadth of his chest. On top of it, like a caricature of the man I'd once known, floated his ruined face. A river of muddy tissue circled the left eye and descended to his jowl, which was threaded with white scars like stitching through sailcloth. I felt a powerful wish to take hold of that flap and tear it down all the way, exposing the creature beneath.

'Well, well, Carver. Don't you look in the pink. You're twice the man you were.'

'Hello, Buskirk,' I said, when I'd recovered from my immediate shock. 'You look very, ah, striking yourself.' I glanced around, so as not to have to keep seeing that face. 'Is there a Mrs Buskirk? Will I have the pleasure of meeting her?'

'Don't be an ass. I'm only tendered to the halt and the lame.'

'No luck so far?'

'One squinny at me usually frightens the poor girls into lifelong chastity.'

'Don't give up. You might bag a blind one.'

He let fly an incongruous snicker. 'I always liked you, Carver. You never went in for cant, unlike the rest of 'em. What about you? Has Hymen caught you in her snare?'

'Ah, no. I'll die a bachelor. I've no time for affairs of the heart. I'm afraid it's work and more work for me.'

'Well, I'll be hanged. Did the old man cut you off? I hadn't heard. Is that why you're churning out all those infernal publications?' He nodded at one of his mournful chairs. 'Grab a pew. If you need a loan then you've merely to –'

'It's nothing like that,' I protested, settling myself stiffly on the horsehair cushion. 'I work entirely for pleasure. Asylum work. A little research. I've been studying the connection between insanity and memory. I try to – well, I try to alleviate human suffering.'

Buskirk swallowed a bubble of mirth. 'Bully for you, old son.'

'Buskirk. Con. May I call you Con? Let's cut the chit-chat. You said in your letter that you had information for me. Are you offering to help me with the writing of my paper? If you are, then spit it out, please.'

He dropped into the seat opposite with a suppressed sneer. Here he was nearer to the lamp. I recoiled from his disfigured flesh, which was fully revealed in the light: the canvas-like ripple of the deep fascia; the muscle laboring below. 'I don't recall you going in much for consultation before.'

'Older and wiser, Con. Especially older.'

I stared at that cratered flesh. While lacking vitality, it was also never at rest. It was working away now. 'Age don't seem to have cured you of the pash you had on old Billy.' He leered.

'I didn't have a "pash", as you call it, on Mr Borden. He became a patient of mine. He was sent to the asylum after – after we all came home. He wouldn't eat, or speak. He was very ill.'

'Billy Borden! The great sailor. The man of the goddamned people. The great navigator. All the goddamned archangels rolled into one.'

'Yes. He was once all those things, and more. And I believe that I did him some good. I've built an entire career on the back of that case –'

Buskirk interrupted me. The sneer was out in the open. 'Let me ask you this, Carver. If our friend was such a skilled navigator, why did it take him two months to steer those men to shore?'

'They were crossing the Pacific in an open boat. You can hardly expect a man to perform under those conditions as if he were at the helm of a frigate in full sail. And they were half starved.'

'So, was he Jesus Christ too? Could he turn seawater into wine? Did he know how to feed eight men on a single fish?' We were teetering close to the red-hot core of the matter. 'He was a fisherman all right. He was a fisher of men. Think about it, old son. Just think about it. Believe me, I haven't reached my present dizzy age without having had plenty of leisure to think about it, and I've come to some pretty ugly conclusions. They ate each other, Carver. That's how they stayed alive for all those weeks. Your sainted Billy is a fucking *cannibal*.'

'Look, you aren't telling me anything new. Borden confessed – he came to terms with what happened on that boat. This was no small part of his treatment. I'll be addressing it all in my paper.'

'Yes, old boy. But that ain't the whole story.'

'It is. Of course it is! I know for a fact that it is.'

'Then why are you here?' asked Buskirk quietly.

'Oh, hang it. If you must know, I've been feeling distinctly flat recently. Perhaps I've come to you for my own cure.'

'Well, why didn't you say so?' He was on his feet in an instant. I looked on as he scuttled over to a massive cabinet and turned the key in the lock. Within a minute he'd come back bearing two embossed goblets and a bottle of something green. 'I normally smother a parrot around this time, when there's no one watching.'

He poured us both a fat measure of the green stuff. I took a tentative sip and straight away felt a blast like the fires of Etna all the way through my nasal cavities.

'Chin-chin, old boy,' said Buskirk, and emptied his goblet in one gulp.

By now it was nine o'clock. There seemed to be no food in the offing, no tedious requirement to dress. I took another sip. 'What's this liquor?'

'Absinthe. Contains all that's necessary to sustain life. Trust me, coz.' He refilled his glass. 'Bottoms up.'

By ten o'clock we were both thoroughly drunk, I – despite the quantity of absinthe he'd put away – possibly more so than Buskirk.

Buskirk turned to me with hot eyes. 'So, Carver. Are you ready to hear me out?'

'Not yet. There's something I want to ask you first.'

'Roll it out, old boy, and let's see if I can crack it open for you.'

'That afternoon on the ship. The whatchamacallit.'

'The *Orbis*.'

'That's the one. We were eating. The wind was up. I felt seasick. I went on deck. But before I went, you were engaged in a – in a conversation with William Borden.'

'Conversation is a marvelous thing. Cornerstone of civilization.'

'It certainly is.'

'More?'

'Just a drop.'

Buskirk poured, and we both took a gulp.

'I learned about hypocrisy from you, you know old boy,' he muttered.

'Hypocrisy? Don't you mean – oh, what's-his-name.'

'Hippocrates.'

'Right on the money.'

He topped up my goblet again. 'See, old man, I've had time to educate myself a little in the years I've been shut up here. I've had nothing better to do.' Lying back in his chair, he eyed me through his ruched lid. 'So what did you want to ask me?'

I slugged back a mouthful of absinthe. It was quite marvelous, the way it simply evaporated in the throat, without putting one to all the trouble of actually drinking. 'Well, Con, it's this. I was on deck, heaving my guts up, and the next thing I heard, Borden had gone for you. He'd charged right at you. And what I want to know is – what did you say to him? What in the name of all that's unholy could you have said, to make him fly out so?'

'Why d'you think it was me, old man? Why couldn't it have been him?'

Because you're a twenty-four-carat piece of shit, I wanted to say. *Because he was someone I loved.* But I wasn't so sure any more. 'Professional opinion.'

'Ah, professional. As in – Hippocratic? The sort that swears it ain't going to do any harm?'

'Yes.' I may have been drunk, but I knew that I was being goaded. 'What's your point?'

'He wasn't eating. He didn't eat the turtle soup. He didn't eat the beef. So I asked him if he'd rather have some other kind of meat. He sat there coiled in on himself like a cobra, but he didn't answer. We all just went on talking among ourselves.'

'About what?'

'About war. *I* was talking about war. Spalding was on the claret. Borden wasn't making a peep. Damned difficult to have a conversation on one's own. I was saying that I thought it a damned shame that we were out on the briny on a man-of-war with forty-four guns but without a hope in hell of ever seeing combat. Then Gilly piped up and said that speaking for himself he'd be ready to die for his country at the drop of a hat. And old Spalding pulled his snout out of the claret to say aye, but would he be ready to kill for it? Because he'd seen war and killing for your country was a damned sight harder than dying for her, and that was the real test of a man, and he, for one, would be ready to eat anyone that Gilbert killed. And then I asked Billy if he'd be willing to do the same.'

'You asked him *that*?'

'That's all, old chap. And before the question was out of my mouth Borden had nearly murdered me.'

'I don't see. I don't see it.'

'Well, I do. I've worked it out since then, old boy. They ate their dead. But the men they ate weren't already cold. They were killed. Our Billy killed them.'

'My God, Con —'

With a lurch of nausea, like one waking from a dream without knowing that he has been asleep, it came to me.

The sacrifice.

Why, yes. One sacrifices the living, not the dead.

Floor after floor opened up in my mind and I began to fall towards consciousness, exactly as one falls in dreams, falling and flailing without hitting the bottom.

It arrived as an intuition, in the way that truth does. And yet I knew.

I'd been duped.

My breath failed me. I shambled to the window, pulling at my collar, and delivered successive blows to the mullioned casement until it opened a crack. I gulped at the air. That sentence – what was that sentence Borden had come out with on the night when I induced him to start eating again? It was going around and around in my brain, round and round, trying to find traction; here it came . . .

The meat was a lie.

A lie, yes. A lie.

Up to this point I'd been falling, falling – but I knew that the bottom was coming now. As I fell my heart seemed to fly upwards through my head. And then I smashed to pieces on the ground.

'Con, listen! I know you've suffered. But I have too. All my life I've tried to do the right thing. I've worked. I've striven. I've applied myself to better the lot of my fellow man. I've gone against many things which our world holds dear in order to do it. In one case, at least, I did terrible wrong. Still I persevered because I thought that overall I was doing right. And now I fear, oh God – I find that I was mistaken. I fear that I was tricked—'

Buskirk laughed long and hard. Since laughter made his left cheek purse up like an anemone, this required considerable effort. 'You've only found this out about the world *now*, old boy? Where have you been living?'

I couldn't say anything more because the absinthe was rushing up my throat. It came jetting out of me in a magnificent heraldic fleur-de-lis of green.

He rose to his feet. 'I'm sorry if the subject makes you sick, old man.' His tone was surpassingly weary. 'D'you know, Hiram, I'm equally sick of it. I'm sick of being a joke. I'm sick of being the chump the Hero of the *Providence* almost had for his damned dinner. I'm sick of being a footnote to that bastard's story.'

Yes, I was going to say. Yes, so am I! But I was vomiting again.

'This is just like auld lang syne. You always were a hurler.' Tears, of anger or amusement, welled in Buskirk's good eye. He dashed at them with a velvet sleeve, crossing the room to pull the bell cord. The great doors wrenched open like the Cimmerian gates and the silent flunkey from earlier reappeared at my side.

'Dr Carver would like to go to bed now,' said my old shipmate. 'Breakfast at nine? I'm not an early riser myself, but I expect after all that puking you'll want to strap on the nosebag before you catch your train. Good night, Hiram. It was nice to see you. We should do this more often. Sweet dreams, cousin of mine.'

AS SOON AS I got back to Boston I ransacked the bureau in the drawing room. Where was the court transcript? I'd been consulting it sporadically while writing up Borden's case. As I clawed at my heap of papers I felt that I would suffocate at any moment. Finally I found it. It still looked just as crisp as it did twenty years ago, just as innocuous . . .

The boat had been cut loose at dawn on the second of January. Perry had died from the pistol shot to his head after five days at sea, and his body had been thrown overboard. Towards the end of that month Monroe had perished as a result of the blow, very likely causing a swelling in the brain, that Small had given to his skull. He died with his head on Borden's knees. He didn't die, however, until Borden had gone over to him and taken his head in his lap. Then Webb died around thirty days later. But of what? Of what? I tore through those fraudulent pages. *Of feebleness*. That was all

Lenox had said. *He was feeble and he gave up after a short struggle for his life.*

I forced myself to take measured breaths. It was like inhaling crushed glass.

We fix it so we sacrifice the weakest. That's the way it's always done.

Buskirk was right. The two men who had been eaten, Monroe and Webb, weren't already dead. They had been killed for the purpose. Borden had executed them. And no one had said a word about it afterwards, not when they were rescued; not at the inquiry. Not Fitzgibbon, who was half mad; not Canacka, not Lenox, not Duggan. They had all – each and every one of those survivors – remained absolutely silent. Borden even more so than the others: even when he appeared to speak.

Oh, his silence was the deepest, the most impenetrable silence of all. The completeness of his silence promised to pull me right under.

It was all a lie. All of it! He'd never trusted me. He'd never looked to me. He'd never confessed; never really spoken to, never confided in pathetic little me. His admissions were a lie, his healing was a lie. And by extension my hope, my ambition, my work – they were all a lie too. I, Hiram Carver, was a lie. It was as if my entire self had been flattened.

Oh indeed, he had made a sacrifice of me.

And she – I'd given her back her lover. But what had I given back to her? What had she married? My imagination shrank from turning that corner.

There were two questions which began to torment me that day. Even then, in pain as I was, I was aware that they were the same question. What really took place in that boat? And if I'd been wrong about this essential thing, then hadn't I also been wrong about the emotions that had tipped Borden over the edge on that long-ago afternoon on the *Orbis*? I understood enough by now, after two decades of co-existing with the mad, to grasp that what happens between human beings doesn't spring from nowhere, fully formed. It erupts from some primal interaction, it finds its origins in those energies that are primitive, irreconcilable with each other, and that will struggle to rise to the surface, until they achieve release . . .

In William Borden's case, I was no longer certain what these energies were, or what I had let loose.

TWENTY-FOUR

THIS MORNING SOMETHING HAPPENED that has left me shaken. After being absorbed in writing the above for several hours (I think that in time I'll grow accustomed to using Papa's study; it didn't irk me nearly as much today as it did last night, in fact it suits me rather well) I went downstairs in search of a cup of tea. Caro wasn't in the drawing room, the parlor, or any of her usual Saturday forenoon haunts. I found her in the scullery, surrounded by pans and scattered utensils, bending over a crate. She was wearing an apron and had a ketchief wrapped around her head. For a moment I mistook her for a servant.

'What's all this? Are you spring cleaning?'

Caro shied a tarnished ladle into the crate and straightened up. 'Since we're not to have the study, I thought this room might do just as well. Better, perhaps. There are no stairs to climb, and there's water to hand. And we'd be well out of your way.'

'Are you referring to the ladies at your Lying-in Hospital?'

'I am. Unless you're going to object to this proposal too?'

'You make me out to be some sort of Herod. Suit yourself, my dear. The kitchen has always been your domain.'

She expelled a *hoo* of relief. 'Thank you, Hiram.'

'As long as we're clear that this will be a consulting room and that there are to be no actual – no actual –'

'Births?'

'Births, deliveries, instances of parturition – what is it, Caro?' Her narrow face had broken into a grin. 'Do I amuse you?'

'Don't worry, Hissy. I won't be setting up a rival hospital to yours here.' She put her hands on her hips, ready to start in on a crowd of dusty old apothecary's bottles. There were rows and rows of them, all with a sediment at the bottom. '*Instances of parturition*.' Caro shook her head brusquely, as if she were trying to dislodge an irritation from her ear.

But I wasn't listening. My attention had strayed to the bottle she'd picked up, which still contained a quantity of something syrupy and teakish.

I pointed to the shelf. 'What are these?'

'Mama's.'

'Why would Mama keep empty bottles?'

Caro smiled a rackety smile. 'They weren't empty to begin with.'

'What d'you mean, not empty? What would have been in them?'

She looked at me in quiet wonder. 'Oh, Hiram. Did you really not know? Here.' She placed the bottle she'd been holding into my hand.

'Know what? What should I know?' I prised away the stopper with the ball of my thumb. The cork was powdery and crumbled slightly, springing free with a weary exhalation. As soon as it was out I realized that I did know, had possibly always known.

My eyes met Caro's.

'Go ahead, Hiram.' She made a ducking motion with her head while raising her fingers to her nose.

I did as she directed, putting the neck of the bottle to my nostrils. The smell was immediately familiar, as familiar to me as the smell of my own body. It was a smell I'd breathed all my life, it seemed, always at a distance, always at a remove; breathed for so long that I'd stopped registering it; a spiced apple smell, like incense, like a child's idea of Christmas, with an underlay of ethanol and the faintest hint of rot. It was my mother's scent. But I hadn't smelled it here at home for seven years, and as I inhaled it the physician in me recognized it instantly.

Laudanum.

Oh, oh, oh. I turned away.

'Hiram, please. Please don't cry. I thought you knew. How *couldn't* you have known?'

'I'm not crying, God dammit. My eyes are strained. They're strained because I'm tired, Caro, *tired*, don't you see? – tired and overworked and yes, *middle-aged*, and – and what do I have to show for it? Can you tell me, hah? Where am I? Where do I find myself?' I faced her, my head ringing with the earsplitting urgency of my own alarm. 'Here in this goddamn HOUSE on yet another goddamn DAY in this goddamn CITY with another week of WORK ahead of me, work, Caro, among the MAD! Trying to soothe the unsoothable fears of the INSANE!' My stomach was cold, with shock and consternation and another, darker sensation I couldn't define. 'And I don't know, oh God, I've never known what I'm doing, don't know what I want, don't know what I lack, but I lack something, Caro, I know I lack it and I can't live without it any longer, just can't continue to pretend that I have the answer to every little human grief, every stupid human question, when I can't solve, can't even begin to understand, the problem of my own SELF, Caro, of goddamned HIRAM CARVER –'

In my distress I was swinging my arms about, and managed to knock a pan from its shelf. It fell, spinning, to the ground.

Caro sprang forwards and bound me in a hug that encircled my whole body. 'Hush, Hiram. Hush now. Get a hold of yourself. You're here with me.' I sagged, sobbing, into the straitjacket of her embrace. 'That's where you are – *here*. With *me*.'

She drew me to the floor. We sat against the crate while I wept and she made shushing sounds. Eventually the torrent inside me became a trickling runnel of shame. The idiot pan lay upside down near me: my belly, my chins, hung in its copper side. I lowered my eyes and there was my nose, rising into sight like a fin. A flag of snot flapped from my nostril.

'Oh Lord. How humiliating.'

'Don't be a foolish boy. Come on.' She dug into her sleeve and produced a square of muslin. 'Have a good blow.'

I blew, with a luxurious feeling of being shriven. But I knew I had to go on. 'You said something to me once.'

'Did I, darling? I'm sure I've said many things.'

'Yes, but this! It was when I'd just started working in Charlestown. You said I didn't care for people. For the people I ought to care for. For Mama and Papa. For you.'

'I can't believe I ever said that.'

'Oh, you did! You did! Maybe not in those very words, but that's what you meant.' I was once more perilously close to tears.

'Forget that now. I was talking nonsense. I'm sorry if I was ever so stupid.'

369

'You may have been right.'

'No, Hiram.' She held me tighter. 'I've always been sure of your love. I resented you for a time, after you were born; oh goodness, yes. When I was a mean little girl. But then – do you remember the cows? On the Common?'

'I do. Those black eyes that didn't seem to have any irises! They never looked away. And those teeth – like stone tablets, all along the bottom jaw, and that hard searching lip. I thought – well, I thought they'd eat me. I thought they'd devour me alive.'

'You were so afraid of them. I didn't know why. But whenever we visited the cows you'd lie in your crib afterwards, at night, and call out for Mama, and she wouldn't come –'

'No. You came instead.' I gazed at her, at her red hair spilling from its kerchief, the blurred outline of her freckled jaw. 'You came, just as you did at Christmas –'

The fool in the pan had begun to blub again.

'Hush, Hiram. Oh, hush now. I'm still here.'

DID I REALLY NOT notice that my mother had found it necessary to drug herself to get through her days? I've asked myself how I failed to acknowledge such an enormity. Or could it have been – and perhaps my blinkeredness about Borden was of a piece with this reluctance too – a case of knowing and not knowing, of not *wanting* to know?

Caro saw the truth of me long ago. How that asylum, crowning its hill, whispers of the will to power, the bitter wish for solitude, a detachment from all ordinary contacts with others –

If I'm to look at things squarely – for it seems, God knows, that I have no choice – then I must admit that, in spite of my own withdrawal from the world, I'd been quietly furious at Ruth Macy's aloofness all those years. Oh, she had shut me out, with her purity, her silence, her money. She had waited for me to deliver her lover back to her, and then she'd closed the door.

But hadn't I made it easy for her?

As soon as I got back from visiting Buskirk in New York I fired off a note to Nantucket.

'*My dear Mrs Borden*,' I began. '*Forgive me for intruding on your domestic happiness. After an interval of so many years I find, quite unexpectedly, that I will be making a brief journey to Nantucket before Christmas. I hope I may call on you and Mr Borden.*' I paused at the end, unsure of how to sign off. On an impulse I wrote, '*Your old friend, Hiram Carver.*'

I was gnawed by uncertainty as to how much she knew; whether she was as much a dupe as I was, or an accomplice. My first feeling when I left Buskirk was one of rage. I would call them both to account. I wanted to punish them *both* for the deception he'd worked on me. Though I was ignorant, surely she'd known! It was inconceivable that she didn't. She wanted him at all costs, and she'd maneuvered me into making him well enough to become hers again.

But by the time my train pulled into Boston station, and I stepped from my lit-up car into the surrounding dusk, I wasn't so sure. She'd got what she'd wanted, all right. But what if she *hadn't* known? What if she'd been in the dark too? If I'd sent him back to her, and she'd married him only to discover that he wasn't who she thought he was – why, then she needed my help now more than ever.

I anticipated her reply to my message with apprehension and a curious sense of elation. Beneath my swirling anxiety was the knowledge, that bore me up even as I pitched about, that I'd soon hear from her, would soon see her, after such a long interlude.

And on seeing her, I would — astonishing, terrible thought! — at last again see him.

AN AGONIZING WEEK PASSED, and then another. Every noon I'd watch the mail cart labor up Pleasant Hill. Once it had parked in the carriage drive, and the mailman had slung the asylum bag into the hall, I'd wait. I was waiting for Ben Schultz, whose job it was, to fillet and distribute the day's letters. He did this while whistling. Very few of our boarders had permission to receive mail. The bulk of it ended up on my desk, and Ben stopped there first. As soon as I heard my study door click shut, and his whistle coming up the stairs, I'd drop whatever I was doing and hurry down.

Each day there was nothing.

Time trickled, where it had previously rushed by. Thanksgiving came and went. I'd almost given up hope when the envelope appeared. It was lying among the bills and inquiries and petitions and other junk, in the very place where so many of her former communications had lain, like an emanation from the past: a letter addressed in that ribbed hand I remembered. I held it up to the light, as if to make sure that it was real. I weighed it on my palm. In a flash of emotion, I brought it to my lips. Only then, with the blood rushing to my temples, did I open it.

The person to whom you write does not exist. If it is me you would like to speak to, Hiram Carver, then you are welcome here. R. M.

It took me several minutes to understand what I'd just read. Ruth Macy! She was still Ruth Macy.

She wasn't married. She hadn't married him.

I knew that I'd been launched onto a polluted tide, where nothing was certain any more.

Everything I'd secretly pictured to myself in the last twenty years – the quiet wedding in the Congregational church, with Mrs Chadwick beatifically gloating, the simple wedding breakfast afterwards in Main Street; all the breakfasts, in fact, eaten on the days that followed in the white-painted breakfast room belonging to Mr and Mrs William Borden – all of it was illusion, all imagination. For the rest of the day I could hardly concentrate on my duties. I made such gross errors that after lunch Ben offered, as deferentially as ever but with a marked hint of exasperation, to relieve me until supper time.

I put on my coat and wandered out onto the hill above the Bartlett mansion, as I used to do as a young man. The air was cool and musky with fall fires. A layer of scarlet leaves rotted gently underfoot. For half an hour I imagined, as in days past, that I was walking through an enchanted realm, and that a red carpet had been rolled out for me –

All fancy, all illusion. I came to the summer house and sat down under the bare rose branches. I suddenly felt spent. I felt old.

Why hadn't they married? Was there some last-minute obstacle, a dogmatic blow struck by Mrs Chadwick's minister, some piece of doctrinal flim-flam that sank all their hopes? No. Ruth Macy didn't care for such idiocy, she was impervious to all such stupid rules. She'd been prepared to take William Borden even if it meant that she'd be cast out forever; wouldn't he have been equally willing to take her on the same terms? I believed she would have married him in any church, at any altar.

Then the dreadful truth occurred to me. He was dead. He hadn't married her *because he had died*. And no one had thought to tell me: in her grief, she'd been too lost to the world to write; the fact of his death had truly wiped all memory of Hiram Carver from her brain, just as I'd wrongly imagined her marriage had. Or. Or – she had wanted to write to me, had known that she *must* write, but had found herself unable to commit the awful words to paper, and had been locked all these years in silent suffering.

Yes, he was dead. He'd died years ago, and she'd been in mourning all this time, and I never even knew –

But then, why didn't she say so now? Why didn't she say that he was dead?

I WAS LESS CERTAIN of anything than ever before. But I'd felt it again, the twitch on the thread, and I began to make the necessary arrangements for my journey. First I'd have to find lodgings on Nantucket. The latest edition of the *Inquirer*, which I picked up at the railway station, had a small section offering accommodation in the town. Among the Husseys and the Gardners and the Wyers touting their rooms there was a Mrs Bunker. The name was familiar. Why yes, I knew *that* name! Though there were probably hundreds of Bunkers on that patch of sand, I took it as a good omen. Mrs Bunker, rather quaintly among the paper's brash boarding-house notices, advertised a 'shipshape bedchamber' in her 'well-ordered seaport dwelling' near the harbor. I wrote at once to inquire if the room was still available, and on receiving a drab note in the affirmative – Mrs Bunker's paper was mousy, her ink was mousy, her prose was mousy, and she herself was no doubt a mousy little person with a dishcloth in one hand and a book of Quaker discipline in the other – I secured it by return of post.

By the second week of December my plans were in place. Shortly before my departure I told Caro and Ben that I'd been called away on urgent business.

'I don't see why you have to rush off now, so close to Christmas,' grumbled my sister.

'Needs must, old girl. It's only a brief trip. Three, four days at most.'

'Where are you going anyway, Hiram? You're being so hole and corner about it all.'

'Now don't nag. I'm just running down to the Cape. I'll be back in plenty of time for the festivities.'

'Hum. I hope so. We've been invited to the Winthrops' for dinner on the twenty-third.'

'Oh God. *Must* we go?'

'Yes. I've already replied.' It is a cardinal rule of Beacon Hill society that invitations, once accepted, constitute a binding contract that can never, ever be revoked. Caro's superior smile, though ironic, was unchallengeable. 'Take this as a fair caution, Hiram. If you're not back punctually, I'll hunt you down and bring you home myself.'

*

I SAILED FROM HYANNIS Port on Thursday, December fourteenth, as a heavy fog was rolling inland across the water. It was so thick that the ferry had to stop and sound her whistle many times, and each time the wall of fog seemed to give us back the echo of our own warning. As we left Cape Cod in our wake I could discern the russet shoulder of the hills, and then nothing at all. For the next hour we were completely enveloped in what looked and felt like a clinging wet shroud. We were steaming into a headwind, our passage was rough, and I took refuge in the saloon. At that season there were very few other passengers making the crossing: two sailors grunting at pinochle, a flushed woman with a weeping nose and a loud catarrh, and an old divine perusing his newspaper between clicks of his false teeth. I arranged my limbs on a bench, propped my head against the cabin wall, and prepared myself, to grunts and the slapping of cards, and snuffling and coughing, and the rustling of newsprint and the snapping of teeth, for the nausea that I knew would come . . .

I must have fallen asleep. What might have been minutes later a bell was ringing fit to wake the dead and the ferry had waggled herself to a halt with a pounding of her rods and a shearing whine of her side wheel. The cabin was empty. I hurried out on deck – I remember that the doorway of the saloon was low and that I had to duck. When I emerged I thought, momentarily, that the fog hadn't yet lifted and that we'd met with an obstruction, another boat, perhaps, and were stopping until it was out of the way. Then I realized that the ferry had docked, and that the air was perfectly clear. The whiteness that lay to every side, in chill featureless drifts, was snow.

My fellow passengers were already queueing up to disembark. I hastened down behind them onto the deserted wharf, feeling as if

I'd been struck blind: all the muddled life I remembered was gone, completely erased. Snow was heaped on the rooftops of the town and in its lanes; on the shop signs and boarded-up stalls. The sun, obscured by wadded cloud, shed a hollow glow through the lowering sky. Though it was late morning, and no lamp was lit, the glare coming from the muffled streets had the harshness of gaslight.

Still half asleep, with my valise bumping against my calves, I followed Mrs Bunker's directions until I arrived, just north of the harbor, at a plain salt-box with weathered gray shingles and projecting window frames. Above the lintel hung a ship's quarterboard bearing the name *Harvest* in gold letters. The pitched roof was topped by a roof walk, and both were freighted with snow.

I was about to raise my hand to the knocker when acid swelled in my throat. It was, unmistakably, seasickness.

My knock was answered by a tidy old person in black – not at all the mouse I'd imagined, but a sadder, more guarded, and more aged woman – who evinced a flinty distaste at the transaction she now had to enter into.

'Thee's the Boston doctor?'

'Hiram Carver, ma'am, yes.' I looked around woozily. 'What a pleasant view you command here.'

Mrs Bunker made a fractional adjustment to her goffered cap, a gesture that might have signaled either assent or dissent; I had no way of telling. 'If thee'll come aboard, thy tea will be rigged out in the parlor in just a minute.'

She piloted me into a bedroom smelling of vinegar and wax, with a hooked rug and a bed bounded on three sides by rails, and withdrew to make the tea.

The timber wall had a low window, like a porthole, facing the ocean. I lifted the hem of the curtain. In the distance I could see the ferry refueling before sailing back to Boston and civilization as I knew it. I was stuck here for the present, and though I'd made this journey of my own free will, the realization that I couldn't leave now even if I wanted to filled me with gloom.

I sat down on the bed and gave an exploratory bounce. Hard as a gangplank.

After washing my face and hands in the basin on the washstand – there was a 'splasher' tacked to the boards behind it, and that modest detail depressed me further – I retraced my steps to the parlor.

This room, armed with an Empire sofa and two rockers, sat poised for any social emergency. Stiff needlepoint cushions were on the qui vive on every seat. On the mantelpiece stood a whaler's lamp, a funny little clock in the shape of a lighthouse, topped by a tiny ship, and an Oriental ceramic cat. Plain white oak paneled the fireplace, but the floor was painstakingly painted to resemble marble. A pair of terrestrial and celestial globes kept vigil to either side of the grate, in which a kettle boiled on a crane.

Mrs Bunker slid a plate of dry biscuit and a cup of black tea in front of me, and withdrew to a rocker.

'Did thee have a smooth voyage?'

'Alas, no.'

I drank. She rocked.

'It has snowed here,' I remarked.

At that moment the avalanche on the roof slipped down and met the street outside with a thud.

'It has,' Mrs Bunker agreed.

I bit into the biscuit. The dry fare, the wooden walls, the smell of vinegar and polish, my bubbling nausea: it was horribly like being on a ship. 'We have no snow in Boston yet.'

''Twill come.'

I looked about desperately. The cat winked at me with an azure-rimmed eyelid. The hands of the clock, creeping around the belly of the lighthouse, reached the twelve and the four, sending forth a volley of pings at which the miniature ship on the top began to careen to and fro.

And then I saw it. Almost but not quite concealed by the open parlor door, hanging above a cabinet stuffed with clay pipes and tobacco jars, was an oil portrait of the old Sphinx who'd driven me to Sconset twenty years before. The eyes, set in a face that was mostly bristle and chin, had the selfsame lapidary squint.

'Why, ma'am,' I exclaimed, 'I believe I'm acquainted with that gentleman.'

Mrs Bunker stopped rocking and gave me a suspicious glance. 'He was my husband. Ezra Bunker.' In her mouth it sounded like 'Bunk-ah'. 'Did thee know him? Has thee had previous business here?'

'Oh, yes,' I said. 'I once had the privilege of meeting Captain Bunker. I remember him perfectly. Am I to understand, ma'am, that you are – that you were – that he is no longer – ?'

'Well, see now, Doctor. He won't be coming home again. He's gone offshore forever.'

I stared at her stupidly.

'I've been a widow this twelvemonth.'

Aha – this explained the amateur tone of her advertisement, and her evident reluctance to prostitute the little salt-box in this way. She was new to landladying. 'I am very sorry to hear that.' I bowed my head for a moment, in the way my father used to do: it was his one convincing bedside mannerism. 'He was a most affable man.'

We resumed our silence. I strained the bitter tea through my teeth, recalling the old cipher. Presumably he'd been less of a cipher to her.

By and by Mrs Bunker spoke, with what seemed to me to be a glimmer of interest. 'Is it business brings thee here again?' She contemplated the possibilities. 'A medical matter, I reckon?'

'In a manner of speaking, ma'am, yes. I was introduced to your late husband by a dear friend of mine. Possibly you know her – Miss Ruth Macy. It's her I've come to see.'

'Ruth Macy! Oh, that poor child. What a terrible sad story. Just terrible.' Having delivered this dangler, Mrs Bunker got up and busied herself about a shelf. 'Well, Doctor.' She returned with a sugar pot. 'Will thee take a spoon or two? I don't care for it myself, but Captain Bunker had a sweet tooth.'

'Thank you. I will.' I stabbed at the Gibraltar-like mass in the bottom of the bowl with the scoop. 'Maybe just a few grains. This is powerfully fine tea. Much finer than any I've had in Boston.'

'Captain Bunker was a man of many parts before he retired. A little whaling. A little trading. Mostly in the Pacific and China seas. This tea, now, was brought back from Canton by Captain Bunker forty years ago.'

'I can tell.' I dispatched the dregs of it, hoping to God that the biscuit didn't come from the same consignment, determined now to steer her back to the main point. 'You appear concerned for Miss Macy, ma'am.'

'Aye, poor unhappy child.' She cast her eyes up at the portrait. 'Captain Bunker was always kind to her. You see – he once knew *him*.'

The pronoun hung darkly in the air. 'Him? You are referring, I think –' my pulse had begun to race, exactly as it did during nightmares – 'I think you are referring to William Borden?'

Mrs Bunker nodded, musing. 'The Hero of the *Providence*. But he was just a boy back then, when he used to call on Captain Bunker. He had all his life before him still. And the Captain and I were fixing up to get married. It was all so long ago.' She uttered a bleak sigh. 'Oh, Doctor, it's terrible sad, to think of her sitting in that great house all alone, breaking her heart. While he –'

'*While he*, Mrs Bunker? What of him? While he *what*?' My stomach tightened in a ferocious knot. 'Is he still living?'

'Why yes, he's still alive. Why shouldn't he be? But Doctor, I can't be speaking about it. It's not right.' She reached for the kettle. 'You'll have some more tea.'

'Ah, no, thank you all the same. Do you know –' I deflected her, my guts still roiling – 'I've rounded the Horn myself. I was a sailor of sorts, when I was a lad.'

Beaming now, she put the kettle down. The rocker started up again. 'Well, I never. I just sensed that thee had something of the sea about thee. This is almost like entertaining a friend of the family. Ain't we comfortable? Who'd ever have thought it?'

'It's a most welcome surprise to me also.' I set aside my cup. 'Ma'am, if I'm frank, I'm somewhat anxious with regard to the professional matter that brings me here. I'd rather it were settled quickly. I've a very busy hospital to get back to. And so I won't be trespassing on your kindness longer than I can help.'

'Now, Doctor, it ain't a trespass. If thee has any messages for – for *her*, I'll arrange for them to be ferried to Main Street.'

'Since you mention it, I was hoping to send a communication to Miss Macy this very afternoon.'

She looked me over as carefully as an old tar taking a sight. At length she made a concession that must have cost her much. 'Thee'd be welcome to use Captain Bunker's own study.'

So I came to find myself at Captain Bunker's 'country' desk, sitting on Captain Bunker's chair, writing a note with Captain Bunker's pen on a square of familiar – not mousy, I now saw, but merely faded; most likely it had also once come from Canton – paper.

'My dear Miss Macy,' I began. 'I have arrived on Nantucket.' *I must see you*, I wanted to say. *I am in agony until I see you again.* Instead I wrote, 'May I call on you at your earliest convenience?'

There followed a terrible twenty-four hours, perhaps the most terrible of my life up to that point.

TWENTY-FIVE

RUTH MACY DID NOT reply that afternoon. By evening she had still sent no message back to me. It was too cold to go out, and though I was deeply agitated I also felt much too downcast to fake an enthusiasm for conversation. So I simply sat and waited.

During this time Mrs Bunker displayed a formidable tact, leaving me quite alone in the study. I'd brought along the case notes I'd so recently begun to write up, and then abandoned, and I made a show of working on these. She interrupted me only twice, to ask if I wanted more tea (I didn't), and to summon me to 'supp-ah'. Between us, at seven o'clock, we consumed, at a drop-leaf table in the parlor of the *Harvest* (as I thought of that ship-like house), a dish of buttered potatoes and two anonymous fried fish. Mine seemed to smirk at me before I stabbed it in the gills. When Mrs Bunker offered me a thimble-sized glass of Captain Bunker's port, I accepted it gratefully.

I was swallowing the last of my port as the lighthouse struck eight and the ship began its jig.

'So, Doctor. Thee'll want to find thy berth now.'

'I will, indeed. Good night, Mrs Bunker.'

I didn't sleep all night.

Why hadn't Miss Macy answered me? Had I offended her in some way? (Thank God I hadn't written what my heart had prompted me to write.) Was she sick? Was she away from home?

Or was she – oh, unthinkable, when I was in such extremity – indifferent to my arrival?

All through that night I could hear the lighthouse clock going *ping-ping* and the little ship whirring, until I was convinced I'd lose my mind. Just as my curtains grew pale I started to drift into a sideways sleep.

With the coming of sleep, so did Mrs Bunker's hesitant knock on the door.

'Will thee take a mouthful of breakfast, Doctor?'

I was up, and washing my face in front of the 'splasher' again.

The parlor table was set with more biscuit, and – I was relieved to see – a cup of coffee.

'Were there any messages this morning, Mrs Bunker?'

'No, none yet. Why, Doctor, thee's as peaky as the snow on the road. Sit tight and I'll poach thee an egg.'

I ate the egg and drank the coffee, and slunk off to Captain Bunker's study. When the wooden joints of the house creaked, or the doors shivered in their frames, I jumped. The crunching of boots at the back around midday had me out of my chair with my ear pressed to the wall, but it was only a woman peddling something. Mrs Bunker began to haggle with her in a high voice like a muezzin's. Each time I assumed a deal had been struck she would start all over, counting up the dimes and cents . . . Finally the boots could be heard retreating on the snow. There was protracted slapping on the kitchen counter, the banging of a pan, the smell of frying.

After what felt like hours and hours the lighthouse pinged once.

'Dinn-ah.' Mrs Bunker set before me a fish that was identical in every way to the one of the previous evening.

I thought – I really thought; it had never seemed less like a figure of speech – that I'd go mad. I bit my cuticles. I recall that I scratched at ghostly pimples on my scalp. I pretended to write, but I couldn't write. I couldn't concentrate. Whenever that clock pinged, I wanted to vomit. Was this how our boarders felt? Was this how they experienced time, as waiting on a deliverance that never, ever came?

My question remains unanswered, because for me, at last, it did come.

I was still trying and failing to write my paper. For the whole of that endless day I'd sat, stalled, over the paragraphs in which I promised to reveal the origins of Borden's sudden mental crisis. It was at the ringing exposition in particular that I stumbled.

> Could it be that the suffering of that moment sprang from the emotion surrounding a much earlier memory, a memory which, though lying well within the scope of his recollection, was so awful, so far beyond the realm of ordinary human experience, that he had never been able to speak of it?

My earlier certainty, in its declamatory shrillness, now lay revealed as the farcical thing it was. I'd begun to fear – a fear I didn't wish to confront, let alone put into words – that the memory of what had happened in the dinghy of the *Providence* had perhaps not been awful to William Borden, or not as awful as he'd led me to believe.

I took up my pen and drew a line across the page. I was watching the ink dry when Mrs Bunker's triumphant tap sounded at the study door. 'Doctor, I've a message for thee.'

She handed me a folded piece of paper. We looked at each other, absorbing the terror of the moment. Yes, terror. That is what coursed through me – nothing less.

I opened it. '*I am at home today at five o'clock*,' it said, and that was all.

'Five o'clock – why, Mrs Bunker, that's now.'

'Thee's ready? Thee's prepared?'

Her benign old eyes searched my face. I glanced at the manuscript spread out on the desk. I was poleaxed by doubt – doubt of William Borden, and of Ruth Macy, but also of myself, and of what I'd come for. 'Ma'am, I hope so.'

AS SOON AS I set off along the frozen length of Main Street I felt it more keenly than ever: the sense that I'd been excluded. It wasn't just the invitation that wasn't an invitation. It was as if everything about the place, which I'd last seen in spring so many years ago, was now designed to shut me out. Was this really the same street? The wintry anonymity of it all was a shock: it wasn't at all the place of my memories. Yet despite its unnatural blankness it was also more crowded, somehow, less isolated, less removed from the world. Rows of newly planted elms cast cobalt shadows on the snow. I passed the veiled stump of a tethering post. And then, as if conjured by my mood of dislocation, the most insanely whimsical structure rose up before me, a strapping Grecian thing straddled by creamy Corinthian columns wide as the thighs of a giant. This edifice was raised off the street on an artificial hill. Beside it, like a sacrilegious twin temple, towered another. Directly opposite these follies were three red brick slabs, like blots of blood on the landscape, topped with jabbing belvederes. The Starbucks and the Folgers, and God alone knew who else, had closed in on the Macys.

There was the house: still bluff-fronted, austere. The shutters were fastened. I put my gloved hand on the shallow curve of the balustrade, mounted to the broad door beneath the transom with its green fan. I heard the sound of my knocking reverberate in the depths of the building. No one came, and after another minute or two I knocked again. This time I was certain that I could detect footsteps. They were faint but rapid, and their quickness, which was immediately familiar, woke an answering quickness in my breast.

The door opened and light trickled from the hall. Ruth Macy stood on the step, holding a lamp.

'Hiram Carver.'

'Miss Macy – good God.' I scarcely realized what I was saying. 'How you've changed!'

This wasn't the woman I remembered, this whitened wraith, with her lace cap and spinsterish shawl hanging at a slant from her chiseled shoulders. After two decades her face, under its cuff of muslin, was still smooth, and as perfectly proportioned as ever. But it had a scantness, a flatness – her whole frail body appeared to share in this flatness – as though compressed by the weight of some great grief. She looked horribly mortal.

'No, Hiram. You're mistaken. I've seen very little change. But you – why, look at you. You've become a man of the world.' She gave a lusterless laugh.

387

I couldn't take my eyes off her. She led me into the very room in which we'd shared confidences all that time ago, and as she walked ahead of me down the gray passage, her spectral arm carrying the lamp aloft, her flattened face turning to me at the end to indicate that I should go in, and find my old seat, I kept thinking that it was wrong, it was all wrong, it couldn't be . . .

The fire that had once burned in her had gone out. She was utterly without her former shine. And that room! It was the same room, and it wasn't. The floor, the furniture, every object, large and small, that had gleamed so brightly then, now partook of this dullness, and I couldn't work out why until I sat down on a chair and found the legs of my trousers smeared with dust. There was a discomfiting, sour mealiness in the air. It was the smell of burnt-out candles and unswept hearths; the smell of ashes, of unwashed skin.

But it was the silence in that house I noticed above all, a silence so heavy and palpable that it seemed like a physical thing, immovable, and yet not inert: it wasn't just silence, but an energy, a stony force, grinding as finely and obdurately as a millstone; a force of silent *waiting* . . .

Miss Macy set down her lamp. 'If you'd like coffee, I will have to make it,' she said. 'I keep no servant here now.'

'Ah, no. But how –' I thought, all at once, of Caro – 'how do you *manage*, all alone in this big house?'

She batted away my question with a paper-thin hand. 'Oh, I manage well enough. It was the noise. I couldn't stand it. There was never any peace.' Her eyes flickered and closed. 'Now I can be quite quiet. I prefer it this way.'

I looked at her aghast: at her dusty hair, her unleavened face, her lowered lids.

She raised her head and caught me staring. 'You've prospered,' she remarked. 'You've met with success. I knew you would.'

'I've prospered outwardly, yes. But by any real measure of success – success as I'd measure it, not as the world would – I've failed.'

'Oh, the world.' Again that wave of the hand. I almost expected to hear her fingers rustle. 'You used to talk a great deal about the world, as I remember. The world doesn't trouble me much, here.'

This was more than I could stand. It was all beyond endurance: the dust, the smell, the silence. But her willed self-entombment, that compulsive banishing of anything external to herself, when she'd once been without walls or barriers of any kind – this was a horror too far.

'Well, Hiram Carver,' she said, 'I'm sorry that your journey has been for nothing.'

I reached for her wrist, but she slid away, further into her chair. 'Please hear what I have to say,' I begged. 'I didn't know, when I came here, what the purpose of my journey was. But I do now. I've come to apologize. I've come to tell you how bitterly sorry I am for having failed you, for having led you to – to this. I believed – I really believed – that I'd cured him.'

'Ah, you believed! He was cured, you said.' A strange shaded smile crossed her face. 'But he never came back.'

'Miss Macy, what in God's name do you mean? Isn't he living here on Nantucket? You fetched him away yourself! *Where is he?*'

'Oh, he is here on the island – on the very edge of town. He did return.'

'Then I don't understand.' I reached for her again, and to avoid me she half rose from her seat. 'I understand nothing!'

'Stop asking me,' she said through her wrenched smile. 'Stop asking –'

'I will not.' I rose too. 'I won't stop until you give me an answer I can live with.'

That awful smile – awful in its vagueness! – perished on her lips. She gazed at me with something of her old directness. 'Hiram, he came back. But he never came back to me.'

'But you were to be married! When we last wrote to each other, you were preparing – you were planning –'

'Yes, I was planning. When have I ever not planned? Oh, I've planned and planned myself to a standstill. I planned to save him. I planned to be his wife. But men are not machines, Dr Carver. They can't be fixed, and they can't be bidden, and they can't be made to mean yes when they say no.'

'He said – no? After all we – you! – had done for him – *no*?'

'He said no.'

With that, Ruth Macy started to cry. I'd seen her cry, long ago, but this was different. It was unmoored. It felt dangerous. She cried as if she were heading for the rocks, as if she wanted to break herself apart. And yet, with that annihilating crying it was as if she'd set in motion a strange reversal, had begun to turn, again, into the timeless creature I'd known before.

I raised my helpless arms in surrender. When she didn't stop weeping, I let them find her and creep around her waist. The back of my neck prickled with excitement and terror. A blistering tenderness ran through my veins. I felt limp, in the grip of desire.

'How could he have said *no*?'

I still had my arms clasped lightly around her. Instead of replying she hid her face in my chest. I stroked her hair, and as I felt her body shake against mine, I understood – but only dimly – what she had been trying to tell me.

I was aware of a shock, a wave of foreboding, traveling along my nerves. But within a few moments it was gone, and in its place was a sudden, wild fancy that it wasn't, perhaps, too late – not for him, but for me.

'You were engaged. *Contracted*. He was well again. He was in his right mind. Didn't you ask him *why*?'

'Oh, Hiram.' The moan that came out of her white mouth was all in the present. 'What am I to say to him? *Why don't you love me now? You loved me once?* I know what they say about me here. *Poor Ruth. Poor Ruth Macy.* To be born with so little art as to love a man who won't have her.'

She was suffering not from love but from lovesickness, and with that cry it was as if I saw straight into her ravenous heart. I had my answer: she didn't know. She didn't know the first thing about it. She was trapped in the labyrinth, and could see no way out.

And by now I'd grasped the most appalling fact. 'You still hope, don't you? You still want him back.'

'I do. I do! I haven't stopped wanting him.'

'Miss Macy. Ruth!' I loosened my hold on her and looked into her blanched eyes. 'You may have to accept that the man you want does not exist.'

She moaned again, faintly. 'Do you think he may be so far beyond recovery?'

'No. I mean that he might *never* have existed. I sometimes wonder whether you and I haven't both been under the sway of an illusion. I wonder, in short — I wonder if William Borden was ever what he appeared to be.'

'Then — what? *What* is he?'

'I think he may be something far worse.'

'Worse?' She repeated the word in a whisper, as if afraid to give it substance. The darkness of the December afternoon seemed to billow around us, engulfing the small circle of light in which we stood.

'If you like — if you really want me to, after all this — I will seek him out.'

'Will you?' She seized both my hands in hers and crushed them between her blue-white fingers. 'But what can you possibly discover?'

Oh, I'd been mistaken in thinking that there was no fire left in her! I felt the heat in her fingers, smelled her smoky skin, and I knew that the willed flatness of her voice still hid a consuming flame.

'I don't know. But I know that my own peace of mind depends on it.'

'I can't help you this time, Hiram. He won't see me. He won't see anyone.'

'Just tell me where he lives. That's all. If he is there, I will find him.'

How I wish, now, that she had not!

I LEFT HER MOST reluctantly. She stood for a little while on the doorstep in the darkening air, watching me go. Within minutes my feet throbbed again, stung by the cold. The elms lining the street glistened like a black fence; in the distance, all the way down to the sea, house fronts, iron railings, guttering lamps seemed to undulate in the icy dusk.

When I stopped at a bend in the sidewalk to wave, I saw with an ache that the house door was shut.

TWENTY-SIX

THE NEXT DAY BROKE fair and calm, with a slate sky miraculously unburdened by clouds. There was no sign of further snow. The horizon looked swollen; every distant rock and promontory stood out. Great Point hung suspended between water and air, and from my bedroom window I fancied that I could make out a striation in the blue that might have been Cape Cod.

The nightmare had begun to lift from my mind. I was convinced now that the violence of Borden's reaction on the *Orbis* all those years ago came from the eruption of a long-buried tension in him. He was afraid, viscerally afraid, in the course of that voyage, that Buskirk had guessed his secret. But Buskirk's remark about killing and eating the dead wasn't the motive for his murderous rage, when it finally came roaring forth; it was merely the spark that lit the underlying tinder. The deeper tension in William Borden, all that time, was not the tension of having to reconcile the knowledge of his own weakness and helplessness with a heroic illusion. It was the tension of having to seem modest, having to seem subservient, having to seem meek in relation to the Buskirks of his world, when he knew that he was stronger than they, quicker than they, more ruthless than they; that he'd once had the power of life and death over others, that this power was bound in him, bone and sinew to him, irreducibly part of his being.

Our sacrifice was accepted. It raised the wind.

It wasn't that he didn't believe in the illusion he'd created. The monstrous truth was that he did believe it.

On coming back to my boarding house the previous evening I'd gone straight to bed, feigning a great weariness. But in the crystal sea-light of morning I couldn't avoid my landlady's winnowing gaze.

'Did she consult thee?' she asked as we sat at our breakfast. 'Was thee able to give her some relief?'

I realized that Mrs Bunker thought I was treating Ruth Macy as a patient. Perhaps I was.

'Well, ma'am, that remains to be determined. I've seen her, yes. I haven't wanted to ask you this, but I feel obliged to, as – as Miss Macy's physician.' I was full of a strange agitation, and unable to finish the oatmeal in front of me. 'She needs our help particularly now. I am trying to understand as much about this sad case as I can. I think you said, ma'am, that your husband knew William Borden before you were married?'

'He did. It was Ezra taught Will to sail a ship. He taught him how to use the instruments. I guess he taught him most of the things as saved his life later.' She swallowed meditatively. 'But look here, Hiram Carver. Those things can only save a man at sea. They ain't a help to him as he is. He's lost.'

'What does he do now? How does he live?'

'He's a shooler.'

'I don't know what that means.'

'It means that he shools,' said Mrs Bunker flatly. She put down her spoon. 'He lives by what he can find along the shore, when the tide is out. And he fishes.'

'Does he live alone?'

'He has a companion. He ain't entirely alone.'

'Who is this person? Is it a man or a woman?'

'It ain't for me to say.' Rising from her seat, she began to stack our bowls. I watched her neat movements, the spare gestures of her body in which there were no lines of youth left. 'Doctor, tend Ruth Macy. But don't go casting thy net for trouble.'

ALL THAT DAY I remained in my room, riveted to the spot by a live anguish that completely drained me of any ability to act. I lay on my bed in a turbulent drowse, staring at the ceiling, ignoring Mrs Bunker's anxious inquiries about my health. After that fair start a cold wind had begun to blow from the east, shaking the window panes and sweeping balled clouds over the water. Towards evening I brushed aside her warning that a storm was in the offing and quitted the house. I intended to walk up through town on the cliff road to which Miss Macy had pointed me, and brace myself for the moment of confrontation that I knew must come, but once I arrived at the cliff I found my legs carrying me further and further away from human habitation.

Beyond the last lots I made a sharp turn off the trodden path, through head-high beach grass, and soon discovered myself above the bluff facing Nantucket sound. I was walled in by dunes on both sides, down which the wind skirled from seaward, as if along a tunnel. I had an urgent feeling that I was looking for something, but I was aware at the same time of how preposterous this was – for to the north of me there was only the toothed and relentless ocean; to the east, the ocean, smothering and encircling; to the west, the ocean, black as jet and now seeming to tip towards the shelf of land on which I waited, to nudge it as if to set it in motion, for wasn't it moving?

My head swam. Was it the sea, or the world that was moving?

I waited there at the verge of the turning world, with a sensation that I was about to be upended, covered by floodwater. The moon rose out of the sawing waves and the beach was irradiated in cold light. At the base of the cliff, half buried in the sand, were the keel and ribs of an old wreck, its arches straining above the white strand like a shattered cathedral. On and on the wind went, keening and complaining in its hoarse dialect about the inevitable wreckage and loss of every human hope and design – a wind that might have come not from the shore of the Cape, thirty miles away, but from anywhere in the world; from the Azores, from the Canaries, from the islands of the great blue-gray Pacific itself –

And still that saw-toothed sea gnawed at the cliff.

Far down on the beach I saw it, a form that seemed, in its sideways, crab-like motion, like the fear I felt made manifest, beating against the wind, trying to gain the shelter of the wreck. But it was quite different to the shapeless dread that had immobilized me all day: it had limbs, it had agency, it had a purpose. On it struggled, trying to find safety in the storm that was sweeping the back of the ocean. I watched it as one might watch an ant, or a fly, crawling across a tabletop.

The wind was louder now, more violent, clamorous. It blew

397

through my mind with an inward scream. I turned to go, and just as I did the creature below, which had reached the ossified curve of the keel, looked up.

It was – I was quite certain – John Canacka. There was a quality about its streaming hair, the set of the shoulders, that I recognized, even after all that time. Its eyes were fixed on me, in spite of the tearing wind, as if it had seen something unexpected, the mirror image, maybe, of what I'd seen. Then it began to stir . . .

A blast of rain swept over the bluff, nearly knocking me sideways. I stepped back from the cliff. When I'd found my footing and gathered my coat around me, and returned, crouching in the sand and grass, to the brink, whoever it was had vanished.

ON SUNDAY MORNING I awoke with the beginnings of a headache and a chill sweat in all the hollows of my body. The cretonne curtains at my window flapped ominously. The rainstorm had passed through but the wind was still high, and was now blowing from the opposite direction to the day before. I could make out brisk feminine sounds in the hall as Mrs Bunker put on her bonnet and cloak on her way to Meeting. After a couple of hours I heard her returning, and struggled into my clothes.

She was hanging up her outer things when I emerged. 'Thee ain't going abroad again, Doctor? Thee came home whipped to pieces yesterday, and the wind's backed.'

'I'll only be gone a little while. I must clear my head.'

'So. Wait just a minute now. Thy coat ain't dry yet. I'll fetch thee another.'

She went out to the press in the kitchen and reappeared with a bundle in her arms.

'This was Captain Bunker's.' She shook out an oiled cape with deep sleeves. 'It will keep the wind off thee. And this –' drawing out a water-ringed sou'wester – 'will keep thy head dry.'

She had removed her Sunday mittens, and I took her roughened hands in mine. 'My dear Mrs Bunker. I don't know what to say. You've been marvelously good.'

'Oh, tush. Captain Bunker would've wanted me to keep an eye on thee.' She clenched my fingers with startling force. Her voice dropped. 'Thee'll be careful, won't thee?'

'I will. It's just a little walk.'

This time I didn't hesitate, but went straight up the cliff, all the way to the top of the road. The recent rain had melted most of the snow, revealing shorn and stubbled fields in the valley below. Bells were sounding in a salvo across the island. The headache had spread from the base of my skull to my temples, and the ringing of the bells seemed to enter my body and to run through my limbs in shivering vibrations . . .

I followed the curve of the headland, edged with shingled cottages that became fewer and more spartan as the way grew rough, until I came to a set of steps cut into the cliff face that led to the beach. My head pealing, I began the steep descent through mats of cranberry and tangled vines. In the distance the whiteness of the sand was broken by pewter pools. The tide was low, the water, flattened by the wind on the sound as if by a colossal hand, resolving into seething foam along the shore. I found my way down clumsily, with the oddest sensation, all the while, that I was being watched.

It was an apprehension, the merest pricking of my skin, and horribly disturbing. I was afraid to turn around: I was certain that I'd be confronted with some abominable thing, the raw-eyed image of my own dread, perhaps, if I did. My misgivings were unfounded, of course. For as I stumbled from the last step onto that shining strand, it opened out before me in a sweep of light.

There he was.

He was hauling a rowing boat to the water. The first thing I noticed was that he was no longer large. He was still tall, to be sure, but stretched thin like wire, thin and strong, as if he'd been stripped to his essence. And then, that he was gray: that once abundant coppery mane of his was as scrubby and hoar as the winter fields. He was whiskered, too, with a brief scraggle of turf-colored beard.

Oh, the ordinariness of that moment. I will never forget it.

'William!' I called out. 'William!' The wind snatched at my voice, throwing its flitters back at me: 'I am, I am.'

He stopped dragging at the boat and started to walk towards me, with an expression on his face between doubt and joy. 'Hiram. Hiram Carver. It *is* you.'

'Yes. I'm here, Will. I've come.'

'I always hoped you would.' His lean arms closed around my shoulders. I allowed the constriction, knowing that I couldn't resist it.

'Did you? When we last spoke, you said I'd never come back.'

'Aye. But I hoped for it.' He bared his teeth at my cape and hat, the sudden smile dawning in his melancholy face as it had long ago. 'Look at you. You're the spit of a man I knew. You could be the spook of that old skipper.'

'Oh, my clothes – I'm staying with Mrs Bunker up in the town.'

'I thought just now I was being haunted. Step out of the wind for a minute. You're frozen.'

The stupid banality of it all! 'Thank you. I can't stop shaking.' My limbs were, indeed, still shivering with a strange silvery thrill. I squatted beneath the hull of the skiff. It was a poor-looking thing, clinker-built, roughly caulked and patched. Borden climbed into the stern – the bottom of which, littered with rope and nets and bits of planking, resembled an ash heap – and brought out a canvas bag. He was himself weirdly dressed, in nankeen breeches belted with a length of frayed string, a pea coat and what might once have been a gentleman's shirt that was now shredded at the cuffs. His boots were finely stitched but cracked across the toes. And yet the whole bearing of his body was still kingly, every movement so assured that something in me cowered. I felt emptied of certainty, as if I'd come to the wrong island, strayed onto the wrong shore, were on the point of confronting the wrong man.

When he swung himself down beside me his sandy knees were as gray as his hair. If I was ghostlike, he was no less so. 'Are you hungry? Have you eaten? I have biscuit. Cold coffee. Pickles.' He spoke like the Lord of the Underworld peddling his pomegranate seed. 'Whatever you like.'

A desperate instinct for self-preservation awoke in me, driving out any sense of the ordinariness of the encounter. 'I'm not hungry.' My brain seemed to thrum. 'Please. Please stop. Stop trying to be civil. Stop trying to be hospitable.'

'Very well. What do you want, Hiram? Why are you here?'

What did I want? I wanted him to be, again and forever, the man I'd known, not this disheartening shadow.

'I want what I've always wanted, William. The truth.'

'I gave you the truth, years ago. I gave you everything I could.'

'No, you did not. You gave me enough to shut me up and to get away from me. You fed me the sort of words you thought I wished to hear. You may think you've escaped me. But I'm here. Here I am.'

'You're mistaken. I've waited for you.' His head loomed in the sea-light. 'I've longed for you to come.'

Though we were here together at last, within touching distance of each other, we seemed to me less and less like real people than like two phantoms of my own imagining.

'What an outrageous thing to say. For me? What about *her*? How could you leave her, after all she'd sacrificed for you?'

'Oh, Hiram. I couldn't let her marry – this.'

'What are you, William? I must know.' I felt as if there were no space between my being and his, as if the answer to the question of him were the answer to the question of me. The shimmer of the water lit up the left side of his body. Oh, he was huge! There was no softness in him anywhere. He was all bone. I saw him, for the first time, as those others in the dinghy must have seen him: enormous, potent, unopposable. As he leaned over me his tongue flickered across his lips. It was like looking at something very old, something barely human. In a moment he would pull away and slither back to the darkness he'd inhabited for so long.

'I'm a sailor, Hiram. I was taking the boat out when you came. Will you go with me?'

'In this *boat*? No! Don't ask me to do that. I can't!'

'If I don't fish, I won't eat.' He got to his feet and regarded me sadly. 'Well, goodbye, friend.'

Turning, he set his shoulder to the gunwale and began to push that old skiff into the surf. It shot forwards with a grinding shriek. The shrillness of the sound made me stagger back, and at that moment I saw him: Canacka, crouched at the top of the cliff, his head a snarl of hair that was almost indistinguishable from the waving grasses.

Ahead of me was the sea. Above was an unavoidable encounter with that savage other.

'Wait,' I shouted, breaking into a run. 'Will! I am coming. Wait for me.'

The boat was bucking and yawing on the tide. I tumbled in and felt the thrust of the water from beneath. The sky rushed at us at an angle, so that I didn't know which way was up. 'How can you bear this?'

'It's my life. I was born to it, same as you were to yours. Sit up, Hiram.'

He waited for me to right myself before he resumed pulling at the oars. The strand receded fast as the skiff cut through the waves, leaving a swirl of phosphorescence in its wake. I looked back at the cliff.

He was still there.

'Who is that?' I asked – though I already knew.

'Fishing chum of mine. We share what we get.'

As the boat smacked the water my blood pounded so hard I couldn't tell if the sensation that we were capsizing was being produced from within or without. Borden rowed steadily, working the oars with a rhythmical sureness that raised the tendons in his neck. After several minutes there was a tranche of ocean between us and the shore. The skiff drifted across a lozenge of shadow into bald sunlight. Far off the cliff reared away, streaked with lichen; below and all around was a dizzying plunge of spangled green.

Borden had been sculling, but now he drew in his oars and started to gather up the heavy folds of a fishing net. 'Hiram, you asked me what I am. I don't know how to answer you.' The waves whispered over his voice. 'Seems to me I ain't ever been anybody I could live with for long. First I was a boy here on Nantucket. Then I was a sailor. Then a dead man. Then a hero. Then a lover. Then a madman. Then a man about to be married. And nothing's come of all of it. Seems to me I've always been afraid. That's the one thing that's stayed the same. In all my life I ain't ever been a free man, a man free of fear, except the once.'

'I don't believe in your fear any more, Will. I don't believe in it any more than I believe in your bravery. I think you've been spinning stories your whole life.'

'Yes, Hiram. I told a story and no one gainsaid it. No one pointed out that it was impossible, that things couldn't have happened that way. And for the rest of my days I've been trapped in that story, and no way out.'

'It's not just you who's trapped. Have you seen Ruth Macy lately? Do you know what you've reduced her to?'

'I'm sorry for it. I've ensnared her too. I believed for a time that she'd free me from the tale I'd told. She set no store by the world. She didn't give a goddamn about my bravery, in any way the world meant it. But she couldn't free me from myself because she didn't know the truth. I wanted to tell her, but I wasn't able to.' He spoke in a tone of low despair, but his gaze was hot with reproach. 'What was I? Come back to this place from the dead. The ghost of their notions of honor. The ghost of an idea. They didn't know my real story. No one knew. I wondered sometimes if you knew. I waited for you to say the word, to give me some sign. You never did. I guess you ain't going to free me either, Hiram.'

'No, I'm not. You're going to do it. Tell me, William. Tell me what you are. Set yourself free at last.'

'I don't know how.'

'You do. We showed each other how, before. It was you who taught me. Do it properly this time. Start at the beginning. Start with where you began.'

'I began right here on Nantucket. Is that what you want to hear?'

'Yes. It is. Tell me what it was like. Tell me what you remember.'

Borden looked out doubtfully at the bay. 'Well, I was nearly twenty years growing on this island.' We'd gone on drifting. The green of the water radiated from beneath us, traveling outwards in wheels that ran to gold where they met the surface. The wheels broke and dissolved, each replacing the one before, as if our keel concealed a secret spring that was inexhaustible. Green, gold. Gold, green . . . Now there weren't many wheels, but only one, constantly expanding and contracting. I glanced over the gunwale, straight into the depths, and realized with a tremor of surprise that I wasn't seasick.

We sat like that for a while as the boat rocked in the current. Though the net still robed Borden's feet, he made no move to cast it. He was staring at that ever-dilating circle with a rapt look. When the words came it was as if they were being called out of him by the ocean itself.

'Seems while I was growing I was always hungry. My pa fished for a living but we ate everything we could find. In my memory of that time we are always eating. In fishing season we go to Sconset for the cod. Cod is easy to catch in spring and summer when it's shoaling, but in winter the cod all streak away like mercury to the New Jersey coast and then we eat clams, cranberry and huckleberry preserve, kelp and sorrel soup, lobsters if we can get them, scallops and crabs. You can always find crabs. Crabs and men are the same. They will eat anything, everything, even each other.'

'Not yet. Don't tell me about that yet.' He appeared to be falling under the spell of the water. I studied his eyes, which seemed, in their fixed communion with its restless layers, to give out a light of their own. 'What about your father? Your mother? What's the first thing you recall?'

'My pa was native to Nantucket but Ma was an off-islander. She was a coof. A stranger. She never felt at home here. From the earliest time I can remember she is sitting me up in my chair and teaching me my letters. The letter A comes first, the beginning of all things.' He flung back his shoulders and began, in a high voice, to recite:

> 'A's for the ARK
> That swam over the flood
> Till the dove did embark
> With the leaf or the bud.'

'So you are a little boy now. What, six, seven? Do you like that rhyme? Do you like ships?'

'Yes. I like them. The Ark is a ship, but not like the ships on Nantucket. It is bigger even than they. I'm walking along the shore with Ma. Cape Cod is just a smutch on the horizon. "See there, that's

America, William. And behind America there's the world. There's Japan, there's China. There's a greater ocean than this one, where a man can make his fortune." She's leaning towards me. There's sand on her eyelashes. She says, "And better than that."'

'What's better than to make your fortune?'

'Why –' now his voice was nipped with feminine indignation – 'to make your name.'

'How do you feel about that?'

'I don't know. I don't know how I feel. I guess it makes me excited. I guess I feel ashamed.'

'Why would you feel ashamed?'

'This is our home. We belong here, not there. I'm ashamed of her and me. And oh – I want to laugh.'

'What are you laughing at? What's so funny?'

'We are. The two of us, stuck on the sand, pointing. We're like beetles with our legs wagging in the air.'

'All right. Enough. Try and go forwards a few years. Did you go to school?'

'I'm being schooled by Captain Bunker in the town.'

'Was this your pa's idea?'

'No. Ma sent me. There's heavy weather between Pa and Ma over it but Pa don't get a say because Ma has a little money, coof money, and he knows he is losing this fight. I've seen him cut a fish loose that can't be landed and that's how he's looking at me now. It's fish or cut bait with him and he lets me go. I already know all my letters and how to figure and I can handle any boat there is, gaffer or smack or lugger. But Ma says the only way off this sand bank forever is to go to sea, not in the way my pa does, as a fisherman, nor even as a whaleman, but as a real sailor, a navy man. Now, Captain Bunker's a real sailor. He's a fellow in the middle of his life with a trim house and an interest in a ship of his own. He's biding at home for a time, fixing up his ship to sail to China and his house to get married. Ma pays a half-cent for me to attend to him there twice a week, and off I go.'

'Does that please you?'

'Oh, yes. Captain Bunker's house is clean and quiet, not like ours. It smells of new paint and wood shavings and tobacco. There's always the same lady in the parlor, with a sister or two, all stitching curtains or pillow cases. They talk among themselves in serious voices but they don't disturb us.'

'Who is the lady?'

'Miss Grace Worth. Captain Bunker's fiancée. She's a sensible-looking body and younger than he. But neither is exactly young and it looks like a sensible, comfortable sort of marriage they are arranging, not like the sea battle over my soul my parents are waging.

'"So thee wants to sail the Pacific," says the captain.

'"I do," I say. "I can sail a boat."

'He's toking on his pipe. "Thee can work the rigging in heavy weather, I expect. Expect thee can reef too."

'"Yes, sir, and hoist and set. And mend sailcloth."

'"A-course thee can. That ain't sailing. That's just housework. That's just staying afloat. Sailing a boat ain't the same as sailing a ship, and no disrespect to your father."

'"Then what *is* sailing a ship?" I ask.

'"Well, sailing a ship is like reading. I expect thee can read too, a smart boy like thee. But this is reading of another sort. This is learning to read the book of the world. Bet thee never even knew it's a book."

'He's tapping his teeth with the stem of his pipe and now he pulls over two globes. One is an ordinary globe like a schoolroom globe, but much larger and drawn so carefully you can see every contour and the detail of each continent, down to the wavelets on the shore. The other has a brace around it like a horse's halter and is hatched and dimpled all over with lines and what might be craters.

'"See here," says Captain Bunker. "The earth with its waters is its own page and the sky with its stars is its own page. And this is how we start learning to read them. We have to know every character. Every possible circumlocution. The whole alphabet and all its tricks of speech. Only once we're fluent readers of the world's signs can we truly sail in her. Until then we're just trespassing and blundering. We ain't speaking her language and we ain't at home. We ain't safe. She will catch us unawares. She will spew us out of her mouth when we least expect it. But if we approach her humbly, as children willing to learn her horn book –"

'He drags on his pipe again and blows out a long feather of smoke.

'"Then the whole world is open to us. Then she will admit us. And a ship is the swiftest and surest way of opening that book. Now this. This is a ship's compass."

'He's lifting the lid of a square wooden box and beckoning me over to take a look inside. It ain't like any compass I've ever seen before. The face is paper card with a nest of black diamonds pointing to every corner of the earth. It tilts a little and there's my own face reflected in the brass bowl of the gimbal.

'"And this is a sextant."

'Another foreign body, with a brass smile and splayed iron arms.

'"Now this will make thee see double. Look here through this spy glass. Double, sure. But what thee sees are the real relations of things. The horizon is here, the sun there. Between them is only light, nothing real, only an angle to be crossed. The geometry of the ocean we sail on is water and sky and light and darkness. It opens inwards into terror or outwards into freedom. Sometimes both ways."

'"Oh hush, Ezra," Miss Worth says, glancing up from her needle. "Thee'll frighten the child."

'But I'm already frightened. As soon as I looked into Captain Bunker's instruments a giddy terror came and nestled in my heart. I've stepped outside the palings of my life. I've glimpsed something tremendous and far flung. But close! So close I know I can't speak of it to anyone. Oh what is it – it ain't the world, as Captain Bunker says. I reckon that's his own word for it, the word he's found to make sense of his life by. But it ain't this. It's some part of me that is out there, some fragment of me belonging to the water and the sky, and to whatever lies behind them. The unfleshly part of me, perhaps. I know, even though I ain't even set foot on a real ship yet, that for me the terror and the freedom of the voyage will be the same.'

He'd stopped talking, and appeared to become aware again of where he was. 'Go on,' I urged. 'I'm listening. Is that all you do – take instruction from the captain at home?'

'No.' Borden gazed back into that glistering, boundless green. I could feel the springiness of the water, like turf. The faraway shore seemed nebulous, so nebulous that it was difficult to believe we'd ever had any connection to it.

After a space he started to speak again.

'When I've been to his house some weeks to study the globes and to learn to read the instruments, not just the compass and sextant but the quadrant and chronometer too, Captain Bunker takes me aboard the *Harvest*. That's his ship. She's a small clipper, sharp-lined as a marlin, square-rigged and tall-sparred.

'"Now," he says, "we'll work the lead. Even though we ain't journeying, we will imagine that we are and we will work it. And once we have done this we'll learn about charts and how to use the dividers and rules. But first we will study how to measure in three dimensions. If thee was the leadsman thee would stand up here in the chains, up against the shrouds. Thee would cast thy line into the deep. Cast it, now. It's marked at every second fathom with a knot. Now call off the depth as thee reads it off the line. Call it by the mark or by the deep, according to the position of the knot."

'I'm already on that ocean, sailing over the face of the waters. In my mind it is night. "But what if it's dark? What if I can't see the knot, sir?"

'"Then thee must call it by touch. Feel for the knot. If thy hands are cold, then touch the mark to thy lips, like kissing. Don't strain. Kiss lightly, now. Thee mustn't work thy gear. Thy gear must work for thee."

'It's the same with the yard work. As soon as the weather turns rough, Captain Bunker has me up on the mainmast, shinning a hundred and forty feet all the way to the top, reefing the skysails.

'"Course, she ain't moving as she would," he shouts. "At sea now she'd be heeling and riding the swell. Imagine a storm at sea, Will.

Thy lee rails are in the water! Don't shorten her overmuch. Use thy sails! *Use* the wind! Bring her home. Imagine that." And afterwards he says, "Did thee see it in thy mind's eye? Did thee feel it?"

'"Aye," I say, "I did."

'"That's the trick of it," he says. "In a storm, don't be straining, neither. Let the others strain and lose their heads. Imagine thee's berthed safe here in dock, just learning thy business with me."

'Well, I'm hungry to learn, and I get the way of it pretty quickly. I'm hungry for the real journey of my life to begin. But, oh – oh –'

'What's wrong? What's happened?'

'Captain Bunker is married. There's Mrs Bunker looking as sensible as before but in a new bonnet, and he's setting off for the China seas. We're all at the harbor and I'm trying not to cry, I'm trying to look as if it's nothing to me.'

'What is making you cry?'

'He was my friend. Captain Bunker says, "I'd take thee with me if I could, William Borden. Thee'd be as handy a mate as ever I could wish for. But I know thy mother has bigger plans for thee." And away he sails. He's gone and left me stranded on this barren shore and I'm still hungry – and still afraid –'

He closed his eyes and lowered his chin to his chest. For a while there was no sound except for the wind and the gurgling of the water beneath our prow. 'Do you have no other friends?' I asked.

'Aye. One. A boy.'

Since after many moments it didn't seem as if he was going to resume, I said, 'Tell me something about him.'

Borden blushed a sore purple red, as if an artery in his body had burst and filled him with a sump of shame. His discomfort was so stark that I found it difficult to look at him. He spoke without opening his eyes.

'Ain't much to tell. At first we ain't friendly at all. He's just a boy, a dark boy half my height and many years younger, and he follows me along the sand. I don't like it though I don't rightly know why. I know his mother by sight. She's always on the beach at Sconset out in the shallows, picking mussels off the rocks, a lone woman with a plug of tobacco in her mouth. My ma don't speak to her. She makes as if they don't recognize each other, saying, "William walk, walk on." His father I know also because he fishes in our boat for a spell. We call him Canacka. He's the color of oakum and mostly drunk, and when he's drunk he will fight anyone, even my father. One day Pa breaks Canacka's arm fighting, and after that he don't go out in our boat again.

'Once I see this boy – his name is Johnny – get larruped. He and his pa have been trawling for lobster all day and the boy has a creel with but the one lobster in it. He goes to his father with the lonesome creature and his pa strikes him with his good arm. He just raises his fist and down Johnny goes.

'And another time I see the boy on the strand, torturing an eel. An old female, about five foot long. He has her in a cannikin and he is jabbing at her with a stick. Jabbing and riling her, and she's darting her pointed head and twisting herself nearly out of that tub to get away. I have a thought, then.'

'What thought?'

'Forgive us. This is us. This is what we do.' A shrug. Borden had opened his eyes, but I felt as if he were staring right through me, without seeing me at all. 'Well, this boy starts to follow me. Under the cliffs, over the dunes. Day after day. He follows me down to the shore, smelling my fear and my hunger I think, our two shapes black on the bright sand. Through the grasses and reeds he comes, a dusky thin thing, nothing but arms and legs and hair, like my shadow at noon. I try to shake him off but he won't be shook.

'At Sconset bluff beyond the cliffs the land sticks out like a shin. There's a place where the rocks are tumbled into the ocean and if you are slow and careful you can get around the promontory that way. That's where I head one afternoon to get away from him, slipping over the weed. There are pockets of the trailing kind called devil's apron strings, and walking on them is like skating. The only boats to be seen are a few dories, trolling for bluefish.

'Still he comes after. I'm quicker and stronger and I'm set to escape him, pulling myself hand over foot along the rock, when I see that he's stopped and sat right down. He just sits there on the mat of weed with his legs sticking out, as if his strings have been cut. Behind him the ocean is jumping, alive.

'"You must go back. You must go back now!"

'I'm yelling. But he looks at me and don't move. He is willing the next wave to take him. I see it come, a sunless bulge of water, shortening as it nears the rock. It goes over him in a frill of white. It clears and he's still there, latched on. There's blood spooling from his hands. I crawl across and a second wave covers us both and almost lifts me right away. Then I am on him. We are pulled sideways with a scraping of knees, our skin all grated off like soap. We're lying together on the rock and our legs are scored to the quick.'

'Is that how you become friends?'

'Not friends exactly. Two creatures joined together in – in

414

unbelonging. Now, that pa of Johnny's is tattooed all over his body, more than any sailor or whaleman I've ever seen on Nantucket. He's so overprinted with ink it's like looking at the page of a book come to life. Just signs and figures in every place. Johnny says that's how the men on his island know each other. "If thee ain't inked, thee ain't a man."

'"But what's it mean?" I ask. "All the different marks."

'"Don't mean nothing," says Johnny, "other than thee's a man."

'Well, Johnny and I decide we're going to get ourselves tattooed and be men. But I feel an aversion to putting a mark on myself that don't mean a blessed thing. I guess everything Captain Bunker has been teaching me about reading the language of the world has sunk in, and I won't be content with nonsense.

'There's a picture on one of the captain's globes I admire. It's like a serpent on its side but it ain't exactly a serpent, more of a long fish twined in a double loop with its tail in its mouth, and underneath in a banner are the words TEMPUS EDAX RERUM which Captain Bunker says means "Time, the eater-up of things". I think this is very fine. This is the tattoo I'm fixing to have, and Johnny says he'll have the same and we're off to get tattooed. The old fellow doing the inking down on the quay is pretty well blued himself, and he says, "The picture won't take jest a minute boys, but the motto will take longer. So steady yourselves." But once he gets going with his needle the pain is so great that we cry off at the TEMPUS part and just have the serpent. Afterwards we're gawping at the blood staining our bellies.

'I say, "It's better like this, because now we two alone know the meaning of it."

'"Kinda like brothers," says Johnny.

'"Kind of," I say. "If you like."

'We do many fool things like that. Fool things that only boys do.

'"Now we are men and we must hunt," says Johnny, "like the men on Nukuheva." So we pretend to hunt for boar at the bay and we run miles along the bending shore. We're chasing something that ain't ever been seen on Nantucket and never will be. But that don't make the hunt any less real and later we're spent, our hearts clappering like hell's bells. Feels like we're many miles from anywhere. Every now and then we come upon low straggling shrubs of beach plum with purple and yellow fruit, and we eat it. We find skates' eggs, knuckles of sponge, horseshoe crabs, and now and again the white breastbone of a bird. We find the penny shells folk say were used by the Indians for money, pilgrim shells, cradles, toenails and razors. We find sea urchins and starfish, and Portuguese men-of-war, curtsying in their rainbow crinolines.

'And we fish. Sometimes we fish for bass and tautog off the pier, but mostly we take a skiff and cast a line for bluefish because they are fighting fish and a greater test of your wits and strength to catch. When we do this we sail out to where the tide is running over the shoals and making rough water. We're looking out for a slick, the oily bloom on the surface that means a school of bluefish is feeding below. On an ordinary day the waves are wrinkled by the wind, but where there is a slick the water's smooth as a freshly laundered handkerchief. Our line is a good strong cord that could hold a twenty-pound fish if need be but is small enough to cut your fingers if there's much sharp pulling to be done. Our hook is an inch and a quarter above the bend and the piece of lead at the top is covered with an eel skin to make a drail. We're running it over the stern, skipping and twirling, through the crests of the waves sixty or seventy feet away.

'Our boat's leaping across the rips. In the next minute there's a break and the line is taut. A fish has taken the hook. It's a big one. I start pulling hand over hand, the fish tearing from side to side, jumping right out of the waves and shaking the hook the way a pup does the leash. The line cuts through the water and through my fingers too as the fish fights me with all his strength. Oh, that fish fights gallantly. We're under swift headway in a badly broken-up part of the rips, and I'm falling about the boat, trying to keep my foothold and pull at the same time, and every time I pull it seems he manages to recover part of the line. But finally I have him near enough to the boat's side and I swing him up and haul him in, as full of fight as ever, and I thrust the helm under my arm, twist the hook from the snapping mouth and throw him into the tub. He's a twelve-pounder at least, a good-size fish for these waters in summer.

'Johnny is screaming in ecstasy with a shrill rising cry, *Aie, aie, aie*. "Thee's gone and caught the king of the bluefish," he cries. "*Aie!* The emperor fish! The chief of all the fish. Now we must sacrifice him and take his power."

'"Quit your mumbo-jumbo," I say, because all at once I'm feeling how much my hands are hurting and I realize now how tired I am after landing that fish.

'"It ain't mumbo-jumbo," says Johnny. "This fish is our *ika*."

'Something in me is being drawn into the game, too, into playing my part. The emperor fish is lying quite still in the tub, looking at me with his great eye, and it's as if I'm snagged on that eye and I go closer.

'"That's right," Johnny's saying. "Thee must lift him up now, Will. Thee must take him out and then thee must cut his throat."

'"Ain't no call for me to do that," I say. "He'll die as he is."

'"No, thee must cut it. Just a slit. Hurry! He must be still living when thee cuts it."

'"And then what?" I ask.

'"Then we must take turns drinking his living blood and then we will have taken his power into ourselves."

'Oh, it's a stupid game. It's no more than a joke, really. When I try to lift the fish it begins to kick and I have to pin it between my knees.

'"Keep still," I say. "Keep still."

'I'm hugging that fish in a deathly embrace and I don't know whether to laugh or cry. "You show me how," I say, but I can see that Johnny is making it up as he goes along, he ain't got any idea how any more than I do. When we put our mouths to the skin of the fish it's more dead than alive but we do it because we've come so far and we'd feel even more foolish not to. Its flesh is wet under my lips and its watery blood tastes like salt, like nothing much, like the blood of any creature anywhere.

'We're done and I feel ashamed and I am angry. I'm angry that I've played such a game, at my age. I steal away from Johnny and hide from him for a few days. But soon we're running about again together, the two of us. I feel afraid, but I don't know what I'm afraid of. I hunger, but I don't know what for. I don't belong here and the part of me that might be found elsewhere seems very far away. I'm weak and uncertain. And coursing through it all is the crash and pull of the sea, with her many ships and all that sail on her. I can't set the two things apart. The sound of the sea becomes to me the sound of my own weakness and uncertainty.

'My ma is sorely displeased. "What are you, William?"'

Again, that contralto voice.

'"You must decide. Are you going to kick your heels around here forever, wasting your time with half-breed savages and fishermen, or are you going to make something of yourself? What will you be?"

'Well, I'm going away as she wants me to. I'm just eighteen, and on this island we count that as a man. I go to Boston harbor, looking to sign up to a ship. There's the *Providence* in dock with her sails furled and her colors flying and her first lieutenant on the quay writing down names in a book with an ill-tempered mien, and the bosun standing by. She's bound for the Pacific on the next tide.

'As soon as I spy that bold ship and hear from the folk on the wharf where she's headed, I'm ready to sign up as a landsman if need be. I'm ready to sign up as anything.

'But the lieutenant sees me and his face clears like mist in the sun. "Mr Duggan," he says. "Let's interview this tall fellow and then we can wet our whistles. After you, sir."

'The bosun is asking me have I been to sea before, and I say I have been acquainted with boats all my life and I know something about ships. He asks what can I do, and when he hears that I can work the sails and set the rigging on a ship he says, "What about the lead?" I say I know how to take a sounding all right. He says, "What, and can you steer too?" I say I can. "Who taught ye?" I say I was taught by a proper sailor, a ship's captain just like his own. He laughs. "Well, God be praised, Mr Monroe, it's as if heaven itself has sent us this lad."

'The lieutenant, that's Monroe, says they are short-handed and he'll take me on as an ordinary seaman, and that is better paid than landsman. He pulls out a flask, holds it up on high and says, "Welcome aboard. Our country, gentlemen, right or wrong."

'I'm feeling as if I will break apart with the solid joy of it. I feel like a made man, a man new made, and truly that's what I am, for now I have a calling and a place in the world where only moments before I was a frightened boy adrift with nothing.

'But my joy is short lived. I'm preparing to go on board and find my berth and cast off all memory of Nantucket, when I hear a voice crying out to me.

'"Will, wait, I will go with thee! Oh, Will, don't leave me!"

'Oh Christ. Oh God, no! There he is like my shadow, always dragging behind me, always following, the proof and sign of my weakness —

'He has tailed me all the way from Nantucket.

'"Go home," I yell. "Go home!"

'"Thee can't send me away," says Johnny, as if he's stating a plain fact. "I am thy brother."

'Well, the lieutenant is looking at Johnny askance. "Is he really your brother?" he says.

'I look too and I see what he sees: this dark child, hair foamy as the waves in the harbor, shoulder blades jerking like a gull's wings. I know I can't deny him, even though I want to more than anything in the world.

'I tender a shrug. But I ain't persuading myself. "Aye," I say. "He is. Yes, he is."

'"What age is he?" asks Monroe.

'"He's eleven or thereabouts."

'"Can he follow instructions?"

'I smile at that. The sense of my defeat is going through me like lead through water. "He can if he wants to."

'"Is he nimble?"

'"He's nimble, sir."

'Monroe is looking me over again and he's calculating. "The captain has no boy," he says. "The young gentleman was to serve him has been taken sick and we get under weigh tomorrow. I don't want to lose a splendid fellow like you. We'll take the both of you, if you're willing."

'That's how Johnny becomes Captain Fitzgibbon's boy.'

TWENTY-SEVEN

W E'D BEEN OUT ON the sound for what felt like an eternity. The wintry sun had shifted towards the west, but though the wind showed no sign of quietening, the sky was still clear, shading into aquamarine where it touched the horizon. I gave myself up to the benumbing blue of that sky and to the rhythm of the ceaselessly rolling waves. Borden was looking at them with a strained concentration; trying to see right down, I thought, into their darkening hollows, to the very bottom of the ocean's uncharted gorge. After some moments the motion of the water began to re-exert its lulling effect on him, and he picked up his story again.

'We sailed. We were a strange ship. A strange crew. A real rag-tag bunch, drawn from the whole length of the east coast of the United States, from Delaware and Virginia and the Carolinas and Georgia, the leavings, it appeared to me, of all the other ships that passed through Boston. We didn't belong to any particular station, but were headed for the waters of South America where we would defend our country's interests. What that meant, no one exactly knew. The Chileans were at war with the Spaniards, was all we knew, but this wasn't our war and we weren't a fighting ship. The *Providence* was a peaceful ship. A peaceful ship, going about her mysterious American business in the Pacific.

'Meantime there ain't near enough of us to carry out the daily round of our duties on her and to keep her afloat. I soon discover that I'll be made to earn my pay twice over. Mick Duggan the bosun has us hauling and hoisting and pumping and caulking until I'm so tired I feel my senses are being scooped out. There's an unceasing blare behind my eyes and a ringing in my ears. My fingers are so chafed from handling the rigging they lose their sense of touch. Then within a few months my head clears and I see a new and surprising sort of meaning in what's happening to me. My body has grown hard and no longer seems like flesh and blood, but like a machine designed by an intelligence other than nature's. It's a machine purpose-built to suit the ship, a man-made body if ever there was one. My arms are like knotted pine and my thews like oak. I can lift a bale of rope and sling a chain as easy as if they're yarn. I am a part of that ship.

'And I am always hungry. I am always eating. We ain't rationed, victuals on the *Providence* are plentiful, we are well fueled, but still my hunger grows. It's a hunger for motion and for speed. It's a hunger for the bounce and leap of the ship at full sail, to feel that power. It is a hunger for the work of sailing her itself. Maybe it's just the sea air makes me so hungry – so I laugh at myself. But I am a sailor to my bones, I have become a sailor through and through, and I can't get enough. The men laugh at me too and they tease me in fun and call me Gabriel for the span of my arms and the color of my hair. Mr Lenox calls me Odysseus, or the Noble Ithacan. But they marvel at me a little also. I'm something of an oddity on that ship.

'There's only one other on the *Providence* like me, and that's Daniel Small. Now, "Small" is a funny name for him because he's nearly as tall as me – by now I'm a veritable sea-tower, a mast of strength, none on deck is taller — but he is a few years older, and he is cannier. He's been working the sea for longer and he has a hunger even greater than my own. And he sees me and nods whenever we haul or mess together, and I know that he has recognized me as I've recognized him.

'Well, the men of the *Providence* need to be strong because her officers are weak. Monroe's a soft-natured man, by which I mean that he has no resistance to anything, and he's been further softened by being daily soaked in whiskey and rum. He's friendly with Duggan, and with Small, and he casts a kindly enough eye on me because I'm often to be seen with them and because, to speak plainly, it's hard not to see me, I stick out so because of my height. The second lieutenant, Perry, is dapper with a slinky gait like a swordsman in an old story. He fancies himself a gallant, and that will be his death later. Little Mr Lenox, our third lieutenant, is smart and polite. He is so polite it's like taking orders from a book of etiquette. *Would you be so good as to ask the hands to douse that sail please, Mr Duggan? Much obliged if you'd pipe us down to dinner.* And so on. At first I think it's all a joke at our expense, but then I see he's in earnest and that this is his native tongue, and I feel a sort of pity for him.

'But the captain, now. The Ape. First time I set eyes on him, I thought I was gazing at a picture on a wall, he was such a gentleman to look at, like the very painting of a navy captain with his crease-less trews and gold epaulets and his turned nostril and his eyes like drops of oil.

'"Ain't no need for us ever to go near him," says Dan Small. "Was a reason the last boy was taken sick, being locked up with that bastard night and day. He bites."

424

'I couldn't see his meaning then. I only spoke to Fitzgibbon the one time and he was perfectly gentlemanlike. He spoke just the way you would expect a portrait to speak.

'I'm splicing a hawser on the fo'c'sle. We've reached Staten Island off the mainland of Patagonia and are readying ourselves to round the Horn in the next days, and I'm alight with a terrified excitement such as I ain't ever known in my life before. I can feel it scorching along every fiber of me like a fuse. It's around noon, the sun shining like a blazon. Suddenly there stands the captain, his shadow etched across my hands.

'"Good morning, Mr Borden," he says. "Isn't this fine weather for our passage?"

'"Aye, sir," I say, and I'm getting to my feet for the salute when he shoos me back down. He's taking me in wonderingly, his painted nostril arched, eyes agleam. "Yes," he says after a moment, "it is true. Two angels, a dark and a bright." He laughs a crisp dry laugh, like varnish cracking. "I have heard good things about you from Mr Monroe," he says. "Very good things. Mind you get us safely round, now."

'And then he is gone.

'Still, I'm troubled by what Small has said.

'"Is the captain kind to you, Johnny?" I ask. "Is he fair? Do you get enough to eat?" We've been at sea a couple months or so, and he is looking cushiony, softer and plumper than he ever did on land, his face washed and his hair silkily combed. There ain't a mark on him far as I can tell. "Does he beat you?"

'"No, never," says Johnny. "He's kinder to me than my own pa. He has never raised a hand to me. I eat plenty."

'"Then why do you appear so downcast?"

'"Well, Will, I am missing you. I don't see you, now that I am the captain's boy. And I am sometimes made to wear a dress."

'"A dress? What sort of a dress?"

'"Just an ordinary dress that the captain has about him in his cabin, when I am serving him in the evening and such. He says it was owned by the boy before me and now it can be mine. But I don't see how that could a-been. Because we's boys."

'"Well, Johnny, if the captain has a fancy to see you wearing a dress then surely there ain't no harm in it," I say.

'But I am troubled. And as to the missing me, ain't a thing I can do about that, because I don't belong to myself any more.'

Borden had been staring at the water as if into a glass, but now his eyes found mine. I remembered how strangely colored his irises were: a resinous, sticky amber, like those of a big cat. His whole face quivered with a look of feral astuteness.

'I told you some of what took place on that ship, Hiram.'

'The money.'

'The money. Yes.' His handsome mouth slanted in derision. 'When we get to the Pacific and begin to scud up and down the coast of South America it becomes clear what our purpose there is. We are there to make Captain Fitzgibbon rich. For two years we do business with every privateer and pirate and gun-runner there is. The money comes rolling in till we're just a floating poke. Fitzgibbon keeps the midshipmen so busy counting specie that we scarcely see them. They sit in his counting house all day, wide-eyed as lemurs, tallying his takings. The purser, Joseph Webb, is a close-lipped sort but one afternoon he comes up on deck sweating like a man in a

426

high fever. "A hundred thousand dollars deposited today," he says. "A hundred thousand on this day alone." And then he says, "Sweet Jesus. Sweet son of a bitch."

'Well, the news spreads like a fast-growing vine and pretty soon we're all entangled in speculation as to how much there is. We imagine the money heaped up in that hold like the fabled treasure of a genie, seams and ridges and seas of it, with the Ape lolling on top and stirring his paws in the shallows. It's a kind of madness, that fantasizing, but we can't stop. We let ourselves run wild with spinning that legend, and none more so than Dan Small. He has a poor man's faith in the magic of wealth, wedded to a bookkeeper's pointy nose for detail, and he talks and talks till we can taste that golden river running down our throats. But turns out even he ain't ambitious enough in his telling of it. Webb came clean later. Fitzgibbon took at least two and a half million dollars in specie on this voyage, though we never saw a cent.

'Still, the rights and wrongs of it all don't concern me overmuch. I have other fears, and sore ones. The officers are asked to the captain's cabin every evening to drink. Monroe steps down willingly enough but Lenox and Perry go with gritted teeth. They go, and when they come up again they look unhappy. They're very particular men, and neat in all their ways. They are gentlemen and there's a boorishness to these evenings that pains them. And then I learn there may be something more.

'After a year or so at sea Johnny is rounder and softer than ever. His skin has a buttery glaze and he wears his hair in a thick braid like a rope of onyxes. He holds his head high, as if he's balancing a diadem there. He don't speak to me much these days. He's a creature apart, following the captain with a sashaying step. The two are mighty close. He is Fitzgibbon's shadow now, always at his heels, or carrying the captain's hand on his shoulder. Does Fitzgibbon let him fondle the treasure, we wonder, do they visit it together, is he given gifts of gold not given to us? There's a peculiar halo about him, as if some of the shine of that hidden money has rubbed off on his person. He is himself like a little gold fetish, like one bewitched. The men sense it and steer clear of him. Sailors are superstitious folk, and by and by, though the captain's boy becomes the butt of their jokes, he is the object of their fear and envy too. They call him "M'Lady". And then the "Captain's Lady". And later they call him the "Ape's Whore".

'Dan Small begins to press me. "Well, will you?" he says.

'"Will I what?"

'"Will you stand by and see your own kin used so?"

'He ain't my kin, I want to shout, he's none of mine. I am a free man now. I am free of the land and of Nantucket. I am free of that place.

'But I wasn't. I wasn't free of that place, or the rules and ties of that place.

'It was Dan Small insisted on the rules. They said he was lawless but he was the greatest stickler for rules I ever met. He was as well-read as any lawyer.

'To the rest of us it seems natural that the captain makes the law on that ship. There is one law on land and another on the sea, and the two ain't always the same. That's the way of it.

'But Small says, "No. It ain't right, Billy. Captain Fitzgibbon has sworn to uphold the law of the United States on these waters.

No rapine. No embezzlement. No extortion, which is the same as embezzlement."

'"But honest profit," I say.

'"Honest profit is not the same as what is happening on this ship. Embezzlement is what is happening on this ship. And on this ship there is rape in clear contradiction of the law. I ask you again, Billy, will you let your brother suffer so and lift no hand to help him?"

'Dan wouldn't let me be. He whispered sedition at every turn. He sowed doubt among the men with his lawyerly ways. He sowed doubt in me. At last he whispered the most terrible word of all, and that was "mutiny". But until the very end it seemed like play-acting, like a part we were rehearsing for in a dream but would never be called upon to perform.

'Then there came a day when the captain overreached himself. Seems to me every man has a natural grasp, and that day he went beyond his and this was his undoing. It was January first of a new year, 1821, the whole twelve months stretching before us like an unwritten page. At midnight on New Year's Eve the year was rung in with sixteen bells and there was carousing and quaffing above and below decks, of rum by the men, and whiskey and brandy and port and Christ knows what other fancy liquor by the officers. Now it was the next morning and we were nursing our sore heads, just idling in still waters, when after breakfast the Ape says, "Trim sails, Mr Monroe, and steer a course to the west as I will presently direct you."

'"Aye, sir," says Monroe, but privately he mumbles to the bosun, "I don't know what this means, Mr Duggan, but captain's orders, look to it."

'And then it was all hands haul away.

'"Well, Will," says Duggan, after we'd been making headway a good while, "this don't sit right by me."

'We were nowhere that we knew of, spun right out onto the black face of the Pacific, not a speck of land in sight.

'"And if that ain't an Englishman, saints help us."

'And so it was – a little English craft, her ensign all jags of red, white and blue, and her captain hobnobbing with the Ape as if they were long-lost cousins. There is a lot of unloading by her men, pale, sorry-looking devils all a head shorter than we. There is more drinking below in the captain's cabin at dinner time. There is the sound of laughter and gibbering and screeching as if a pack of baboons has been let loose, and the smash of bottles and the slamming of furniture falling over. When the foreign captain weaves his way back down the spar deck it's dusk, and no sign of Fitzgibbon. The moon is up and shining like the unblinking eye of God. And the *Providence* is sinking lower and lower into the water, as if dragged by invisible hands.

'I'm in my berth during the second dog-watch because I will be on deck later when Dan Small comes to me. "We will overthrow Fitzgibbon tonight before the end of your watch with Duggan," he says. "We're as good as in the desert here and not a living soul to apprehend us. The Ape is dead drunk. Tonight is the night. Are you with us, Billy Borden?"

'"I don't know," I answer truthfully. "I am so afraid. I do not know."

'"Well," says Small, "find your courage. Think of your brother. He won't be harmed, I swear. I will come for you." And he embraces me long and hard.

'Midnight arrives and I take the middle watch with the bosun as we have determined. Monroe comes and goes, and bawls orders, and is so drunk he can't tell the helm from the mainmast, but Mick Duggan and Lem Price and I keep the ship sailing true. We don't rightly know where she is headed. No one knows. The stars are so bright and thick you feel you could reach out and stroke them with your fingertips and the moon has its sleepless eye fastened on us as we sail further and further away from any civilized shore. Those minutes and hours seem never-ending and the fact is I don't want them to end.

'Then six bells strikes, and up comes Dan Small, as he swore he would, and all hell breaks loose.

'It all happens in a moil, before I can understand what it means. The officers are driven up on deck stinking like a brewery, and the captain with them. I am there, but it seems to have little to do with me. Monroe and Perry are struck down. Small's boys have cut off Johnny's ear and he is naked except for the crimson mantle of his own blood.

'"You said you wouldn't hurt him," I holler. "What about the captain? If you harm him now you're as good as dead."

'"Well, what's to be done with him then?" asks Small.

'I am afraid, and he is just as afraid, I can see it. And in that minute I know what to do.

'"Put him in a boat, Dan," I say. "Fling them all in a boat."

'"No, no," cries the captain. "You disloyal bastards, this is my ship. You are sending me to my death."

'Then Duggan surprises me. "Ah shut up, you bugger," he shouts. Johnny is clinging to his ankles. "Shut up or I'll put a smile in your neck myself."

'"Well, Mickey," says Small, "is this fair? Is it? Is it, Billy? Will it be murder?"

'"No, no," cries Duggan.

'"No," I say. "I will get them a mouthful of food and some water. They are near dead already. It won't matter much."

'Dawn is breaking like a bower of roses, a crazy beautiful dawn, the most beautiful dawn I've ever seen, and the moment comes when it is time to let them go. Johnny is lying at the bottom of the dinghy in a ruff of blood, his eyes gulping at me as if he's coming to from a long sleep.

'I could be free of him now. I could be free of him forever.

'"So, Billy," says Small. "Cut them loose. Cast them off!"

'Well then. I hardly know what happens then. There is the boat. There is the horizon, pink and buckling. There is the little part of me that lives beyond it all. There is Johnny in the boat, his black hair snaking about his shoulders and his face rimmed with blood. And I say no. Who speaks? I don't know. I don't know which part of me speaks.

'And I jump into the boat as if I am jumping towards myself.'

Borden's eyes were still fixed on me. The gold-green reflection of the water was trapped in them, inexhaustibly refracted.

'Dan Small begins to stamp and roar in a voice like a demon, and he is firing away at us. It's me, in his bottomless fury and despair, he is trying to kill. He is aiming at me. We row for an entire day, until the stars appear again and our hearts are ready to crack. But I know Dan won't follow me. He has set his course, and I must set mine. And as that first night falls, and the next day breaks, I realize that I'm alone, quite alone for the first time in my life. I have seven souls with me and none of them is any goddamned use in this venture.

'Well, I will do my housekeeping, I say to myself, and to hell with you, Ezra Bunker. I am in a boat now, not a ship, and I have to darn my sails before I do anything. But once I've darned them I'm no clearer than I was. I am afraid. I am lost.

'*Thee ain't lost*, says Captain Bunker. *Thee has a quadrant. Can thee shoot the sun?* No, say I. We are south of the equator. It's too bright. It will make me blind. *So what must thee do?* asks the captain. I will take a sight by the Southern Cross, I say. *And then what will thee do?* asks he. I will use the lead. *Thee has no lead, boy.* Then I'll make a log line. *Good lad*, says he. *Where will thee go? Study thy globe here.* What globe? say I. *Why, this one. The one I am showing thee now. Thee can't head for the Galapagos. The wind will drive thee back. The trades will bring thee to the Marquesas, but that devil will be waiting for thee there. Cruise south. Don't work against the wind. Head south and then ride the variables east to Chile or Peru.* We will all starve, I protest. *Ye will not. Thee knows how to speak this language.* Are we still in harbor, Captain Bunker? I ask. *No*, he says. *But thee will have safe harbor soon enough.* What about these other men? I ask. *This is thy voyage, Will Borden, he says. Only thine. Thee's their safe passage.*

'You'd think it would be silent in that boat, on the open sea, but the ruckus never ends. There's the whanging of the waves against the clinkers, and the soughing of the wind, and Duggan singing out Our Fathers to his God, and the Ape licking the drops from Monroe's whiskey flask and chattering to itself, and Lenox making conversation, I swear, just like a man in a drawing room trying to fill an awkward pause. Webb says nothing, just sits. Johnny says nothing, just shakes like an animal that's escaped the hunt. Monroe seems to have no memory of himself though he sometimes says my name. He is blind. The butt of Small's pistol caught him a crack on the temple and his eyes are loose as pearls. And there's the cheeping sound that is the noise of Perry dying. He dies with a froth of blood on his lips. When we cast him out to sea a bloody arrow shoots from our wake.

'"There'll be sharks coming after that blood," says Webb. "And you starving us!"

'Maybe he's maddened by the sight and smell of the blood. Maybe he's afraid of what may happen next. Maybe he's near to a shark himself in his madness and hunger and fear. Next thing I know he's come at me with his jackknife and cut me across the ribs. It's a deep cut, but not the deepest. Worse is, I know I ain't safe from him now, and won't be again.

'I wrest the knife from his grasp and say, "Goddamn you, if you kill me you are killing yourself also. I'm your only salvation here."

'I scarcely know what I mean by these words but I mean them with every ruck and swell of my breath. I feel as if I'm on fire, my whole body is on fire. I feel no pain from the cut to my ribs, though I am bleeding.

'Webb falls back and starts to weep. "You say so, but you starve us and without food we'll die, and that's certain. Prove that you love us, you bastard."

'"I will prove it," I say.

'And the very next morning at sunrise as I'm keeping watch over their sleeping forms a turtle flies into my lap.

'Lenox is awake, and sees it, and claps his hands and whoops,

"Hallelujah! Praise be! Wake up, Mr Webb. Oh ye of little faith. You fucking doubter, you fucking Thomas, wake up."

'"Shut up, Mr Lenox," I say, "and come here."

'Well, he slides along and in spite of all his education he drinks that turtle's blood as naturally and eagerly as a babe sucking at its mother's teat. And then the others, all except Monroe, wake up and we all drink, and once we've drunk we drink again.

'We're sated for a short while. Our bellies are appeased by the blood and stringy flesh of the turtle, even Webb's.

'But then the ocean turns rough. And once the waves subside we find we're glued to the black bowl of the Pacific. We are gummed there. There is no wind. Not a smear. Not a lick, to unstick us. We're dead in the water. Above us by day is the sun under the lid of the sky, hot as a bread oven. At night we're canopied by a net of stars. The warrior, the twins, the two pups, Canis Major and Canis Minor; the whale, Cetus, the cloudy river of Eridanus and at the zenith, Auriga, the galloping charioteer. To read that rushing sky, to be more than a spectator to the universe, to hear the stars speaking – when we were sailing in the *Providence* I thought there was no better thing than this. But that was on the ship and now we're adrift in a darkness in which sea and sky are one. The moon has been a friend to us for thirteen nights, and now the moon is gone. I try to cast a line but nothing comes near us. No fish, no bird, no living creature. It is as if we are cursed. It's then I feel my betrayal of Daniel Small, with the rim of the world turning in a black circle around us.

'"It's the Ape has put a spell on us," mutters Webb. "It's the Ape and his Whore."

'"No," I say. "No! It ain't. Be quiet, Mr Webb. Hold your tongue."

'I know it is me. I know it's my cursed fear and disloyalty that has done for us. In that hour I know there's no escape from myself.'

Borden's neck, as he spoke, was tensed, his eyes moving from left to right and back again, as though he were seeing these events as unfolding scenes rather than remembering them.

'Oh, those windless days and nights we spend on that dead dark water. It hurts to blink. It hurts to swallow. We're like men of coal, our skin is so blown. Our legs are swollen like tubers and our bodies gemmed with sores. Monroe is dying athwart the bows. The Ape has crept under a tarpaulin in the stern. Webb is still breathing. His stomach is bloated with gas in foul mimicry of his old fleshliness. With his wrung face and stretched black belly he looks like the Ace of Spades. But Lenox – Lenox is starving like one to the manner born. Language ain't left him yet. He's sitting upright against the gunwale, reciting verses in a raveled voice, the voice of a seer, or one of the bards of old. Twining verses about seafaring heroes going to war and returning to their wives, their homes. I'll always remember those words. *Of all creatures that breathe and move upon the earth, nothing is bred that is weaker than man.* He was a thin body to start with, and now he's like sea-glass, the light seems to shine right through his skin . . . "*Truly we are creatures of labor and suffering, and nothing for long,*" he says. "*I envy any man whose life passes quietly, unnoticed by fame. I do not envy those who must lead others.* I don't envy you, Mr Borden."

'Johnny is the thinnest of us all, his roundness all melted away like his luck, and I know he'll be dead soon.

'Monroe may be dying but he won't die easy. He's battling his death, he won't be reeled in. "Billy," he says. "Billy, Billy."

'*Forgive us*, I think.

'*Die*, I think. *Die now*.

'He does not die.

'And then one night the moon comes back. It's been slowly waxing and now it's here again to guide our way. The dinghy is bathed in light like sunlight and for a wild minute I imagine I'm out on the sound again at Nantucket, riding the rips, my hands bloody, and I know what I will do. I slip over to Monroe in the bows and cradle his head on my knees. I feel for his pulse and it's still there. As I draw out my knife I look up and see Lenox watching me.

'"It's a necessary sacrifice," I say.

'"Who decides this?" asks a voice – is it Lenox? "Who will be our priest?"

'"I decide it," I reply. "I'll take the burden of guilt on myself."

'"Will you absolve us?"

'"I absolve you. I absolve you of everything."

'Monroe is lying in my lap. I take his head, his ears, between my hands.

'"Billy," he croons. "Billy, Billy, Billy."

'"Keep still," I say. His throat is long and lean and still full of words when I cut it. Once he's stopped kicking I put my lips to the wound and take a pull.

'"Come, Mr Lenox," I say. "Come now. You know how."

'He does not want to come, but he comes. Afterwards he's silent as he never has been.

'Webb comes third to the feast. He drinks with his eyes lowered. "But will we eat too?" he demands. "Will we?"

'So I get to work with my knife and he eats in the same way he has drunk, with his eyes downcast.

'The Ape has come out from beneath its cover and is hanging from the gunwale. I extend a slice of liver to it on the point of my blade and it snatches the liver from me with a whimper.

'Johnny won't taste Monroe's blood. He turns his face away when I try to raise him up. But I smear it around his lips with my finger, and his tongue darts out. I put a strip of Monroe's flesh between his teeth, and his throat has swallowed it before his brain knows what it's about. He eats and eats.

'"How can there be a death and not a grave?" says Lenox. "How, Mr Borden?" He is weeping. "No," he says, "I will not shed any tears now. It is improper for tears to be shed during holy rites. See, our sacrifice has brought the wind. The gods do strange things, things that baffle us mortals, to save those they love."

'He's right about the wind. It's rising in the west for the first time in many weeks, rising with a freshness and a promise of deliverance, and I know then that we've reached the variables in spite of my stupidity and my miscalculations and my failure of courage.

'The wind lifts us up and we begin to sail. But before the moon has run her course once more Monroe's flesh has all long since been eaten and we are starving again, and still no land in sight.

'We lie in the boat like the sloughed skins of men. Webb is looking at Johnny and sucking on Monroe's shinbone. We've sucked his bones clean, there's nothing left in them, and soon we will try to swallow the bone itself.

'"That boy won't live," he says between sucks. "I ain't come this far to die now. You must kill him next."

'"No," I say. "There will be no more killing."

'"You've killed one man, Mr Borden, why are you so delicate now? Don't you want to live?"

'Do I want to live? I don't know. I know that if I die, Webb will rule in that boat. If I die, Johnny will most surely die too, if Webb don't die first. He is eyeing Johnny as if he can already taste his marrow. I don't know what he will do, what he still has the power in him to do.

'I'm afraid to sleep, either by day or by night, and leave Webb unwatched, and as the hours pass I find I'm unable to tell night and day apart. Everything is shadowed and bright at the same time. The sun roasts us, striking sheets of flame off the black ribs of the ocean. The moon is so fierce now that we can all see each other quite plainly. There is nowhere to hide.

'I'm able to hide from myself least of all.

'On one of these nights Johnny speaks. I can hear it as clearly as I do my own breath, coming and leaving through my mouth. He's lying near me with his head turned to mine. The light of the moon spills over him like water. His face is milled to blank bone by hunger, his lips pulled wide across his teeth. It's an unearthly sound he's making. A speaking beyond words, like the groaning of creation, without beginning or end, dark and undammed.

'That dark saying pours through me, wave upon wave, until time seems to run back on itself and the stars to leak away.

'I am empty of fear. I swim towards Webb through the moonlight and draw him into my arms. He resists me but he's weaker than I am, and when my knife enters his throat I push the blade in all the way and it ain't difficult.

'Lenox starts up his chant.

'"Oh, Artemis!

Oh, goddess who lets her brilliant light roll through the
    dread blackness of the night!

Accept this sacrifice which we offer to you!

Accept the pure blood from this neck!

Accept it and grant us a safe journey!"

'I am sawing away at Webb's flesh when the Ape creeps out
from under its canvas with its forepaws extended. At first I think it's
asking to have a taste. But it refuses the meat I offer it. And then it
addresses me in a human voice.

'"Let me be next, William Borden," it says. "Let me die."

'"No, sir," I say. "This is your punishment. To live. Like the
rest of us."

'After we eat Webb, we sail on for what must be another week.
Just another seven days. The length of time it took to fashion the
land and the sea and the whole universe. In that time – such a little
time, after all, compared to how far we've come – I lose myself. I
surrender. There is no *I* that wants. There's no *I* that hungers. There
is only want. Only hunger.

'I am one with the imperishable dark, and I am free.

'On our sixty-fifth day at sea we are rescued, and towed to shore,
and returned to the world of men. It's the start of Lent and the
whole world is about to fast. The whole world is covered in ashes.
The world seems gray, without color, not at all as I remember it.

'That is all a matter of record. But that ain't my real and abiding
memory.

'This is what I remember. This is the memory that won't leave me. The black waves, white and black. Someone weeping, on fire under the moon. The edge of the sky sharper than a blade. The cleaving wind. Bright midnight, rolling around where noon should be, and the day breaking in darkness.

'The wind, flowing under my knife. From my knife.

'A feast at which I am both priest and sacrifice.

'The mouth of that darkness, which is my own mouth, and time dwindling away.

'Hiram, once I devoured time.'

'No, William.' I'd been listening to him with a growing sense of dismay and loathing – loathing at myself, for having loved this fallen creature – and now it crested at that word 'devoured'. We'd been pitching for the last hour on the incoming tide and were close to the shore again, in the shadow of the cliffs. 'You slaughtered those men. You made a sacrifice of them. You've just confessed it.'

'I did it to save that child.'

'You saved him to save yourself. And now you're tied to him forever, aren't you? You're bound to him till the day you die.' But an awful ticking had begun in my ears, and I could hardly hear what I was saying.

Borden's eyes shone with a cavernous intentness. He extended his arms like the yard of a ship. 'You absolved me, Hiram.'

Tick, tick. 'Not of killing. Not of *murder.*'

'Have you never killed? Are you innocent?'

I pressed myself against the gunwale, out of the shadow of those arms. 'I don't want – I don't.' *Tick, tick, tick.* 'Don't make me remember.'

'You must. I have. Now *you* must.'

'It was hardly equivalent.' Yet I knew that it was. Though every nerve protested, I found myself reaching back. 'There was a patient – a patient of ours. Of mine.' The words came reluctantly. 'His name was – oh God, his name. Thornton. His name was Adam Thornton.'

'I remember him. How he suffered. I remember the sound of it.'

'He suffered, yes. There was nothing I could do – nothing.' The ticking sound in my head became louder and louder. It was my frantic pulse that I heard, but it sounded like the relentless and crushing motion of the universe itself. 'He wanted to see his wife. I encouraged him, and I – I did nothing. I fed his hope, my own sense of power, and then I did nothing. I knew everything, and he knew nothing – and when he couldn't bear any more he took his own life.' Each syllable was like a hammer blow, and the last blow discharged a shattering truth I'd never spoken aloud before. 'But it was I who took it.'

A hideous radiance had broken over Borden's face. 'Can't you see it, Hiram? We're the same, you and I.'

'We aren't. We aren't the same!' The twinned chambers of my heart seemed to enlarge and to expand like a monstrous, hinged screen, completely enfolding sense. 'I've tried to atone for what I did. I failed then, with Thornton, but my consolation, always, was that I'd healed *you*. I cared for you, Will. I looked after you. What have you done in return? You've lied to me and misled me. You've tricked me and compromised the only thing I have – my life's work.'

'Why do you blame me for your failings? You speak as if I've spent all these years sitting on your shoulder. I never made you do anything. Never.'

'You made me eat. You led me to it.'

'You wanted to eat. You wanted to be one of them. You pretend to resist them, Hiram, but you are one of them. You always were. Look at you.'

I glanced down at my solid legs, my caped paunch. I'd eaten, and gone on eating. But he, so thin, so pure, this thing of bone – what was he but a ghoul?

'I know why you're here now,' said Borden.

'Why? Why am I here?'

'You've come to devour me. You've already devoured whatever else there is.' He put out his hands and took my face between his palms. His heavy brow, still so square, with the depthless yellow eyes slanting beneath, swung towards me.

'Don't touch me. Let me go!'

I was aware that I was trying to scrabble away from him, but he was much stronger than I was and I hung there, twisting. 'That's what you've always wanted, Hiram. It's what you want more than anything.' His mouth came closer, as if to speak, or to kiss –

Horror rose up in me. I lashed out as hard as I could at his empty eyes, that approaching mouth.

'No, William. I don't want it! I wish *you* were dead.'

His hands left my face. In the space of a heartbeat he'd retreated to the stern, neck bent, jaws agape in a noiseless cry.

I jumped from that boat. The water came up to my waist and I struck out for the shore without looking back. I remember wading through the glittering waves, and falling and getting up again, not knowing whether Borden had come after me, and gaining the strand and clawing my way up it before I could get free of the water. And then I was running, the wind slamming into me, running back up the beach to the cliff. The pressure in my head was blinding. In my panic I didn't know where I was running to. I'd headed unseeingly for the steps and begun to climb, up and up, through the matted cranberry, up through the jutting scrub, and it was only once I'd reached the top and realized that I couldn't climb any further that I finally stopped.

No one was waiting for me. The watcher in the grass had gone.

I peered down. There was the silver shore, deserted. The wind spun like a top, driving wheels of sand across the bluff.

Borden hadn't followed me. There was no trace of the boat. It was as if the flood had swallowed it up, and I was the last man left standing on the face of the earth.

I found the shelter of a rocky shelf and sank against it, gasping. I was very near the drop. Below me, the ocean beat at the foot of the cliff. I had been seeking something. And now I saw that this thing was here, the thing for which I had no name. It devoured the stones and drove tongues of water, flame-like, into every crack. It shivered with an eternal, unassailable truth. It had nothing to do with speech, or any of the things I'd held so dear. It was vastly impersonal. It was the sparrow that fell, dead, to the ground. It was the caterpillar sleeping in its chrysalis and the fish hatching in the cusp of the wave. It was the worm curled around the heart of the rose. It was Hiram Carver, chattering on a rock. It was the rock and the wave that smashed the rock.

I felt, all at once, as if I were stretched over a divide. On one side was my life with its hope and its ambition, its loves and derelictions. On the other was a natural blackness, as dense and irresistible as a dying star. I thought that I might step one way or the other and that it wouldn't matter which.

The sandy shale beneath my feet was loose. It would be easy to walk into that empty space; I wouldn't even have to walk deliberately, I could just stand, and let the slippage of the ground carry me forwards.

I stood. The air seemed to go dark, as if night had come without warning.

I looked up and saw that I was braced on the cliff in the shadow of a gigantic sea-bird, pinions outstretched in the wind, that hovered two or three feet above my head. Even today I don't know what sort of bird it was, whether albatross, sea raptor or another creature entirely. It was white as new milk and its undercarriage was bowed with living muscle. It made no sound. It simply tarried in the air, with a perfect and careless power. Then the wind shifted and it rose with a silent pulling of its great cords. The ashen light of the sky came spilling over me.

I think I cried out. My heels slid and I fell heavily onto the shale. I lay there, clinging to the rock on which I'd been sitting moments ago. The wind blew so keenly that it felt as if it were blowing right through my body. I might have lain there for several hours or only for a few minutes; I've no idea which. I remember that I was bleeding from a slash to my elbow, and that I left blood on the rock, but I felt no pain.

I felt drunk; delirious.

I felt empty, light, as if I'd been rinsed through by acid.

I got up, as if floating – when? Ordinary ways of measuring time were meaningless – turned my back on the sea, and dived into the wind.

*

AS I ROUNDED THE bend of the road into town and crept up to my boarding house Mrs Bunker was waiting for me at the front door with a lantern.

'I was on the walk and spied thee coming up along the cliff,' she called out when I was within earshot. 'Thee was head under in the gale.' Seeing my deathly face, she ran out and dragged me into the hall. 'Why, Doctor, where has thee been? Has thee been in the *water*? Thee's shaking fit to churn butter!'

'I must write a message. May I have pen and paper?'

'Why ever?' She took one glance at my sweating features and drew me close. 'Thee looks as if thee's met with a ghost.'

But she brought me the paper, and a pen.

Still floating and diving, I scribbled a note to Miss Macy: '*I have seen him. I fear I've failed you again.*'

Then my writing arm seemed to grow quills, red shooting filaments of feathery pain. And my legs! They were singed all along the nerves, riveted and bolted through with shafts of fire. I felt myself soaring. I soared higher and higher, away from that fearful shore, into the face of the sun. At last, unable to sustain the illusion of flight any longer, I plummeted into the sea's dark embrace, and sank. It was cold, and it was not. It was hot, and it was not. It was precisely as hot and cold as my own blood.

I sank as far as it's possible for any human being to sink, or so I thought.

TWENTY-EIGHT

W HEN I ROSE FROM the sea it was into a narrow patch of
light. I was surprised to find a woman sitting there, knitting
a stocking. The light flowered from her needles. I was convinced that
she was knitting this stocking for me, and meant to pull it over my
shins, which felt bare. I uncovered my outstretched body and saw
that I was in an unfamiliar bed.

'Don't, Caro,' I said. 'Please don't. I'm hot. I'm too hot.' And
then I tried to get up.

The woman thrust me down with a surprisingly corporeal arm.
'Lie back. Thee's over the worst but thee ain't ashore yet.'

'Mrs Bunker.' The room was darkened except for a candle, but
I knew the dun of her widow's peak, her ruffled cap. 'Why, is this
your house?'

'It was, last time I looked.'

'How long have I been asleep?'

'Thee's been *asleep* for little over a day. Before that thee was
tossing about like a barrel on a wave for four nights and crying out
that thy arms and legs were on fire.' She pulled the sheet back up
and smoothed the cuff of my pillow. 'I called Dr Coffin in to take a
peep at thee and he said it was a bad case of the grip. But if I didn't

know my place I'd say thee's once suffered from the breakbone fever. Captain Bunker was laid low with it the time he shipped home from the Sandwich Islands, and after that he never had the grip but he near expired from the pain in his limbs.'

'Ma'am, you may well be wiser than many a medical man. But I'm still alive, all the same.' I dangled a calf over the bedframe. 'I think I'll try my legs.'

'Stay abed for a minute. I ain't watched with thee these five nights to see thee go under now.'

'My dear woman, surely you didn't sit up with me?'

But the sallowness around her eyes confirmed it. 'I did. So I've shares in this vessel, see. Lay thee down, Doctor, and I'll fetch thee a bite to eat.'

She went out to the kitchen. As soon as I was alone I was seized with a deep unease. Splintered images came hurtling at me: the ocean, with a small boat drifting across its face; a cliff edge, darkness, and then, mysteriously, a broad and motionless wing . . . No sooner had they arrived than they twitched away like the hem of a dream, so that I wasn't sure if they were memories, or shapes cast up by my recent fever. I tried to raise myself on my elbows, but felt so dizzy that my head fell back on the pillow. And yet I knew that there was somewhere I had to be, and someone I had to see.

A minute later Mrs Bunker returned with a bowl of thin porridge.

'I have the most awful feeling, ma'am,' I said, 'that I've left some business unfinished. Once I've had this I really must get dressed.'

'Wait now,' she insisted. She let me pull myself up on her forearm and settled the porridge firmly in my lap. 'Just eat.'

She watched me thoughtfully while I sucked it down. When my

bowl was empty she took it from me with a solicitous constriction of her eyebrows. Setting it on my bedside locker, she wiped her hands. 'So, Hiram Carver. I didn't intend to go heaping more trouble upon thee until thee had all thy strength again to bear it. But I can see thee'll never be quiet, and that keeping thee in the dark ain't going to make thee quiet neither. I'll have to tell thee.'

'What is it?'

'Well, Doctor. There ain't no easy way of saying it. He's dead.'

'Dead? Who's dead?' I must still have been slightly delirious, because I thought that she was once again talking of her husband.

'William Borden.'

Borden. A name as close to me as my own. A name that seemed to seep up from my deepest foundations, like blood. And with his name came another, the echo of a dream. Mercy. Pity. Ruth. William Borden and Ruth Macy – it was Ruth Macy I had to see. I'd given her my promise that I would find him. And I had. Hadn't I?

'He's not.' I laughed a dismissive laugh. 'I spoke to him only –' *Yesterday*, I was going to say, *I spoke to him only yesterday*, when it came to me, with a sickening shuttering of time, that our meeting on the open sea had taken place nearly a week ago.

Mrs Bunker looked at me sorrowfully. 'Oh, Doctor,' she said in a hushed voice. 'Thee never did, did thee? That was a foolish thing to do.'

I stared back at her, seared by a shocking flare of knowledge. My tongue cleaved to the roof of my mouth. Eventually I felt it move; felt rather than heard myself whispering the words, 'He can't be dead.'

When she said nothing, I asked, 'But how? *How* did he die? And when?'

'They found him washed up along the sound two days ago. At

449

Jetties beach, where the tide comes in. He must have fallen from the cliff in the dark.'

Fallen. I recalled that I'd almost fallen there myself, days ago. Or had I been about to jump? I was no longer certain.

'Mrs Bunker, what day is this? What's the date?'

'It's Friday morning. The twenty-second. Thee's not to fret thyself. Thee can stay here as long as thee likes.' She got up and left the room. When she came back she had letters in her hand. 'Now look,' she urged, placing them in mine. 'Thee's not to fret thyself, does thee hear?'

'When did these arrive?'

She began to straighten my sheets. 'While thee was keel out. And if thee has any sense thee'll not be going there now.'

Ruth Macy had sent me two notes. The first, written on Monday, was short: '*You have failed, you say. I must know what he said to you. Please come, Hiram. Please hurry.*'

The second was sent on Tuesday. It consisted of just one rending sentence: '*You don't reply, and you don't come.*'

I threw off my bedclothes. 'I must go to her.'

Mrs Bunker stayed me with a somber look. 'Bide here a day. Go tomorrow.'

'Why not today? What's today?'

'She is burying him today, Hiram Carver.' Her eyes were black with a stern authority. 'Let her grieve.'

I DIDN'T GO THAT day. But when Mrs Bunker brought me my porridge the next morning I pushed the bowl away and prepared to get up.

She held on to my wrist. 'Doctor, I've an ill feeling about this. Stop here. Thy wits are still scattered.'

'They may well be,' I said bluntly, 'but I can't stop. Let me go.'

'I'll call Dr Coffin.'

I shook her off. 'Call your medical man, Mrs Bunker. Call your undertaker. But I'm going, all the same.'

I could feel the disapproval in her rigid old fingers as she helped me out of bed, and though she left me to dress myself, her disapprobation seemed to fill the whole cottage. It took me a long time to put on my underthings; my trousers, my shirt, my waistcoat, which Mrs Bunker had laundered; my socks, my puckered shoes. I had very little strength remaining in me, and I was quaking as I shrugged on my jacket. When I came out to the hall I found her at the door, bearing my coat on her extended arm, like the figure of Destiny in a copybook. She handed it to me without a word.

I went first to the hilltop cemetery signposted at the north-western edge of town. The lane running behind the last houses was rough and muddy and it was slow going, made slower by the weakness in my limbs. It was close to noon when I found the gates. I half expected to discover a woman among the graves, all in gray, flat as a winter shadow.

But there was no one there. The hill was covered in patches of thawing snow, the lichened headstones cottony in the sunlight. I made my way among them, reading off the names: Wyer, Starbuck, Paddack, Hussey, Folger, Ray, Gardner, Coffin, Chase. There were few Bunkers, fewer Macys; the Friends must have buried most of their dead elsewhere. Here, in a corner of the field, were the Bordens. Asa Borden. Maria Borden. Reuben Borden. Judith Borden,

Beloved Daughter of Maria and Reuben. Thirza Rebekah Borden. Peleg Borden. Jethro Borden. Also, His Wife.

Whorled clouds cast roving shadows on the water of the bay below the town. In a portion of the cemetery that was still unpopulated, an unprinted page beside that catalogue of names, was a single hyphen of freshly turned earth. I stopped and waited there for something, some meaning, some insight, to announce itself to me. Nothing came. Gulls skimmed overhead. A breeze rose. Small grasses trembled at my feet.

Was this where he lay? Was this him?

That disturbed soil seemed, to my inflamed senses, to communicate an accusation. That William Borden's death was chosen and not an accident – of this, reeling under the onslaught of a thousand confused impressions, I now had little doubt. But the realization paled in the stark blast of the main fact. He was dead, and it was only then, encircled by the black ocean, listening to the cry of the gulls and watching the distant waves shiver in the wind, that I felt the full force of it.

I would never – no, never, however much I longed for it – speak to him again.

It was an hour later, perhaps more, when I reached Main Street. Time and space appeared distorted, and the town itself to have grown thinner and more twisted; to have become, to my racked sense of perception, not just indifferent to my progress, but positively malevolent in its obstructiveness. The noonday sun had vanished and the wind had kicked up, chasing a switch of cloud before it. The façade of number 99 was sunk in a wine-dark dusk. I knocked loudly. There was no answer, and I knocked a second time. As I waited I was rocked by the fear that something unspeakable had happened to her, too, and my terror drove me to hammer on the door with all my might.

From somewhere in that shut-up house, at last, came a dreadful voice, before which I quailed. It was dreadful because it was, in spite of its hollow note, so intimately known to me.

'Who is it?' asked the voice. 'Who's there?'

'Hiram. Hiram Carver.'

'What do you want?'

'I must see you. Please let me in.' There was no reply. In a lower tone, I said, 'I've been to his grave.'

The door opened with a groan like the unsealing of a tomb. As it did, an involuntary cry escaped me. The woman standing there was emptied out, not a shadow, but the shadow of a shadow. Her unfastened hair floated over her shoulders in a pale net. The face she lifted to mine was the face of some ancient creature; the blue face of a siren, guarding the wreck of a lost ship.

When I leaped forwards it was – I am certain – from the purest impulse to comfort her. 'I would have come,' I said beseechingly, grasping at her sleeve. 'I was very unwell. I didn't know.'

'So I heard. Let me be.'

Ruth Macy drifted down the hall, a diver returning to the deep. I saw her arrive at the threshold of a distant room, the tail of her dress dragging across the dusty boards, and go in. Darkness closed around her. She was slipping away from me into the abyss. I faltered on the lip for whole minutes, afraid to enter the unknown. Then I broke free of my paralysis and hurried after her.

I found her in a shuttered office illuminated by a lone candle, surrounded by banks of paper. She was seated at a desk. Drawers were pulled from their grooves onto the strip of carpet in front of the fireplace, disgorging yellowed account books, bills of sale, fretted registers. Ravenous flames, fed by torn-out leaves, smoked in the grate. While raking dreamily through her papers she occasionally tossed one into the fire. In her blue-veined skin and shattered movements I recognized the signs of a nervous debility that mirrored my own.

'What in heaven's name are you doing?'

'I am clearing away all this trash. I've decided to put my affairs in the hands of an agent. I'm going to sell up.'

'The factory? Your entire business?' I tried to disguise my shock with what I hoped sounded like rational inquiry. 'What, *all* of it?'

'Why, yes,' she said vacantly. 'I plan to live a much simpler life from now on.'

'Stop a moment. For God's sake, stop.' She was intent on burying herself alive. I struggled against the sense that a fundamental law of the universe was being transgressed, as much as against what seemed to me a precipitate and ill-thought-out plan. I knew that I had to fight with every part of my will to drag her, and myself, back into the light. 'Ruth!' I insisted, when she continued to throw her life into the flames. 'Why won't you speak to me? Oh, please speak!'

She looked at me with an inexpressive, drowned look. 'What did you do to him, Hiram?'

'Nothing. I did nothing! Nothing deliberate, nothing that was intended –' Out of the shadows the image of Borden's face swung at me: his open mouth and exposed neck, lowered in self-abasement like an animal submitting to the knife. He'd fallen from that cliff, but hadn't I also nearly fallen?

Then it flashed on me that she was still ignorant of the truth. She was still innocent! But her innocence, if so, was unnatural. It was chosen, deliberate. The thought filled me, first, with sorrow, with a piercing sense of loss, as if she and I, having just lately peered down at the chasm together, were now irrevocably separated by the horror of what I alone knew. Alone, yes – I was alone, quite alone. *She didn't want to know.* She had stepped away from me, back into her stubborn veneration of him, and left me to face the drop on my own.

Grief and rage sluiced through me. He was dead, but I was yet living. I remembered the last words of his story, which might have made me laugh if they hadn't fetched up so tragically short of reality. *Priest and sacrifice.* What gibberish. He was a self-deluded butcher, and I – God knows, I'd only ever tried to help her. And *still* she preferred him to me –

'I think you should hear the confession he made to me before his death.'

'No. I have no need to.'

'I think you do. I think you should know what he said. What is this hold he has over you? Why are you so afraid to break it?'

'I'm not afraid.' She got up from the table. Her vacant tone had changed and was now harsh. I sensed, with a lurching heart, that she was on the point of disclosing what I had wanted to know for so long.

When she stood up, her chair had fallen over, slamming into a sideboard bristling with silverware and gewgaws. They vibrated like the shaking of the wind before a storm. She was still poised across the carpet from me, her faded head raised, her brow creased, pressing her hands to her stomach. I felt a terrible sense of disorder, as if we were waiting in a whirlwind.

The truth came at me in a rush. 'You knew,' I brought out. 'You always knew.'

'Oh yes,' she said softly. 'I knew. I guessed – long ago.'

Waves of darkness beat all around me in that silent house. At that moment I saw, truly saw, what danger she was in. We were both at the brink, but of the two of us I was still further from the drop. 'Let me help you,' I pleaded.

She didn't respond. She was where I could no longer reach her, her ears deaf, her eyes whitely staring.

'Ruth,' I said. 'Ruth!' I sprang to cross the distance between us, to seize her. Clasping her by her thin shoulders, I pulled her against me.

'You are not well,' I breathed, still gripping her tightly. She was a raft of bones in my grasp. 'Look at you! He's almost destroyed you too. *He* has done this to you! You need my help. I can save you!'

'Save me?' she cried. The words poured out of her like scalding steam. 'Oh, Hiram. You – *you*! Save *me*?'

'Listen to me,' I begged. 'Oh my darling. He may not have wanted you, but I do. Don't think you can just shut yourself away from the world like this.' I was shouting now. 'Come back home with me. Let me keep you safe. Safe!'

But I could scarcely hold her; it was like handling something white-hot. 'You wanted him for yourself!' she shrieked in untethered fury. 'You wanted him, and when you couldn't have him, you killed him with your talk! With your endless, endless talk –'

I guided her snarling head firmly towards my mouth. She seemed to relent for a moment, then turned her face to mine and bit me hard on the cheek. Her voice, when she spoke, had a grave power. It was guttural, deep as a man's. 'I would rather lie chained at the bottom of the ocean for all eternity, Hiram Carver, than go home with thee.'

'You bitch!' I gasped. I could feel blood running down my chin. 'You mad bitch!'

She was crying now, howling, doubled over, her arms wrapped around her middle, as if bisected by grief. The noise was unbearable.

I started to walk out of that room, holding my hand to my cheek. I walked neither fast nor slowly. I had as little dignity left as any man when he is walking away from the woman who has rejected him. But when I got to the door that ghastly crying attacked me like a physical object. It was the strangest thing. It was just like being assaulted with an axe. I felt myself tear, and begin to bleed, from a far worse wound than the one to my face, and I ran. I crashed into the hall, and out onto the street. It was slippery, and I almost fell. I caught the balustrade and hung there, winded. Still that howling drove on, carving through the walls of the house, right through my skull.

I ran and ran, all the way down Main Street. The town erupted in a blister of bays and parapets and porticos, of doorsteps that flew up out of nowhere and stray cobbles that caught at my heels. I ran across the square, along the bleared length of South Water Street, up past the harbor to my boarding house. But even as I ran I knew that I'd never get that noise out of my head.

The door of the *Harvest* was wide open. Mrs Bunker was keeping watch on the step.

'Mrs Bunker!' I cried out when I was nearly there. 'I must go! I can't stay. I must leave at once. I must get away – Oh I must –'

'Doctor, there's someone to see thee.'

'Oh Christ. Not your quack!' I started to laugh, an unstoppable laugh that came from the pit of me. I held out my wrists. 'You've called him, have you? Lock me up! Take me away! This whole world is insane. I'll have no part of it any more, Mrs Bunker. I tell you, I'll have no part!'

Mrs Bunker stood aside. I saw that the parlor door was ajar. There was an explosion of green, a collision of skirts, and Caro appeared in the doorway.

'Hiram, I'm here. I've come.'

I REMEMBER COLLAPSING INTO her arms. I remember her throwing my clothes and papers into my valise. I remember her settling my bill, and embracing Grace Bunker, the two women leaning together wordlessly in the hall, in a prolonged moment of farewell. I remember her elbowing us onto the last ferry out of Nantucket before Christmas Day, and rolling me up in a rug in the saloon, and holding my hand in both of hers all the way back. But how did she come to be there at all? In my fogged and hysterical state it seemed like a miracle, and then, as we drew closer to Boston and my senses began to clear, like a mystery, but in fact the explanation, which she gave me once we were home in Mount Vernon Street, was simple.

When I didn't return after a week, she'd come to find me, just as she'd threatened to. She had no idea where I'd gone. Since Ben Schultz was none the wiser, she'd resorted to searching through the papers in the drawing-room bureau. And there, beached among my things, she'd found my copy of the *Inquirer* with a circle scrawled around Mrs Bunker's advertisement.

She'd booked her place on the next ferry and sailed straight over. She'd even missed the Winthrops' dinner.

And so I came home for the last time.

CHRISTMAS WAS A GRIM affair. For a week or more after being resettled in Mount Vernon Street I was unable to shake the conviction that I didn't belong here at all; that this was merely a way station, and that I'd soon be gone again. I was possessed by a desire for flight such as I haven't felt since I was a very young man. I cancelled my forthcoming lecture and left Ben entirely in charge of the asylum. My role there struck me as meaningless, temporary; how could I ever have mistaken it for my life's purpose?

I didn't sleep at night – I seemed to have no need of rest – preferring to roam the house instead. In the dark it was transformed into something exotic and strangely menacing. I foraged for scraps in the kitchen, cramming them into my mouth with a voluptuous sense of transgression: crusts of bread dipped in milk, chunks of apple, cold bacon rinds. One midnight I climbed up to the old nursery and stood at the dormer window on the landing for what must have been hours, gazing at the iron shadows cast by the elm and marveling at my own willingness to submit to this imprisonment for so many years. By day I lay on my bed in my dressing gown, or dozed jerkily in a chair.

At New Year, Caro took me in hand. She insisted that I shave, and dress, and pay calls and visit my patients, and start to keep regular hours once more.

'Come along now, Hissy. Get up. You know you must.'

'Why must I? What if I don't want to live this sort of life?'

'Don't be absurd.' My sister gave me a look in which exasperation was not unmixed with compassion. 'There *is* no other life.'

In sullen fury, I did as she commanded. When I managed not to fail this test, producing a tolerable impression of myself, she suggested that I should try to drive out my lingering depression by making a record of all the things that had so recently tormented me.

'Maybe you could approach this narrative differently, Hiram. Write it as a memoir. Write it for your own peace of mind.'

At first I resisted. Why go on with this farce of 'Carver's Cures'? Whom would I be trying to cure now, if not myself? I didn't think there was any purpose to such an exercise. But I indulged her, and as the weeks have passed, and the words have come, so, oddly, my sense of belonging in the world has returned to me. It is now late February, and I am eating and sleeping, and going about my daily existence as if it alone has always been real, and that other time – those youthful months at sea, my years of knowing William Borden and Ruth Macy, and that ultimate, terrible week on Nantucket – the shadow.

And yet. The memory of those days, and of the flawed but hopeful young man I once was, has left a deathly aftertaste. If I measure the distance between then and now, I'm haunted by a sense of failure so absolute it feels like ruin.

I know that I won't ever finish the case study I began in the fall, before making my last journey to Nantucket. It's irrelevant now (it was always irrelevant). It has been overwritten by what I have set down here. And in a real sense it has been overwritten by Borden's own words. This is, I concede, not a work of sole authorship, but a collaboration, just as my life has been a collaboration. Let him, in his version of himself, right or wrong, have the final say. I no longer know if mine is any more accurate.

Although I wanted nothing more than to be free of this world of ours and to flee its many forms of incarceration, here I am: not simply trapped, but inescapably installed as one of its keepers. I am powerful. I am enlightened. I am sane. But I know that my power is an illusion; my knowledge, my very sanity – illusions, too.

Not only mine. There are times, as I dine in the great houses of Boston, or get ready to commit another lost soul to the asylum, when I almost sink before the fact – so plain I'm amazed at our conspiracy of silence about it – that we are all hungry, naked, heading towards a death we can't avoid. We are all at sea, sailing over dark water.

Not one of us is safe.

TONIGHT I HAVE REREAD the account that I have tried to give of myself. Looking over these pages, I see that I've done what I at first doubted I could do. I've retrieved the shape at the bottom. I've resurrected William Borden, as best I can.

But whose shape is it? His? Or mine?

I grope my way downstairs from my father's old study, which now belongs to me, and pause at the threshold of my bedroom. The clock on the landing strikes twelve times and to my surprise I realize that I've been awake, writing, for the whole of Saturday night. For a moment it's again as if I've never seen the place before; as if I'm about to walk in on myself unawares. My bed is unslept in; the curtains are hanging open. As I kindle my lamp, I catch sight of my reflection in the glass above the dresser. The midnight darkness – it's Sunday morning, the start of a new day in this year of grace, 1855 — pocks my face. I hold the globe up to my features: the left cheek wreathed with bite marks, the jowls, the arrogant chin, the bloodshot eyes, with their intent, infernal glare —

I can hear Caro stirring along the corridor, in the room she's occupied since she was a girl. Since my breakdown in the scullery yesterday we haven't said much to each other. The truth of that moment was too painful to be sustained. A bedspring squeaks. A few seconds later a finger of light reaches beneath the crack of her door. I have an overwhelming desire to go to her, to take her hand in mine and anchor myself to the present — to speak some word of regret, or love.

Dearest Caro. I'm sorry. I'm sorry for everything I've done, and failed to do. Let me in. Absolve me.

But the glimmer has already been extinguished, swallowed up by that spinsterly solitude. I know that we'll face each other at breakfast tomorrow as if the stunted life we lead, in which what is most real is least often acknowledged — this refined barbarism of ours, this socialized savagery — were somehow normal. And as the years pass, the banalities I will go on supplying will become ever more effortlessly insubstantial, effortlessly cruel.

Ruth Macy is sealed away from me forever, in her tomb-like house. She is as far beyond my grasp as if she really had gone to the bottom of the ocean. I feel an exhausted tenderness for them both, followed by a sudden flood of pity — a pity I'm unable to extend to the raddled prisoner that is Hiram Carver.

I take off my clothes, my fingers thick around my collar stud, my cuffs, my trouser buttons, and put on my nightshirt. I sit down on the bed and dim my lamp. At last, heavy with a sense of defeat, I swing my legs under the covers and lie there, listening to the crashing of my pulse.

I remember that afternoon on Sconset bluff, when I looked out at the ocean and felt the heartbeat of my own life, the terror of it. Would I do it justice? Would I be able to cup it in my hands?

What an awful thing it is to be alive.

Who, given the choice, would choose it?

These nights I seldom dream. But just as I am drifting off, I'm quite certain that I can make out a sound that I haven't heard for what seems like a lifetime. It is a low creaking, like the creaking of miles of cordage and chains, the creaking of a ship's rigging as the anchor is weighed and her sails begin to fill. The room is too warm — when I got into bed the embers of my evening fire were still glowing — and as I turn my face to the window in half-sleep I am grateful, even though the sash is tightly shut, to feel the stirring of the wind.

ACKNOWLEDGMENTS

T HE ASYLUM FOR THE Insane in Charlestown is loosely based on the psychiatric hospital that later became known as McLean, and is today located in Belmont just outside Boston, Massachusetts. Two decades before Dorothea Dix set out to reform the care provided in mental hospitals across America, a system of compassionate management was already being practised at the Charlestown asylum, founded in 1818. (Though the section of land over the bay from Boston which it occupied became part of Somerville in 1842, I've stuck to the original name throughout.) The buildings on which Carver's asylum are modeled, with their ornamental gardens, no longer exist. The original house was erected in 1793 by the Boston merchant Joseph Barrell and the wings were added in the next century. Anyone interested in reading more about the buildings will find a full description in Nina Fletcher Little's *Early Years of the McLean Hospital* (1972). They were bought in 1895 by the Boston and Maine Railroad, which demolished them and razed Pleasant Hill, and the spot where they once stood is now occupied by North Point Park.

The characters in *Dark Water* are invented and do not represent historical figures. I am, however, deeply indebted to Sylvia B. Sutton's account of the program of 'moral treatment' offered by the early superintendents of McLean, Rufus Wyman and Luther V. Bell, in *Crossroads in Psychiatry: A History of the McLean Hospital* (1986), in particular to the Annual Reports quoted there; and to Alex Beam's delightful memoir of McLean, *Gracefully Insane* (2001). Carver's tongue-in-cheek reference to killing off irrational thoughts through 'sheer lack of exercise' is Sutton's. Mansfield's remark about science being 'the topography of ignorance' is Oliver Wendell Holmes's, made to a class of Harvard Medical School students in 1861, and quoted by her. The details of Miss Clayborn's madness are drawn partly from Beam's account of the illness of Jones Very of Salem and from the records of a patient known as 'Julia Bowen', whose list of permissions is in the McLean archives. When Carver suggests that only a fit of insanity can help us stand in a true relation to the world, he is paraphrasing Ralph Waldo Emerson's remarks about Jones Very in Emerson's 1841 essay 'Friendship', which is quoted by Beam.

In creating Sarah Clayborn and Adam Thornton I have also relied on Rufus Wyman's lecture 'A Discourse on Mental Philosophy as Connected with Mental Disease', which was delivered before the Massachusetts Medical Society on 2 June 1830, as well as on monographs by two former McLean patients, both of whom were detained in the Charlestown asylum: Elizabeth Stone's *A Sketch of the Life of Elizabeth T. Stone, and of Her Persecutions* (1842) and Robert Fuller's *An Account of the Imprisonment and Sufferings of Robert Fuller of Cambridge* (1833).

Readers who would like to know more about the development of psychiatry at McLean and in the USA generally will find Albert Deutsch's *The Mentally Ill in America: A History of Their Care and Treatment from Colonial Times* (1937) indispensable. Mansfield's opinion that 'when a man once becomes insane, he is about used up for this world' is Luther V. Bell's, and is quoted by Deutsch.

The ships are invented too. Captain Fitzgibbon bears some resemblance to Captain (later Commodore) John Downes of USS *Macedonian*, who ran a banking ship in the Pacific from 1818 to 1821, but whose cupidity never provoked a mutiny. (Downes was, coincidentally, a lieutenant on USS *Essex*, the men of which were responsible for the burning of the Taipivai valley on Nuku Hiva in 1813, an event I've moved back by about seven years.) By 1855 there had been just one mutiny in US naval history: the *Somers* mutiny of 1842 in the North Atlantic, and I have followed the proceedings of the court of inquiry in that case for certain details of Van Tassel's opening defense of Captain Fitzgibbon. The other notorious mutiny of the time was on the *Globe*, a whaler, in the Pacific in 1824. I have drawn on sailor George Comstock's first-person report of how the mutiny unfolded, quoted by Edouard Stackpole in *The Mutiny on the Whaleship Globe* (1981).

The most famous nineteenth-century instance of survivor cannibalism at sea in an open boat occurred in 1820 after the sinking by a sperm whale of the Nantucket whaleship *Essex* – not to be confused with the US navy frigate. An account of their ordeal was published the following year by her mate, Owen Chase. Chase's narrative was used by Herman Melville (who was far more interested in the whale) as source material for *Moby-Dick*, and has been brilliantly reimagined in *In the Heart of the Sea* (2000) by Nathaniel Philbrick, and by Henry Carlisle (who has also written about the *Somers* mutiny in *Voyage to the First of December*, 1972) in *The Jonah Man* (1984). Almost as sensational, sixty-four years later, was an act of cannibalism among the crew of the *Mignonette*. When this English yacht foundered in the South Atlantic in 1884 during a passage from Southampton to Australia, her captain and mate, afloat for close to a month in a dinghy with only two tins of turnips, killed and ate the cabin boy, and made no secret of how they had survived. I have based some of the conditions in the dinghy of the *Providence* on the survivors' statements given by A.W. Brian Simpson in *Cannibalism and the Common Law* (1984), which also inform Neil Hanson's gripping *The Custom of the Sea* (1999).

I owe a debt to all of these, but most of all to Melville. It's impossible to write about ships and the sea in nineteenth-century America and not to collide with him. The image of a man-of-war as a floating city in chapter One is, of course, his (*White-Jacket*), and the sensational description of the Marquesas in chapter Eleven is his too (*Typee*).

Ruth Macy's observation that the trivial nature of women's work prevents them from entering 'the universe of truth' comes from a diary entry for 1853 by another unconventional Nantucket woman, Maria Mitchell. See *Maria Mitchell: Life, Letters, and Journals* (1896), compiled by Phebe Mitchell Kendall, who also gave me Miss Macy's irreverent gloss on the old Quaker practice of 'dealing' with transgressors. Carver's fear that he'll incur the wrath of Miss Macy's ancestors by breaking one of her coffee cups is patterned on the recollections of Hilda Gibbs in Frances Karttunen's *The Other Islanders: People Who Pulled Nantucket's Oars* (2005).

Fellow admirers of Ernest Becker's *The Denial of Death* (1973), and the writings of Otto Rank, will recognize them as contributing to Carver's thoughts about heroism.